THE SEA SWORD

"I am the worst student of mage-craft you have ever had," Claire said to her father. "I can barely start a fire. I do not shape-change or farsee. The gods have never spoken to me. What is wrong with me?"

"Sometimes it is difficult for them to reach us, child," said Geoffrey. "I saw the goddess many times before I acknowledged her. I thought I was mad." He chuckled. "After I spoke with her, I knew I was—for only a madman wishes to speak to the gods, and have them answer."

Avon Books by
Adrienne Martine-Barnes

THE FIRE SWORD
THE CRYSTAL SWORD
THE RAINBOW SWORD
THE SEA SWORD

THE
SEA
SWORD

ADRIENNE MARTINE-BARNES

AVON BOOKS ◆ NEW YORK

THE SEA SWORD is an original publication of Avon Books. This work has never before appeared in book form. This work is a novel. Any similarity to actual persons or events is purely coincidental.

AVON BOOKS
A division of
The Hearst Corporation
105 Madison Avenue
New York, New York 10016

Copyright © 1989 by Adrienne Martine-Barnes
Front cover illustration by Romas
Published by arrangement with the author
Library of Congress Catalog Card Number: 88-92123
ISBN: 0-380-75456-8

First Avon Books Printing: March 1989

AVON TRADEMARK REG. U.S. PAT. OFF. AND IN OTHER COUNTRIES, MARCA REGISTRADA, HECHO EN U.S.A.

Printed in the U.S.A.

K-R   10   9   8   7   6   5   4   3   2   1

This book is for my brother,
Philip Sebastian Martinez,
and my sister,
Bernice Amanda Martinez,
gone, but well-remembered

THE SEA SWORD

PART I

They sat in unnatural silence, the many expressions of the goddess, willing their strengths to pierce the distance that stood between them and the humans who were both their servants and their hearts' masters. With each year it became more difficult to reach the earth, and more needful.

Alone of all the gods, Hermes moved amongst them, carrying out his duties as messenger. He ordered them to appear at the trial of their sister, Bridget, and they ignored him. All knew it was empty form. No goddess would attend that mockery of justice, except perhaps Eris for mischief. No, even she was with her sisters, in the cool, plain halls of Heaven.

His duty done, Hermes saluted the assemblage with a bow, a smile, and a kiss on the tips of his fingers which scandalized the more stuffy of the goddesses, and left them to their deliberations. They looked at one another, and at themselves, at the ways in which men had divided and separated their unities, had weakened and dismembered their totalities, and sought some beginning point. It was diffi-

cult, for they were confined by their aspects, by attributes hung upon them by centuries of worship. The love goddesses could not speak with wisdom, and the wise goddesses could not speak with love.

Then one spoke who was neither wise nor affectionate, but so fearsome in her aspect that the goddesses themselves shuddered when her raging voice began. She was Time itself, and Death and Wisdom, as close to wholeness as any present, and eldest, in her way.

"The Darkness we have striven against has eaten worlds, and we are no more. Here, in this place, we have chosen to make our stand, and for that purpose, we did seize the person called Eleanor from her place and time, and set her in another. And she has served us most faithfully, in her life and in her children. But with the bringing of the Sword of Fire into the world, our voices grew dimmer. Now, none of us can speak to our children except as ghosts. This is painful, for they cry out to us, as we yearn to speak to them. The harmony is broken by those very weapons which we must make manifest to battle the Darkness. We did not foresee this. I did not foresee this."

It was a great admission, and the goddesses held their breaths to see if the divine rage for which the speaker was renowned for would follow. Even Heaven could not contain Her if she loosed her anger. But only a howling blast of wind which tore at draperies expressed her displeasure.

"We must acknowledge that if we persist, we also might cease to be."

"Oh, no. They need us!" Gentle Isis spoke, then quailed beneath the red-eyed glare of her sister.

"While our foolish brothers and husbands try to fix blame for what has gone awry, we must decide if we can take the risk, and continue with our plan."

"Who can reach them now? You, Saille?" The speaker was grey-eyed Athene, always calm. Ever her father's advocate, her presence with the goddesses was a measure of the graveness of the situation.

"I can still speak to Eleanor, and also to her daughter,

Rowena, but Eleanor is old, and waits for her final rest, and Rowena is weary with the waiting, and does not listen."

"Then, you, Beth of the Birches?"

"I have lost my devotee, Dylan SilverHand, and his daughter, Orphiana, like Rowena, waits and ages."

"Artemis?"

"When I can reach Helene, which is rare enough, I feel her rage. She fears to lose her babes. And she will not betray me to her spouse and share her pain."

"Persephone, can you still speak to Geoffrey Flute-Mage?"

The Lady of Hades gave a bitter little laugh. "That boat crossed the Styx years ago. I had him for such a little time. We are too weak, too voiceless."

All eyes turned towards the terrible black-faced mother of Time, the red-eyed goddess Kali. "I am not weak." The pillars rattled at the sound of her voice. "I will do the deed, though I will not be loved for my efforts. The girl is mine." She ignored the sound of weeping that came from several quarters along the hall.

And Hel, icy death mother of the North, nodded. "And I will take the boy, though it will cost me a child."

"And what of the little one, Anna?" A silence returned to the hall, as no goddess could be found to speak for the girl. The wind of time blew leaves through the halls of Heaven.

I

Geoffrey d'Avebury stood by the window of his study and looked out into the garden. Below he could see Helene, his wife of nearly a quarter century, motionless. She seemed to be speaking to what looked like a moony mist in the middle of a sunlit plot. Her face was transfused with delight, but he felt a chill that was out of place with the warmth of a late summer day in the city of Baghdad. He had no doubt that she was communing with her goddess, wild Artemis, and it made him uneasy.

He had, in truth, felt mildly uneasy for days, for no particular reason. He was settled, for the first time in many years, in one place, and his family was all about him, well and healthy. There had been so many years when this was not the case, and he had never realized how much he disliked dragging around the Levant, tidying up, until he was finally permitted to stop. The goddess, through her agent, Hermes, had sent him hither and yon on errands of mercy, from Cairo to Byzantium, and he had fulfilled these demands long after his heart stopped being in it.

5

He turned away and returned to his writing stand, frowning over the words he had penned. For twenty years he had struggled to create a second volume to the *Chronique d'Avebury* which he had stolen from his aunt Rowena as he set out upon his adventures. The events were clear enough in his mind, but there was so much more, such profound feelings, that he never managed the correct, spare style demanded for such a work. Helene had read the pages, and so had his children, the twins. Claire and Roderick, and the younger girls, Dorothea and Anna. He did not hide from them the tale of the Sword of Light, even if his own part in it was less than heroic. He never forgot that his own parents had hidden their history from him, and that it had cost him greatly. And, over Helene's mild objections, he had taught his children what he could of magecraft, instead of letting them discover it for themselves, as his father and grandmother had done. He loved them passionately, and he wanted to protect them from the intrusion of any fear of themselves, or of the deities who seemed to take a special delight in plaguing the lives of his family.

Geoffrey had not been able to give his whole energy and time to these pursuits, for he had been much occupied with going from place to place and using his musical mage-craft to renew the war-ravaged Levant. Then too, rearing children was, he had discovered, very time consuming. It was also rewarding, but sometimes the epic gathered dust for months while he changed diapers and spooned gruel into toothless pink maws. His eaglets, he called them, and they had grown into very handsome birds. Helene displayed a near indifference to her off-spring until they were old enough to learn to ride and hold a wooden practice sword, and that had been hard for him to bear. She seemed not so much unloving as puzzled as to what she should do with a howling infant or a feverish toddler.

Roderick favored his mother, being short and red-haired, and Claire was tall and spare, like himself. Dorothea resembled his father, Dylan d'Avebury, in her dark good looks, and enjoyed the hearth more than the field, while Anna was a tiny version of his mother, all golden haired and azure eyed. Geoffrey loved them all quite whole-heartedly and sometimes wished they would stay little forever, even as they grew into interesting people with ideas of their own which often surprised him. Soon, he was sure, Roderick would go off upon his quest, but he would have the girls still.

A throat-clearing cough made him turn. His eyes met a merry, mischievous face, ever youthful and yet old, beneath a flat-brimmed hat. Geoffrey felt his heart skip a beat and he smiled.

"Well, Hermes, have you come to see your god-children? I wonder if that poor priest had any idea who he was entertaining when you signed the baptismal record? I wonder what I was thinking of to have them watered?"

"It has been an amusing experience, I confess, keeping an eye on Claire and Roderick. I think the priest suspected I was not quite what I seemed—but, is anyone? As for why you did it, I think you wished to give them every advantage. But, no, I did not come to visit the children, nor for the pleasure of your company, dear friend. Well, maybe just a little. It is time, Geoffrey, for them to be about their tasks."

"Them?" He felt his heart stumble with fear. "Roderick, certainly. I have been expecting it. He is well-trained, prepared to be a hero as I never was."

Hermes looked solemn. "All your children are well-prepared for their quests, as well as they can be. You and Helene have done your jobs well."

Geoffrey felt his stomach twist, and his heart thudded. "All?"

"Claire will go east, and Roderick and Anna will venture west, and then to the back of the north wind."

Geoffrey let the rage race through his blood and tasted the bitter bile in his mouth. He waited until he could master himself a little. He felt again the betrayal that had marked all his commerce with the gods. It would not serve him to rant that he had been trapped in a generations'-long scheme without being consulted. That had begun before he was born or thought of, and he was only a step in a plan he did not pretend to comprehend. "And Dorothea?"

"She will remain here, and wed, and give you grand-children to spoil." The young god gave him a look of such compassion and affection, as if he understood how hard it was. He rested his hands on Geoffrey's shoulders and kissed him lightly on one cheek.

"She is well-named then—gift of the goddess—for she will be all I have left. I suppose I should feel privileged to give thrice where my parents and grandparents gave but once. Helene is not going to like this." It was a feeble way of saying he hated it.

"Helene has never liked it. It is why she has never been as motherly as you would have liked, to shield herself from the pain of fresh loss."

"You mean she knew and did not tell me!"

"Artemis told her years ago. Geoffrey, Helene would rather bite her tongue out than hurt you."

"Yes, she would. I would rail against the unfairness, but it would do me no good. Three children seems a great price to pay for the whims of the gods, my friend."

"Not whims. A plan—conceived in desperation—which has borne unexpected fruit. It sits bitter on my father's tongue. Comfort yourself with that. *He* never meant those swords to pass into kingly hands. That was your grandmother's doing, and once begun, it had to continue." Hermes gave a sharp laugh. "In truth, by your steadfast refusal to become servants of the swords, you frustrate the schemes of the great with a vengeance only I can appreciate."

Geoffrey pondered this a moment, remembering a conversation with the Queen of the Underworld, Persephone herself, in which she had told him that the sword of light must be passed onto another. In the end, Michael be Avi had snatched it up ungiven and used it to drive back the forces of the Shadow that had threatened to engulf the entire Levant. Now Michael ruled in Jerusalem, one eye burnt away by an arrow of Artemis, and the rainbowed sword lay within the holy temple. Once he had desired it, but Helene and the children held a greater attraction, and he felt no regret. Perhaps the gods were at cross-purposes with the goddesses, as men sometimes were with women, he thought.

"I was prepared to give Roderick his sword and horse—but Claire and Anna! Oh, they are skilled in arms, but they are only girls. Tell me they will be safe."

"I cannot, Geoffrey. They are brave and resourceful, as their mother was, as you were, and that is all they can take with them. I cannot promise they will succeed. There is only hope."

"Hope! My heart can break on hope."

Helene felt the mist before she heard the voice. It caught her in mid-stride, and, as always, it gave her a sense of peace and a thrill of terror. It was the most awesome sensation, and she was never certain that it would happen again. As well, she was uncertain that she wished it to.

"Mother!" She whispered the word, and felt the swell of love in her chest.

"Dear child. It is time."

She felt her face, which had smiled into the mist of the Goddess Artemis which enveloped her, stiffen, and she felt her body tense. A dry swallow closed her throat. "So soon?"

"Is it? No, they are twenty now, the twins. I have looked upon them, and seen something of myself and bright Apollo. He is so impetuous! They are wonderful children, daughter. You have raised them well."

"Perhaps, but well enough? I cannot bear it. I thought I was prepared, but I hate it. It is not fair. Anna is still a baby. Roderick has not learned to curb his temper. Impetuous is putting too nice a touch on it. He is headstrong and incautious. Why couldn't he have been more like my careful husband and less like me!"

There was a silence, and Helene wondered if she had offended her beloved matron and caused her to depart. There was a kind of wryness in the answer when it came, a rare bit of humour in the very sober goddess. *"Even the gods cannot answer that, Helene. Anna is a child, but she was born old, and so her age is of no matter. Roderick will do very well, I think, once he gets the wind knocked out of him a few times."*

"If he doesn't get himself killed first. He is going to be furious when he finds out he has to take Anna with him."

"His angers never last. And what have you to say of Claire? Have you no thought of your first-born?"

"What thought should I have?" I never desired children, only to be safe, only Geoffrey and my Lady.

"Will you let her depart into danger feeling that you have no care for her, that you find her unworthy?"

"I am not easy with her, and I never have been. She used to look up at me when she was at the breast. Her eyes were still grey, and she seemed to see right through me. She made me feel so wanting, somehow. Anna, for all her purity, never made me feel so unworthy. It was as if Claire had nothing but edges, and I was afraid I would fall off."

"She has great compassion."

"Does she? Odd. I would have called her merciless, myself."

"They are hardly the same, mercy and compassion, and it is true. Claire is merciless, but yet she is compassionate."

"I would not know, being, I think, quite lacking in that myself."

"It is not an emotion either of us excel at, daughter. But, speak to her, for you will never forgive yourself if you allow her to go off believing that you do not love her."

"Just once I would like you to tell me to do something easy. I *can't* talk to her. I don't want her to go off on the business of the gods to begin with. You sound as if she will not return."

"None of you will ever see Claire after she leaves this house, except perhaps in dreams."

"You mean she is going to die? No, no, that cannot be. She is to be a sword-bearer, and all of those have survived. I suppose she will meet her beloved on the road, as I did. I hope she is as happy as I have been. Geoffrey is the best reward for all that I endured."

"What is death?"

"You frighten me, Mother Artemis. I am worried enough without more. And I dare not show it. Geoffrey would see it in an instant, if I . . ."

"Claire will do what she has to do, as will Roderick and Anna. The situation is desperate. No longer can the gods be heard by men, for the imbalances which we allowed to battle the Darkness distort the paths of converse. It was needful for this to occur, for the swords to come out of their hiding places and enter the world of the now, but it was not without difficulties. Even now, my sister faces extinction over the matter. But that does not concern you. You must send each of your brave and chosen children out to their tasks with your blessing, no matter what it costs you. And you must do it though you know you will never see any of them again, and you have always known this, in your deepest heart."

Helene of Byzantium, who had faced a thousand dangers in her life, stood absolutely still, her arms still lifted into the presence of the goddess. She felt her anger and her fear and sorrow, and she let them play across her heart and mind. *I cannot defend my own children.* The pain of that pierced her. She bowed her head in submission, and wept.

II

The young man stepped out from the Porch of Maidens into her path, his eyes moist with fervor. "Mistress, I adore you. I wish to marry you."

Claire d'Avebury, startled, paused in mid-stride, and considered this astonishing avowal. She had been far away, pondering a dream, and she chided herself for inattention. There had been too much of that lately. She kept finding herself staring out windows or standing in the middle of the garden, with no clear memory of her intentions, just a sense of being draped in mist. She felt as if something was trying to touch her, and could not manage.

She was tall, a full head taller than the man who had spoken to her, and brown as a nut from days on horseback. Her hands had never held a distaff, but were hard and callused from hours with sword and shield. Her long brown hair was gilded from the sun, and she wore a green linen tunic and wide trousers gathered at the ankle, male garb that revealed small high breasts and a tiny waist.

"I do not think so, Giorgios," she answered, and began

to continue down the street. Several veiled desert folk, men and women, emerged from the caravanserie and looked at her with disapproval. Her mother, Helene, had never tried to force her into conventional dress or manners, and when she had asked why not, Helene had shrugged and said she never paid any attention to such small things, lacking a mother to teach them to her. Helene always treated her children in a rather unconcerned manner, rarely giving them her full attention, except while instructing them in arms or horsemanship, and Claire had sometimes wondered if she and her brother and her two sisters were entirely welcome.

"But, you must! I have already told my father, and he is going to talk to your father, and it is almost arranged."

As this was the common way of things, Claire was not surprised. Her rage, therefore, startled her. The thought of Giorgios's sweaty hands on her skin revolted her. Claire did not think her father, Geoffrey, would agree to such an arrangement. On the other hand, he was a little vague, his head always in a book or writing on the tale of his life, and he might say yes without thinking. He was so gentle she found it hard to believe he could transform himself into a fearsome beast, except she had seen his shape-shifts, and those of her younger twin, Roderick, who had begun manifesting them while still a toddler.

They had been wrestling in the garden, and she was already the larger child. Roderick had gotten frustrated at being beaten, and turned into a large version of a garden snake. This had frightened her into screaming. Her cries had brought Geoffrey and Helene and several servants from the house. The servants would have slain Roderick but for her father's quick intervention.

The memory reassured her. Her father might be a little vague, but he was not stupid, which was more than she could say for Giorgios Mendrinas. Claire considered further. She was, after all, a female, and already old for marriage, almost twenty-one. What if Geoffrey thought all the mooning about house and field she had been doing was a sign of burgeoning passion. What was she going to do with her life, after all? Roderick would go off on some great adventure soon, as his father and grandfather had done before him. She spent a wistful moment thinking about her great-grandmother, Eleanor of Avebury, who would be in her eighties, if she still lived, in distant Albion. Claire had fastened on that portion of her family chronicle almost the first time Geoffrey had read it aloud. She looked at her calloused hands and despaired. They were not suited to womanly pursuits.

Seeing her hesitation, Giorgios laid a possessive hand on her forearm, and Claire felt her blood roar. "Soon we will be wed," he said smugly, "and you will give me strong sons."

Claire twisted her arm away. "You . . . pimple! You could not father strong sons without the help of several friends."

Giorgios went white beneath his olive complexion, and grabbed at her wrist. Claire twisted out of his grasp easily, slammed his narrow shoulders against a wall, and pinned his throat beneath her arm. He gasped like a beached fish, and clawed for his neck. With an ease of long training, she jerked his legs out from under him and sent him sprawling to the paving stones. Resisting an urge to kick his chest until the ribs split, she turned and walked towards home.

After a few steps, she stopped herself. She needed some time first, to gather her wits. She hated the feeling of imminent hysteria that throbbed in her chest, and she knew she never behaved well when she acted in its grip. It had been with her for days now, a nagging flutter beneath her breasts, and it made her feel slightly ill. It was those dreams.

Retracing her steps past the still fallen Giorgios, Claire walked into the bustle of the caravansary and headed for a cook-stall. Two camel drovers were engaged in an exchange of insults in the midst of an appreciative crowd. Claire watched the wagering on the outcome. The nomads were great gamblers. She bent an ear to the heated vituperation, struggling with a dialect she followed with some difficulty. Still, she caught the jist of it, and chuckled.

Claire dug out a coin and put it into the greasy hand of the cook, then hunkered down beside the little brazier and pointed to a skewer of chicken and onions. The man turned the skewer and reached for a flap of soft, flat bread without lifting his head. The crowd cheered at a particularly magnificent turn of phrase, and a camel bellowed as if he too enjoyed the jest. The cook tucked the food into the bread and handed it to her.

Rising, Claire moved away from the center of the bazaar towards the shade of a copper merchant's booth. She had always enjoyed the feeling of the caravansary, especially the sounds of many tongues. Sometimes the quietness of her father's house oppressed her a little. She could not enter into her sister Dorothea's cheerful domesticity, and realized she found the idea of doing so rather alarming. Why didn't she yearn to get married and settle down? She was a woman, and women were supposed to desire such things. That, at least, was what all her nurses had told her. Her mother had never suggested any such future, and for the first time this struck Claire as a peculiar omission. All she ever got from Helene was lessons in archery and sword craft and horsemanship. These were given with a kind of intensity amounting to near madness, as if her life depended on these skills. Why, she wondered? I am not going off to great adventures.

Claire frowned and munched her meal. She had never found it easy to talk to her mother. It was as if a wall existed between them, and she always felt faintly inadequate around Helene. As if her hands were dirty. Except, as her family was fond of pointing out, Claire's hands were never dirty if she could help it. She was closer to her father, and her brother was closer to their mother. Sometimes it seemed a little unfair. He was going to get to go off and do marvelous things, and she was going to be left behind with a pointless life. She loved her fierce, short twin, but sometimes she hated him just a little bit. She felt like that about her whole family sometimes, and it shamed her. How could Dorothea be so happy mending linens. She sang to it. Claire was the least musical person in the family, and had to struggle with even the simplest song. Instead, in secret, she danced, as if her body could sing wordlessly to music she alone could hear.

She could not remember anytime when the sound of a dombek and flute did not make her feet itch with a need for movement. Sometimes, on hot, restless nights, she would creep into the courtyard and dance with her shadow in the moonlight, her arms and legs making strange elongations, her hands gesturing in ways she had never seen before. Every movement seemed important. The dawn would find her sweaty and exhausted, loathing the stink of her own flesh. Sword practice was easy by comparison. Why couldn't she sing or play the lute or flute, or feel as she ought.

It had been worse of late. Sometimes she felt possessed, and it was not a pleasant possession. The dreams! Claire almost gagged at a sudden clear memory of one of the nightmares that had left her with dark circles beneath her glass-green eyes. She had been dancing in blood. Every step she took, the earth spouted red fluid. She could smell it. Her unfinished meal slipped from her fingers, and a cur dog gobbled it before it hit the dry soil. All she wanted was some peace, to be free of the terror that pounded in her throat. She would have run somewhere, only she could not imagine where in the wide world she would feel any differently.

Claire turned away from the shade of the stall and wandered aimlessly across the bazaar. After a minute she realized that she was heading for the spot where Achmed usually plied his tales, and felt a little better for no reason. Achmed was the oldest person she had ever met, and he had a fund of stories that outshone those of any other story teller she had ever heard, and even rivaled in marvels the half-unbelieved chronicle of her family. She liked the variety of his stories, and she respected his skill. Also, it seemed to her that often his stories gave her clues to herself, as if he was telling the tale just for her. She kept a record of the stories, first a literal transcription in Arabic, then a literary translation into Greek, sometimes setting them to paper simultaneously, using both hands in that particular trick she had—the Arabic with the left, the Greek with the right. She could do it with a sword as well, and she had never forgotten the expression on her mother's face when she had shifted from right to left in a practice combat. Helene had been stunned. Afterwards she had grinned at her tall daughter and hugged her fiercely. Claire could still feel the warmth of that rare embrace.

Achmed was nowhere to be seen. Instead, his spot beside the baked brick wall of the caravansary was occupied by a stranger, a sort of man she had never seen before. His head was covered with matted locks, and he wore a filthy cloth draped around his loins and a cord across his shoulder and down his chest. His legs were bent in what seemed to be an extremely uncomfortable position, cross-legged like any bazaar man, but with the feet pulled up onto the calves, the flat of the foot turned skyward. He was motionless. His thin chest did not seem to expand or contract with breath, and his skin did not twitch beneath the flies that crawled across it. She was repelled by his filth and fascinated at the same time.

Claire started to leave, and found herself hunkering down a few feet away instead. After a few minutes she settled her flat bottom on the dirt and pulled her legs up onto her calves in imitation of his posture. It was more than uncomfortable. It was downright painful. How did he stand it? Maybe being barefoot would help. She was contemplating pulling off her short boots when he gave a little snort and moved.

The man opened his eyes and stared at her. They were black as olives, rimmed with heavy lashes. Then he smiled. The transformation was remarkable. Claire forgot all about the matted hair and the filthy garment. He was beautiful. It was as if he pierced something with his smile, as if he had put an arrow into her flesh. She was so startled she let her ankles slip off her thighs and gave a little yelp of pain. Letting go of the position was even worse than holding it.

"Who are you?" she asked, rubbing a calf that was now knotted with cramp.

The man seemed to consider this question as if it was terribly important. Claire wondered if he understood her. She had never seen such intensity, even in her father. The stranger was somehow more alive than anyone she had ever seen before. She contained her impatience and waited for a reply.

"The wind. The river. A leaf."

A madman, she thought. How sad. She had seen all sorts of madmen in her life, babbling nomads and self-styled prophets and priests of strange gods, but never one who smiled with such serenity. A happy lunatic. That was different, at least. Most of the others she had seen had been filled with something hideous and hateful that she had drawn away from. His speech was heavily accented, but understandable.

"*Salaam,* oh, wind," she said, and touched her brow and chest with a half bow. It was always good to be polite to the madmen of the world. It was harmless. Claire wondered if he was quite as harmless as he appeared, and was puzzled by the thought. "What has happened to Achmed the story-teller?"

The smile faded. "He is gone to his fathers. Three nights past. And I have waited for you here, in his place. I knew you would come."

Claire had an urge to leap to her feet and run home, but she kept her seat. Her green eyes flooded with tears at the loss of her old friend. She halted them in their course, feeling them brimming all along the aching flesh beneath her eyes. She tucked her knees up and put her head down on them. Her heart ached in her chest, and it seemed as if the world was a very dark place. She felt so empty. It was not just Achmed. It was everything. Her shoulders shook with soundless sobs, dry-eyed, until the first anguish spent itself. Then she pulled herself back into her ordinary, daily self, the sober and dutiful face she hid the riot of conflicts behind. She smoothed her cheeks on her sleeve and tucked a stray wisp of hair off her high forehead.

She looked at her companion and realized that her mask was only half in place, and that it meant nothing to the glossy black eyes of the madman. He could see right through her, she was sure. It was uncomfortable, but at the same time restful, as if for a moment she could set aside her disguise and simply exist. Claire felt almost giddy, as if she had drunk a great deal of wine very quickly. She gave a deep sniff to clear her nose and then a little sigh. Then she frowned over what he had said.

"Waited for me? Did Achmed charge you with some message? Anyone in the bazaar could have come for me."

"But, I did not know who you were. And, after my journey, I needed some quiet."

More riddles. She felt irritated. Her temper flared for a second. "Let me understand you. You waited for me, but you did not know who I was." He was a madman. She had almost forgotten for a moment. She felt acutely uneasy, and entirely relaxed at the same time. "Why?"

"I was sent."

"Sent? For what purpose?"

"Who can know the purposes of the gods?"

Claire gave a sharp bark of laughter. Her father had asked the same question many times. The whole thing was ridiculous. She would just stand up and walk home and go about her life, her pointless, meaningless life. But she could not move. It was as if all the strength had just drained out of her. She was tired. A bleak future of mock combats and copying her father's manuscripts, or marriage to some pudgy merchant rose in her mind's eye. She wished the earth would swallow her and end her misery.

Putting her palms on the dirt to rise, Claire had the sensation of tingling run up her arms. A smell overwhelmed her for a second, a tang of blood, and was gone.

The half-glimpsed dreams that had troubled her all through the months of summer welled up with brilliant clarity for a moment. She flinched and snatched her hands away, as if they burnt.

"Sometimes they speak to us, and we cannot hear," the man said.

"Sometimes we do not want to," she answered tartly. Whatever it was, Claire was certain she did not really want any part of it.

"True, true. When She came to me, I did not wish to hear her. We are all uneasy in the service of the mighty."

"I think you have mistaken me for another. I serve no one."

"For whom do you dance then?"

Outraged, Claire glared at him. How did he know? Her dance was secret, private. Were the servants gossiping about her in the bazaar? There was no logical explanation. Even if they had been, this madman was hardly the sort to listen to idle chatter. She pushed the anger aside and shrugged. I dance for myself, she thought.

"What do you want from me?" Claire spoke more sharply than she intended, and felt a tell-tale blush colour her cheeks.

"I wish only to serve you, and guide you to Her."

Claire decided abruptly she did not want to know who "her" was. She caught the slight emphasis in his words and felt cold all the way to her marrow. She was terrified and excited at the same time. She felt as if she stood in a doorway, and beyond it lay something so great she could not grasp it. It was something she wanted so much she could taste it—and it tasted of blood.

She looked into the serene, dark eyes of the madman. "Have you eaten?" she asked simply.

He laughed, and it was the sweetest sound she had ever heard. "No, but fasting is no burden to me."

Claire glanced at the ribs that stood out clearly against his dark skin. "I would not have guessed, your flesh is so sleek with victuals."

He made a comical face. "Yes, no matter how I starve my flesh, it will not release me."

"Is that what you want?"

"All desire is illusion."

The words seemed to explode in her mind, and little stars danced in her eyes for a second. She had always known that, and longed to escape the yearnings that burned within her. She wished for adventure, for her brother's place, for something she had no words for except the movement of her body in the moonlight. Why did she want a destiny beyond the hearth? She longed for Dorothea's domestic content, and wondered if she would ever find it. "Including the illusion that desire is illusion," she said, the words tumbling out without thought. "Come. And, pray, give me the courtesy of a name. I cannot tell my father I have brought the wind home, even if it is true. Fathers do not approve of such flights of fancy."

"I am called Djurjati." He paused and waited for several seconds. "And you, young woman?"

"I am Claire d'Avebury."

Claire rose and turned towards home, bemused. She looked over her shoulder and found his smile warming her. Part of her wondered what her father and mother would say to her dragging this stranger home with her. The rest did not care, so long as she could feel the stillness of his black eyes.

III

By the time Claire had reached the gates of her home, she had nearly forgotten her companion. Instead, she had remembered her encounter with young Giorgios and had the panicky sense that some sort of trap was about to close on her. She felt more angry than frightened, but still frightened enough to notice. She settled the stranger in the garden and charged into the house, ignoring a question from her sister Dorothea as she climbed the stairs to her father's study.

She began to reach for the doorknob, then heard an unfamiliar voice. Her father answered, and she turned away, then felt a fresh panic. What if it was Giorgios's father, or his emissary? Claire burst through the door.

Geoffrey was alone, seated at his untidy table, and he looked very tired. He coiled a finger into his beard, and she noticed he was getting grey along the temples and around the generous mouth. Claire looked around, but there was no one in the room but the two of them. Where could his visitor have gone? There was no other way out but the hall she had been in. There was no place to hide in the big, sunny room.

Claire dismissed this puzzle and walked towards the table. Geoffrey looked up and smiled at her. It was such a tender look, an expression which was almost her first clear memory of another human being. His ink-stained hands had brushed away her baby tears and washed the dirt out of scuffed knees. His lap had always been available, though she often had to compete with a large volume, and less often with her brother. But the book would be set aside, and she would always receive his undivided attention. A bad dream or a broken toy were each greeted with utter seriousness, never as an interruption, and she had felt more than loved. Claire had been too big for lap camping for years now, but she still could summon up the sense of certainty it had given her. They had moved from place to place, from city to city, over her childhood, and their house in Baghdad was the first she remembered living in for more than a year or two. Only her father was always there, for her mother was often absent upon military errands against the remnants of the Shadow that still lurked in the wadis, or the fierce, nomadic peoples who came in wave after wave, from the heart of Asia.

"Is something wrong, my child?"

"How do you know?"

Geoffrey pondered this. "When one of my daughters arrives wide-eyed, rosy-cheeked, breathless and sweaty— especially my most particular and fastidious child—I naturally leap to the assumption that all is not quite well in the world."

"Ah." She felt awkward and clumsy. At the same time, her fingers itched to straighten the stacks of manuscript, dust the table, and shelve the books around him. Claire could not abide clutter, and her father's study always comforted her at the same time it disturbed her. "It always seems like magic when you know how I am, as if you could see into my mind."

"Only when you wear it on your face. My magicks are

not useful for seeing the truth; for that I must use my heart. Sit down. Your arrival is not unexpected."

"Then you did have someone in here. I thought I heard another voice. Where did he go? Was it someone from Janos Mendrinas? Did you turn him into a . . ." As she spoke, she wondered where her father intended her to sit. Every chair and bench in the room was covered with books and scrolls. He was studying Egyptic, with Helene as his impatient tutor, and had recently received a fresh batch of papyri from Cairo.

"Mendrinas? Odd. I had a missive from him two days ago, but I have not opened it. Is it important?"

"No! Just cast it into the fire and do not answer it."

"That would hardly be good manners. It is bad enough that I let it slip my mind. It is around here somewhere." Geoffrey reached for a pile of papers which slid away and threatened to cascade onto the floor at his touch. Claire held herself back from springing to rescue them. Her father got very cross, as angry as he ever got, if his papers were touched. "Ah, here it is. I was using it as a place mark on this fragment I have been trying to translate. It really needs Helene's hand, but you know how difficult it is to get her to settle down." He looked a little sad when he said this. "But you cannot keep a falcon in a cage," Geoffrey added as he snapped the heavy seal and peered near-sightedly at the writing.

"Father!"

"Shh. This is fascinating." He waved a long hand at her.

"Fascinating! It is disgusting."

"Yes, it is, but fascinating nonetheless. Just because I do not like something does not make it less interesting. Master Mendrinas seems to feel that an alliance between his house and mine would be of mutual benefit, as long as you are well-dowered. You know, I have never thought of that. I do not think about money very much."

Claire groaned. "I *know.* I learned to deal with irate tradesmen before I was eight, and was very relieved when Dorothea took it over. She is much better at it than I am."

"I am sorry I am such a poor father."

"You are the best father in the world, but a poor house-holder."

He grinned. "You have your mother's tart tongue. Now, what is this nonsense about?" He dropped the letter on the table.

"Giorgios Mendrinas has some idea of being in love with me—or with the money he imagines I possess. He had the effrontery to speak to me in the street. I . . . knocked him down."

"Good for you. Do I know him, this Giorgios?"

"Yes. He took some rhetoric from you last fall."

"Oh, yes. Rather a stupid boy, running to fat around the middle."

"That is the one. And I will not marry him. Please, do not try to force me."

"Claire, I have never been able to make you do anything you did not wish, and I am not about to try. Besides . . ."

"What?"

Geoffrey looked at her with enormous tenderness, until Claire was almost uncomfortable. "I love all my children, and I have tried not to favor one over the other, but you have always been the dearest to me. I never thought about you growing up and leaving me, though I suppose I knew you would wed one day. I still think of you asleep against my shoulder while the fire gutted and I read. I would have kept you small if my magic could have done it. When your mother insisted on training you to the arts of war, I was terrified, but I could never deny Helene anything. You always smelled so sweet as you slept. I love being a father —and perhaps a grandfather."

"But, I do not want to be a mother. And certainly not with Giorgios."

"No. Not that." He looked at the motes of dust floating in the sunlight. "I have spent many years preparing to let my son go off on his adventure, only to find I must lose you as well."

"Do you mean I will accompany him when he goes?"

They were twins, and loved each other as twins do, but she rather doubted Roderick would be pleased to have her along.

"I wish it were so. But, no. The gods are not done with us yet, curse them. You will go alone, as your mother has always known. I wish I were brave enough not to fear for you."

Claire was torn between a desire to comfort her father and another to crow like a cock. Unable to choose, she stood absolutely still before him, until she could feel the swirling, spilling force that churned within her belly. She had never understood what that sensation was, but it had always come to her in times of stress, as if she had swallowed the sea. It was like a voice speaking in an unknown tongue, and she always ached to comprehend it. But like her dance, she could not control it, and sometimes that frustrated her.

"Why?" Claire asked finally.

Geoffrey d'Avebury gave his first born and dearest child a wry look. "Why" had been her first word, after she had pushed a clay cup of water off the table and watched it smash to pieces on the floor. Unlike her brother, who had babbled cheerfully from his twelfth month, she had waited another half year before she began to speak, though she had meowed at cats and tweated at birds and tried to imitate the sounds of wheels on pavement and rain falling on rooftops. Roderick, Dorothea and Anna had said *imi*, mother, and *abu*, father, and many, many "no's" in their first halting speeches, but Claire had only asked why. All the children used a muddle of language, picked up from their parents, and from servants; Greek, Hebrew, Arabic, Latin, Aramaic and Persian, even Turkic, the strange, harsh tongue of the fierce Asiatics who had troubled the peace of the region for the last two decades.

"Why am I not brave enough not to worry, or why must you go off into the East?"

She tucked a wisp of sun-bleached brown hair into place and straightened a fold in her tunic. He marveled at her tidiness. "Why am I going? Where am I going? How am I going?"

"I can only answer that last with any certainty, and say on horseback. I will feel better knowing you are up on Absolom's broad back. The gods must tell you the rest."

"They have never spoken to me."

It was such a final statement, and held such a body of pain that Geoffrey winced with empathy. Perhaps he had made a mistake, letting them know so much of the history of their forebearers. He had been ignorant when he began, but he had had no expectations either. Claire had read the chronicle written by her great-aunt Rowena many times, and his own, halting, clumsy effort as well. She knew of his trafficking with Hermes and Persephone, of his father's love for Beth of the Birches, and their great-grandmother Eleanor of Avebury's long affection for both Briget and the cool willow goddess, Saille. It had never crossed his mind that his first born might yearn for such intercourse, since he had spent his first twenty years attempting to avoid just that. But then, a great many things did not occur to him, like dowering his daughters or paying the tradesmen.

"Sometimes it is difficult for them to reach us, child. As you know, I saw the goddess many times before I acknowledged her. I thought I was mad." He chuckled. "And after I did speak with her, I knew I was, for only a madman wishes to speak to deities—and have them answer."

Claire sat down on the edge of a book-laden chair and glared at him. "I have never seen a thing. No voices call me. And I am the worst student of the magical arts you have ever had. I can barely start a fire. I do not shape-change or farsee. I am as likely to petrify a loaf as freshen it. What is wrong with me?"

"You are slow to begin, as I was. You were late to walk, to speak. Only in your reading did you excel, and I had hopes that you might be a scholar. But you have little interest in my moldy old tomes."

"Father, I am sorry I have been such a disappointment." It was true. She pursued learning to please her father, not to enlarge her mind. "The things in books are . . . so far away."

"Claire, you have never disappointed me. Infuriated me and given me a few grey hairs, yes, but disappointed, no. When each of you was born, I spun great, wild dreams—foolish plans. And then you grew into yourselves, into strange, interesting individuals. I soon forgot my ideas in the wonder of my children. You are my blessing, my reward. I survived in the hope that one day you would exist, and I would feel your sticky fingers in my beard. You are all that I imagined, and much, much more. To send you off into the unknown . . . stills my heart. I would rail at the Fates, but it would do no good. It is like debating the sea . . . or your mother."

Claire thought that the gods must be very cruel, to subject her father to such distress, and was almost glad she had never had the chance to speak to them. She would probably say something rude. "But, didn't you like it? Your adventures *sound* exciting."

"There is nothing exciting about being shipwrecked or being ravished by wild women. Terror is not exhilarating, Claire. I was frightened all the time, first for myself, then for your mother. Bravery is a kind of madness, I think."

Claire chewed her lip for a moment. She had never heard Geoffrey speak so bluntly, and it made her want to squirm. At the same time it made her feel very adult. It was so untidy. She straightened the edge of her tunic across her knees. "You sound almost angry."

Geoffrey ran long fingers through his curling hair. "Yes. Very, very angry. And bitter. I have not had great pleasure in my dealings with the gods, except my friendship with Hermes. All I wished for was a quiet life of fatherhood and study. Instead, I have spent twenty years dragging around the Levant, from the ruins of Byzantium to the Empty Quarter of Araby, working to heal the balances of the world. I do not wonder that my father was sullen and morose, because, in truth, the gods have used us. It was for a good end, but we are pawns nonetheless. I had accustomed myself to seeing Roderick off on his part of this work, but I never thought to see my daughters away as well."

"Daughters? All of us?"

"Dorothea alone will remain with me."

Claire leaned her elbows on her knees and rested her chin on her clasped hands for several minutes. She tried to imagine herself traveling alone, and felt her belly churn. Secretly she had always wished for adventure, but, being female, she had resigned herself to some vague domestic future, when she thought of it at all. She had envied Roderick just a little. It had always seemed a shame that she, the first born, had gotten the inches but not the sex, while her brother was so short, but male. Sometimes he teased her that she had stolen his height while in the womb. There was never any malice in it, because Roderick was full of kindness. Still, she had felt quietly unhappy that she was a mere girl, and a clumsy one at that. She could manage a drum, but no more demanding instrument, while her sisters and brother took to flute or oud almost without instruction. With sword and shield she was capable, but she lacked Roderick's quickness, and only in her ability to use either hand with a weapon was she singular. She could write with both hands equally well too, and draw any bow with ease, while Roderick was quite hopeless at archery.

Now she had the chance to realize her secret desire, and she rather wished she hadn't. She did not feel right. It was as if she had lost her footing, lost her place in her own dance. "Where will I go?"

"East is all I know."

The stranger who said he was her guide. How was she going to tell her father about him. Before she could frame her words, she had a vision of enormous mountains where the snows stayed from century to century. Something flew towards a peak, something huge and terrible. A body like an enormous serpent appeared out of the mist above the mountains. It had great white eyes, and they sought something. In an instant she knew it was herself, and her heart rose in her throat. She wanted to hide under the table, but she was frozen. Blunt nails cut into sweating palms as she struggled to conceal herself. Finally she managed to blink, and the vision vanished. Without a word, Claire ran out of her father's study and into the heat of the garden.

IV

The stranger she had brought home from the bazaar was folded up in his peculiar posture again, motionless in his trance. She tried to remember his name—the wind, indeed—and she never had gotten around to mentioning him to her father. Djurjati, that was it. She wondered what it meant. Claire chided herself for a moment, then chuckled softly. Two hours before she had been wondering what her life would be like, and now she wished she had not. In the sunlight, the monster she had glimpsed was powerless. Geoffrey would not mind if she dragged half the bazaar home. He never worried about things like that. And he was too busy worrying about her already. Dorothea would fuss like a mother hen, but otherwise her guest would go nearly unnoticed.

Claire sat down on the stone bench beneath an olive tree and tried to sort herself out. She was going on an adventure! She chewed the idea over, and was not sure it was good. No, she was thrilled at the idea, and frightened of the reality. She felt unprepared, or was it something more.

Unworthy. The word arrived unbidden, and her shoulders
sagged a little. She never felt quite good enough. It was as
if there had always been some summit she could see but
never climb.

The thought of mountains brought back the vision of the
terrible eyes. She would, she was sure, meet those gleaming orbs somewhere, and she wondered what would happen. And what was the part of the stranger? What had he
said? He had come to guide her? Where? For what purpose? There were too many questions, and Claire wanted
only answers—clear, concise answers. It was a thing she
had always longed for, absolute certainty. Perhaps it was
all the changes she had endured as a youngster. She hated
the memory of it. Changes of city, of house, of servants, of
the very language. And people! Why could they not remain the same? Why did they get old and die, like
Achmed, or turn into strangers, like her mother?

As if the thought had conjured her, Helene appeared at
the edge of the garden, her imp face more solemn than
usual. As she walked towards Claire, the younger woman
noticed how old her mother seemed. There was silver
amongst the coppery curls, and deep, grim lines that an-
gled down beside the small mouth. Only the slight softness
that swelled beneath the green of her tunic spoke of her
womanhood. Claire wondered that those breasts had suck-
led her. She had not memory of it, or of any caress except
occasional praise for a practice fight well-performed or an
arrow well-spent. Helene was never unkind, just distant.

The older woman sat down beside her, and the strong
little hands clenched and unclenched several times. "Well,
daughter." She seemed to be at a loss for any further
words, and Claire let the silence grow between them as she
gazed at the motionless man now almost invisible in the
deepening shadows of the afternoon. She could see a muscle spasm along Helene's cheek, and realized her mother
was as upset as she had ever seen her.

Finally, she answered. "My father says I am to travel

into the East, but, as usual, he is a little vague about the details."

Helene laughed until tears trickled down her sun-browned cheeks. It took Claire a minute to realize that not all the tears came from merriment at Geoffrey's haziness over the minutia of daily life. Her mother was crying. Claire was horrified. She had never seen her mother weep. She tried never to cry herself, in imitation of her mother. Beneath the horror, she discovered she felt slightly betrayed. She did not want Helene to behave this way!

Her mother finally got some command of herself. "Yes, of course. My darling Geoffrey will probably wander about the house for several days after he is dead, because he will not notice the difference. It will terrify the servants."

Claire found this fancy rather alarming. She thought of the grandparents, Dylan and Aenor, whom she had never known because they had died shortly after her father set off in search of his destiny, and of Hiram, Helene's father, who had perished in the destruction of Byzantium, and felt a fresh panic. "He is not ill, is he? You will not die when I leave—promise me you won't. Or I just will not go!"

"Oh, no, no. At least, I believe I have several decades left to me, and your father as well. What put that in your head? Ah, that blasted history. I cannot decide which is worse—ignorance or knowledge. Your father and I began with so little sense of our destinies, while you and Roderick have so much. On the whole, I think knowledge is the heavier burden. It will make you hesitant."

"Hesitant?"

"You will get into a mess and pause to wonder what I would do, or Geoffrey would do. You must not. It is why I have trained you so hard, so you will act quickly and without much pondering. It is why I permitted all of you to learn what you could of the ways of mages, though I have no love for mage-craft."

"But, Mother, you are as skilled as Father in that."

"Perhaps. But I think magic is as two-edged as any other blade. I can put an arrow in a man's eye at a hundred cubits, but it does not mean I love to kill. There is a great difference between doing something well and enjoying it."

Claire chewed this over for a moment. "Oh. I suppose I do not do anything well enough to see that."

"What is this? You handle sword and horse superbly, and your archery is a pleasure to behold. Your spell casting becomes more proficient, though you were slow to start. I think you grasp the principles behind them much better than Roderick or your sisters. Your father has often told me he never has to explain anything to you twice."

"But—it is not ever perfect! And somehow, Mother, it is not real. Magic is a plaything, like my dolls." Claire paused. Her parents had *talked* about her. She found this difficult to imagine. Most of her memories of Helene and Geoffrey were of furious arguments alternating with passionate forgiveness. They would scream at each other in six tongues until they were exhausted, then Helene would curl up in Geoffrey's lap like a cat. Their reconciliations always made her ache with envy. It was such a shameful feeling.

"Perfect! You cannot get perfection. It is . . ." Helene lifted her hands in a futile gesture. "Perfection is an illusion. It is the least real thing in the world."

Claire gaped at her mother, then turned her eyes towards the still figure in the shadows. Helene followed her glance and gave a sharp exclamation. "It is all right. I brought him home."

"Well, I did not think it just materialized in my garden. Astonishing. My most fastidious daughter brings home a ragamuffin *fakir*. I thought I was past surprise."

"Fakir? Is that what he is. I have never seen his like, but he said he had been waiting for me in the marketplace for three days. I could not leave him there. But, I forgot him, almost, because of things. Giorgios Mendrinas proposed to me in the street, and my father tells me I am to go off to Asia, and I think this is the most confusing day of my life! And I do not like it!"

"No, you never could endure uncertainty."

"What do you mean by that?" Claire was instantly defensive.

"You do not remember, I suppose, but when you were small, you would eat only certain things, day in, day out, no matter what Cook had planned or prepared. And you put your clothes out on the chest each night, very neatly, so you knew what you would wear the following day. It used to rebuke me, all that orderliness, as if the irregularity of our lives was an affront to you."

I still do, Mother. "I was never sure where I was," Claire answered, a little chagrined that she still behaved like a child. "You were gone so much, and Father would mope around and scribble for days. I mean, he took care of us quite well—in a dreamy sort of way. And sometimes I felt lost." *I always felt lost.*

"We have not been exemplary parents, have we? I am afraid, Claire, that I never really tried."

Claire looked at her tiny, fierce mother and saw a stranger. She heard the pain this admission cost the older woman, and wished the subject had never arisen. At the same moment, perversely, she was glad it had. Her mother's distance had always been hard for her to understand. "Why didn't you?"

Helene gave a great sigh. "I *knew*, before you were born even, that you would go off into peril—and I could not bear it. For nine months I carried you beneath my heart, knowing that some day you would follow in my footsteps and bear a sword of power. I would have preferred ignorance, but Artemis would not let me possess it. She has been the only mother I have ever known, and I have loved her, but she is not kind. I could not tell you, or Roderick or Anna. And, worst, I could not tell Geoffrey. Oh, he always knew that Roderick would go away, but he wanted to keep you girls by him, safe, just as he wanted to preserve me from harm."

"That is cruel. Why did She do it?" Claire's cheeks were hot with outrage.

"Claire, you had to be prepared. Otherwise I might have

let you moulder over an embroidery frame like any other girl."

Claire giggled. "With these great hands?"

"They are beautiful, like your father's. I could only give you what I had, which was my skills at sword and horse. If I have appeared unloving, it was not true. When I put you to my breast the first time, all I could think of was that you would be torn away from me. Foreknowledge is a terrible thing. And the way you looked at me when you began your training. You hated it. You hated the sweat and the dirt, though you never complained of the work of it, the way Roderick did. Men, I think, are naturally a little lazy, always sighing after paradise and trees heavy with figs."

"Mother, will I ever see the Goddess?"

Helene frowned. "You have not, then?"

Claire chewed her thumb for a second. "I do not think so. Sometimes I feel as if something is nearby, but I cannot see it. It is like a heaviness in the air. And, after what you have said, I am not certain I want to find out what it is. I think the gods are very . . . It is threatening, like the time before thunder. But, if I am destined to serve, I would prefer to know what I am in service to. Why have I not seen Her?"

"That, at least, I have a clue to. There is War in Heaven —and, in a way, it is all our faults. Mine, Geoffrey's, his father's, and his grandmother's. The swords are part of it, but also the blood."

Thinking of her dreams, Claire flinched at the word. "The blood?"

"We are a blood-line, Claire, as much as your horse Absolom is part of the blood-line of my stud Achilles and your father's mare Marina."

"What does that have to do with the gods? Everyone is part of a blood-line, Mother."

"The gods, in their pride, conceived a plan to restore themselves to their former glory, but they handed it over to the goddesses to manage. As I said, males are rather indolent. They did not consult. They ordered. Typical. The results have not pleased them, I suspect, for things have not turned out as they wished. I think we can put *that* at your great-grandmother's door, because she behaved in a way that the gods did not even conceive of. She did not seize power; she gave it away. So, we became king-makers, not monarchs, for which I confess I am grateful. Being a queen would not have suited me at all! Much too proper. So, the swords which should have opened the gate-way to the gods shut it in their faces instead. One conse-quence of this is that it is more difficult for them to manifest themselves to us. They are very angry."

"How do you know?"

"I do not. This is a great deal of guesswork, from things my Lady has let fall over the years. The end of the world is coming, Claire, and you will be part of it."

"That is a cheerful farewell gift, I must say! I do not want to end the world. I want to heal it, like you and Father have." Claire found she was shaking with rage, and it surprised her. All the dreams of blood seemed much too real.

"Well, if you survive, you will do that." Helene seemed calm and remote, but Claire could see a pulse throbbing in her throat, a rapid flutter of flesh that spoke of anything but serenity.

"If the world is going to end . . ." she began to argue.

"Child, the world ends every day, but earth abides. It will just be different. Better or worse, I cannot guess, but it will be different."

"I am so glad we had this little talk, Mother," Claire snapped, her nerves screaming. "Now I can go off happy in the knowledge that if I do not die along the way, nothing will ever be the same. I don't want to change the world or end it. I want . . . I don't even know what I want anymore." It was a cry of anguish.

"Confusion is the human condition, Claire. You better get used to it."

"You and Father are not bewildered!"

Helene laughed. "Daughter, the day I am not confused

and uncertain and unsure of six things I was absolutely sure I knew, I will order my shroud. You have great strength, but your weakness is your need to be certain."

Claire started to sulk, then stuck her tongue out at her mother instead. Helene grabbed Claire's shoulders and pulled her head forward and kissed her on each cheek, then in the center of the forehead. The girl felt a tingle across her brow, as if something asleep within her was restless. It was as if she had an eye that was trying to open. She was caught between the comfort of her mother's rare affection and a desire to retreat into the safe sureties with which she had tried to surround herself. Clumsily, she kissed her mother back.

"I have something for you, Claire."

"What? More dire predictions, or some good advice?"

Helene dug into her belt pouch and pulled out a small, black stone. "I carried this away from the temple of Artemis more than twenty-five years ago. It has virtues I cannot grasp, or use, and I have kept it for you. You will know how to use it when the time is ripe."

Claire looked at the bit of rock resting in her palm. It looked quite ordinary, but it felt heavy. For a second she imagined she held a world in her hand. Her wrist almost ached with the weight of it. She was overwhelmed with a great exhaustion, and her shoulders sagged. Had Helene really carried the thing around for all these years? How? No one could be that strong.

Slipping it into her own waist pouch, the sensation of weariness left her. "Thank you. You never gave me anything before. Oh, your knowledge and skill, to be sure," she added hastily, wishing she had not spoken, "but nothing solid." She found her cheeks were warm with embarrassment.

Helene nodded. "I wish I could have been a different sort of mother, Claire. Not better. I have been the best I could all my life. It took me awhile to understand that. I hope you will grasp it someday. But I wish I could have acted differently with you, been closer and more giving. I never desired children. That does not mean I did not *want* you. But I have always felt quite bewildered by all of you. I do not understand you. I do not comprehend how Dorothea can be so blissful mending linen, or how Anna even exists! She's so . . ."

"Spectral?" Claire offered the word to stem the babble of confession. She did not want to hear her mother's admissions of confusion. And, more than anything, she wanted to escape the sense of equality that was beginning to grow between them. She did not want Helene as a peer, but as someone to look up to. Claire nearly giggled in spite of herself. Helene was so little!

Her mother made an open-palmed gesture of helplessness, then gave a brief shrug. "I do not believe her feet *really* reach the ground. Do you recall at all how I was when I was carrying her?"

"A little. You went around stomping a great deal, it seemed to me, and you looked very red the whole time." She let herself breathe a little easier to be back on safe ground, away from the sense of being an undesired child and an incomprehensible person.

"Did I? It is not fun to carry a saint in your belly."

"A saint? Is she? I mean, I know she is very good. Sometimes too good." Claire felt like squirming as she said the words.

"Yes. She is. Now, imagine carrying that much pureness around for nine months. I knew the moment she was conceived, and I spent the entire time feeling soiled with myself. *All* of you rebuked me in the womb, made me see all my spiritual short-comings, but Anna was by far the worst. I was never so glad as when the labor started."

"Rebuked you?"

"Claire, you are not like other children. I do not mean simply because of your abilities as mages, or shapeshifters. Those inheritances were bred into you, quite deliberately, I believe. But there is more. I *know* how the Virgin felt with Jesus—and I am not surprised he was an only child!"

Claire gaped at her mother. Helene was the least imaginative person she knew, so she accepted these statements as facts. "Why is that so dreadful?"

"It was like being cut to pieces by light. I do not know. It hurt, Claire. After you and Roderick, I swore I would endure no more. Artemis informed me I had no choice in the matter. I remember how you felt, like a lotus in my womb. A lotus made of knives. So, Dorothea was born. Do you know why I called her that? Because Aphrodite herself had to put in an appearance to get her started. I had never needed any urging to share your father's couch before. But after you and your brother came, I would not bear his touch for months. You were a lotus like the moon, and Roderick was blue, somehow. Dorothea was a rosy bloom. And Anna! Anna was so golden, like the sun burning me up from inside."

"I am sorry, Mother." Claire found her hands had clenched into fists. She understood a little of the pain Helene had just voiced. Anna always made her feel even more untidy than she usually felt. "I never knew I injured you."

Helene turned on her with a fierce glare, green eyes half ablaze. "Being alive is an injury, Claire. Learn that lesson, and you will manage quite well." She rose and stalked away, leaving Claire feeling like a monster. Her whole world seemed to be breaking to pieces, and she had the irrational conviction that it was her fault, somehow. She tried to conceptualize how it would feel to have a flower made of blades inside her, and decided that virginity was much better. Who would desire a girl like her, in any case? She remembered the terrible eyes that had sought her in her father's study, and shuddered. She was glad for the first time in her life that no deity had ever spoken to her. They might order her to marry a demon or something worse.

Claire got up and went over to where the stranger sat in the shadows. What had Helene called him. A fakir? A holy beggar. She felt less disoriented as she approached him. She sat down facing him, folded her legs under her, and closed her eyes, hoping his calm would enfold her. She felt his holiness and she liked it. It was very odd, for it was not unlike the way she had felt as a child when she climbed into the safety of Geoffrey's lap. It was insane, for she could not think of two people less alike than the unwashed fakir and her scholarly father. She was revolted by his filthy hair and dirty breechcloth, repelled as she always was by any sort of uncleanness, but her heart swept that aside in a brisk gesture of negation. A warmth filled her, a sense of gladness. Nothing mattered but the sweetness of his presence.

All sense of the present faded away, and Claire felt she slept, except that she had never been so awake in her life. Her eyes seemed glued shut and wide open at the same time, and her flesh transparent. Her bones seemed to reach into the earth and feel it.

Blackness swirled. Two huge red stars spun towards her through the darkness, and terror gripped her heart. A smell filled her senses, a scent like all the rotting dead since time began, and with it another feeling, of warm blood pooling up around her legs, her waist, lapping her nipples, caressing her long neck, filling her mouth, her eyes and ears. She wanted to scream. Her mouth was full of blood. She could taste it.

The stars became eyes, enormous, merciless eyes. A mouth gaped. A hideous tongue lolled out. Teeth like arrowheads pierced the tongue and blood spouted up. Claire wanted to protect the tongue from the teeth, somehow. She was frozen with fear, and she tried to lift a hand to help the poor, injured organ. The red eyes glared and the mouth closed around her head. Claire screamed as the teeth bit through her neck, as blood filled her, within and without. Pain. It seemed to go on forever. She felt herself die, become nothing. It was good. Blackness swirled.

Claire found herself asprawl on the ground. Her face was soaked with sweat and coated with dirt, as if she had rolled her head around. She tasted blood and found she had bitten the inside of her cheek. Shuddering, she wished she could escape her body. She hated being dirty. A gash on her forehead oozed sluggishly and her skull throbbed.

The sense of her own death persisted. It struck her that she would indeed perish, and soon, and that Roderick and Anna would die upon their quest as well. She did not know how she *knew,* but she was quite certain. So be it.

Her father would not know, nor her mother. Geoffrey would move both heaven and earth to protect his children, no matter what schemes of the gods' he might disrupt in the bargain. That thought comforted her, because she could not bear the idea of her father losing any of his children. Perhaps the gods would lie to him. She prayed so as she had never prayed for anything in her life.

The *fakir* opened his eyes, and Claire felt his calm penetrate the bleak desolation within her. He was a dirty, odd stranger, and she loved him intensely, immediately. He would guide her, even onto death.

V

When they reached the delta of the river, the reed clogged channels and the little islands with their nomadic population, Claire could smell the sea beyond. It blew away the stagnant odor of the Euphrates, low and sluggish at summer's end, and refreshed her. She felt almost excited as they transferred from a low draft river vessel to a larger sea-going one. In all her travels, she had never actually crossed any open sea for the simple reason that Geoffrey refused to set foot in anything larger than a dugout. He had protested mightily at her decision to cross the gulf and the Indian Ocean, rather than take the caravan route across the desert, retracing her companion's journey of some several months, and he had been outraged that she had chosen to leave her horse, Absalom, behind.

Claire had been surprised at her decisions herself. She was not sure why she had made them. It was not a clear, logical choice, but a kind of knowledge she had within her. All she could remember of her encounter with the terrible being who had bitten her head off was the smell and the pain, and her own conviction that she was going to perish. But she also had a sense of direction, perhaps for the first time in her life, and she *knew* she must make haste. To rush towards her own demise was madness, but she had a sense of correctness that had allowed her to defy her father for the first time in her brief life. It had also let her ignore her brother's fury, and his near-begging that they must trade tasks. She did not want to think of her precious Roderick facing either the lolling tongue and slavering chops of the red-eyed goddess, nor of him encountering the terrible white eyes that sought her from the icy mountains.

. Claire could hardly tell him any of this, for it would only have added to his sense of ill-usage and his feeling that he was being given a less than heroic task. She hardly understood it herself and hated the feeling of uncertainty she had. It was as if her head really had been snapped off, because she was not thinking as much as acting on some intuitive level she had never experienced before. It disturbed her, because she had copied her father's logical approach to problems for so long. And suddenly she had stopped.

The waves rolled into the shore, and a dozen dhows stood by narrow wharves. Her companion, Djurjati, eyed the scene impassively. They walked out with their bundles of belongings, and Claire inquired of various captains until she found a ship that served her needs. She had spun a small spell upon herself, so she looked like a Greek youth, for the sailors would not travel with women aboard, unless they were slaves, and only then reluctantly. Females, they believed, caused storms at sea.

Claire and Djurjati settled on the deck of the dhow they had chosen. The fakir promptly folded himself into his meditations, and she let herself study him. The sailors eyed his actions uneasily, and the girl, anticipating trouble, cast the illusion that he was merely sleeping. The creak of the rigging of the single triangular sail, the minor shifting of the boat, and the shouts of the sailors as they prepared to cast off, faded from her consciousness as she enjoyed the blue of the water and sky, the smell of resin-caulked timber and spices, and the breeze against her skin.

She could not remember ever having felt so involved with her senses as she had been for the past several days.

Claire ruminated on this, and wondered how she could have lived twenty years without paying attention to the world. It was as if she had been asleep, and was now awake, vividly alert. Claire felt she was a different person, and she was not certain if she approved.

Frowning over this thought, Claire barely heard the cries as they cast off. The ship slid away from the wharf and the helmsman shouted directions. The little vessel wallowed into the swell, and the sail bellied with the wind. It was a beautiful sight. She watched the curve of the white canvas against the blue of sky and water and felt her heart lift at the utter simplicity of it. It was perfect!

"It is illusion." The voice of Djurjati broke into her thoughts, and Claire was surprised at how angry she felt. She did not move a muscle as she struggled to quell a fury that was not unlike that of the red-eyed terror. She could not believe she contained such rage. Where did it come from? Surely she was not angry with him. He only spoke what he believed. "The world is only a dream."

For some reason, this made her even more furious. Claire rolled the words around in her mind and tried to grasp what angered her. Djurjati had spoken this way before, and she had listened without any response. He was her teacher and her guide, and she knew she loved him, even if she did not know why. He was wise. She was sure of this.

Or was he? What was the nature of delusion? It was a question she would have liked to discuss with her father. She would never see Geoffrey again, or Helene, or her brother and sisters. They were no dream. They were the best people she had ever known, and she wished to fly home and tell them so.

Claire thought of the pages of her father's unfinished history of his adventures. Each incident had several versions, as if he was trying to sort out fact from lie. There was pain in those pages, not just the horror of the days of the Shadow in the Levant, but of Geoffrey's own terrors and doubts. He never spared himself or put himself in a good light. He was always self-critical, and with a start, Claire realized she had always done the same of herself, in imitation of her adored father. He could heal all manner of hurts, but he could not heal himself. *We injure ourselves by our longings. Is this what Djurjati is trying to show me when he says the world is a dream?* For a moment Claire felt she understood, and then it was gone.

Leaning her back against the side of the ship, she felt the spring of the waters beneath her. It was a good feeling, a simple, clear being. The sun sparkled on the water, and the ship gathered speed as the wind quickened. *If the world is only a dream, then all my father's work is nothing. All the service my family has made to the goddess is meaningless.*

Claire decided the thought was unbearable and felt the anger surge, then fade. She let her shoulders relax and breathed the air. Somehow, in the past few days she had lost her ability to care about complex things. The more Djurjati explained to her the tenets of his religion with its seemingly endless series of re-births and rituals for achieving release, the less she wished to learn of it. He was very kind, but firm. She was a woman, a vessel of impurity, and the best she could hope for was to be reborn as a man, so that, after many lifetimes, she could cease existing altogether. Claire had lived her whole life amongst peoples who held females in small esteem. Her mother had told her this was only a fear of women speaking. The girl had wondered how anyone could be afraid of something they despised.

She rolled her head against the side of the ship, feeling the planks and sensing something of the nature of the wood itself. She put her hand against the deck. What a wonderful thing wood was. How could she have overlooked this? The more Djurjati insisted the world was illusion, the more she found to treasure in it. It was perverse of her, she knew, but so powerful was her sense of doom, so sure was she that she was going to die very soon, that her only experience of the goddess she had longed for would be to perish by her hand, that nothing else mattered.

Claire looked at Djurjati and tried once again to discover why she found him so loveable. It was certainly not his unkempt person. She had to struggle with her basic revulsion at untidiness. And it was not his mind, which she regarded as filled with superstitions and just plain foolishness. But he shone. His aura was clear and pure. Like Anna's. She let a slow smile play across her lips as she thought of her beautiful baby sister and Djurjati. What had her mother said? That Anna was like a saint? So was this strange man. And yet he thought himself impure and unworthy. He wanted to be perfect just as much as she did. The path he had chosen was one of prayer and fasting, of contemplation. She wanted to shine as brightly as he did before she died. It seemed a singularly foolish reason, and a selfish one, to follow him.

When she had recovered a little from the sheer terror of her vision, Claire had discovered she possessed knowledge she had not had before. As she had accepted the imminence of her death, she also accepted the other notions that now occupied her mind. She wished she were like her ancestor, Eleanor of Avebury, who, in addition to being brave and resourceful, had had a specific task to perform and a set of instructions to follow. Saille and Briget had talked to her. Claire felt a little envious of that. Granted, she had spoken to her god-father, Mercutio di Maya, who was the god Hermes, on several occasions, but he had never advised her or instructed her. He was, in truth, a part of the family, as much as Geoffrey or Helene, and she never thought of him as a deity.

Claire was startled by this train of thought. She blinked and pulled her head back in a little gesture of surprise. She banged the coping with the movement and rubbed her skull reflectively. *I never wanted to talk to a god. I only wanted to speak to Saille or Briget or Artemis. No, not Artemis. She is my mother's.* The girl found herself quivering a little at the very idea of communing with the goddess who had been Helene's guardian and guide. It was almost indecent, like lusting after one's father.

She brushed the thought aside and tried to dig out of her reluctant brain the scraps of knowledge she had found after the visitation of the red-eyed intruder. *I have seen the goddess. It just was not what I desired or expected. I never imagined it would be so terrible. I wanted the goddess to hold me and love me, the way Mother never did, and instead I got something else. I never dreamed I would be invited to die. And here I am, rushing into the arms of death, like a woman to a lover. I do not even have Djurjati's faith that I will be reborn in some better form. In truth, I think that the idea of being reincarnated endlessly, until one can achieve non-existence, is most peculiar, and silly! If that is true, then the purpose of life has not meaning, and I cannot bear that. I want to heal the world, not end it.*

Claire remembered how she had played with her father's magic flute as a little girl. She could feel the music it held within it, just as she could hear the same music when she sat in Geoffrey's lap. Although she could not whistle the melodies, she had them in her bones and blood, and they were full of beauty and grace. They were healing songs. But once, she recalled, she had held the flute and, for a moment, heard the monstrous melody which, if played for any length of time, might rend the world. She had that within her too, and sometimes when she danced, she felt that song course along her flesh, drowning out the sweet music of grace. It filled her and possessed her, and she could not imagine how her gentle father had created such a thing.

Then she *knew*. He had not. The two songs had been since time began, and they were one. Healing was a kind of destruction, and destruction a face of creation, not a separate entity. It was not complex. It was utterly simple.

Claire thought of the red eyes and foul maw of her vision, and felt a curious sorrow. The being that would slay her could not hear the healing song any longer. She had been cut off from it by some means. *Perhaps if she eats me, swallows me, some of the song will get into her and heal her.* The girl felt herself blush. *What pride. Such ambition. We cannot heal the gods, can we?*

For four days they sailed, down the gulf, and Claire discovered that the worst part of sea voyages was boredom and confinement. She was used to several hours of exercise on horse or in the field every day, and there was not room for anything like that. For the first time she missed her mother as a sparring partner, and, more, she missed her entire family; Dorothea singing as she bustled about the house, Anna juggling bright balls of light and smiling, even her parents arguing. And, fiercest of all, Claire missed Roderick, and wished they could have parted with more affection. The memory of his final words still ached. *You took what was mine, and I shall never forgive you.*

Djurjati instructed her. He taught her the rudiments of his tongue, using common objects where his command of Arabic failed. Much to her surprise, his language seemed akin to both Greek and Latin, rather than the Arabic they used as a lingua franca, and she was able to advance rather rapidly once she accepted this rather astonishing idea. She asked him what the letters looked like, and discovered he could neither read nor write, and, indeed, regarded such accomplishments as unnecessary to her purposes. Claire was a little shocked.

In between language lessons, Djurjati tried to teach her his beliefs, and only her respect for his spiritual beauty checked her impatience. Claire wanted to tell him her thoughts, to enter into the sort of argument she had experienced not only with her father, but with scholars in every city from Cairo to Baghdad, but she sensed it would make him unhappy, and kept her tongue behind her teeth as much as she could.

As the sun began to sink in the west, she asked him a question that refused to remain silent. "What is your intention in instructing me?"

Djurjati hesitated. "I am your guide."

"My guide to what?"

"To show you the way."

"The way to what? You had a dream, you have told me, and you journeyed with the caravaners for half a year, to find me and take me back with you."

"Yes. But I must show you the way to *moksa,* to release."

"Why? You have told me I cannot achieve it, because I am only female."

Two deep furrows creased his dark brow. "I forgot. So complete is the illusion you cast about yourself that I forget. But, you will remember what I teach you in some other life—and I will acquire grace."

In unconscious imitation of her father, Claire coiled her fingers into the illusionary beard she wore. "Are you certain of these things?"

"To be sure."

"How?"

"What do you mean?"

"By what means do you know that you can be reborn?"

"It is written." He used a word which, after some trouble, Claire understood to denote revealed wisdom, not necessarily words on paper. She nodded. She was beginning to realize how difficult it was to distinguish between what she believed and what she knew. He was as much in the dark as she. She gave a little sigh. Helene was right. She was never going to be certain of anything.

A sailor gave a shout and pointed towards the sea. The sky to the west was streaked with rose and pink, but the waters before the ship lacked any reflection of these colours. It was a dull grey, and murky. The master, a vigourous man in his forties, dashed forward and peered overboard. Then he looked anxiously towards the horizon to the south and barked several orders. The sailors scrambled about, and the helmsman turned the ship to a new course.

The wind slacked off as they turned, and after a few minutes, died completely. They were heading east, towards the faint outline of the shore, as the stillness gathered. Claire caught some muttered phrases from the men. They were worried about something more than this sudden becalming in the middle of the gulf.

A thick mist congealed upon the murky grey waters as the last of day faded into twilight. It seemed to terrify several of the crew, and the master shouted them into silence after an outburst of hysterical incoherence from one or two. Claire could see the sweat that beaded his brow, and studied the now advancing fog with interest. She could see nothing in it to arouse such terror, and, puzzled, she reached out with her senses to probe it.

Her first impression came from her ears. The mist had a sound, very soft, very low, but a distinct tone. As she concentrated on it, identifying it, Claire felt the hair at the nape of her neck bristle. It seemed harmless enough regular creak, almost like the sound of an oar in its housing, but it was still unnerving. She breathed slowly to calm herself.

The smell of the mist filled her, and it was overwhelming. It was the scent of salt, of weed, of fish, and, in itself, not unpleasant. But it was concentrated, so that she was nearly sickened by it. She pulled her extended senses away sharply, and pinched her nostrils with her fingers to shut out even the memory of the odor. A glance at Djurjati revealed very human apprehension, and Claire was relieved. She had half expected to find him immobilized in trance, as if nothing was happening.

The mist began to gleam faintly, and several sailors backed away from the prow of the ship, until they were as far away as they could get without jumping into the water. Their eyes were wide, the whites flashing against their tanned faces, and Claire could see they were holding back screams. Another clot of sailors surrounded the master, speaking quietly but with great intensity, and one pointed in her direction. She wondered if her illusion had broken, and her sex had been revealed, then realized he had gestured at her companion.

The mist swelled and bellied, and it was incredibly beautiful, like the shiny surface of many pearls, every colour from white to black. Something was coming. The steady creak was discernible now without any magical aid, and the sea smell drowned out any other, even the vile stink of fear sweat she knew was seeping from her body. There was a scream from somewhere, a shrill shriek of terror.

The glowing pearls of mist solidified into an object, and Claire could not be sure if it was artifact or animal. It was like a ship in the form of an enormous fish, but, as well, it was a huge fish with a sail afixed to its back. The prow was a mouth, a maw that moved up and down, creaking rhythmically. There was no other sound. The water parted before it silently, and there was not a whisper around her.

The sailors beside the master stared up at the great mouth moving towards them. It towered above the top of the mast, gleaming in the now deepening twilight. The two of them dashed across the deck and reached for Djurjati's seated figure. Claire moved without thought or hesitation.

Her sword came out with an ease of long practice, and the hilt smashed one sailor in the jaw while her foot caught the other in the chest and sent him sprawling. He rolled to his feet and charged as she shifted the sword from right to left, caught his extended arm with her right, and pulled him headfirst into the gunwale of the ship. It was a trick Helene had taught her, and Claire had an instant of pleasure that she had executed it so handily. She turned back as several more sailors rushed to help their comrades.

One grabbed Djurjati's slender body and pulled him to his feet. Then he ran forward with his squirming burden towards the creaking jaws of the ship-fish. Djurjati reached a hand out and poked the sailor with a single finger. The man gave a howl and dropped the fakir. Claire kicked and slashed her way through the knot of sailors who were stupid enough to stand between her and her guide, hardly conscious of the terror that pounded in her blood. She was barely aware of her actions, that she was disabling rather than killing, because her only clear thought was to reach her friend.

There was a crashing sound, and the jaw of the ship-fish crunched off the bow-sprit of their vessel. Claire felt as if time slowed for a moment as she watched the huge mandible close and re-open. A voice echoed in her mind, her father's voice, clear and precise, and she found her body following the instructions even as she put a boot into the groin of another sailor. Her sword went into her teeth, and she tasted steel and the tang of blood, while her hands englobed an unseen ball. For a second nothing happened, and Claire was afraid. She was such a poor magician. The blue mage-fire bloomed in her palms, and she hurled it into the maw just as it tore off another hunk of the ship.

A fist struck her between the shoulders, and she grabbed her sword out of her mouth as she rammed an elbow into the belly of her assailant. She heard a faint grunt just before a boom deafened her. Claire whipped around and watched the ship-fish explode into a shower of pearlescent shards. A pillar of fire four times the height of the mast pierced the mist, and a rain of round stones began to batter the deck. She grasped Djurjati's hand and pulled him into such shelter as the overhang of the tiny cabin afforded.

The curious shower did not last long, but when it ceased, the entire vessel was ankle deep in spherical objects the size of eggs. The ship wallowed low in the now blue waters of the gulf, and the master shouted to his men to remove the debris. Cautiously, one sailor picked up a double handful of the stones. They were a dull grey in the twilight, and seemed to be covered with soot. He felt no ill-effect from contact, and started to toss them overboard. A pale gleam from one made him pause, and he brushed it against his grimy trousers. A pearl the rose of a woman's breast lay in his work-calloused hand.

Claire watched the sailors rush forward to claim their

unlooked-for treasure, and tried to decide what to do. The men had tried to feed her friend to whatever that thing had been, and they would undoubtedly wish to finish the job as soon as they got over their excitement. In the Levant, it was very poor manners to murder those who have eaten bread with you, but it did happen. They would certainly dispose of her as well, if she gave them a chance, for sailors were less eager to travel with mages than even with females. There were methods to become invisible, but she doubted her ability to manage that. She was still in shock that her fire-ball had worked. She had never been very good at that one.

If only they would forget what happened. As soon as she had the thought she saw the solution. Claire visualized the past few minutes as vividly as she could, with as much clarity as she could, concentrating on small details, like the sound and smell of the mist. When she was satisfied that she had done the best she could, she dismembered the picture, piece by piece. The sweat poured down her face and stung the little cuts at the corners of her mouth where the steel had broken the skin.

Shaking with exhaustion, she remembered the vision. The mist was still there, and the ship-fish, but no vestige of the fight across the deck remained. All there was was the explosion and the hail of pearls, battering the heads and bodies of the sailors. The shards of the body of the ship-fish cut flesh and knocked men unconscious. It was hard; there were so many tiny details to create. She did it with care, even as panic fluttered in her belly.

Finally satisfied that it was as good as she could manage, Claire gathered the memory into a mental globe. She pictured a flute, her father's flute, against her cracked lips, and "breathed" into it. She felt her spirit quicken the vision, and she held it until she had a sense of balance and fullness. She paused, examined her handiwork, and then released it. The spell swelled. Claire could nearly "see" it. It was like a ball of glass as it enveloped the little ship.

Then it was gone, and the master and the sailors paused

in their activities for an instant. Confusion played across their brown faces, then a kind of slackness followed. Claire tensed as she leaned against the rough wood of the cabin. If she had failed, she would have to fight her way out of this.

"Wonder what destroyed that thing?" asked one.

"Who cares. Will you look at this pearl? We will be lucky to make shore with this load. We are rich, man, rich. We can each buy a dozen ships."

"Or a hundred. And women! By Iblis, women."

The girl let out her breath. She was filthy and exhausted, too tired to rejoice. Abstractedly, she picked up a few pearls and dropped them into her bag, then slid down onto the deck and stretched out. After a moment, Djurjati sat beside her and pillowed her head on one of his thighs. He stroked her head lightly. As sleep began to claim her, she heard him whisper, "You are *maya*."

VI

Djurjati disembarked the ship with more relief than Claire had ever expected to see him express. She hid a little smile, because it did not seem proper to laugh at the sudden humanness of her teacher and guide. Then she shrugged. He would not care. It was one of the things she loved about him. He didn't care about manners, and he never worried about being perfect, except in his adoration of his god.

She hurried after him, suddenly afraid of being lost in the press of people along the docks. The smell of India was incredible. It was rank and green, like crushed flowers, and hot as she had never experienced heat before. And people. There were so many. The docks teemed. The streets were thick with bodies, with vivid faces, dark-skinned and fine featured. They screamed and bargained and bustled to and fro, ignoring men resembling Djurjati who sat motionless in the midst of traffic, and ducking to avoid large cows who seemed to run wild in the narrow ways.

The man led her away from the wharves into the city

itself. They passed buildings whose walls were covered with carvings of people engaged in the most graphic forms of love-making, and Claire was glad she had cast a small illusion about herself, so that she appeared to be a youth rather than a woman. She kept sneaking glances at the big-breasted women and long-waisted men, their faces filled with serene delight as their bodies coiled in such specific copulations that she blushed hotly. Pretending to be a man made her feel less conspicuous about her wide-mouth gaping. Claire wondered what the purpose of the buildings might be, and thought they must be brothels. She asked Djurjati, and was told they were temples, which shocked her into silence for several blocks.

They passed food stalls steaming with spicy scents, and booths of cloth or copperware in small bazaars. A clamour of cymbals announced a train of brightly dressed people in garlanded carts on some festive errand. The people in the street waved at the procession in a friendly way, and the merry-makers waved back. Claire had thought Baghdad the most colourful city on earth, but she changed her mind as she followed her teacher. The smell made her feel giddy, and the noise was overwhelming after the quiet of the ship.

A huddle of starved looking people caught her eye. They edged along the road, and other pedestrians avoided them. "Are these people ill?" she hissed at Djurjati.

He did not even glance at them. "Pariahs."

Claire gave the people another look and could see nothing about them to merit their obvious exclusion. Djurjati had told her of this sort of people on their journey, about the division of priests from warriors, warriors from merchants, merchants from peasants, and finally, peasants from these untouchable pariahs. She had struggled to understand their supposed impurity, the idea that their very birth was a punishment for misdeeds in previous lives, and had not succeeded. She had dealt with priests and merchants and beggars all her life, and it had never crossed her mind to think of them as part of a greater scheme of things. A great many of the things which Djurjati had told her were confusing and troublesome, because they contradicted each other. He had assured her that she was very high caste, because her father was a sort of *brahmin* and her mother a kind of warrior, and then he had told her that caste was all part of the illusion of the world, and added that women were the most delusive part of all, and that they could not achieve release. At that point Claire had decided that she had come to the limits of her confusion, and refused to think about it any more. Now, watching the pariahs slinking along, she was furious. The beggars in Baghdad were better treated.

A howling mob of men pushed through the street ahead of them. Claire stared at them for a long second, and lost sight of her teacher. There was something strange about them. She could not put her finger to it for a moment. She hurried to follow Djurjati and frowned. The mob surged and screamed, and she was glad of the extra inches she had, because it gave her a good view of them.

Then it struck her. The people were oddly lightless. She was so used to seeing the little glow of body light around everyone that she did not miss it immediately. She found her mind filled it in unless she made a deliberate effort to look. They were Shadow.

Stunned, Claire looked around her in the streets, to check her observations carefully. The shaven headed man in the white garment shone like a topaz; the shuffling pariah in rags gleamed like an amethyst. The people in the mob ahead were utterly empty, without so much as a flicker of light. Somehow she had expected all the people of Darkness to be obviously horrible, but these people looked normal except for their lack of aura.

"Djurjati, those people ahead."

"Yes?"

"They . . . what are they shouting?"

"They are deluded. They are concerned with the question of which goddess is greater, Durga or Sri. It is most strange. I have never seen anything like it. The goddess is one and many. It is not to argue over. She takes many forms so that all may find a face to worship. She is the energy that moves, and that is all."

"They are shouting about the goddess?" Claire found that idea did not make any sense with what she knew of the effect of Shadow. She decided that she was mistaken, and did not say anything about their auraless appearances.

"No, not precisely. I know that you are very precise." Djurjati gave a little smile, to let her know this was a gentle joke, for they had gotten into some vigourous disagreements on the boat when she had demanded exactness. "They are shrieking about which one is superior, which I cannot say I think is speaking of the goddess. It is very disrespectful. And they are going somewhere. Ah, a temple. Oh, my."

"What?" Claire wished she had progressed further in her study of the language.

"They are going to the temple I was planning to visit. Perhaps we should go to another. I confess I do not like the look of these men."

"They do not have any auras, teacher."

The fakir gave her a look. "You never told me you could perceive those."

Claire gaped at him. "I . . . I thought everyone did. Everyone in my family does, and has for generations, I think."

Djurjati let his shoulders sag a little. "It took me years of meditation to achieve that ability, to see the light of the world, and you were born with it. No wonder you make my eyes hurt when I look at you. No wonder She sent me to you. Truly, you are a remarkable being."

"For a woman."

"You are *maya*. And casting a veil of disguise about yourself leads me astray. I forget that you are a woman, and by law must always lean upon a man, deceive him, and that you cannot achieve release. The law is the law. Dharma is the law."

"The law is an idiot," Claire muttered. Her mother had rarely spoken of her own childhood in Byzantium before its ruin, but she had frequently expressed the bitterness that lingered over her father's refusal to value her, simply because she was not a man. She had taught all her daughters never to permit their sex to diminish them, and Claire was glad of the lesson. She loved Djurjati, and she respected him, but she knew that she could not accept all his ideas without question.

"We will go to the temple of Ratri. This street should take us there."

They turned down a little street, crossed a large bazaar, and turned a corner. Before them was a pile of rubble. The stones were blackened with soot, and the graceful carved hand of a statue pointed towards the merciless blue sky in mute supplication. There was blood here and there, dried and rusty, and the smashed pieces of many idols.

Djurjati squatted down over the broken hand and looked from side to side. His face was impassive, but his red-rimmed eyes were troubled. Claire crouched beside him. "Was this where we were coming?"

"Yes. What has happened since I left? I have never seen such a thing. There is madness here. I thought I had left fear behind me, child, and now I find I have it still."

There was a gobbling scream, and several men scrabbled out of the ruins of the temple. They hurled pieces of broken masonry at Claire and the fakir and shouted. The girl ducked and darted back, and Djurjati followed her. As she passed over a corner of the ruined temple that was almost intact, she felt a presence, and almost stumbled. It was not like the terror of her dreams, or the vision she had had in the garden. This was gentler, softer, sweeter.

They are trying to dismember me, daughter. They are tearing my body apart.

What can I do?

Help me, help me.

Claire paused and looked at the distorted faces of the men swarming towards her. She did not need any translation to understand that they wanted to kill her and that they had had something to do with the destruction of this holy place. She had been in and out of holy places all her life, and she knew how they felt. She did not question the sanctity of the ground she stood on, nor the urgency of the voice in her mind. The lightless men howled.

With a leap, Claire sprang over the fallen blocks and drew her sword. She charged into the pack of attackers, hacking and cutting with a fury she could not believe. She almost enjoyed killing the lightless men. They had injured something precious, and the price was death. She slew, and felt nothing, no sorrow, no remorse, only a slight pleasure.

When she stopped, when all the men lay dead or dying around her, Claire turned. Djurjati was motionless, watching her. He had an expression of great sadness on his bony face. She felt herself blush with shame. She had disappointed him, and she knew it. She had defended some portion of the goddess, some face of the Lady, and it had cost her the respect of her teacher. Claire wanted to cry, and felt her face go stony. There were too many conflicts, too many demands. She was not strong enough for this.

The days passed, and Claire found she was no more comfortable with the clamour of India than she had been upon her arrival. The sheer number of people overwhelmed her, and the warm lushness of the air was breathless. She had gotten used to the powerfully spiced food and the absence of *kavya*. She rather liked the hot drink called *chai*. It had a delicate flavor. The Hindus served it with milk and a great deal of sugar morning, noon, and night. It helped keep her awake while Djurjati instructed her.

They had never spoken of the slaughter at the temple. It lay between them like a festering sore, and the intimacy that had developed on the ship was lost. The pain of that hurt Claire, but she knew she could not explain to Djurjati why she had done what she had. The reminders of her act were everywhere, for there were packs of lightless people roaming the streets of cities and the highways between them wherever they went. They attacked temples everywhere, and many cities were reduced to being battle-grounds of torch-bearing mobs of madmen.

For all of this, she found herself falling in love with the land and the people. Claire struggled with the language, and there were whole days when they did not see a single Shadow-struck person and it was possible to concentrate on listening to her teacher. They walked from village to town, from town to city, sleeping in temples or under the sky. She almost forgot sometimes anything but the tongue, the rhythm of it, the rise and fall of the syllables. It got into her bones, until at night she dreamed in it as she danced in her sleep. The dance and the language became one after a time, and she was barely conscious of her fluency. Claire found she had forgotten everything except the present, the smell of each day, the sound of Djurjati's voice as he detailed some story of the many gods of the land or revealed some abstruse philosophical point. It all blended with the colours of the fields, with garlanded wedding parties, burning *ghats* where the bodies of the dead were cremated, the bright, flowing garments of the women, the brown and green of the fields, and the earth beneath her feet. Her family, her history, her future, became a dream, and there was nothing but the moment.

Claire knew she was happy, though she could not imagine why. Every step she took brought her nearer to something she had no name for, something wanted and unwanted. She listened to Djurjati's sincere recitations of his scripture and felt only a deep content. The conviction of her own imminent death never left her, but it did not seem to matter. She could not remember ever feeling so replete, and it was sufficient.

In the third week of their travels, they entered an enormous city, the biggest one Claire had ever seen. It stood on one side of a river, the Ganges, which Djurjati informed her was sacred. Since he had told her that the waters of this river flowed from the heavens into the matted hair of his deity, Siva, it seemed perfectly reasonable that the river was holy. All of India was covered with sacred places, it seemed to her, and the scattered mobs of lightless men and women who wandered across it profaned that. She felt a deep, passionate caring for this land, and for its holinesses, and she did not regret her killings.

Still, the sluggish flow of the river looked perfectly ordinary, and rather dirty at that. Claire longed for one of the great baths of Baghdad, but she had gotten accustomed to the absence of such places and the way the Indian people immersed themselves in any source of water they happened to be passing. She had not felt clean since they started their trek, no matter how often she scrubbed in the river, and she did not anticipate the Ganges would be any different.

Counting on her fingers, Claire realized it was well past the middle of September, and close to her birthday.

"Djurjati, what day is it?"

He checked his stride for a moment, glanced at the soaring entrance of a temple, and answered. "It is the solstice tomorrow. The festival will begin soon. All the city will be decked with flowers. Come. We will go to the temple."

It was as if she had suddenly awakened from a long dream. Claire was choked with apprehension, and for a second she was immobilized. Then she knew that the sense of her own death which had haunted her for weeks was immediate. And it hurt. She did not wish to die. She followed her guide in a haze, barely noticing the huge buildings they passed. She could not understand. She had come there to die, not to serve any purpose. Alone, and in a strange land, she would perish, and never know why. It seemed unbearable.

But, except for the sweet voice in the ruined temple, no goddess had ever deigned to speak to her, as they had to her father and her mother, and probably to Roderick and Anna as well. She was not even sure why she had come. For herself, she had come for the comfort of Djurjati's eyes, and, finally, for the sense of content that had marked their journey together. She had come to meet her death and to run away from the knowledge of it at the same time.

Claire let her thoughts whirl, and felt both betrayal and rage. This is how her father must have felt when he had found out that he would not really be able to restore his mother's health and preserve his parents' lives. But she could not complain of having been lied to, because nothing had spoken to her at all. She must not be angry, because there was no one to be angry with.

Stumbling into the dimness of a temple behind Djurjati, Claire paused to remove her dusty sandals and wash herself in a stone basin. She felt very tired. Then she started as she saw the idol looming above the vast, tiled floor. There was no mistaking the red-rimmed eyes and lolling tongue of her vision, and she could almost smell the blood and the stench of corruption, though the temple was bedecked with flowers. She looked up into the merciless face and felt her heart sink.

Claire tried to wrench her gaze away, and almost managed. Then she saw the weapon the idol held in its left hand. It was a sword, but a sword like none she had ever seen before. The edges were rippled, like the waves of the sea, and in the hilt was a pearl as large as her fist, silvery-blue, and round as the moon. It was not like the crescent blades she wore at her slender waist, not like the straight ones the Greeks preferred. There was no doubt in her mind that this was the weapon of water mentioned in the pages of her great-aunt Rowena's history of the family. She paused a moment to wonder where her brother was, and how he and Anna fared, and wished she could see across the leagues that separated them. Did they know how much she loved them? Had she ever told them?

Then the sense of being hunted distracted her. At first she thought it was the nightmare figure before her, the being in her vision. Claire realized it was the cold, huge eyes that had found her in her father's study. For the first time since she had been a child, she felt little, and worse, helpless. She looked at the sword in the hand of the statue and wished she possessed it. Then she shook the thought away and looked for her companion in the shadows.

There was no one. She was alone. Claire strained her ears for any hint of sound and found a silence more profound than anything she could imagine. The shouts and cries of the street were gone. There was nothing. It was as if the world outside had vanished or never existed at all. Only the sense of the terrible eyes which sought her persisted, and she felt an icy coldness curl around her.

She forced her limbs to move. Claire found she was moving across the tiled floor, towards the statue and, in some fashion, away from the eyes. The closer she got to the statue, the more her throat closed with fear, but it was a different fear than she felt of the distant eyes. She turned to go around the patterned floor and found herself immobile. The silence pressed down on her. She tried to shout, but no sound came from her mouth.

Claire struggled with her terror for what seemed an eternity, caught between the looming presence of the goddess before her and the searching eyes behind her. Painfully, she twisted her head back and forth. Finally she turned to the statue. A throb came to her ears. It was such a welcome sound that for a second Claire did not care what it was. It seemed like a heartbeat. It throbbed again. The noise seemed to explode in her skull. She clapped her hands over her ears, but the noise continued.

The pain of the throb rattled through her over and over, until it became a drum and her feet began to move. She stepped on something sharp, a bit of glass, hidden between the tiles, and barely noticed the cut. Every sound and every movement was an endless agony, and every footfall seemed to shake the building, if not the entire cosmos. Her feet followed the pattern on the floor, and she felt the pattern connected to everywhere on earth. For a moment, she saw a chamber full of pattern, and saw herself, a tiny figure, balanced on a minuscule portion of it. There was a firepit and a great serpent swayed beside it. Then the drum sounded and she lost all sense but that of moving, even though her body screamed with unfleshly agony. It was the dance, the dance she had struggled with in the moonlight, the dance she had done in dreams. It was all that mattered.

Claire could feel her skin sheen with sweat in the humid air, and she could feel the protest of her muscles and tendons, but she could not stop, even as the breath in her chest grew more ragged. The thud of the drum in her skull forced her on, its pace increasing and becoming more wild. There was a noise behind her, a sort of terrible rending, and the girl leapt and whirled.

The statue stepped off its pedestal, four arms moving like striking serpents. Claire would have run, but she was petrified with terror. The arm with the sword descended towards her. Years of ruthless, pitiless training took command.

Her sword whipped out as she twisted to avoid the blade in the hand of the living statue. Her feet took wing, and she darted away, then ducked behind the terrible figure. She could smell the stink of rot and the tang of blood as she whirled past the black skin. A scream rattled her bones as the statue turned to pursue her. Claire felt her heart falter at the sound.

The red-rimmed eyes glared at her. Claire felt the rage in them, in the whole quivering body that lunged at her. The anger seemed to pool out of the goddess like fiery blood, and the girl could feel it seep into her, soak into her flesh and penetrate her bones until there was nothing in her but that rage. She flew at the figure, swinging her sword in a mad dance that seemed almost to please her fearsome opponent. Claire pulsed with anger, with a desire to destroy everything that lived. Including herself.

The wavy edged sword of the waters swept towards her, and Claire bobbed and shifted her own weapon to her left hand. She lifted her right hand into the descent of the blade and felt the metal sever flesh and bone. So much pain. There was so much pain in the world. She watched a fountain of blood gout from her injured arm with complete dispassion. It showered the looming goddess with a sheet of glistening red, and Claire knew that soon the pain would end. She would die. Then there was a searing sensation that made a nothing of her agony, as if the stump of her arm was on fire.

Claire felt her body shudder, and she wondered if her father would know. She wished she could have spared him. Then she watched detachedly as the gleaming chops of the black-faced goddess opened and descended towards her pounding head. The rotting stench of the mouth filled her faltering senses. As she waited for the teeth to snap her head off, for her pain to end, she felt an enormous compassion for the endless torment of the ravening monster above her.

Her sword clattered to the floor as she lifted her remaining hand to touch the cheek above her. *Before I die, I want to kiss you, Mother.* She did not know to whom she spoke in her heart, Helene or the hideous devourer whose arms now embraced her. Claire raised her lips to the blood-spattered chops of the goddess. *My torment will end, but yours goes on forever. I wish I could change that.* Then the mouth closed around her, and the throb of her heart was silenced. There was nothing.

VII

Someone was moaning, and Claire wished they would stop. Her skull pounded, and there was terrible pain. It surprised her, and then angered her. Being dead should not be so noisy or so painful. After what felt like an eternity, she decided she was alive, and realized that the moans were her own. She opened an eye cautiously, then closed it again. The light hurt! Everything hurt. She could still feel the teeth clamping down around her throat.

Weakly she tried to lift her arm to touch her neck, and found it did not move. It seemed to be tied down. She forced her eyes open, wincing at the light, and saw that she was wrapped tightly in a thin sheet. The effort exhausted her, and she let her head flop back and her eyes close. She held back another groan.

The pad of bare feet nearby made her turn her head and open her eyes. The headache stabbed her, and she made a little mewling noise. Djurjati bent down and looked at her. His glossy black eyes were wide with concern, and tenderness. He had a basin in his hands. He dipped a cloth in it, wrung it out, and washed her face and neck. It felt wonderful. He rinsed the cloth out, folded it, and laid it across her forehead. The water he used was scented with some flower. She breathed it in.

"What happened?" Claire whispered.

"Shh. Not now. You must rest. You must eat and recover your strength. Later is soon enough to talk."

"Why am I wrapped up like a mummy?"

"To keep you from fighting. To keep you from harm." He sounded sad and tired. "I will bring you soup."

Claire found she lacked the strength to argue. Besides, there was something nagging at the back of her mind. As the headache eased, the thought demanded attention. Djurjati returned and lifted her head with a lean arm and held a little cup to her lips. The sharp tang of *laban* mixed with the dusty taste of lentils filled her mouth. It was a broth, with nothing in it to chew, and it was cold. It washed away the vile iron taste in her mouth. There was some mint in it. Claire savored the clean, green flavor among the other tastes, and decided it was the best thing she had ever drunk. It hurt to swallow, as if her throat was bruised, but she did not care. She was too tired to care. Djurjati washed her face again, and Claire felt how dirty she was all over as she slipped into a light doze.

A voice howled in her mind, a terrible, harsh voice. There were words, but she could not grasp them. Distantly she could feel her aching body flex and flail against the bindings, and Claire knew she was trying to dance, not fight. It was such an urgent, wild dance. Her heart pounded with the rhythm of the dance. And then the words were clear, just for an instant, like a blow to the head, and she understood. Her muscles went slack. The dance was gone, for now. A sense of loss touched her, a profound longing to return to the dance forever. Her heart ached for the dancer, for the black-faced, lonely goddess, and then healing sleep claimed her.

When Claire opened her eyes again, it was night. She could hear shouts and cries not too far away, and she felt weak. And hungry. Her whole body seemed to be an empty belly. Her headache was gone, mercifully, and it no longer hurt to move it. She started to sit up, but the bindings restrained her.

Djurjati was at her side almost immediately. His face, in the flickering oil lamps of the room, was troubled. "How do you feel?"

Claire had a wild urge to giggle. She felt like a herd of camels had run across her several times, and she did not think her companion would appreciate the jest. "Alive. Unexpectedly alive."

"Good." He cast an anxious glance over his shoulder. "Can you walk, do you think?"

Walk! Her legs felt like old tree stumps. Her arms seemed leaden. Claire felt drained of blood. "If I must. Release me."

Djurjati hesitated, then unbound the cords that held the sheet in place. Claire sat up as he pulled the cloth away. Her tunic was rank with dried blood and old sweat, and her mouth curled with disgust. She lifted her right hand to brush the soil away, and stared at the stump of an arm. For several seconds she could not comprehend what she saw. She reached out the fingers of her left hand and touched the empty space beyond the wrist. The end of her forearm gleamed with the hideous whiteness of scar tissue, and it looked as if it had been burnt. She swallowed a scream and gave a little whimper instead. She remembered the arc of the sword as it cut flesh and bone, and knew it had not been a dream. She had dreamed she died, and lived, and staring at the stub of her wrist, she wished she had. Claire wanted to stretch out on the pallet and perish.

The sounds from the street increased and Djurjati spoke. "We must leave this place. They—those lightless ones— have been going from temple to temple, destroying. You have paid a great price for the sword of the goddess, and now you must bear it away."

Claire looked at the man stupidly for a second, then followed the gesture of his hand towards the object lying

on her cloak a few feet away. The lamplight played along
the wavy edge of the blade and gleamed upon the great
pearl in its hilt. A dull, rusty smear remained on the steel.
That is my blood, she thought.

The entire thing seemed unreal, and Claire was surprised to find herself standing up, then bending forward to
clasp the hilt of the sword in her remaining hand. A surge
like a wave of the sea swelled up her arm and over her
body. She tasted salt in her mouth, and smelled again the
ocean. A wave entered her blood, pressing the pain of her
injury away into some secret cavern within her, and giving
her a sense of renewal. Not wholeness. She would never be
whole again, never be perfect. But she was strong enough,
holding the enchanted blade, to remember the words she
had dreamed, and to walk and move. She would do her
duty, perform her task. Had she not paid for the privilege?
She thrust the naked blade into her belt.

Claire pulled the boots she had not worn since her arrival in India out of her pack, then discovered she was
unable to put them on one-handed. That small thing nearly
broke her. Tears of frustration and rage welled out of her
eyes, and she cursed the gods in all the many tongues at
her command. Djurjati shushed her and helped her on with
the boots, as if she was a child, then helped her put her bag
across her right shoulder. He picked up her bow and
arrows, and his own few belongings, and led her into the
temple proper.

The din was incredible as they reached the tiled
chamber where the idol stood glaring. Claire kept her eyes
on the floor, still feeling the throb of the dance, until she
could resist no longer. She took a look at the statue, and
saw her own scimitar now clasped in the hand of the figure. Then a dozen or so people bearing torches burst into
the room. They howled incomprehensibly, and began to
strike the pillars with sticks. The girl and her companion
hugged the shadows and crept towards the doorway as
more people pushed in, gibbering.

Finally, one man rushed up to the statue and thrust his

torch against the naked leg. There was a cracking sound, and a hand reached down and plucked the fellow up and drew him screaming into the lolling mouth. Claire was frozen in horror until Djurjati dragged her away. The statue made smacking noises with its lips as it ate the man, and reached for another. It gave a belch that shook the ceiling, and a large block fell, crushing two people. *I guess I just whetted her appetite,* she thought in a kind of hysterical daze.

Claire felt weak, but she followed Djurjati into the street. The air was thick with smoke and the night was alight with the glow of several fires beneath a sickle moon. Mobs dashed back and forth, and it took all her concentration to keep up with him.

Finally, they found a quiet neighborhood with a sleepy bazaar in its warrens. Claire sank down where he pointed and leaned against a wall. Her body screamed for sleep, but every time she closed her eyes she saw the terrible mouth and the red-rimmed eyes. Claire "heard" the whirlwind voice that screamed at her. She tried to quell the vision, but she was too tired and too weak. The words told her something, but she could not really grasp the meaning.

Her back rested against stone, and her legs and bottom sat on hard packed earth. After a few minutes, she noticed that, and realized she felt much more than rock and dirt. She brushed her forehead with her upper arm and tried not to look at her mutilated wrist. It fascinated her. Claire held up her stump and stared at it in the flickering glow of the city. She had been prepared to die, but instead she was hideously injured. She longed for wholeness, and for healing until her heart ached.

And then, just for an instant, she thought she heard her father's flute. Claire stared and looked around for the sound. No, she looked for Geoffrey and Helene in the shadows of the bazaar. She looked for rescue, for waking from this terrible nightmare. A momentary hope that they might appear by some magic was replaced with a despair that wrenched her. She wished she was little enough to curl up in Geoffrey's lap again. A bitter laugh swelled up in her throat as hot tears brimmed in her eyes. She raised her hand to brush them aside before they fell and shamed her, and banged the scarred stump into her cheek. If only I had never longed for adventures, she chided herself. I never could do anything perfectly. How am I going to change the world with no hand. I cannot even do magic without two hands. I am crippled. The thought shamed her, as if she had done something terribly wrong, and she hated it.

The tone of the flute came once more, and Claire sought in vain for its source. Then she realized that the sound came from within her, like the dance, but resided in the earth she sat upon as well. She pressed her palm against the dirt beside her and felt the tickle of power that denoted magic, and the voice of earth. It welled through her renewing her a little, easing the ache and hurt.

If I weren't so tired, I would dance. The thought tore the fragile healing just begun to shreds. I cannot dance again, not like this. Why couldn't I have just died! And why do I have to go on? Will you be still, curse you! As she mentally shouted this last thought at the howling voice in her mind, she began to laugh hysterically. The final little reins of control snapped as she ordered the goddess to shut up and saw it for the ridiculous act that it was. She was nothing, and no one would listen to her.

It took a moment to realize the howling was gone, stilled for the present, and Claire watched her terrible merriment vanish in surprise. Then Djurjati appeared out of the shadows with a bowl full of cold rice and spiced vegetables. Claire looked helplessly at her dirt-crusted remaining hand and wiped it on her filthy trousers. She felt so dirty. The man pointed at a structure in the middle of the compound, and Claire struggled to her feet, knocking her elbow against the sword and slashing her trousers on its wavy edges.

A sheath. I need a sheath, she told herself as she crossed the bazaar and pulled the dipper that hung beside the well off its hook. She plunged it into the dark waters and poured it over her head and shoulders. As the coolness touched her she knew that she had to seek the covering that belonged with the sword. That was part of what the voice had been shouting about. Where?

Her head snapped around so hard she heard a pop of spine. She looked northward, towards the icy mountains where the snows did not melt from century to century. Somewhere, there, the sheath was hidden. And dreadful white eyes sought her, something more terrible than even the goddess she had battled. Could anything be worse? Clumsily, she washed as she struggled to overcome her fear. Then she trudged back to Djurjati and cold rice.

It was delicious. Claire forced herself to eat slowly, not as ravenously as she wished to, and found that while her mind was hungry, her belly was not. The act of eating restored her sense of self-control. She chewed and swallowed long after she was sated, as if they were the most important things in the world. With a great detachment, she watched the increasing glow from the city's heart. The heavy smell of smoke drifted in as the breeze shifted. It seemed almost indecent to be eating peacefully while a great city was set ablaze. She ought to *feel* something, some emotion. This was not a spectacle to watch. It was a terrible thing. She ruminated on this as she finished her meal.

"I need other clothes," she said suddenly.

He shrugged. "These things mean nothing."

Claire found she had not patience for a lecture on the meaninglessness of the world, and bit back a sharp reply. Instead, she said as firmly as she could, "I have to go up in the mountains, and I need warm clothes."

Djurjati pondered this. "The mountains. It is cold, yes. But you do not need clothing to warm you. I feel neither heat nor cold, by my austerities."

"Nonetheless, I require clothing."

"Very well. If you insist." He seemed rather disappointed. "What did She tell you?"

Claire opened her mouth, then closed it. She could

never tell anyone about what had happened. There were no words. What could she say? She bit my head off, cut away my hand, gave me her sword and took mine in its place. Those were drab facts, but they were the least important part of what had happened. There had been a moment when she had been one with the awesome being, when she had known all that had been and all that would ever be, and it had been nothing beside the torment of unceasing rage. How could she tell him that the gods suffered, not because of man's imperfections, but for their own ineffable reasons. And how could she confess her desire to somehow ease that pain. It was too ambitious a thing, that silent yearning of her heart. It was too new, too fresh, a tender shoot of something she needed to nurse within her bosom.

Then she realized that Djurjati did not ask from idle curiosity, but because she had had an experience he had wished for and laboured for. It had been denied him, for all his strivings, and she had gotten it unasked for. He might be beyond envy, and she believed him to be, but she understood his longing. She had yearned all her life to speak with the Goddess. And it had been so awful and so different than anything she had dreamed of. She wished she could fulfill his need. It was impossible. Her mouth tasted of the bitterness of betrayal. Her own, and the cruel trick the gods had played on Djurjati. She was too weary for all this.

"She told me to get some warm clothes and go to the mountains."

Several days later, Claire watched from the deck of a small boat as another mob of shouting people raced through the growing rubble of a town. She felt sick and helpless. They had traveled up the Ganges, by boat and on foot, and in every place they stopped, it was the same. Riots and burning, senseless killing and destruction were everywhere. It was as if the spirit of blood-thirsty Kali had infected the populace, and they had gone mad. She felt it was her fault, though she could not imagine how. Worse, she had no power to stop the insanity, or even to help.

Claire was remote from herself, from her pain, and in a sense, even from what went on about her. She watched an enormous figure of the elephant-headed god Ganesha, several tons of animated stone, as it thundered down a street, smashing buildings and trampling people. Behind it, a statue of Siva danced gracefully, a sword-wielding hand lopping off heads as it advanced. Claire stared in sudden awe. She was too tired, after days of watching such destruction, to feel horror any longer. It seemed that all the many gods of India had sprung to life and were entering into the madness. Abstractedly she realized that the idols killed some people and ignored others.

Claire snapped to attention at this, and watched more carefully as the oarsmen drew them away from the wharves of the town. How could she have missed it before! The statues killed the lightless ones, the shadow-struck folk, and left the others alone. They were defending the city and the land. Heartened by this realization, she turned her eyes towards the distant line of the mountains that loomed on the northern horizon. Were they really so tall, or was it a trick of the light?

As distant as the mountains were, the chill they held was already evident. The vegetation along the river's edge was less lush, the trees somewhat smaller. She listened to the sound of the water, the steady thump of the oarlocks, the voices of the boatmen, and the receding howls of the mob, and felt soothed. Each day since they had left the ruins of Varanasi, she had recovered more of her strength, and something of her peace of mind. She had learned how to do simple tasks one-handed, which was difficult and often frustrating, particularly when her right arm moved as it would have before her battle with Kali. It was almost as if a ghostly hand existed about the scarred flesh of her wrist.

Claire held up her stump and studied it as dispassionately as she could. At first she had been unable to look at her arm without disgust, and rage as well. She had almost wept over her lost hand, and sometimes she could feel the tears like a hot tide waiting in her eyes, pressing against her. She dammed them up, held them back. She would not surrender to sorrow, to feeling sorry for herself, no matter what. Anger she permitted herself, and fiery hatred that made her shake all over, but only for a few moments at a time. She wished she had died. Instead, she swallowed her loathing, and tried to accustom herself to her mutilation. In one town which had so far escaped the terror that seemed to be sweeping the land she had acquired a small leather roundel studded with brass. She could put her arm through the straps and used the shield awkwardly but adequately. In the same town she had found a leather worker to make a clumsy sheath for her sword. She had wondered if covering that object of power with such an ugly thing was perhaps wrong, but the sword seemed not to mind. That it was, in some sense, alive and intelligent she had no doubt, and she spoke to it sometimes—a greeting at daybreak, and another at bedtime. The sword never answered, but it gave her a sense of quietness in return. Often her left hand curled around the huge pearl in the hilt, and she sensed all the waters of the world lapping against her palm.

The scar tissue of her right arm was shiny and white against the brown of her tanned skin. The bones were hidden under the flesh, and it looked as if it had been burned. Claire remembered how she had had a sense of heat just after the goddess injured her. *I have been touched with divine fire. That is what I get for wishing for the moon. Why is the goddess so cruel to me? Nothing prepared me for this.* Unconsciously she lifted her remaining hand to touch a thin red line, another scar, that circled her throat like a garrot.

As she studied her arm, Claire remembered how her hand had looked. There had been a crescent scar around the thumb from a practice bout with Roderick, and the veins had shone blue through her brown skin. For a second

it seemed to hover in the air, her hand, the fingers flexing.
Then it was gone.

Claire sighed and lowered her arm. She pulled a small
store of paper out of her pack, her pen and ink, and braced
the pages against her knee. She stared at the river a minute,
then began to cover the paper with elegant Arabic script.
She was grateful she could still do this. Writing out her
thoughts and feelings cleared her mind, and helped her
keep the tears at bay.

Djurjati came from the bow where he had been meditat-
ing and sat down nearby. "Why do you write, child, and
for whom?"

Claire completed her sentence and looked up at him.
His glossy black eyes were puzzled, and he looked weary.
No, he looked unwell. She had been so wrapped up in
herself that she had not noticed how sallow he had become
in the past few days. His skin looked dry. How could she
explain the making of a memoir to a man who was illiterate, who believed in his own irredeemable impurity, and
the emptiness of the world. It seemed quite silly against
that reasoning. Why had she followed him?

Recalling their first meeting in the caravansary at Baghdad, Claire realized she had been drawn to his stillness,
and that she had loved it. It had seemed such a contrast to
her own unhappiness and restlessness. She had mistaken
her fascination with his state of being for real affection, but
as they had traveled together she had come to care for him.
She found she did not love his belief that the world was a
dream which must be denied. For her, the real dream was
his serenity, which she could never enter into. And she
longed for it.

She found herself lacking in the patience to create his
stillness, for she discovered, to her daily surprise, that she
was glad she was alive. Despite her hours of despair and
her rage at what had happened, she still felt a certain delight in the simplest of things. The taste of food, the smell
of the river, the sound of one of the boatmen humming

tunelessly, the feel of the boards beneath her legs, each seemed infinitely precious to her. She looked at her stump resting on the pages and found she could rejoice in what remained while raging against what was gone.

"I write to myself—and perhaps for my father. If I can find a way, I will send my words to him. Why does it matter to you?"

Djurjati squirmed a little. "I am your guide. I want to show you the way to *moksa.*"

Claire made a little tutting sound. "Why? You say I cannot have release, because I am a woman, and you say all desire is illusion." She wondered who was the teacher and who the student.

"I see your light shining like a beacon, and I see that somehow you are holy. But still you persist in seeing the world. I wish to help you stop."

She smiled for the first time in days. "Master, I have no desire to stop. Perhaps I cannot. My mother told me I was bred for this task." She flexed the injured arm. "I always longed to speak to the goddess, and have her answer, and when it happened, it was unlike anything I could have dreamed. I thought she would be the loving mother my own never was. Instead, she hacked off my hand, and . . ." Claire touched the scar around the base of her throat. "I do not know why. Part of me rages, but another part accepts all this. I have this weapon, and it draws me into the very mountains of the gods, for a purpose I do not understand."

"There are no purposes!" Djurjati spoke more emphatically than he normally did, and a light sweat sheened his skin. "There is only the Void." He did not sound as serene as he usually did. "I never had a student before, and I feel I have failed. I have taught you nothing."

Claire shook her head. "You have taught me greatly, master, and I will always treasure it." *By your very asceticism, you let me see how precious life is, but I cannot tell you that because it is exactly the wrong lesson. I came here to die, because I thought that some purpose lay in sacri-*

*fice. All sacrifice is folly, vain folly. I hope I gave her a
belly-ache!*

The city of Hardwar, at the headwaters of the sacred
Ganges, was quiet when they arrived. A mizzling rain fell
in the streets, misting the mountains beyond. Claire felt
relieved. The mountains frightened her. Somewhere up in
those snowclad reaches a monster awaited her. She almost
laughed at her fear. Could anything be more terrifying than
the mouth of Kali? If only she was not quite so in love with
the world.

Claire had a much more pressing concern than the distant threat in the mountains. Djurjati was ill. There was no
question in her mind of this, though the fakir denied it. It
was a fever. He shivered and coughed a great deal, and
rejected any suggestion of treatment.

As they settled into a hostelry near the main bazaar,
Claire wondered if she should go on with him. The thought
wrenched her. If only she could do something. He had
cared for her when she was ill, and she wanted to return the
kindness. No, it was more than that. She was afraid he
would die, and leave her alone. She felt terribly alone already. She did not think she could bear it if he left her.

Djurjati stretched out on a pallette and settled into a
profound sleep while Claire mused over a steaming cup of
chai, white with milk and sweet with sugar, savoring the
aroma of it and enjoying its warmth. It was cold here, a
wet, harsh cold that slowed the blood after the warmth of
the plains. The clothing she had gotten down river was
inadequate. She watched the fakir sleep and felt useless.

When she finished her *chai*, Claire decided to go into
the bazaar to look for clothing and other necessities. She
wandered from booth to booth, fingering thick wools, rank
with smoke and some unknown perfume, and simply
watching people. They seemed subdued, uneasy even. She
haggled with a vendor over some heavy trousers she hoped
would be long enough for her legs, and bought a jacket

worked with red embroidery along the front. They made an awkward bundle under her handless arm.

A brown hand darted towards her pouch, and Claire caught the wrist and twisted the arm above it, dropping her purchases on the still wet pavement. The thief gave a howl of pain and kicked at her. She brought her stump up and smashed the forearm against his cheek, feeling her phantom hand curl into a fist, and he crumpled onto the street. Then she retrieved her belongings as several people eyed her. Some were lightless, and she hurried away. The mist cleared a little, and the mountains gleamed whitely against the sky.

Claire returned to the hostelry and found Djurjati tossing in his sleep. She did not need to touch his skin to know that he was burning up. He had thrown aside his coverings and she could see how his ribs stood out beneath his flesh. She reached forward to begin a healing spell, and stared at her gleaming stump in dismay. Magic was a two-handed task.

For a moment she was too stunned to move. The realization that all her father's patient teaching had been for naught shook her badly. Although she had never felt very capable as a mage, she had accepted magic as a given in her existence. Claire had never valued it overmuch until this moment when she grasped its loss. She tugged the blanket back into place over her friend, and brooded over a fresh cup of *chai*.

Claire felt bewildered as she sat beside the moaning fakir. *This was not at all what I expected. I thought it would be like my great-grandmother, Eleanor's adventure. I would go out and fight the Shadow, serve the Goddess, and save the world. I thought the goddess would love me. Instead, she took my hand, took my head off, and left me helpless. Why should I go on? Why am I being punished like this? I cannot understand, unless it is as Djurjati says, from previous lives I do not recall. And that is such foolishness.*

Methodically, she examined herself, looking for a reason, a rationale, for what had happened. As she thought, Claire became more and more angry. She had lost her hand and her magic, and now she was about to lose her friend. It was not fair. She did her best, even if it was nowhere close to perfect. Was she so flawed that the gods must punish her for longing to serve them?

The rage throbbed in her throat, making the scar around her neck itch. She wanted to climb into the heavens, take her sword, and slaughter all the gods that ever existed. Claire could hear, somewhere deep within herself, the thudding drum that had drawn her into the dance and the duel. It seemed to resonate in her loins, until she felt like a fire roared in her most private place.

It had always been there. A portion of her had always known this rage, and feared it. Some particle of her had known that she was bred to serve, and never to have any life of her own. Claire understood then that the death she had foreseen in Baghdad was not of her flesh, but of her very existence. Unlike her father, she had no children to anticipate. Her womb was seared by the fires of heaven, and it would remain empty of all else. She was not flawed so much as fragmented, for she was perfect for the purposes of the goddess. The problem lay in her own ambitions and yearnings.

This was why Djurjati was her guide. He was meant to teach her how to surrender her personal desires, and she had rejected the lesson. She had to save this man. It was more important than the sword or the Shadow.

Claire closed her aching eyes and begged for counsel. She stretched her mind across the leagues, and sought her father. Emptiness echoed. It was too far. She knew what Geoffrey would do. He would play his flute. But she had not music in her but the throb of the dance of Kali.

God-father! The word snapped into her consciousness like a whip. The young god Hermes was as distant as Geoffrey, but she demanded his presence anyhow. *Tell me what to do.*

All is illusion. The whisper of Djurjati's words rattled

through her mind. Frustrated, Claire felt a rush of rage, and the heat of mage-fire blossomed in her belly, gouted up into her heart, and flowed along her arms. It tingled in the hand that was, and the hand that was not. She flexed fingers real and unreal.

Claire brought her fingertips together, until she could feel her left hand meeting some resistance. Then she opened her eyes and peeked. Above the white scar of her stump, a ghostly hand glowed with the blue of mage-light. It flickered and wavered a little, and she focused on remembering it in vivid detail, down to the scar on the thumb. It hurt. Where the wrist had been severed and cauterized, it burned, and this increased as she strengthened the vision. The pain was almost overwhelming, and she longed to stop, to give up, and leave her friend to his fate. But the sight of the thin, fever-wracked body sustained her. He had not left her in the temple of Kali, and she would not abandon him.

With a great effort, Claire reached out with both hands and drew the heat out of the fakir's body. It was like a thread of fire, and she moved her hands as if she were winding a ball of yarn, gathering the fever between her palms even as her own flesh, real and unreal, screamed in voiceless agony. Before she was half-done, she was exhausted.

The writhing thread of fever surged against her, and Claire paused and wondered if she could go on. She noticed the sweat that beaded her skin, and the foul smell of her body and the room. She swallowed, drew a breath, and thought with longing of water. She wished a river would cool her and cleanse her. She remembered the sweetness of the Ganges, the good smell of clear water as she had bathed in it above Varanasi. It was the river which flowed from Heaven and washed away all sin. After the burning of Varanasi, it had seemed a blessing, as if she was indeed reborn.

The pain diminished, and she felt her flesh cool. Refreshment flowed into her cramped legs, up through her belly and out along her weary arms. Claire quickly returned to her task of winding the fever out of her guide. It went on and on, until, after what seemed like hours, she jerked the end free of his matted hair. The fever lay in her hands, a tiny ball of sickly fire, and she had no idea what to do with it. It was not the sort of thing to toss aside. The end writhed like a worm seeking a hole. It poked towards her real hand, and she jerked, nearly dropping it in her fright. In a second of fury at her own fear, her mage hand closed around it, and there was a flash of light and a spark of heat against her illusory palm as she crushed it. She screamed once. Then both the hand and the fever were gone. She felt ready to lie down and die, but a slow smile creased her face as the man opened his dark eyes and looked at her.

VIII

For days they climbed, sometimes on foot, sometimes on the backs of small ponies or riding mules. The mountains still loomed above them. Claire began to understand why the people lived in awe of them, though for the most part she was too busy struggling with cold, shortness of breath, and exhaustion to spend much time thinking about it.

Djurjati had completely recovered his wiry strength, as if the fever had never been. But he was somehow a different man, as if the thread of heat she had drawn out of him had taken something with it. He dwelt less on the subject of *moksa,* the release from the cycle of endless re-births, than on tales of his childhood in a little village by a river, or stories of the great hero Rama. He told, too, tales of Krishna, an avatar of the god Vishnu, who had spent his youth among the cow-herders. Claire was mildly shocked by the amorous adventures of this god with the *gopis,* the female cow-herds, as she had been by the graphic carvings on the temples when she first came to India. Somehow she could not manage to reconcile what appeared to be unrestrained lust with the austerity that characterized her companion, the less so when he told her it was all the same.

Some of the sweet content that had touched her at the beginning of the journey returned. Each morning, before they set out, she conjured up her phantom hand, steeling herself against the pain which never seemed to become more bearable, until she could command it into being almost between one breath and the next. All the years of discipline at her mother's side stood her in good stead, and she recognized it for the great gift it was. She understood practice and she understood discomfort. The pain of her wrist, where the sword she now bore had severed flesh and bone, was an outrage that brought sweat to her skin in spite of the chill of the mountains, and left her reeking. After a time she stopped loathing the stink of her body beneath its woolly garments. She never quite stopped longing for a hot bath, clean sheets, and a comfortable bed, but Claire found that these things now had a dream-like quality. It took all her strength to simply keep going, to practice her magic as much as she could bear, and not to despair.

After some days, Claire realized she was both lonely and homesick. This notion surprised her one afternoon as they rode shaggy ponies in the company of a merchant train. One moment she was studying the mountains against the sky and noting the paucity of birds, and the next she was pitched into a yearning to see her sister Dorothea. To be hugged by Dorothea, who was a great one for embraces, was her desire. Then she thought of Roderick for the first time in weeks, and wondered how he and Anna fared, and where they were. She thought of her father and had a great longing to sit in his cluttered study and hear his voice. Before they had left Hardwar, she had found a caravaner going west, and entrusted to him the precious pages she had penned coming up the river. She wondered what he would think of her account of her adventures, and if she would ever see him again. Or her mother. Claire felt tears brim at the thought. She missed Helene most of all, oddly. That night, in the travellers' rest, surrounded by snoring gurkas and the smell of woodsmoke and unwashed bodies, she began a letter to her mother. It seemed to bring her closer, and it helped a little.

They had gone north from Hardwar for ten days, until they left India altogether, and entered another land where the people were small and slant-eyed, dressed in trousers and coats instead of veils and dhotis, and spoke a singsong tongue that defied her linguistic skills. Claire had never found any language she could not learn the rudiments of in days, and she realized that this was because all of those she knew, even Hindi, were related in some fashion. But this tongue was completely different, and it frustrated her, until it occurred to her that she might enspell herself to understand it. The thought was easier than the deed, for she had no ready model in her education to begin from. It took three days of mental sorting through her intellectual baggage to find some tools that might serve her purpose, and another two to cobble together a device to implement it. This had been the easy part, for the actual making of a new spell was both difficult and painful. Nothing she did eased the agony of doing magic now, and it seemed to her that this effort was even more so because she was serving her own needs, not healing another's wounds. That it was necessary she was certain, and she held to her intention until she accomplished the thing, and gave herself a raging headache to boot.

It was not until she had recovered from her exertions that Claire grasped what she had done. Never in all her studies had she imagined that she could create a new magical process, alone and unaided, for she had always felt so quietly inept. She wrote the method down, and looked at the words curling across the paper, as if some other person, a total stranger, had scribed them. She did not know who she was any longer, and it frightened her. Then she felt a flush of pride in her work, a warm sense of a job well-done, and that, in a way, frightened her even more.

Djurjati watched her quietly during those days, and said nothing. She could sense his presense hovering nearby, and she wondered what he thought. Finally, she got the courage to ask him.

"Am I different, master?"

"Yes, child, you are."

"Do you approve?"

"Approve? What is that? Can I approve of the mountains or the sunset? What a futile pastime. I neither approve nor disapprove. This has nothing to do with what is."

"Teach me."

He gave a snort of laughter and shook his head. "I came to be your guide, to teach you, in my pride. I thought I had done with pride, you see, but I was deluded." He sighed. "The light thickens."

"What?"

"When I first saw you, there in the marketplace, I was stunned by the brightness of your being—and later by your complete unawareness of it. It let me perceive my monstrous pride in my own hard-won clarity, and see how my humility was mere vanity. I was glad when you put on the mask of a boy, for I could not bear the conflict of your femaleness and your purity. It made a nonsense of all that I believed. If those sailors had fed me to the fishes, or the fever had claimed me, I should have been relieved, for then I would not have to confront myself. Twice you have saved me from death, and thus I see that the goddess is not done with me yet."

Claire shrugged against the stiff wool of her jacket. "I cannot see myself, master. And I think you make a great thing of it. You shine for me, I shine for you. What is the loss?"

"No loss, to be sure. But a marvel, a miracle. Your aura grows deeper and richer. It is like speaking with a saint— only a very . . . how can it be that you are exalted and commonplace all at once?"

Claire chewed her lip and flexed her stump as she thought about this. She remembered Dorothea, so tranquil in her daily living, and how she had always envied that quality. She thought of Anna, who was remarkably soul-bright, and remembered what Helene had said about carrying a saint around in her womb. But, more, she found memories of her nurses and several serving women who had had a steady glow about them, not of any magnified sanctity, but of a simplicity she could not explain. "I think most women are, master, if men will just pause to see it. I think this is true of humans. We are all quite ordinary, and also shining. I never understood that until I saw those poor people who had lost their light."

"You sorrow for them?"

Unaware that she spoke with more passion than was her custom, Claire answered, "Yes, certainly. They did not ask to be afflicted, any more than you desired fever. I do not think they even knew what had happened to them, only that they have come to hate everything that formerly they loved, so they must try to destroy it."

"But, surely it is their *karma* to be afflicted."

"Karma! Why must you burden yourself with past lives, when living the present one is difficult enough. All my life I have tried to be perfect, and look where it got me." She waved her scarred stump at him. "This is not punishment for something I did. I do not know why I lost my hand, but I do know it was not done because I was wicked." Claire gave a sudden grin, hiding her pain and confusion. "Maybe it was done to show me I could lick the Darkness one-handed." She barely noticed a tear rolling down her cheek. "I was pre-destined, my mother said, to be here, and perform these tasks—which I am not even clear about. I bear the Sword of Waters, and I have only a glimmer of what I am to do with it, which is come to this chilly land for some reason. But I do not believe we can be accountable for things we did in other lives, or even that other lives exist. I do not accept that we are born to suffer, because the world is so fair a place that we must love it."

"You are most compassionate."

"No. I am just a woman who has learned to value simple things. I refuse to get confused with unnecessary complexities."

"Unnecessary complexities?"

"All those systems, those castes and hierarchies, they are the real *maya,* teacher. In the end there is nothing but the moment. I wanted all my moments to be perfect, by which I meant that I held them in these two hands and commanded them. But, what you can command is such a pitiful thing. Now, I must take my moments as they come, because I cannot hold them fast in my grasp. That is hard, for I am a very grasping woman. But it is not a punishment for deeds. We were not made to suffer, but to rejoice. Do you not know how Kali rejoices in her terrible dance?"

"Have you ceased to fear then?"

Claire shook her head and chuckled softly. "Hardly. I am afraid all the time. But, that too is one of my moments."

They came to a small city and parted company with the merchant train, got food, and continued on foot with a taciturn guide, going east through the foothills of an enormous range. Claire was fascinated and surprised by the shifts of the terrain. They might climb over snow-encrusted paths for half a day, then drop down into a little valley where it was almost summer, not winter. At night, they stopped in villages of twenty or thirty tiny houses, rank with unwashed bodies and the smell of shaggy yaks. Claire learned to drink the bitter *chai* with yak butter churned into it, and to eat the rather flavorless gruel, *tsampo,* that was the staple of the diet. She dreamed of the spicy curries of the plain which had seemed so alien a few weeks before. Too, she dreamt of *kavya,* of sitting in her father's study while he read the pages she had sent, like a ghost. Her legs ached from climbing, her lungs hurt from the thin air, and she had a persistent headache. She was quite weary of rocks, snow, and rushing rivers that had to be crossed by swaying suspension bridges that made her giddy. Then she would remember how she had died in the arms of a goddess, and see the many colours of the snow, the shape of the rocks, hear the call of the birds, especially the croak of the vultures who consumed the dead in this land, and the weariness would depart, leaving contentment in its wake.

They came to a valley that seemed unnaturally quiet, even in the silent land, and the guide looked about him uneasily. Claire asked him if anything was amiss, and he answered with a single word that she understood as "spirits," or perhaps "ghosts." Despite her magic, and her increasing skill, her command of the language was still very limited and rudimentary. As story-telling was the main entertainment of the villages, she was learning a larger vocabulary daily, not to mention a wealth of lore, but the concepts behind the words often still eluded her. She extended her senses but found nothing supernatural to disturb her.

The feeling of unease persisted as they crossed the short grass. The sky was cloudy, but only lightly so, and the little valley was warm by local temperatures. A light snow began to powder the landscape. They hastened towards a shelter the guide assured them existed at the other end of the valley as the day darkened. Without any warning, a howling blizzard closed over their heads, blinding eyes and deafening ears momentarily. Claire stood lost in the swirling whiteness, looking for Djurjati's familiar aura until she found him a few feet away. She reached a hand towards him.

There was a growl above the wind, and something huge swelled in the whiteness. Then there was a scream and the sound of tearing cloth and flesh. Claire caught a glimpse of something tall, white as snow, and clawed. Red blood spattered its chest as it swung towards her, dropping the gutted body of the guide.

She drew the sword by instinct, and felt it surge in her hand like a wave of the sea. It was alive, even through the glove that covered her skin, and it nearly knocked her off-balance. As the creature lifted a great, clawed hand to slash her, she took a step backwards, and fell to one knee. She heard the swipe as it missed her head, and smelled a fetid breath as she rolled into a somersault and came up, whipping her little shield off her shoulder and onto her stump.

Claire danced to the right, kicking up drifts of snow, as the thing charged again. It was tall, and as it lifted its huge claws, it left its furred belly undefended. She raised her shield above her head as she ducked into the exposed belly and plunged the sword deep into the body of the beast. It howled as she tore the sword out of the flesh, dragging bits of guts out with the terrible wavy edges of her weapon, and she darted back. One of the claws struck her shield, and the force of the blow nearly knocked her down.

Half-blinded with snow, and almost breathless, she slashed at an unprotected leg, then tried to get behind the beast. For all its size, it was quick, and Claire kept having to try to keep out of range while attempting to disable it. There was another sound, a long, thin scream, somewhere close but somehow distant, and she felt her heart contract with terror.

Djurjati! She whirled towards the sound, then snapped back as the beast closed on her. It was limping, bent to one side, but still eager to fight. Fury filled her, and she loped off the clawed hand that reached for her. Blood spouted out and fountained over her as the thing howled with pain. The blood was warm against her chilled skin, and it got into her eyes. She rubbed her brow against the felt of her sleeve quickly. Then she thrust into the torso of the screaming beast, up under the ribs, into heart and lungs, as it tried to pull her away. Its claws were not made for grasping. She could feel them rip her back as she pulled her weapon out, and hoped her many layers of clothing would keep her from serious injury. The creature sank into the snow, and she had a glimpse of an almost human face, with great, round eyes, before she turned to seek her teacher in the blinding whiteness.

The wind whipped her skin, and her eyes teared, but she finally saw the broad back of a second beast, almost invisible in the snow, bending over. Claire rushed forwards, fueled by fear and rage, and drove the point of her sword into the neck of the beast, pressing on until she saw the bloody steel emerge below its head. Then she tore it out, half decapitating her foe, as the blizzard vanished as suddenly as it had appeared.

Snow remained, but only a thin layer over the dried grass, and blood reddened its whiteness. Claire gave a quick glance at the still forms of the two snow creatures, then ran to Djurjati. His slender body was torn diagonally, from shoulder to hip, and his face was clawed and partly eaten. One soft black eye gazed sightlessly at the sky, and one hand lay in a mute gesture of supplication on the crimsoned snow.

Claire knelt beside him a long time, too stunned and tired to even cry. The cold penetrated her knees as night came. She had saved him from death by water and fever, but still he had perished. Her mind refused to accept it. Surely there must be some way to bring him back.

The increasing cold finally drove her into activity. Claire stood up and found the blankets in her pack, and those of her companions. She wrapped one around herself, cleared a space of snow, and sat down. She ate some dried meat without tasting it. She was not really hungry, but she ate because she needed the strength. The sound of wings roused her, as one of the white vultures who consumed the dead circled in the night above her. It was a practice which revolted her, and she resisted an impulse to slay the bird as it flew.

Claire tried to think what Djurjati would have wished for. Her frozen mind responded sluggishly. His desire, of course, would be to be burned and have his ashes set adrift on sacred Ganga. A lack of firewood was an insurmountable barrier for what seemed like hours, as the vulture landed and began to feast on one of the snow creatures. Then she realized what she must do.

Her practice had made the conjuring of her right hand faster but not less painful. She ignored the searing sensation about the scarred wrist and created the phantom hand, then gathered her energies. Another bird joined the first and she formed a ball of mage-fire between her fingers. With an enormous effort, she cast it upon the stiffening corpse, trying vainly to recall any appropriate prayers.

The body went up like a torch. A fire like a beacon rose against the sky, and for a moment she thought she saw a ghostly, golden image of Djurjati among the flames. It seemed to smile, and then was gone. Tears welled in her eyes and choked her throat. The sobs shook her whole body as the vultures flew away. He was gone, her friend. The pillar of flame continued to rise until the whole valley was nearly day bright. Claire wept as she had never cried before, for her loss, for her friend, and somehow for herself. A sense of being utterly lost and alone overwhelmed her.

The fire began to die as the moon rose behind her. Claire rubbed her face against the rough wool of the blanket and realized how cold she was. It seemed like too much effort to do anything about this, and she wondered abstractedly how long it would take to freeze to death, and if it would hurt very much. After pondering this for several minutes, she knew she was not going to do any such thing, and stood up. She dug a little jar out of her pack and staggered across to the still warm ashes of her friend. Clumsily she scooped some into the container, crying again, then cursing as she stoppered it. Someday she would take them back to his river. It was the least she could do.

Still cold, she flapped her arms to get her blood moving, and saw her shadow in the moonlight on the snow. It brought back memories of hot, sleepless nights in her father's house, and before she knew it, the dance had taken her. Awkward in her boots and clothing stiff with clotted beast blood, she lifted her arms and legs in the strange gestures she had always known. The vultures returned to their messy feeding, and she barely noticed, so bemused was she by grief and exhaustion. Claire did not think of perfection, as she always had before, but only of the dance itself.

She was barely aware of something disturbing the feeding birds until she noticed a small, golden figure coming across the valley towards her. It seemed to be some sort of dog, though it gleamed in a way she had never seen on any hound, and she paused in her movements. Its feet did not quite seem to reach the earth, and as it got closer, it was as large as a pony. It came a few feet away, then sat on its haunches like a cat, and coiled its plumy tail about its feet.

Claire stared at the beast, and the beast looked back with huge, round yellow eyes. Whorls of brindled fur, like golden thread, curved across its squarish face, and down its shoulders and hind legs. It opened its mouth and displayed sharp teeth, then breathed a mist out into the air.

A smell like flowers joined the stench of blood and the scent of ashes. Claire felt the sweetness of it, tasted it almost, and struggled to deny it. She was outraged, as if her grief was being taken from her, and she dragged her eyes away for a moment, concentrating on the naked head of a vulture as it plundered the eye of a snow beast. The world was a wretched place, not worth saving. How could she do anything when she could not even save her teacher's life?

But she could not evade the piercing sweetness of the strange creature. Claire could not hold her breath that long! The thought made her give a little laugh. Once, during a particularly grueling archery lesson with her mother, Helene had become exasperated. "Girl, will you stop being so stubborn? You cannot learn this by turning blue holding your wind!" *How can I laugh at a time like this? How can I not?*

Claire hunkered down until she was eye-level with the curious beast. It lolled its tongue, and she was reminded of the hideous tongue of the goddess. Cautiously, she extended her remaining hand, well aware that the strong jaws of the creature could snap it off in a thrice. It did not appear unfriendly, but she should be careful.

To her surprise, Claire found she did not wish to be careful. It seemed as if she had been forever at being cautious, at being restrained and contained. What she really wanted, she decided, was to embrace the shaggy head of the beast, and coil her fingers in its marvelous coat. She had not held another living being in weeks. She ached for it.

As if it knew her thoughts, the creature rose and minced across the space between them, extended its rather flat nose and touched hers. It was cold and moist and infinitely precious. Its breath mingled with hers, free of any kind of normal smells of cat or dog or horse.

They remained frozen in their postures until Claire tenderly reached her hand to touch the golden coils around the mane. It made a little noise, not quite a bark, a sound of delight, and buried its muzzle against her breast. Claire overbalanced at this movement and fell backwards while the creature nuzzled her eagerly, as if it too longed for touch. She wrapped her arms around the neck and felt the sweet warmth of flesh and blood under her fingers. A tongue caressed her cheek and she had a sense of ecstasy. Her grief was not gone, her loss, her sense of terror and rage. All her emotions were there, side by side, immediate and distant simultaneously. She had an instant of clarity. It all seemed very simple again. She surrendered herself to the sweetness of it. For a moment she understood that she was injured and that she must heal herself before she could heal anything else. Then it was lost in the honeyed breath of the beast as it filled her being.

IX

At dawn Claire pushed aside the bundle of blankets she had
wound around herself and stretched. Her breath made a
little white mist, but it was not very cold. The beast, curled
up beside her, raised its curly head and looked at her intel-
ligently. She touched its cheek tenderly, to assure herself
that it was real, and gave a silent thanks to whatever power
had sent it to her. She felt lost, and felt her loss of her
teacher and companion, but the strange beast made it just a
little more bearable.

The carrion birds were still gorging on the remains of
the snow beasts, their handsome white wings contrasting
with the ugliness of their featherless heads. She was still
filled with the harmony she had found the night before, and
looked at their greedy feasting with indifference. She was a
little hungry, but not enough to breakfast with vultures, so
she rose and sorted through the remains of the three packs,
taking only what she could carry. Her garments were foul
with blood and dried sweat, torn in several places by exertions or the fury of the beasts, but there was little she could

do about it. Nothing remained of Djurjati's clothing, now burned, and the birds had destroyed those of the guide. In any case, they would have been too small. She was grateful that her boots were still serviceable, though the soles were showing unmistakeable signs of wear. Claire had a moment's regret for the fine leather boots she had brought from Baghdad, but they had given up days before, and these which she had replaced them with were not so well-made.

Prepared to depart, she looked at the beast inquiringly. "Well, Aurelian, my golden friend, which way now?" She spoke in Greek from habit, and noticed the name she had given the creature with a slight grin. Her face ached where the muscles pulled her mouth into a smile. Then she wondered if she should ask her question again in the local tongue.

It rose, shook all over like a huge dog, and trotted towards the end of the valley. Claire shouldered her pack, her bow and arrows, reslung her little shield with some awkwardness, and followed the beast. It slowed until she caught up, then positioned itself on her right, as if it knew perfectly well which side of a left-handed swordsman was correct. She puzzled over this as she walked, but for the most part she let her mind roam. She was still tired, and a little giddy, from the altitude and from hunger, and the brightening day had a hazy quality that lent itself to mental wandering. They paused near midday in a meadow of small flowers, and she ate, offering some of her meagre food to the beast. Aurelian turned his head aside, and she decided he was perhaps too magical for ordinary food. Her own belly seemed to have shrunk over the past weeks, and she hardly ate enough to keep her moving, judged by the standards of Baghdad.

Close to dusk, they entered the confines of a good-sized town or small city, perched beside a fast running river. The snow-clad mountains stood behind it, and dominating the place was an enormous building. It gleamed in the last rays of sunlight, and she wondered if the king of this country resided within it. From what she had gathered from her guides, there were several kings, as well as spiritual leaders who seemed to rank above them. She asked a toothless beldame who stared at her from the doorway of a brightly painted house what the place was, and was not surprised to find it was no palace but a monastery. The city itself was called Shigatse, which told her nothing.

Claire shrugged. She wanted some hot *chai* and a meal, even if it was the bland gruel she had eaten in small villages. More, she longed for a hot bath and fresh clothes, though she doubted that the first existed anywhere in this chilly place. Small children stared at her wide-eyed, and at Aurelian, from the protecting cloaks of their moon-faced mothers, and tradesmen grinned at her somewhat uneasily. She had settled, days before, on a male guise somewhat older than the one she had adopted to begin with, complete with illusory right hand for appearances' sake, but she realized that Aurelian drew attention. She would have to think of a spell to cast over him. Somehow she doubted that was possible, and she was too weary to care. She asked one man where she could find lodging for the night, and was directed to the great monastery.

Chanting rang out as Claire reached the gates, accompanied by gongs and bells. A servant answered her call, led her to an anteroom piled with thick, felt carpets, and informed her that she must wait until evening meditations were complete. He looked some askance at Aurelian, but the golden beast ignored him and sprawled at her feet with an expression of disdain on his flattish face. She eased her pack off and sat down heavily. The walls were painted with pictures of many-faced, multi-armed beings she recognized as cousins to the deities of India, and she contemplated these until someone brought her a cup of *chai*. The first time she had tasted this drink, greasy with butter, she had nearly gagged, but now it seemed delicious. Apparently the on-going ritual did not prohibit this courtesy, and she rejoiced in this small thing. She felt as if her life had shrunk into many tiny moments; the taste of tea, the smell of wool and incense, the rhythm of chant and gong, the feel of the chair beneath her tattered garments. Other matters, swords of power, plans of the gods and even the loss of her hand, seemed unimportant. It was just good to sit quietly, in a warm place, with a strange golden animal pressed against her leg.

After a time she felt a little restless, so she pulled her pages out of her pack, settled her chair near a small table, and began to write. Hesitant at first, then more fluently, she set down the events of the previous day. The words flowed across the paper as she chose phrases from the rich poetry of Arabic, comparing Djurjati to sweet water in the desert, to rich food and the golden corn of harvest. Her grief returned, and she wrote of her loss with all the passion which the language offered her. Greek was the tongue of thought for her, but Arabic had always been the vehicle of her emotions, learned from servants who filled the places of her preoccupied parents, and later from savants come to consult her father.

Claire did not notice that the chanting had ceased, and mumbled a thanks when another cup of *chai* was brought to her. A fresh presence in the room finally penetrated her mind, however, and she looked up. A monk, by his shaven head, and a high ranking one by the richness of his garments, waited in complete serenity a few feet away. She wondered how long he had been there as she set her pen aside and scrambled up to make an awkward bow, nearly upsetting the ink in her haste.

The monk had the same sort of inward turned look she knew so well in Djurjati's face, though he lacked the underfed spareness of an aescetic. Still, his expression brought back her dead companion with a sharp, fresh pang. He was short, as were all the people of this land, flat-featured and dark-eyed. He had enormous dignity, and, besides that, an aura of great power. His red robes concealed his body, and his face was unlined by age. Despite this, Claire suspected he was much older than he seemed, and felt awkward. She was a child by comparison, and an imperfect one at that.

His scrutiny of her was no less penetrating, and a little frown marred the smoothness of his brow. "Welcome, traveler." He made a little gesture she could not interpret.

Claire bowed again. "I thank you for your hospitality."

The monk shifted his weight from slippered foot to slippered foot. "Hospitality?" He eyed Aurelian. "Yes, I suppose so." He took a seat on a carved chair and waved her to her place. "I am abbot here."

She lifted her brows in surprise. "I am honoured by your condescension, Lord." This was true. She had gathered that the abbots here were great men, powerful as monarchs and mages of some repute as well. They were rarely seen by the common folk except on festal occasions, and she had not anticipated ever speaking to one. "I ask only a place to sleep for the night."

"We do not permit women here," he replied obliquely. "Not even nuns or saints."

Claire chewed her lip. She was a little surprised that he had seen through her spell, but not overly so. He was, by the liniments of his aura, as dynamic a mage as she had ever encountered, her father notwithstanding. "I did not know, Lord. I am woefully ignorant of your ways, and if I have transgressed, I beg forgiveness. Perhaps, in your graciousness, you will direct me to a resting place."

Aurelian moved from his reclining position into a sitting stance beside her, and regarded the abbot with huge golden eyes. The beast exhaled deeply, and the honeyed flower scent of its breath drowned out even the incense rich odor of the chamber. The abbot looked back, and she could sense some sort of struggle going on. It passed in utter stillness, leaving her with a feeling of having lost her eyes for a moment, in a flash of unseen light.

"What are you?" His question broke the silence abruptly, and he appeared rather startled as he spoke the words.

Claire was puzzled over the phrasing. Not "who," but

"what." *Well, what am I?* All the answers which came to mind were ones of identity and relationship, not of any essence. The hard-won simplicity she had constructed since departing Baghdad shattered in a welter of conflicting images. She made a mental grab for herself, then let go, permitting all the chaos of her secret questions to have their voices. She looked at the tatters of her serenity as if from a great distance, as if she were a hawk looking down at the rumpled earth. It hurt, for she had come to prize the ability to live only from moment to moment, and now she felt the pressure of the past and the future once again.

For some measureless time she was paralyzed. Then she recalled her first meeting with Djurjati, when he had told her he was the wind, and found herself again. "Perhaps I am a dream," she answered slowly.

The abbot nodded. "Dreams are welcome here."

Claire never understood what compromise the abbot reached between the rules of his order and his personal conscience, but she was grateful to be fed and given a place to sleep. A young monk took her to a chamber and offered her a heavily embroidered robe. He informed her that if she would put her soiled garments outside the door, he would see that they were cleaned.

The little room where she was taken was spotlessly clean, and her heart rejoiced in the order of it. She had almost forgotten the pleasure of complete privacy and cleanliness. A ewer of hot scented water and a soft towel stood on a carved wooden stand. She stripped to the skin and scrubbed herself scrupulously, luxuriating in the warmth of the water. Then she put on the bright garment, and set her own clothing outside the door, as she had been told.

On the wall there was an embroidered hanging of a beautiful goddess. Claire stared at it while she ate the gruel which was brought her, and drank more *chai*. Seated on a lotus, in the yogin position she had learned from Djurjati, the goddess smiled and filled the chamber with peace.

Claire smiled up at the tranquil face, and stroked Aurelian's curly mane until her eyes ached for sleep. She stretched out on the narrow bed, wriggled her battered toes under the woolen blankets in great content, and shut her eyes.

Snow. A great expanse of snow seemed to stretch forever, and she walked across it. She could hear the crunch of her boots against the ice, but otherwise there was silence. She sought something she could not name. Her heart ached with yearning.

There, far away, there was a gleam of white that made the snow seem dirty. She trudged towards it, weary but eager. It felt as if she had been walking towards this moment since time began. She was so tired, and her labours were hardly begun. The knowledge came unbidden, and she wanted to sink down into the snow and rest. The scar around her throat was a line of anguish, and her severed wrist throbbed. She "heard" the wild music of the dance distantly, and her feet itched to enter it. Would she ever arrive?

Then, she was there, before the lambent figure of the smiling goddess. Her hands were curled in graceful gestures, and she shone with a light that dazzled the eye and pierced the heart. She felt her knees bend. Snow, crisp and chill, caressed her ankles and calves. She wanted to look away, and could not. The almond eyes studied her, and she felt all her imperfections revealed. She wished she could hide her injured arm from the serene gaze, and more, herself. The awful red eyes of black-faced Kali were not so terrible as this look. She yearned, almost, to return to that foul embrace, to lift her lips again to the blood-smeared stinking mouth. The beauty of the goddess before her frightened her as the hideousness of the other had not. If she was tired, how weary must Kali be, who held within her all of time. She wished she could bear the burden for her, if only for an instant, that Kali might know the rest she herself longed for. The extent of her ambition shocked her, and shamed her. She was not fit. She was so imperfect.

The smiling goddess moved one hand in benediction, and she felt herself dwindle into a mote. She was nothing, and that was good. She savored the sweetness of emptiness, until she noticed the contrary fullness of the Void. And, after a moment or an eon, she realized she was the Void itself, vacant and teeming, nothing and everything, time out of Time. She could not longer perceive any distinction between life and death, between her minuscule self and the shining serenity before her. She reached her scarred stump towards the goddess, and it was not ugly. It was not anything.

The figure nodded, and turned in a flutter of curling draperies. She pointed into a darkness, and the woman peered into the churning blackness. The searching eyes which had sought her long before, the eyes of the snow-clad mountains, looked out of the swirling emptiness. A sound like thunder boomed. She was afraid, so afraid. She tried to deny the fear, struggled to surmount it, and recapture the tranquility of a moment before. But it was like the sea. She drowned in her terror, surrendering finally, as the pale eyes watched her out of the darkness. Nothing could save her. She had no friends, no guardians. Only fear. It was her most steadfast companion. It would never die, or desert her, or deny her. It demanded nothing but a place within her, close by the hearth that was her pounding heart.

How could she fear? It was unthinkable. She must be courageous. She must never be a coward. Her mother was never afraid. Which one? The mortal or immortal? Her heart throbbed with the rhythm of the dance and with the Black Mother who had consumed her flesh. Then she knew. Even Kali feared. What, she could not guess, but Kali could be afraid, was afraid. If the goddess could fear, could bear fear, then she must as well. She let herself surrender to it.

It smashed her like a fist, a great howling terror that made the fear of the searching eyes in the darkness into nothing, a mere thrill of fear hardly worth noting. The

*cosmos filled with the enormity of terror until the stars
themselves screamed and exploded into light. It was not
fear of anything, just blind, unreasoning, soul-shattering
terror, greater than darkness, greater than death. It pervaded every particle, drowning all. A scream tried to force
its way out, to express the overwhelming sensation, but no
sound came. Her throat was choked with ice.*

*The benign figure on the lotus was unmoved. Terror
danced in the tranquil eyes, but the round face remained
serene. The goddess smiled with her fear. The woman
stared in awe at this calm acceptance of something so
overwhelming, and stretched out to encompass it. She felt
a whisper of response, as if the goddess reached out to
meet her, as if the lambent arms embraced her trembling
shoulders. The heart-shaped mouth seemed to touch her
forehead, above the brows and between the eyes, where
her mother Helene had placed a kiss in a dimly remembered time. There was a sharp sensation, like a pinprick
passing through her, not painful, but not pleasurable either. It pierced her, and the fear swirled into a mote among
others, each potent and capable of deluging the cosmos.
For an instant she saw the essential balance, felt it, understood it. Joy could be as terrible as fear. She was not
certain she could tell them apart as they swarmed across
the Void. And she knew it did not matter.*

Claire turned in her sleep, put her arm out from beneath
the covers, and reached for something. Her hand found
Aurelian's head, touched the moist nose and fondled the
round ears. Then she buried her fingers in his mane,
clutching the golden coils of fur, made a small noise of
content in her throat, and slipped into dreamless bliss.

A scratching noise dragged Claire into wakefulness, and
she opened her eyes and looked at the goddess on the
hanging above the foot of her bed. The drone of chanting
came to her ears, and then the scratching sound again.
Aurelian was sitting up and watching the door alertly.

"Enter," she said. It was a servant, with steaming tea,
gruel and her clothing over his arm. It was clean and

mended, and she thanked him. Then she sat down with
more appetite than she had had for weeks, wishing Djurjati
was with her to explain her dream to her. She talked to
Aurelian instead, and he gave her musings such grave attention that it was almost comical. She dressed, packed up
her belongings, and prepared to set out. She was going into
the mountains to find the eyes which hunted her. It felt
good to be certain of something for a change, to have a
clear sense of purpose.

The abbot joined her in the chamber where they had
spoken the day before. Claire thanked him for his hospitality, and offered him a gift of one of the huge pearls she had
picked up from the deck of the ship. Then she said, "Lord,
will you tell me the name of the goddess who graced my
chamber last night?"

He looked her up and down, then nodded. "She is Tara.
She is Mercy."

"Yes. She is." Claire drew a second pearl out of her
bag. It was a rosy pink and as large as the grey one she had
already given the abbot. "I would give this to Her, for her
beneficence to me."

"You are very blessed."

Claire thought about her dream, about Djurjati and Kali,
about her lost hand and the sweet presence of Aurelian. *I
have fed the goddess. As privilege goes, that is a peculiar
one, but privilege it is.* "I am indeed blessed." *But nothing
has been as I expected.*

Claire considered hiring another guide, and decided
against it. Aurelian knew where she was going, even if she
did not. It was so difficult to endure the uncertainty of both
the present and the future, but she had not choice. She said
as much to the beast as they left the city, and he barked in
response.

It was cold and overcast, and she wondered what day it
was. She had lost track of time, and she tried to reconstruct
some reckoning. Even her internal calendar of moon cycles
was absent, and had been for more than four weeks. Claire

pondered this and wondered if she had somehow gotten pregnant without remembering it. It seemed to have happened to several women in myths, but they had been raped by swans or had showers of gold fall upon them, all of which had struck her as extremely unlikely even when she had been young and gullible. No. She could hardly have been unaware if she had a new life quivering in her womb. Then she shrugged and guessed that it was about the end of the tenth month, and that her body had ceased its monthly release because of the hardships she had endured.

There was a decent road out of the city, one well-traveled and clearly used. She caught up with a mule-train loaded with bags of barley flour, and passed them with a friendly wave. The mule drovers eyed her suspiciously, and made gestures to ward off bad luck, and returned no greeting. Aurelian's presence at her side clearly did not inspire confidence in the peasantry.

They paused in a tiny hamlet at midday, and Claire got a meal and some tea. She watched a woman churning in an ornate device, handsome polished wood with good metal work. The yak cream was worked first, then tea, boiled to a thick paste, was added, and the mixture was churned into a smooth consistency. Later it was cut into cubes, or molded, wrapped in oiled paper for travel, and boiled in water for drinking. She made a note of this for her father, then chuckled at herself. She was no scholar, but she had acquired the habits of one by being Geoffrey's daughter. It gave her a sense of connection to him, and to her family.

Claire followed Aurelian's lead, and at evening they were in a dense forest of great fir trees. There was a modest wind, but the trees sheltered her from the worst of it, and she settled down beside a tiny fire. Claire had never seen such arborial giants as those which loomed around her in the gathering night, not even in the mountains of Lebanon where her family had spent one winter. She savored the simple novelty of it, along with tea and barley cakes. She was becoming a little bored with the diet, but like much else, it was of little consequence. She was not really

hungry, and ate more from habit than from need. It was a
little puzzling, she decided, for she ought to be ravenous
all the time, considering everything. Well, perhaps the altitude had robbed her of her appetite.

Claire bedded down for the night, Aurelian beside her,
and found that sleep eluded her. She had never felt so
awake. She listened to the wind in the trees and enjoyed
the rich scent of the resin and green needles, coiling her
fingers into Aurelian's coat, quietly content. The fire faded
into embers.

The wind died to a whisper, and the night as nearly still.
Claire sat up with her elbows on her knees and listened.
There was a low noise, like something being dragged,
something very large and very heavy. Another sound
reached her. It was a snuffling noise, like a horse with a
bad cold, and the hairs at the nape of her neck bristled. She
pushed the blankets aside and stood up. The breeze brought
a smell that was not forest or ash. It was like hot brass, and
she could almost taste the metal in her mouth. Aurelian
stood beside her, his curled tail lifted high, his flat nose
pointed into the shadows.

There was a low moan, and a crashing sound. Wood
shrieked as it splintered. She could hear a tree or trees
being uprooted and falling into others. The smell of metal
mingled with the sweetness of Aurelian's breath and the
rankness of her woolen clothing. She rested her hand on
the hilt of the sword, feeling the silkiness of the great pearl
beneath her roughened palm, and tensed.

Claire saw the huge white eyes before she perceived any
other feature in the darkness. They loomed above her, near
the tops of the trees, gleaming like twin moons that glowed
with their own light. She knew them for those which had
sought her so far away in her father's house. They were
different though, less fearsome somehow. She braced herself and drew her sword.

The thing gave a great grunt, a sound almost like
speech, and a head emerged above the tops of the trees. It
was enormous, as large as a modest house, and scaled like

a serpent. It was also horned and bearded, like a goat, and noble in a hideous sort of way. It exhaled a breath of brass and steam, and ashes flew out of her fire and stung her eyes.

As she brushed her face clean with her sleeve, Claire saw a five-clawed forearm reaching towards her, and backed away hastily. Aurelian regarded the monster with golden eyes, but offered no sign of combat. The beast appeared curious, not threatened.

Perhaps the monster was not hostile. Maybe it was just huge and stupid. Claire hesitated and wondered what to do. What would Helene do? Fight or run. The terrain was rotten for either. A tree crashed to earth a foot away from her bedroll as the creature lifted its other claw-hand, holding a mace which shone greenly in the darkness. So much for dumb and friendly. Some intelligence rested in the shining eyes.

It lifted the mace and looked at her expectantly, almost hopefully. The thing was looking for a fight, but Claire was not sure she was up to giving it one. It made another sound, and again she felt it was speech, not any animal noise. Then the mace descended, smashing to earth a foot away from her and sending clots of dirt in all directions. It spoke again, as if pleading for something.

Claire felt nothing, no emotion. She was not afraid or angry or anything at all. Her long trained reflexes took command unbidden, and she charged forward as it lifted the mace, exposing the belly below its arms. There the scales ceased, and it was soft and furred and vulnerable. The sword surged in her hand, alive and eager, but she barely noticed its power. She was empty of any desire to slay the beast, or of any feeling at all.

For an instant the point of her sword rested against the furred breast. Then she buried it in the flesh, thrusting to the hilt while the monster gave a scream that shook the trees. She pulled the sword out and a trickle of clear liquid followed, spattering. A drop hit her cheek and rolled down to her lip. It was without taste, like water.

At last I perish. At last I am free of this form. What grace! What liberation!

Claire understood the words as the creature began to shrivel into a mist, the scales steaming faintly in the night. The great head shrank, the glowing eyes faded. They seemed to look at her with gratitude, and she felt ill. And then angry. She was so sick of death. She felt tears well in her eyes and let them fall unheeded. She wanted to cast the sword aside and never lift her hand against a living thing again. How could her heart hurt so much over a monster? She had not felt like this when she had destroyed the ship-fish or killed the snow beasts.

Aurelian thrust his head under her hand. *There, there, mistress. Do not sorrow greatly.*

Claire looked down at her companion in surprise. Then she became aware that she was "hearing" the words in her mind, and that she could "hear" as well a number of other voices in the forest. Small animals and birds were discussing the event like gossips in the bazaar.

What's all that ruckus.

Some two-leg killed that big lummox that's been hanging around.

Good riddance. This wood is going straight to the devil, I say. Nestlings not listening, and I don't know what all else.

I hope the two-leg goes away soon. You know what they are.

Oh, go back to sleep.

Bewildered, Claire turned her gaze back to the remains of her foe. Several objects lay on the ground, as if they had been contained within the enormous body of the beast. Curious, she bent down to examine them. The first thing she noticed were the eyes, no longer glowing white orbs, but a pair of perfectly matched emeralds so green they were nearly black. She touched one with a careful fingertip, and found it warm, not cool like a gem. Uneasy, she drew back and chewed her lip thoughtfully.

Take the eyes, mistress.

Claire looked over her shoulder at Aurelian. "Why?"

Her companion gave a little dancing movement. *You never know when you'll need an extra pair of eyes, mistress.* Aurelian lolled his pink tongue out comically and his golden eyes gleamed with merriment.

"I feel like a scavenger," she muttered, not moving.

Oh, mistress, we are all vultures. It is the way of the world.

"Why can I hear you and understand you?"

The blood of the dragon fell on your lips, mistress.

"Blood? It looked like water to me. And dragons are fire-breathing beasts."

Take the eyes, mistress.

And stop arguing with me, Claire added mentally, as she removed from her pouch one of the long white silk scarves that the natives used as gifts. She spread it out on the needle-covered earth and plucked up the jewels and set them on it. Carefully she folded the silk into a neat package and stowed it in her belt-bag.

A few feet away she saw a flash of colour, and stood to investigate. The remains of a heavily embroidered robe of silk lay torn into pieces beneath what seemed to be flower petals. The petals were beautiful, even in the near darkness. They shone slightly, like peacock eyes, and she touched one with her breath held. It took her a moment to realize these were the scales of the dragon. She picked up several and carefully put them away, then picked up the pieces of the robe and examined them. She laid the pieces out like a puzzle, using the embroidered figures as a guide.

Claire studied it. In cut it was not unlike the garments of the local folk, a loose robe meant to be fastened at the left side. The wearer must have been tall, for the robe would have been a little long for her. It was entirely covered with embroidery in a repeated pattern like lapping waves. She wondered how the dragon had eaten a man but not digested his clothing. Then she folded up the pieces into a neat bundle and pushed it into her pack. After she did it, she stood puzzled for a moment. *Now, why did I do that.* She shrugged. It felt proper.

Claire looked for the mace which the dragon had struck at her. She could find no trace of the object, though she could see the depression it had made in the earth where it hit. Finally, she saw a tiny wand, no thicker than her smallest finger and not much longer, hidden among the debris. It was cool to the touch, made of a pale green stone, and she could sense the potency within it. Beside it lay another piece of stone, white and milky, and shaped like a claw.

Take those too, mistress. With some reluctance, she put the things in her pack. They made her uncomfortable in a fashion she could not put into words, and that bothered her.

She was about to return to the fading embers of her fire when she saw something else. It was half buried in forest debris, but a little flash caught her eye. She squatted down and reached for it, then paused. It seemed somehow familiar. Claire frowned over the fleeting memory, then plucked the thing up gingerly.

It was a scabbard, and it almost wriggled in her grasp. Claire turned it towards the faint light of the fire and saw the patterns traced along the supple leather of the sheath. Not leather, no. Snakeskin.

As Claire recognized the sheath as that which belonged to the sword she bore, she felt her heart go still. She had spent too many hours poring over the illumination of Orphiana, the Earth Serpent, in the *Chronique d'Avebury* not to know the object. She glanced from sheath to the last few scales of the monster among the dried pine needles. The dragon had eaten the man who had held the scabbard. The understanding slowly sank into her mind, filling her with desolation. Deep in her silent dreams she had nourished the hope of a passion like that which held Geoffrey and Helene, and by all accounts had held Dylan and Aenor, her long dead grandparents, together through any adversity. The sword and the sheath were one, as wife and husband were one.

Now she would never know that love. A great, stupid

beast had destroyed. It was wrong. Claire stood up, squaring shoulders and jaw, swallowing pain and anger. Her eyes stung with tears and she blinked them away fiercely. She was alone. She had always been alone. No one, not even the gods, would know that it mattered. Stony-faced, she looked into the fire, and added a handful of needles, so it flamed and sparked.

Claire sat down on her bedroll and put some pinecones on the flickering flames. She watched sightlessly as the sparks flew up into the darkness. She breathed slowly, calming herself, emptying her mind as Djurjati had taught her. She was glad of that training now. She thought of her teacher and grieved at his absence. It was a real sorrow, more real than the loss of some man she had never even met. What will I do with all my love, she wondered.

Aurelian curled up against her thigh and put his head into her lap. Claire coiled her finger into his coat and felt numb. The sheath rested in front of her folded knees, gleaming in the firelight.

I love you, mistress.

Claire stroked the silky head across her lap and took what comfort she could from that.

X

Claire strode along the road with Aurelian beside her. It was a veritable highway after the tracks of the mountains, and trains of merchants and pilgrims moved along its width in both directions. After days of solitude, the chatter of so many people was battering, but she enjoyed the cheerful smiles and the shy but friendly greetings she received from time to time. The local custom of extending the tongue as part of the greeting still struck her as strange, but she always politely answered in kind. She understood more of what people said, which she attributed to the effects of the blood of the beast she had so reluctantly slain. Aurelian attracted a great deal of attention, not all of it positive, so she did not spend as much time in the little *chai* houses that stood every few leagues as she would have liked. She had dealt with fearful, superstitious peasants in the many lands of the Levant, and she knew perfectly well that they often killed things that they did not understand. She wished she could think of some way to disguise him, as she had herself. It was quite impossible. Aurelian was simply *too* magical to have any spell put upon him.

She saw the city well before she reached it. It was large and again dominated by an enormous building which she assumed was another monastery. It struck Claire as strange that a land as poor as this one should construct such luxurious dwellings for their holy men, when the common people lived in great poverty. She shrugged the thought aside. Different countries, different customs. All she wanted was a lodging and a bowl of *tsampa*. She was thoroughly bored with the millet porridge, but it was hot and filling. She wasn't really hungry. She wanted the comfort of eating, to fill up the loneliness that sometimes threatened to unwoman her. Ever since she had sheathed the Sword of Waters it had gnawed at her, an empty future with neither spouse nor children.

There was no wall around the large city that she could see, and it bothered her a little. Cities had walls. On the other hand, no army she could imagine would try to conquer this country. There was a guard by the road where she entered, and he looked her up and down, but made no move to prevent her. He stared at Aurelian, and the beast looked back, and leaned against Claire's hip, so she could feel the warmth of his body through the worn wool of her trousers. She opened her mouth to ask the guard for directions to a lodging place, but a shaven-headed monk stepped in front of her and bowed before she spoke.

"Will you come with me, Master?" he asked.

Claire hesitated. She was tired and dirty, and not at all sure she had the patience for polite converse with any more holy men. Then Aurelian touched her hand with a moist nose. *Yes, mistress, yes.* She looked down at his golden eyes, shifted her pack, and followed the monk who had not waited for her assent, but had turned and started up the wide street. She was not afraid. She had not felt afraid since her dream in the monastery at Shigatse, and she almost missed it. *Every time I meet a goddess, I lose something. First my hand, then my fear. I would prefer not to*

*lose anything more. What is left. My life, I suppose. And I
have not the capacity to even be afraid.*

They climbed the steep streets lined with brightly co-
loured houses. Accustomed to the brown and white simplicity of the cities of the Levant, Claire found the ornate
decoration rather gaudy, but charming as well. A dog,
braver or stupider than his fellows, rushed out and charged
Aurelian. When it got close enough to jump for the golden
mane, Aurelian swatted the canine aside with a soft thump,
and the dog went rolling tail over head across the street,
barking feebly. Her companion curled his tail a little
higher, and perked his ears. *How rude,* he commented as
bystanders pointed and chuckled. Claire found herself
laughing with them, and a kind of pain in her chest eased.

She climbed what seemed like several thousand steps
behind the monk, entered a cavernous hall with an overpowering reek of incense and yak-fat candles, and was
taken to an audience chamber like the one she had seen in
Shigatse. Claire set down her belongings wearily and
flexed her shoulders. She looked at the bright hangings,
then sat down and examined her boots. They must be replaced before she went any further. The boots she had
brought from Baghdad were long gone, and these which
she had bought to take their place were falling to pieces.
Her trousers too. All the walking she had done had worn
the wool to the thinness of cotton. The bright red embroidery on her jacket had faded to sickly rust, and where her
pack rested on her shoulder the material was nearly threadbare.

A slender monk interrupted these decidedly non-spiri-
tual considerations, and Claire leapt up from the chair to
bow. He was young, not much older than herself, but so
serene that he seemed truly ancient. He glowed with a silvery aura that quite took her breath away. His robes were
stiff with decoration, with silken embroidery and thick
gold thread couched down in fantastic patterns, but he
somehow wore them with complete simplicity. He smiled
at her as she bowed, and she decided he was truly beauti-

ful, and probably very holy. It was, she thought, the kind
of serenity which Djurjati had aspired to and never found,
and which he mistakenly thought she had. She had only to
stare into the dark friendly eyes to understand that she had
not even a glimmering of it within herself.

"You have come," he announced calmly. He waved her
back towards her chair. "We will not wait upon ceremony."
He gave a little laugh. "I am wound about with ceremony,
from dawn to dawn, and sometimes I would forgo it. But
that would scandalize my brothers."

She followed these comments easily, if not with entire
understanding, but was at a loss for any appropriate response. "Was I expected then, Rinpoche?" Claire finally
managed to ask. She was not certain she had chosen the
correct honorific, but she knew it meant "precious," and
she thought she had never met anyone who fit that title
better.

"Awaited, let us say. Prophesied, perhaps? Yes, prophesied." He folded his small hands together and looked at her
contentedly. There was a small twinkle in his black eyes,
quite unlike the serious abbot at Shigatse. "I am the Lama
Ch'im Dragpa. I welcome you."

"I am humbled by your gracious welcome, Rinpoche. I
am Gauri." She had given up trying to get her given name
into the local tongue, and simply used the one Djurjati had
given her. "How may I serve you?"

"What a remarkable creature you are." There was no
possible reply to this, so Claire brushed a wisp of hair off
her forehead and smoothed the wrinkles in her trousers.
"You have come to battle the Darkness."

"I believed that was my purpose here, but, in truth, I am
no longer certain." *All I ever wanted was certainty, and all
I seem to find is confusion. Why did Djurjati have to die,
and why did I have to kill that poor lizard thing. It seems
as if I have seen nothing but death since I began.*

"We can never truly know our purposes. I was born in a
barn at the edge of the city, but by certain signs and portents, it was known that I was the Dalai Lama reborn.

Thus, I was reared here, schooled and prepared. There are moments when I wonder if some error occurred—if I am fit for this great office which enscribes me like a *yantra*." He made a graceful gesture to a huge, circular painting on silk which hung above them on the wall. "I do not remember the byre, but still I yearn for it, because, in my heart, I am a simple peasant. It is my *karma* to occupy a place I feel unworthy to fulfill—to be a man beyond my own imaginings."

Claire nodded slowly. She lifted her illusory hand and touched her heart. "You are very wise. I feel so lost, because I do not know the person I am any longer. I do not know if I am a hero or a healer, or just a fool." She did not add madwoman, because it seemed unnecessary.

"But, you are all of that! Is it not wonderful?" He clapped his soft hands together gleefully. "Ah, but you are too weary for my play. We will drink tea, and you will rest."

Claire was tired, but she could not rest until she knew more. "What was the prophesy?"

The lama released a stream of words that made absolutely no sense for several seconds. True, it was spoken in the local tongue, but it was some ancient variant which her mind refused to deal with. Then she felt herself shift into Arabic, heard the words with at least a modicum of understanding, and nodded.

> " 'With the golden leopard of snow
> The healing man
> Who is more than a man
> Will come, will restore
> The dreaming dragon.' "

Claire had heard any number of wild prophesies in the bazaars of the Levant, and none of them were any better than this one, but at least she could recognize Aurelian. And herself, if a woman was more than a man. She had never thought about it that way.

Is that what you are, Aurelian? A snow leopard.

No one knows what I am, mistress. He looked incredibly smug as he replied, and Claire swallowed a giggle and curled her hand into his mane. Then she wondered where they kept a dragon in the monastery, considering the size of the one she had met in the forest, and, for that matter, why. The lama was right. She was tired.

After the customary cup of *chai* a young monk led Claire and Aurelian to a guest room. He showed her another chamber further down the corridor where a pool of water bubbled and steamed. Claire almost wept with joy at the sight of it. There was a faint smell of earth gas in the chamber, and she realized it must be a hot spring. The monk gave her a robe of the softest wool she had ever touched, showed her soap and towels, and left her to herself.

Claire put the bar across the door and undressed. She did not think anyone would invade her privacy, but her appearance as a middle-aged male did not extend below her waist. The water in the pool was incredibly hot, and it felt wonderful. She soaked for a time, then scrubbed herself pink and washed her hair in the water. Finally, relaxed and exhausted, she pulled herself out of the steaming pool, dried herself, and put on the garment she had been given. The wool felt soft against her skin, and she realized she was tender all over. She collected her things, made certain her illusion of maleness was intact, and returned to her bed chamber. Aurelian greeted her with a small yelp, and she stretched out on the narrow bed and listened to the roll of the chanting as it rang along the halls. The bed was a little short for her inches, but she was too tired to care. She dozed lightly until a scratching on the door roused her.

The chanting had ceased, and she had no idea how much time had passed. Aurelian stood up and watched the door as she opened it. It was the young monk again. He had a tray with a bowl of *chai* on it, and a pair of slippers in his other hand.

"Master, after you have drunk your fill, I will show you to the place where the Rinpoche waits."

"Thank you." She understood perfectly. Take your time, but hurry. She accepted the tea and the slippers. Her bare feet were cold and battered by the hardships of the road, but she had barely noticed. She had the remains of several blisters on her toes, and a place on one heel was rubbed almost raw. She had not felt this. Claire realized that she barely gave her body any attention since she had lost her hand. She just pushed along the road, without rhyme or reason. She ate out of habit, not out of hunger, and she slept the same way. It brought her no refreshment she could discern. She sighed and put the slippers on, finding them a decent fit. The owner must be a large man. She drank her *chai*, and then put her belt around the robe, unwilling to leave the sword out of her sight. Her fingers touched the sheath, with its intricate pattern of scale, and she felt a tingle like excitement.

The monk led her through a maze of corridors, Aurelian padding beside her. The walls were painted with bright patterns and hung with paintings of various deities. Several times she saw a representation of the sweet-faced goddess of her recent dream, and she gave each a little bow. The monk watched these obeisances without comment, but his eyes were alive with curiosity.

The chamber he took her to was very large, hung with tapestries and embroideries, and crowded with belongings. There were carved chests and tables covered with some substance which looked like red glass. One wall held a series of bins, and these were stuffed with rolls she recognized as codices. Between the tapestries were strange scroll paintings, long, narrow pictures of misty mountains or a single bough of pine. They were unlike anything she had ever seen, so subtle and indistinct that they barely seemed like paintings at all. There was one, of a horse, which caught her eye. Six or seven lines, quick, brief brush-strokes, and yet the steed almost breathed.

In the center of the room stood a raised bed, draped with

heavy brocades and surrounded by small yak-fat candles. They gave off a smell like burning wool which combined with the scent of the incense made the room close and stuffy.

A man lay in the bed. His skin was a sickly yellow in the flickering candlelight, and soft, pale hands were folded across his chest. Claire could see neither any aura nor the rise or fall of the breast beneath the hands. He was tall, even in the bed, and his hair was black and straight.

The lama stepped out of the shadows at one end of the room, smiling his beatific smile. He beckoned her towards the bed with a small, plump hand, and waved her escort away with the other.

Claire approached the bier and looked down at the dead man. His face was smooth and rather flat, and she guessed his age might be as much as thirty. There were lines beside his eyes that seemed to indicate he was fond of laughing, and he had a generous mouth. The lids of his eyes were sunken, as if no orbs rested beneath the skin.

Claire looked up from her examination and met the gaze of the lama. "Who was he?" she asked.

"He is a ruler of men, a leader of men. He has been in exile for many years, and now it is time that he should return to his people."

Claire frowned. The man was lifeless. "Forgive me, Rinpoche, but I do not understand."

"Wake him."

"What!" The man was surely dead. If she could have raised the dead, Djurjati would be beside her now. Even her father could not do that.

"Rouse him, healer. He only sleeps. His spirit wanders."

"I do not . . . he is not alive, Rinpoche."

"No. He dreams that he is dead. Call his spirit back, and wake the dreaming dragon."

Claire shivered all over. She lifted her hand to her throat and felt the scar. She had died in the many arms of the goddess, or dreamed she had. Sometimes her head did not feel quite attached to the rest of her. She was terrified for a moment, and she almost reveled in it. It was a familiar sensation, one she thought was lost, and it was pleasurable to know that she could still be afraid. It vanished before she could really enjoy it, and she realized that it was not fear, but the memory of fear, which had gripped her.

"His light is gone, Rinpoche."

"No, it merely wanders. You can call it back. Between the dream and the reality, what is the difference?"

Everything, she wanted to argue. She looked at the man who had, he said, become someone beyond his own imaginings, and saw, indeed, a simple peasant garbed in ornate robes. Everything was illusion. Including death? The world was a dream, but whose? The gods?

Claire looked down at the still figure on the bier. "What happened to his eyes?"

The lama studied the still face of the man. "Perhaps they were stolen." He gave a little shrug.

Claire clenched her left hand until the nails dug into her palm. This was madness. Then Aurelian nosed her arm, and pawed at her pouch.

The eyes, mistress, the eyes.

Claire stared stupidly at the beast for a second, then dug into her belt pouch. Her fingers felt the bit of leather she used to clean her blade, and the small whetstone she kept for sharpening it. They brushed the odd, heavy stone Helene had given her in what seemed another lifetime, and finally found the silk-wrapped jewels she had taken from the floor of the forest. She pulled the package out, set it below the folded hands, and opened the soft silken scarf. The gems glowed greenly in the flickering yellow light of the many candles. She picked them up in her left hand, and felt the energy that they held.

Claire looked at the man again. She studied the body minutely, noting a little smear of ink on one finger that so forcibly put her in mind of Geoffrey that she wished to weep. There was a scar across the knuckles of the right hand which spoke of some long past dispute or accident.

Within the smooth hair of his head, Claire saw a tiny spark of white. She blinked and looked again. There was no mistaking a bit of aura no larger than a speck resting at the crown of his head. Had she missed such a mote in Djurjati? Had she cremated him when she could have brought him back to life? She banished these fruitless speculations with a soft curse.

She reached for the gleam with her illusory hand. A faint ripple of energy, a mere whisper, touched her fingertips. She picked up the green gems from the man's chest, and she could sense them throbbing against her nail-torn palm. Claire could feel power beginning to move across her body. Still, the speck remained a speck, and she had no idea how to accomplish the task the lama demanded of her. She drew her false hand away from the skull and turned aside, bothered by an itching concern she could not quite pin down. She looked sightlessly at the dynamic figure of the horse on the scroll on the wall, and found herself wondering how Anna was doing with Absalom, her horse.

Then it came back, the lesson which disturbed her at present. It had been five years before, and they had been in the ruins of Byzantium where Geoffrey hoped to recover some of the books from the libraries of the mages of that city. Claire had been trying to imagine what the place had looked like before its destruction, before earthquake, fire, and the pillaging of Turkic nomads had reduced it to heaps of broken rubble. She asked Helene to describe it as they walked past the ruin of the House of Wisdom, where once a thousand lamps had shone through an alabaster dome and been a beacon to sailors across the Bosporus.

Helene had gazed out at the sea, deep in memories, for several minutes, and Claire had restrained her impatience with difficulty. Finally, she had answered. "It was a fair place, but it was evil. The mages were evil. Beside them, the Shadow was a nothing."

"But, why?"

"Why? You always ask that. I did too, when I was your age. I was fifteen when the city fell, when the wards failed and the elementals were freed. They were necromancers, Claire, the mages. My father was several hundred years old when I finally . . . he was a long time dead before I ended him."

"But, why is necromancy evil? Father always tells us that any magic can be used for good or ill, that the magic itself is innocent, and that it is the mage who chooses the result."

Helene gave a little snort of laughter. "That is philosophically correct. Your father is a very moral man, Claire, and very scrupulous. He is so good." There was a little hint of pain at the words which the girl could not interpret. "But, necromancy is . . . all magic can corrupt, daughter, but necromancy corrupts in a particular way. It brings the dead to life, or extends the life of the living in such a way as to deny death. Death must not be denied, Claire. The mages here denied all the gods, and banished dreams as well, because the gods are concerned with death and life, and dreams give us knowledge of that."

"They *banished* dreams?" Claire was astonished. "Tell me what happened."

"Pest! All right. Here is the tale as I heard it in my youth, for whatever it is worth. The Roman Emperor Julian, sometimes called in the west The Apostate, learned certain magics from the gods, even including the secrets of Artemis. He made himself immortal. For all I know he lives yet, sleeping beneath this rubble in his cave of diamond. I explored large parts of the undercity as a girl, but I never saw more than a third of it. But I was assured that Julian lived still, and slept somewhere close by. We can never know what really happened in the past. We barely know what happens in our own lives, so the past is always a muddle of truths, and half-truths, and outright lies. It is never clear and simple."

Helene gave a little sigh, and continued. "But Julian built the city and gathered around him men of like mind, men whose task it was to prolong life, and he proscribed all mention of the gods, except himself, of course."

"Did you ever meet him?"

"Hardly."

"But, if he was immortal and . . ."

"He should have let the gods be and worried about the ambitions of his students. A group of them banded together—the Council of Mages—and overwhelmed him and put him to sleep in this cave. I do not know why they did not kill him outright. I would have. Perhaps they could not, or perhaps they were afraid to. And then they went on existing, century after century, increasing in knowledge which they mistook for wisdom, clinging to life for no other reason than to have it, and bickering among themselves for supremacy. It was no pleasure to them, certainly, for they were all walking dead. Let the dead lie, I say. I hate this place."

The bitterness and anger of her mother's words was fresh in memory. Claire sat down abruptly on a high-backed chair. How could she do what the lama asked? Death was real. It was not a dream. Or was it? If only she could be sure, be certain what was the correct thing to do. She chuckled at the thought. Helene was right. She did not understand what happened in her own life. But, if death was the absence of life, then the man on the bier was not dead. A flicker of existence remained to him. But how could she blow the ember into flame?

She pursed her lips. Then she remembered drawing the fever out of Djurjati and wondered if she could by some means pull something in instead. She would need something to attach the man's aura. Claire realized that she had reached a decision, and it surprised her a little. She did not *want* to do this deed, but she felt compelled to. She had no choice. *I wonder if any of us have any choices but the whims of the gods.*

Claire got up and walked back to the draped bed. She took several deep breaths and steadied herself, planting her slippered feet at shoulder-width apart, and drawing the strength of earth into her before she ventured further. It flowed into her, refreshing her in a different way than her wonderful bath had. She could feel the throb of Kali's dance and the ripple of the Earth Serpent as well.

She formed the mage-hand above her right wrist, surprised yet again at how painful it was. Claire flinched and trembled, then centered herself again, removing herself from the pain as sweat began to pour down her body beneath the soft robe. Aurelian pressed against her hip and his sweet breath began to mingle with the incense and the smell of the many candles. His golden aura began to invade her flesh, upholding her and strengthening her in a fashion she had not experienced before. Her mouth tasted of ripe peaches and she felt as if a tender breeze caressed her brow.

Slowly, she reached for the mote of aura. When her mage hand met the spark, there was resistance, like a great wall, and she could go no further. Claire sought some means to penetrate the barrier, but it remained impermeable. The man was very strong, even in death. After what seemed like several eternities, she realized that what she was attempting must seem a violation of his very being.

Speak to him, mistress.

Please, let me help you, she told the mote.

Who are you? I cannot see. My eyes, my eyes. I must see.

Aware that she still clutched the gems in her left hand, Claire moved them over the still face. Carefully she placed them on the closed eyelids, and sensed something amiss. She had been so certain. Aurelian nudged her elbow lightly. *Backwards.* After several seconds she exchanged the two gems, and immediately felt better. *Why, I nearly made him cross-eyed.* Then she held her palm above the gems, letting her energy excite the crystals, until they seemed to melt into light and disappear.

Her left palm, above the man's face, seemed to sizzle, as if the flesh was being burned away, a pain as great as that which seared where her wrist had been severed. It lasted for only an instant, before she snatched her hand away, but it shook her focus, so she saw stars dancing before her closed eyes. The thousand stars coalesced into two gleaming ones which seemed to pierce her brain.

Who are you!

With the insistent question, Claire felt the resistance to her presence retreat for a moment, and she caught the mote of aura with the power of her mage-hand. *A friend,* she replied, as she extended the mote into the aetheric realm, seeking to draw the wandering spirit back into the body on the bed. It was so weak! She spun a thread of herself into the spark of the man without considering the consequences. She had to strengthen and enhance his energy! Then she was caught, like a fly in a web.

It was so close, an intimacy which she had never imagined or experienced before, even when she had touched the goddess, and it would have terrified her if she had not left her fear on the snow-clad soil of a dream. As it was, she felt the memory of fear, the sense that she ought to be afraid. Claire ignored the flutter of reflexive panic, the sense that she might lose something precious of herself, and permitted her training to take command. It was her warrior self, not her mage, that emerged. This was a battle. Her breath paused as she struggled to match the energy of the man, and felt the union seize her and whirl her away, until she had not clear sense of herself as individual at all. There was nothing but the spinning thread of light consuming her and drawing her away into some nameless void. There was no direction there, no sense of place. She was just lost.

Something brushed her, sweet as sun-warmed honey, and she saw two golden orbs float before her in the limitless emptiness. She turned towards them, reaching out with invisible hands to grasp their light, and felt herself plummet into somethingness again. A glow surrounded her, penetrated her, pierced the disordered shards of her being, then filled her to overflowing. She was a cup too full. It brimmed and spilled, a cataract that poured and poured, until she could sense where it divided around a grain of sand that was like a boulder. For an instant, for an eternity, she watched the abundance divide, bewildered. One stream was blue, the other green, and she must choose. How? They were so beautiful. She wished only to watch them forever, without pain or thought. But, something nagged, and after a time she followed the blue torrent back into wretched solitude. Her entire body screamed as it lost sight of the other stream and plunged into separateness.

Claire came to her senses with her left hand coiled so tightly into Aurelian's mane that the hairs had cut her skin, and blood trickled out. Her mage hand flickered and faded, and her right arm flopped against her side. Then her knees gave way, and she would have crumpled to the floor but for the immediate support of the lama. He barely came to her shoulder, but he was strong, and he half dragged her to a chair.

"Chai," she gasped, as if he were a servant. Her mouth and throat were parched, and she ached from the soles of her feet to the roots of her hair. No, she decided, even my hair hurts. She was so dazed she barely remembered what she had been doing for several seconds. She leaned back against the chair and brushed an embroidered sleeve over her drenched face.

As the lama brought her a cup of greasy tea, the man on the bed moved. His eyes fluttered, and his head rolled towards them. He stared at her, and Claire wondered what he saw. I must look a mess, she thought, and laughed. Her tidy chamber in Baghdad seemed as remote as the moon. She longed for it, for the safety of it, with a fierce wave of nostalgia. She wished the stuff in her cup were *kavya* instead of tea. She longed for a steaming platter of *pilau*, yellow with saffron and beaded with plump raisins and morsels of chicken, and the fresh scent of her own clothing after Dorothea washed them.

Claire's wide mouth curved in a grin as she remembered these amenities amid the incense reeking air of the huge chamber. The man's lips smiled in response. He lifted his head and looked at the rich coverings across him, frowned a little puzzled, and thrust them aside. Then he swung his legs over the side of the bed and looked at her again.

His eyes were dark, as black as soot, but with a glint of green in them as well, and perhaps a pale amethyst. He blinked as if he had some difficulty focusing, and knuckled them. All around him danced an aura as bright as moonrise. He looked at Claire, at Aurelian, at the lama, and back at the woman. The lama handed him a bowl of tea, as if raising the dead were an everyday occurrence in his domain, and beamed happily at both of them.

The man lifted the handleless bowl to his lips and sipped, then made a face. "I will never become accustomed to your tea, Rinpoche."

The lama chuckled. "You will not have to. Soon you will be where you belong, Lord, and you can have all the many things you have missed in your exile." He waved a small hand at the furnishings of the chamber. "These reminders of home are hardly adequate."

"Oh? Have you raised an army to follow me, to overthrow that dog's-head my mother took to her bed? Curse her, and curse all women for treacherous beasts."

Claire listened to these words and felt a pang. She was only tired, she told herself fiercely. It did not matter what opinions this stranger held. She had done her job, and if she got no thanks for it, well, that was that. If she could but forget the joy she had had in the moment when they were one. Tomorrow, she would go on her way. Aurelian would take her wherever she was going, and she would never see this man again. She would do her job and serve the gods, and have done with it. Claire resolutely banished the bleakness that nibbled at her and drank her tea.

"Lord, you must not be bitter. It does not become your person."

"I have always been bitter, Rinpoche, but I have not spoken of it. I feel—so odd. My eyes seem to be misted, and my body hardly my own. I was at my desk, reading a poem, and then I remember nothing. Only emptiness and pain. Such pain. Who is that man who sits there? And why

does the *keelin* sit beside him, and not come to me? Am I
not the Emperor?" He sounded cross, and Claire felt she
could hardly fault him. Returning to the body was rather
shocking, as she remembered from her waking in Varanasi.
It was so puny and confining after the vastness of the Void.

His shoulders drooped beneath his robe. "I am a fool of
an emperor. Why would I wish to return to the intrigues of
the world, the whispers of the court? Why must I imagine
that the people long for my return—or even remember my
existence? Why do I dream I hear them crying out for me?
Everyone I trust betrayed me. Even my own mother. She
was so lovely. Who could believe that such wickedness
could hide in such beauty."

"Tch, tch. You must not distress yourself over the
choices of others, Lord. Have you learned nothing here?
You cannot walk another man's path, only your own."

"Oh, I have learned from you, Rinpoche, but betimes
faith is a small comfort. When I was a boy, I was trained to
sit upon the Dragon Throne, and I believed it was my
place. Everyone was kind to me. And then, in a nonce, I
was thrust aside like refuse. I am grateful for the haven you
have given me, but still I dream of restoring the Celestial
Kingdom and driving the barbarians back beyond the Great
Wall. Who *is* that man?"

The lama turned and looked at Claire, and gave her one
of his quick grins. It was immensely reassuring for no reason she could discern. "This wizard has brought you back
from death, Lord. But, I can tell you little more. One does
not inquire too closely of wizards. It is not seemly." Or
healthy, he implied. Claire liked the little lama more and
more. He was so simple and so lively, as if the world was a
joke he continuously appreciated. He was such a contrast
to Djurjati, who had often been sadly lacking in any humour. Her teacher had been terribly earnest, as she was
herself.

The lama, on the other hand, did not confuse being serious with being solemn, and she appreciated that. He was
up to some mischief. Of this she was quietly certain. His

unnamed guest, this exiled emperor, must have been extremely trying at times. Not always. Those laughter lines around his mouth and eyes were well established.

The emperor cocked his head to one side and studied her with the strange eyes. The candlelight reflected in them, not gold, but green and violet. "Are you really a wizard? I have always wished to meet one, but I never thought to see one who was so young. Or perhaps you have discovered the elixir of life and merely appear youthful. Who are you? I am Ts'u Meng Lung. I feel as if I have seen you before, from a great distance, but you were different. My eyes are behaving most oddly. Your face keeps changing. No, not your face. Your beard keeps vanishing!"

Claire coiled a finger into her illusory beard and wondered what to say. She glanced down at Aurelian, seeking advice.

This is not the time for disguises, mistress.

With a sigh, she released the spell that hid her sex and age, and even that which disguised the hideous disfigurement of her right arm. It was almost a relief. She was weary of pretense. Aurelian pressed against her, comforting and soft.

Lung gave a sharp hiss of breath. Claire could not imagine what of her appearance could cause such a reaction, and touched her face to feel the well-remembered features. Yes, she still had the normal complement of eyes, nose and mouth. Her wide forehead was smooth, though very sensitive between the brows, where Djurjati had assured her a third eye existed. Still, it did not seem to have actualized itself with a lid or lashes. She lowered her hand.

"I do know you! I saw you in my dreams. I saw you dance in moonlight."

Claire could not decide if he spoke of his own memories or from some lingering residue of the eyes of the dragon he now possessed. Who had watched her across the world, the man or the monster? "I trust it pleased you, Lord."

"Pleased me! I thought I was going mad!" He began to laugh hysterically. "Now I am certain of it!"

She was half-tempted to agree with him, since her own sense of sanity seemed to have fallen to the floor of Kali's temple weeks before. But she shook her head. "I am here. I am real, flesh and blood. And you are real too."

"True. How simple. How practical. How like a woman."

"Your exile is ended, Lord," the lama said. "This bright one will take you home at last."

Lung considered this, kicking his slippered feet against the side of the bed discontentedly. "It is not what I expected," he said finally.

"I do not think it ever is," Claire answered. The lama grinned and nodded, as if she had said something clever.

PART II

Light swarmed. It cascaded in glistening motes like rain-
bows, then spun into a whirlpool of colourless colours. It
was both white and not white.

Leave me alone!

Child, listen to me!

No, I won't. He said you were Tara. He said you were
Mercy. Tara the Merciless. I name you.

Child, you cannot deny me.

The lambent countenance coalesced in the center of the
swirl of colours, serene and insistent. No distress marred
the lovely face, and the woman wished she could make it
frown or cry or anything but smile beatifically.

I hate you!

I know, sweet child. I know. But nothing has happened
to injure you.

You lie! I am lost and alone. Djurjati, my teacher and
my friend, is dead. I have no one to pass the Sword onto.
How can you say I am not injured.

Hush. It is but a dream.

It is a nightmare. I cannot continue. I am too tired. My heart hurts. I wish I had died in Kali's arms!

You did, child, you did. It is all a dream.

Then why can't I wake up and stop dreaming?

Someday, someday soon, you will wake and the dream will end. But, now, now you must take the Essence of Waters and cleanse the heart of Asia of its Darkness. You must take the young dragon back to his people and restore him to his throne.

Why not ask me to bring down the moon as well. That man. He is nothing. He is a weak, vain fool. Young dragon, indeed.

Did you not see his spirit when you woke him? Was it not strong and powerful and worthy?

Yes, it was beautiful. But that was a dream. He is not like himself!

Are any of us, dear one? Come, take up your burden with a glad heart. Go forth bravely, and restore the earth. You long to heal. Heal!

I am so tired.

I am always with you. You have only to invoke me for aid.

But, you are only a dream.

The cosmos sighed, and the serene face swirled away into rainbows, and then there was only the light. It dimmed into nothing, and silence reigned.

XI

Claire sat astride the largest pony the lama had been able to provide, her long legs cramped by stirrups which were too short, and stared at the immense expanse before them. It was desert and it was mountain, and it was unlike anything she had ever seen before. She had visited many deserts, the golden sands beyond the Nile, the bone-bleached whiteness of the Negev, and even the Empty Quarter of Araby, parched and arid. None of them compared to this vastness at the top of the world. The thin air was scentless, except for the comforting smell of horse, the stink of her woolen garments, and Aurelian's faint odor of honey. It was so still, so silent. She longed for the call of any bird, even a loathsome vulture. It was dry and cold and empty, and she found herself shivering a little.

Ts'u Meng Lung sat on another pony and studied the terrain almost cheerfully. "Big, isn't it?"

Claire wanted to snarl at him, but she held her tongue. He was not the person she would have chosen to accompany her into the wild, had she been offered any choice.

He was too soft and too pampered, though she admitted to herself that he never uttered a single word of complaint at either the constant cold that wore away at her strength and temper, or the difficulties they faced. Nor had he questioned her authority, once the guides who had brought them out of Tibet had left them. He pounded tent pegs, very poorly at first, and saw to the animals before himself, with grace and good humour. His smooth hands were now rough with the beginning of real callouses, and he was in the habit of staring at them, turning them over in the firelight, as if they were strange growths that had sprouted at the ends of his arms. His expression held something like regret, as if he had lost something precious.

But she had had no choice. The lama had been serenely firm, Aurelian insistent, and the voice of her dream and memory absolutely adamant. She was to take this pleasant, scholarly exiled monarch back to his people and his land. He barely knew one end of a sword from the other, though to her surprise he was a skilled archer, even better than she had been when she still possessed two hands. She carried her bow and arrows still, strapped behind her saddle, but she never expected to use them again. They were a fragile link to a home she did not ever anticipate seeing again, like the fine linen napkin embroidered by Dorothea's skillful hands, which lay folded in the bottom of her pack. The rare coney or rock dove foolhardy enough to show themselves ended up spitted and cooked over the tiny brazier, and, if nothing else, it made a change from endless bowls of *tsampa*, and extended their supplies a little. The pack mules were already lighter by several bags of millet, barley, and the dried yak or sheep dung which served them as fuel.

The short day was almost gone, so Claire began looking for a campsite. Once the pale sun set, the cold was almost unendurable to her, and she dreamed of hot, breathless Levantine nights. And walls. She longed for real walls and roofs and paved streets. Sometimes she let herself think of baths, but that nearly broke her control. The things she yearned for were not at all the ones she had thought she would miss.

A slight depression with some sparse vegetation growing in it appeared a likely place, and Aurelian indicated his approval by sitting down in the middle of it and looking quite pleased with himself. He was their guide now, and Claire nodded at him.

She let herself smile, and felt her lips split and bleed from the dry air. "We will stop here," she announced, then licked away the horrid coppery taste of her lips. It brought back the smell of the goddess and made her shiver with more than cold. Claire kicked free of the miserable stirrups and dismounted. Her knees protested and her thigh muscles spasmed. Cursed things! She stamped her feet and did several knee bends, then walked to one of the mules to begin unpacking the little tent. Lung dismounted, took his bow and arrows, scanned the skies and searched the ground. He gave a little grunt and slipped out of the hollow, his thick soled boots barely making any sound on the rocky ground.

Claire watched him vanish and angrily yanked at the ties which held the tent on the mule's back. The knots surrendered, and the bundle rolled off the back of the patient animal and fell on her toe. She gave a yelp and then just stood and cursed, embellishing her normal repertoire of Greek and Arabic obscenity with some she had acquired in India and Tibet. It took a full five minutes to complete the recital, and much refreshed, she unsaddled the horses awkwardly. They moved off to graze on whatever withered grass and leaves they could find.

"I am being a real sour-puss, Aurelian."

Disappointment is always difficult, mistress.

"Is that what it is? Disappointment. What a foolish, stupid, pitiful emotion. I got what I wanted—adventure. But I am not enjoying it. I miss my hand. I miss my home. The best thing that has happened that I can think of is I don't have to go around looking like a man any longer. But, you know, I sort of miss the beard." She chuckled in spite of herself.

It was an excellent beard, mistress. Here, let me help you with that. Aurelian took a corner of the floor canvas and pulled it away. In a few minutes, working together, they had it as smooth as the ground would permit, and she lugged the little brazier to the circle in the center of it and settled it down onto the ground. Then she carried the bedrolls, saddles and food bags onto the covering and started collecting such burnable stuff as there was nearby.

Lung returned with two small birds in one hand and a large rabbit hung from his belt. Together they set the tent up, and then he cleaned and gutted the animals while Claire got the fire started. When night fell, they tethered the horses and the mules together beside the tent and retreated inside. An appetizing aroma of roasting bird made her mouth water. Lung filled a little kettle with water from the now rather shrunken skin bags and set it to boil on the brazier. It steamed a little in the dry air, and after a while they drank greasy *chai* from small wooden cups while the birds finished cooking. The wind moaned softly around the tent and the silence lay between them.

"Do you think we will be able to find water soon? You and I can thirst a little, but the animals cannot."

Claire stared at Lung after this question, her mind casting up pieces of Arabic poetry. Her nurses had sung them for lullabies, enchanting paens to cool, clear water and grasses green and tender. Nomads had uttered the words as blessing, as greeting and farewell. *May you never thirst.* It made her want to cry. How many houses had she entered where the tiles of the floor were a pattern of blue and white, like waves? The vastness of the waste before them and the need for water seemed nearly overwhelming for a moment.

"I hope so."

"Your face. What were you remembering?"

"Remembering?"

"You have an expression betimes. Your jade eyes glisten and your skin glows like cinnabar, and I know that you are gone into memory. It touches my heart when I perceive it."

Jade eyes? Cinnabar skin? The jewels eyes she had given him must be playing strange tricks. "Water is the subject of the poetry of the peoples I have known all my life, and your question brought it to my mind."

"Will you tell me some?"

Claire reached out to turn a bird while she thought. She could speak to him with ease in his own tongue, though she suspected she did it poorly. Chinese seemed, like Tibetan, a language more sung than spoken, and she was not very musical. The effects of the drop of dragon's blood upon her mouth had given her fluency, but her mind remained anchored in the patterns of her childhood. Problems she approached in Greek or sometimes Latin, feelings in Arabic or Hebrew or Aramaic. To these she had added Hindi, and the complex religious matters in which Djurjati had instructed her, then Tibetan and Chinese. She could translate an Arabic poem into Greek, and knew it would lose some undefinable property, some quality of its beauty, and she was quite daunted by the prospect of attempting to do even that well into a tongue that she knew was richly poetic in itself. She felt no confidence in her linguistic abilities for literature. She had too great a respect for poetry as an art to risk making a muddle of it. It would not be anything like perfect.

Claire made a wry face at herself. She could almost hear Helene chiding her. *Here I thought I was all done with trying to be perfect. Then it sneaks back in on me.* Across the fire, Lung watched her with quiet expectancy, and Aurelian lolled his rosy tongue at her, laughing.

She closed her eyes, relaxed her shoulders, and breathed very slowly, putting herself into a light trance, one where her judgment was set aside. Then she spoke a poem, then another, without the least understanding of what she said or how well she said it. When she came back to herself and opened her eyes, Lung was smiling at her.

"That was splendid."

"Was it? I haven't any idea what I said."

He nodded and sighed a little. "It cost me greatly to

leave behind all my books, many of which were of poetry. They have been faithful companions in my exile. It was expected—when I was sent to the lama—not this one, his predecessor, who promptly took to his bed and perished, after which great confusion reigned for many months while they sought a successor—that I should become a monk. I was but a boy of twelve. I showed so little aptitude for prayer that even the most patient of the teachers realized that this was not my way, and let me be. I came with a dozen wagon loads—one for each of my years—of goods, half of which were lost in the passes of the mountains. I had too a body of servants, tutors and two eunuchs of the court. It was a fearsome journey, and many of my company died. Not all of them. One eunuch survived. Two of my tutors remained, and a handful of lessor serventors. I think that, in truth, my mother hoped that all of us would die, or that we would be killed by wild tribesmen along the way. Then she could pretend it was Fate, and not her doing at all. I suppose she believes me dead. But, when the servants were no longer there, the poetry remained. The classics, the words of wisdom. And I had, too, my painting. I have had much pleasure in the brush."

Claire nodded. "I did not see any servants. Where were they?"

Lung shook his head. "Everyone who was sent with me was old. The youngest was a huntsman in his fifties! Those who survived the trip have died over the years I have waited to return."

"How long is that?"

"I have been in Tibet for twenty years."

For no reason she could express, Claire was mildly exasperated. He had just been sitting around her entire lifetime, waiting? For what? Her? So she could help him regain his throne, as her great-grandmother, Eleanor, had helped Arthur in Albion. If he was that spineless, she did not think he would make a very good ruler. "Why didn't you do something?"

"It was not time," he replied serenely.

Claire found this incomprehensible. It made her angry, and the scar around her throat itched with heat. She tugged at the collar of her jacket to scratch at it, and heard his startled gasp. Her face flushed with embarrassment. Although she had never been overly vain, the disfigurement of her scarred wrist and throat shamed her deeply. Lung had, with enormous tact, made no reference to her missing hand, neither asking her how she had lost it nor treating her as if he were even conscious of it. Since they had left their Tibetan guides, he had simply done such tasks as required two hands, like re-saddling the horses or putting up the tent, without question.

Hastily, she pulled the jacket back into place and hid the scar. The wind began to rise, and Claire listened intently. It was not the start of a sandstorm, but merely the normal evening wind. At least, she hoped she was experienced enough to know the difference. Except the mouth of Kali, she could think of nothing which filled her with more sense of terror than a desert storm. And possibly this passive man across from her, with his foolish hopes and vain expectations. What was she supposed to do—conjure an army out of stones? Or dragon's teeth, like fabled Cadmus?

"I think the birds are done," she muttered.

Lung looked at her, his quiet countenance troubled, but he only nodded and pulled two smooth sticks from a narrow case that hung upon his belt. The first time she had seen him use these implements she had been astonished, and his grace with them still fascinated her. He plucked the birds off the brazier with the tools and set them on brass plates heavily chased in the Tibetan manner. Then he removed a little knife from his belt and rapidly cut the doves into small pieces. He took care over the task, and arranged the dismembered fowl in a pleasing pattern. He did that with everything. If he made the fire, he put the dung cakes and bits of firewood into the brazier in a discernable order.

"Why do you do that, Lung?"

"What?"

"Put everything orderly?"

"Does it displease you?" He looked worried.

Claire laughed. "Certainly not. I am myself a tidy person. My family used to scorn me for it. But, you also make things . . . beautiful."

"We Han believe that beauty itself is an expression of the order of Heaven, so that even the simplest thing must be according dignity. My tutors taught me well, even when I was very small, because as Emperor I would be expected to embody the Mandate of Heaven. It is not thus among your people?" He handed her a plate across the brazier. "Are you ready to try these again?" He clacked the tips of his sticks together. "It is really very simple—and much neater than using your fingers."

"All right." Lung rolled up onto his knees, took another set of sticks out of his pouch, and positioned them in her left hand carefully. She moved the tips opened and closed several times, then conveyed a morsel of bird to her mouth without dropping it. This pleased her immensely, and she chewed thoughtfully. The birds did not have much flesh on them, but Claire was full before her plate was half empty. She set the sticks down, and put the dish aside.

Pulling her knees up under her chin and hugging her arms around them, she considered his question while he continued to eat. She had heard of several heavens in her life. There was the one the nomads spoke of, full of running streams and grass, and the noisy, bickering halls of Olympus, the lotus-lit Void Djurjati had told her of, and the song-filled cloudy place the Christians all seemed desperate to get to. But she had never come across any people who made a ritual act of the most simple things, as he did, in order to reflect heaven.

She liked it, she decided, both the idea and the practice. It soothed her spirit, which always yearned for the order she had created around her in her scattered, wandering youth. But she had always stopped at neatness, and had never gone the step beyond. She had happily settled for austerity in the midst of chaos, without even glimpsing the possibilities of beauty within it. Really, she never thought of beauty at all. That was a kind of perfection that was well beyond her grasp. Claire recalled the way Dorothea arranged the table or folded her linens. She would have understood Lung. She always made things so wonderful, even if she did not have a mandate from Heaven.

"No, no one in my people makes things beautiful for heaven's sake. But, I do not really have a people. I have a family, but no more than that. And it is a very small family—my parents, a brother, and two sisters."

"How sad. So many girls."

"I never thought of daughters as a sadness—and certainly my father did not. But Djurjati—my former companion and my teacher—told me that girls were a curse in his country, that they are impure. I could not quite understand why this could be so, that one sex should be so great and the other nothing. Oh, I know the nomads hold ideas like that, but you are an educated man, a civilized man."

"Women cause trouble. Like my mother."

"I do not understand what happened, precisely."

Lung chewed thoughtfully. "I do not either, I suppose. My father, the Emperor, was, I think, not a strong man. I do not know. I hardly saw him. He was busy with the war against the barbarians when he was not busy with the intrigues of the court. Young as I was when I was sent away, I already knew the endless intrigues, and I also knew my mother sat at the center of them. They called her the Spider Empress—but never to her face. The children of my father's other wives, and those of his concubines died of illness or accident, if they were boys. Girls, being worthless, she did not bother to destroy. Ministers who opposed her found themselves facing the headsman or being exiled to distant provinces. But, despite all this, she cared for me—I thought."

Claire felt sorry for him. He had been lonely all his life. "And then," she urged gently.

"My father died, and the barbarians swarmed across the empire like maggots on a corpse. And my mother invited their leader, their Khan, to take my father's place—both his seat upon the Dragon Throne, and his place on her couch. She married him—and sent me to Tibet. Unless some child of my father's siring was born unknown, I am the last male of his lineage, and the only legitimate claimant to the throne. The Khan had other wives already, but I somehow doubt they have enjoyed long and happy lives. My mother permits no rivals—not even me."

"Do you really wish to go back to that, all the intrigue and vying for favor?"

"It is my duty. Without me, Heaven cannot speak to Earth. I owe it to my people. And, I believe, that it must have been ordained, or else I would have perished long ago."

For a moment she wanted to scream at him. *It is all a trick, all a terrible game the gods are playing, using you and me as pawns. Heaven ordains nothing. Nothing we do matters. You are a fool if you think what you do matters. You idiot!* Claire could not decide if her final furious epithet was for herself or the man.

At the same time, she understood duty. Geoffrey had taught her duty, both in word and in his ceaseless crossings of the Levant to bring healing wherever he could. Helene had taught her duty as well, with her construction of temples to her goddess, and by her many campaigns against the invading nomads and such pockets of Darkness as lingered here and there. Perhaps the Shadow was never really defeated. Perhaps it could only be held in check by force and duty. And perhaps it was in her blood, to go on when it seemed pointless or even hopeless. She remembered the pages her father had written, of how he had felt when he had realized that he could not preserve his mother's life, as he had hoped to, as he had been led to believe he could. He must have penned the moment when he had found his mother, singing in the Elysian fields, waiting in death for her husband to join her, at least a dozen times. The despair of that meeting was undeniable, and Claire had never failed to be moved, no matter how often she heard it or read it. But he had gone on, and she would as well. She just wished she could recapture the light-hearted spirit of adventure she had felt for a moment when she set out, before she met Kali, before Djurjati was torn to pieces by mindless beasts. The last final flicker of it had died when she had recovered the sheath of her sword from the remains of the dragon in the forest. The hero she had secretly hoped for was gone, if, indeed, he had ever existed at all. She was alone.

Aurelian turned a golden gaze upon her, a look of rebuke on his flat face. Claire smiled. Not entirely alone. Whatever this strange beast was, he was a gift. It would have to suffice.

"Have you considered, Lung, that you may be neither welcomed, nor even recognized? After twenty years, even your own mother might not know you."

He nodded. "I have, indeed, pondered the matter. I have no means to prove that I am the Son of Heaven—and I confess I know that I am hardly the kind of man who attracts armies to follow him. I remember General Wu. No one could mistake him for other than a soldier and a great warrior. It was something about his bearing. I used to adore standing above him, while he reviewed his troops. It was very exciting. The drums throbbed, and the tramp of a thousand feet, all moving as one. He was loved by his men, and even popular with the peasantry. That was his downfall. My mother intrigued to disgrace him, for she saw him as a rival for my father's favor. This, despite the fact that he was her own brother. I did not know this, but my tutor explained it later, after we came to Lhasa. And Tin, my eunuch, told me as well."

"Why did she fear a general?"

"In the past, when the portents have shown that the mandate has been withdrawn from the present dynasty, the new emperor has usually been a general or a warlord."

"And were there signs of this, that your house no longer served Heaven?"

Lung looked uncomfortable. He refilled the little pot with water and set it to heat. The steam began to rise and the dry air of the tent seemed less dry. "Yes. You are most perspicacious. The crops failed twice, and there was famine. The rivers overflowed their banks. Hailstones the size of skulls rained out of the skies. The barbarians advanced, and after the fall of General Wu, they swept in like locusts. My father's virtue was insufficient to halt them. And . . . people even whispered that the fault lay with the Empress. A few faithful ministers even told my father this. But, her hold on him was too powerful. She ensorcelled him completely. And cast him aside when he could not longer serve her purposes. He was not even properly interred with his ancestors!"

Claire chewed her lip thoughtfully. "And you expect to challenge the Empress and regain your place. My mother is a warrior, and she taught me much of strategies. I know how to devise a campaign, how to supply an army, how to deploy troops—in theory. My experience is limited. But, I do not know any means to raise an army out of nothing, to support a claimant who cannot even prove his legitimacy."

"The Rinpoche said . . ."

"A great many vague, ambiguous things that any number of interpretations can be made of."

"You will not aid me then."

"I did not say that, Lung. I merely hope to devise some stratagem based on reality, instead of wishful thinking. Or hoping. You need allies. I am here to help you. That much is clear to me—crystal clear. I just cannot see how—and I want to." *I have my orders, and like a dutiful daughter, I intend to follow them, but I will be damned if I will do it blindly.*

Lung rocked back and forth on the folded blanket that he used for a seat. "You remind me of the Empress, though I cannot say just how, for she is all daintiness and beauty." His sallow face reddened as he realized how tactless his choice of words had been. "I do not mean you are not lovely. . ."

"But I am a big, one-handed lummox of a woman, with

too much jaw and too much nose, and a barbarian into the bargain."

Lung laughed. "I would not have said lummox, but, yes, you are a very large and rather . . . overwhelming person. Are your sisters large as well? Your brother, is he a giant?"

"No. Poor Roderick. He takes after my mother, who is very small—dainty, as you said. So is my sister Anna. She comes to here on me, and has golden hair and eyes of blue. My sister Dorothea and I are like my father, very tall. And if you find me overwhelming, be happy you have not met my mother. What she lacks in inches, she makes up for in temper. What have I done which makes you call me overwhelming?"

Lung frowned and unwrapped a cake of rancid tea. He dropped it into the heated water and stirred it with one of his eating sticks, then wiped it clean on a little cloth he wore over his belt, and used the pair of them to turn the rabbit over. "You are so contained," he managed finally. He removed the pot from the brazier and filled their bowls with *chai*.

"What?"

"If I were to name you in the Han way, I should call you Pure Jade, for you are like a vessel which cannot be broached. You have been. Your hand has been taken, and tonight I saw the wound around your throat, but still you are somehow complete and inviolate. You shine so stilly. It is difficult to find the exact words. But, I would pity the man who was tempted to contemplate any trifling with your person, for I think his mind would break at the thought."

Claire shrugged. *I even look like a perpetual virgin! Why doesn't that please me? Why do I still long for what I know will never be? Why have the gods cursed us with hope?* "I do not feel the least contained, Lung. I feel lost. Except for Aurelian, I would not know where I was and what I was about. I do what my mind tells me, what the goddesses I serve demands, but my heart is not in it. There have been times when I would gladly have laid down by the side of the road and never moved again."

"How do you continue?"

"I have no choice." She touched the enormous pearl in the hilt of her sword. "This will not permit me. I am, I think, upon the sword's journey, or yours, but no longer my own." Claire found she could not add that she knew the man who should have wielded the weapon was gone, that she had no one to share her strength with, or the love that refused to cease its longing. "There was a time, a space of days, when I was content, when all the pieces of me seemed in harmony. I can recall that as one recalls a moment in spring, when the grass is wet with dew and the trees are white with blossom. Perhaps I can reclaim it, some day."

"You never speak of your pain or ask for help."

"What good would it do?"

"I would like to help you, Gauri."

Claire almost winced at this use of Djurjati's name for her, for she had never gotten around to telling Lung another. It brought back so many memories. "Thank you. You do, I think. Let's get some rest. It is late, and tomorrow will be a hard day."

They settled into their bedrolls on each side of the brazier, carefully preserving the division of the tent as they had since they began. Aurelian lay on his belly, with his forepaws before him, and watched the door of the tent. Claire rolled onto her side, her eyes towards the wall, and closed her aching lids. Sleep refused to come.

After a time, assured by the regular rhythm of Lung's breath that he slept, Claire got up, added a precious dung cake to the fire, and removed her journey pages. It had been days since she had set words to paper, not since the monastery in Shigatse. She wrote, half for herself, half with her father in mind. After a time, she left off the recital of events and addressed instead the disordered emotions which troubled her. It brought her a little ease, and more, a sense of perspective. The thought made her smile, her chapped lips cracking once more. How many times had Geoffrey complained in his own efforts, of his desire for that quality. Objectivity, he insisted, was the basis for all historic documents, and it eluded him as it eluded her now. She decided it was impossible. No one could really be logical or completely objective about themselves.

With a sense of mild revelation, Claire saw how she had trained herself to contain her feelings, to keep them under a tight rein, in order not to distress her father. She learned very young to avoid displaying anger, unlike Roderick who made no effort at all to control his explosive temper. Geoffrey always looked so pained at any anger, and Claire could not bear that. And after a time she had simply extended her restraint to everything. She did not want to be a bother, to be any trouble. After all, Geoffrey and Helene had important, adult things to tend to. Let Roderick be the trouble-maker. She was determined to be a good girl. No, she was going to be a perfect girl.

She almost moaned remembering the times she had felt sad, or even happy, and had said nothing to her father, lest she interrupt his work. Claire said nothing to anyone, after her seventh or eighth year, after she was too large to sit in Geoffrey's lap for comfort. She had closed herself up like a frost-kissed bud. And she had followed Djurjati because something in his eyes touched that unopened flower. His gaze had contained something of the companionship she yearned for and kept hidden away, lest it intrude and cause trouble. She had always thought of her father as the kindest, gentlest man in the world, and he was, in a vague, distant way. But his attention was so often elsewhere, on his studies or the logic of his magicks. The only way to be close to him was through scholarship, and she had applied herself to the task of learning ancient scripts and arcane knowledge to please him.

It had not pleased her. Claire studied this insight as she might an unfamiliar serpent crawling out of the bushes, to see if it was harmless or deadly. Nothing had ever pleased her, neither scholarship nor martial skills. She did them as well as she could, after patient struggle, because she would permit herself nothing less. And she saw that she had hoped to create some perfection in the hope that her parents might approve and find her worthy. Only it had not mattered. Geoffrey and Helene had not wanted her to be perfect, had not expected it of her, and neither of them had been fooled into believing she took a real interest in the things she did. Geoffrey knew she had no real taste for his scholarship, and Helene knew she loathed the sword and shield.

Pure Jade, hah! She was a camel pat with ambitions of greatness. Was she ever going to be really satisfied with what she had or who she was? Was she always going to be plagued with longings which even the goddess could not answer? What an untidy, unholy mess she was! And the most shameful part was how she managed to fool people into thinking she was otherwise.

Claire tried to imagine what would please her, and beyond such immediate needs as a hot bath and a soft bed, could imagine nothing. There were no words to express the ache within her. She felt so empty. She remembered the moment when she had drawn Lung back into the world of the living, the sense of complete abundance, of overflowing richness, that had been hers for an instant. That was it.

She glanced at the sheath of the Sword of Waters. Its interlaced patterns shone with a light of their own. He who should have held it was gone, and with it, all hope of fullness. She would be empty and alone all the days of her life. It was unbearable. No one would love her as she longed for. It was too wretched to endure.

Claire swallowed, and the scar around her throat burned like living fire. She squared her jaw and shoulders with the same grim determination she had brought to every difficulty in her brief life. She would not be wretched. She would do her duty, do her job, and somewhere, somehow, she would find some quality in it to sate her need. She could live with loneliness. She had done it all her life. It was nothing, an inconvenience. She folded her pages and thrust them into her pack.

Closing her eyelids over tears that brimmed and slipped down her cheeks, Claire leaned her head back and opened her mouth in a wordless, silent howl of pain. Her body shook with unvoiced sobs. She did not see the violet gleam of dragon eyes watching her beyond the fire.

Tara, if indeed you are merciful, help me to love myself. I have nothing else. There was no answer but the wind outside the tent and the soft sound of the dung fire crumbling into ash.

XII

With Aurelian as guide, Claire and Lung continued across the trackless waste, cold in the day, and colder at night. The monotony of the landscape gave them no sense of progress, and the water bags hung slack and nearly empty. A wind blew from the north, sucking the moisture out of their bodies and dulling their minds with its constant harassment. Claire remembered, finally, how the nomads of Araby covered their faces with veils, to keep the sand out of their breath, and suggested to Lung that they do the same. There was little in their supplies that would serve such a purpose, so Lung tied one of the white silk Tibetan gift scarves around his nose and mouth, and Claire dug out the embroidered napkin that Dorothea had insisted she take.

She started to wrap it about her face, and realized the impossibility of fixing it without two hands. It had her furious and exhausted all at once. She swallowed her near tears. "Would you tie this for me, please?" She extended the fine linen square towards Lung with her remaining hand.

"Certainly." He opened it, then spent a moment examining the cloth and the work on it. Then he folded it along the opposing corners, into a large triangle, and stepped behind her. He put the cloth across her face, covering her eyes for a moment, then positioned it properly across the bridge of her nose, and drew the ends behind her head. She could feel the touch of his breath against her hair, and she had a momentary temptation to lean back against him. He was half a head taller than she was, a veritable giant compared to the Tibetans. Claire repressed the desire to feel another's touch, to be held and comforted, and felt the brush of his fingers as he fixed the napkin.

What, she wondered, would Dorothea think of this odd use of her farewell gift. It would probably amuse her pragmatic sister. Still, it had a slight scent of home, an elusive whiff that was both reassuring and heart-rending. By days' end it would be grey with grime, but for now the crisp white linen was like a kiss upon her cheeks.

Claire looked at her sturdy, short-legged mount with disfavor, then swung into the saddle a little awkwardly. "I would give a great deal for a bigger horse," she told Lung.

"True. I would as well. One of the blood-sweating horses of the west would be a blessing. But these little fellows are strong and patient. We must hope your golden friend takes us to water soon, however. If we give the horses and the mules a full ration at nightfall, we will be fortunate to have a cup of *per-cha* between us."

Once ahorse, conversation was impossible, which left Claire to worry in silence over the problem of water. They were still in mountainous country, and making, she guessed, perhaps thirty leagues a day, up and down, but rather less in real distance. Were they actually progressing? Towards what, she wondered. East and north of them lay the land of Han, China. Caravaneers had spoken of it in the bazaars, but in almost fabled terms. None had ever actually ventured there to her knowledge, not in years. The Turkic folk had made the Road of Silk, as they called it, very dangerous, and since the destruction of Samarkand, once a great emporium, in the year of her birth, trade had diminished and faded.

Claire wondered if she could raise a rainstorm, and shook her head. The rule of Air had never been her strength. That was Roderick's element, and he was welcome to it. Her father, with his flute, could probably whistle up a lake, if he chose, but her exhausted mind felt this too was beyond her.

When Aurelian sat down in a small declivity, indicating they would go no further, she was almost in despair. There were a few sere bushes, grey dry leaves clinging to brittle branches, and nothing else. She exchanged a look with Lung, who shrugged. They set up the tent together, watered the horses and the mules as quickly as possible, and crept into the enclosure. A meagre supper of dry barley cakes and the cooked breast of a bird that Lung had killed the previous day was consumed in uneasy silence.

Claire pulled her wooden tea bowl from the fold of her jacket, which acted as a sort of pocket, and looked at it. She imagined it filled with water. Surely there must be some way. Lung watched her. His face was grimy from his black hair to the bottom of his eyes, and fairly clean below, which made him appear rather sinister in the miserable light of their small fire. His dragon eyes glinted green and violet. If only she could conjure a water seller out of the Baghdad bazaar! How startled he would be. And angry. If only she was not so weary.

Her hand brushed the great pearl in the hilt of her sword, and her fingers tingled. Claire looked down at the pale, gleaming surface as if she had never seen it before. In truth, she had not. Every time she looked at the sword in its sheath, she remembered what she had lost. It was not easy to look at a thing which had removed her hand. Accustomed to its weight upon her hip, she was hardly more conscious of it than her boots or jacket.

But it was the Sword of Waters. Clumsily, she unbuckled it from the belt and laid it across her knees, which were tucked under her tailor fashion. The sheath rippled like waves in the flickering light, and she ran her hand from hilt to top, sensing its properties as best her sluggish mind could manage. It was so powerful and she felt so weak. Claire admitted she was a little afraid of it. She did not feel as if it belonged to her, but that if she was not careful, she would belong to it. It would consume her and drown her. And, parched as she was, the notion was nearly desireable. It was not hers to keep. She was only a bearer of the sword, as her mother had been before her. That he to whom she should have passed it was perished did not alter anything. But she could use it, if only she could think of a way. It was more than a weapon to slaughter foes.

The sense of water pervaded the tent as she moved her fingers across the interlaced surface of the scabbard, then up the curving metalwork of the quillons. The air seemed more moist, and a faint tang of salt joined the smell of burning dung and camphor-reeking wool. All the waters of the world churned in the complex traceries of the sheath. Claire felt an urge to draw the wicked, wavy blade from its covering, and had a vision of a deluge sweeping away the tent and occupants, overflowing the surrounding desert and mountains, until finally it found the sea, a thousand leagues distant. How could she control such energies? It was too vast, and she was too small.

Never attempt any magic until you have defined the problem. Geoffrey had said that over and over. She needed some water, but not the waters of the world. Claire realized she had been longing for water without limitation, out of her thirst and her exhaustion. But that portion of her which was devoted to order and tidyness had not permitted her to act heedlessly. *Well, I am glad my pickiness has some use! Now, what do I do?*

"Can I help you, can I assist?"

Lung's question, spoken with great formality, broke into her thoughts, and she looked up and glared at him for a second. It was an expression which usually caused her family or her servants to excuse themselves with all due haste, and remove themselves with whatever grace they could muster. The exiled emperor gave no sign of being in any way discomforted by what Helene called her basilisk stare, and merely waited expectantly. She bit back a curt reply, remembering how he had said that she never asked for help. He must be very brave or very stupid to be willing to risk her wrath, and Claire did not think Lung was at all stupid.

"Not unless you have spent some years in the study of magics."

He considered this. "I have some knowledge of the principles of Tibetan wizardry, as well, of course, as the geomancy which is the ritual of the Dragon Throne. My tutors, both before and after my exile, schooled me most strictly in these practices." He paused for a moment. "Perhaps if you tell me the problem which furls your bright brow, you will arrive at a more propitious understanding of it."

Claire nodded. "We need water, and this sword is all the waters of the world. At least, this is what I think, what I understand of it. No scroll of instructions fell at my feet when I acquired it." She gave a mirthless laugh. "This is the essense of the waters of the earth," she said, touching the hilt. "This scabbard, however, is a portion of the body of the Earth Serpent—who just happens to be one of my ancestors." She shook her head, and some of her hair escaped from its braid. Curse the stuff. She should just hack if off. It just got in the way, and was foolish vanity.

"I barely understand it myself, and I do not even pretend to understand the powers of the sword, but I think that this is only for earth water—not for air water. I have no sense of a way to make it rain down, but I feel I can bring water up, you see. But, how much? I hesitate for fear of dragging half an ocean up here, which would do us no good, because we need fresh water, not salt. Also, I have no longing to yank some river out of its course and bring drought and famine somewhere I have never even heard of."

"Yes, I see. You cannot be hasty or impulsive in so grave a matter. But, you are never subject to impulse, are you?"

Claire looked at him, mildly astounded. It was true. Roderick was the one who jumped into things. She was always careful. Too careful, perhaps. As Geoffrey said, there was no virtue which could not become a vice. And hers was the desire to be perfect.

"No, not often. I am a very poor gamester. I do not make wagers or take chances."

"Yet, you are here. Is not your journey a great gamble?"

"True. But, it is my duty, and I was not given a choice in the matter."

Lung laughed. "So, here we sit, duty-bound and saying we must, when in truth we are only doing what we wish."

Claire made a wry face at him. "It is so. I always yearned for adventure, and I leapt at the opportunity when it came. It was most impulsive, and I have had cause to regret it." She gestured with her scarred stump. "Much cause."

"And if you knew the cost, the price you would pay, would you really have folded your graceful hands and been content to remain at home?"

She remembered Kali and Djurjati. She remembered the first time she breathed Aurelian's honeyed scent. "No, because even if I could have foreseen the events, I could never have glimpsed the manner in which it would touch my heart. To observe the dance is one matter, and to perform it quite another. If I had chosen to deny the goddess, I would have spent my life watching, not living." *And Kali would not have been denied, in any case.*

"So, truly, you do not regret your impulsiveness."

"No, I suppose I do not. I thank you for helping me to see it."

He nodded. "Thank you for permitting me to serve. Now, tell me what you know of the properties of that which you bear so unwillingly."

"I know that this is one of several swords made by an

ancient smith out of the essence of each element. The first, the Sword of Fire, my ancestor Eleanor bore and passed into the hands of the king of her country. The next, the Crystal Sword of Earth, my grandfather got from his wife, and then it was also put in the king's hands, but another king. My mother held the Rainbow Sword of Light, until it was taken by another."

"Taken, not given, as before."

"Yes. He was a most holy man, with an unholy ambition—or so my parents told me. This is the Sword of the Sea, and there is another, which is my brother's task. It was the final work of the smith, and it is the essence of all that grows, of Wood. The swords are powerful, but they are incomplete. Their power is destructive. But, as each sword was made, the Serpent of Earth encompassed it, giving a portion of herself to be a sheath, and this alters the essence somehow, and constrains it. Together, they are complete and harmonious. And, sacred, I think."

She paused for a moment. "They are wedded. And, in each generation before my own, the scabbard was the gift of the man, of my father, my grandfather, and his before him. It was a pattern, or perhaps a ritual, a joining of the female and the male. And now that is broken, and I do not know what to do. I have not drawn the sword since I put it into its scabbard, and..." Claire felt her throat close up and the scar around her neck tightened like a noose.

Lung was silent for several minutes. "The sword is wedded, but the bearer is not. It is complete, but you are yet incomplete. And so you fear that should you attempt to wield its power, you will be... what? Overmastered. Enslaved?"

"Drowned," Claire replied, with great simplicity.

"Yes, I see. A most perplexing problem. But, it seems to me that you have not considered what powers the sheath might have beyond containment. It is a vessel, to be sure, but every ewer has an inside and an outside. But, if we think only of the emptiness of it, awaiting fullness, we forget that beyond its edges is another sort of vacancy."

Claire grinned at him. "I wish you could meet my father. That is exactly the sort of thing he would think of. It was always hard for me, because I have a difficult time grasping . . . manyness. Multiplicity? It makes my head hurt. I am very good at visualizing one thing at a time, and very poor at seeing many things at once."

"But, nothing is only singular, or even what it seems to be."

"Yes, but I want it to be! I think it would be a very good thing if rocks were rocks and camels were camels, and no more than that."

"Can you tell the dancer from the dance?"

"No! But that does not mean I do not wish to!"

Lung waggled his slanting eyebrows at her comically. His eyes glinted violet and his thin mouth curved into a huge grin. "Wish as you will."

Claire ran her hand along the sheath, touching the energies in its complex traceries. She had no guide, for never in the history of her family had there been any mention of the scabbards possessing their own distinct powers, beyond empowering the swords to do their work. She felt herself tumble into a thousand waters, from oceans to tiny freshets. There was still water, lakes and ponds, and rushing torrents and rapids roaring over great cliffs, waves as tall as houses and others no deeper than a hand. Beneath it all she could feel the siren song of the sword itself, longing for release, yearning to envelop the earth. She tried to quiet its seductive call, and wondered if she would ever be strong enough to wield the weapon, now it was entire.

If only she could isolate one thread, one drop. It was too complex, too confusing. She did not dare to take the risk. She could not take the chance, lest she err. Was that why she had been such a painfully slow student of the magical arts? Claire paused and drew her touch from the scabbard and stared sightlessly at a point beyond Lung's head. She remembered how it used to shame her that Anna could farsee almost as soon as she could toddle, and that Roderick could transform himself into half a dozen shapes by his

sixth birthday, when she could do neither. Her entire childhood had been a series of small humiliations because she
learned so slowly. She had felt like a camel amongst
horses.

Claire remembered how she had constructed the spell
that let her understand the tongue of the Tibetans, the days
she had taken to sort and assemble the magical tools, and
how she had checked and tested each portion over and over
before she drew them into a cohesive whole. Roderick,
with the same need, would have scrambled together the
elements in an hour, or a day at most, and come up with a
satisfactory result in no time. But she had never permitted
herself the liberty to act on impulse, or quickly, for fear of
making a mistake. Any number of Roderick's early efforts
had been quite disastrous. He had tried to get straw once,
and ended up with a huge, odorous pile of very fresh dung.
How he had laughed. Everyone had roared, except Claire,
who had stood outside the circle of her family, oozing disapproval. Roderick was never afraid of risk. He had all the
qualities of a real hero, and she had none, unless grim
determination counted as an asset.

Her single hand clenched into a fist. She needed so
much control, over even the smallest portions of her life,
and she was so afraid of not possessing it. Or, did it possess her? She thought of Lung's metaphor of the ewer, and
wondered if her self-containment was not a prison she had
built herself, to keep out all the terror. What terror? Of
what had she always been afraid, a fear so great she would
not even give it a name. She knew she must, that the fear
would rule her unless she named it and knew it. To name a
thing gave power, the power of the word. *But, I already
know I am afraid of making mistakes, of being less than
perfect. Why cannot I master that?*

"'You cannot leave! The child is not even weaned
yet!'"

The shout of those words came back, and with them a
rush of terror and something else. It was Geoffrey's voice,
and Claire knew she was not the child he referred to. He

was so angry. She remembered she was huddled beside a chest, the cool tiles pressing against her small knees, her little hands curled into fists so tight the nails bit into her palms.

"I am going, and you cannot stop me. I will not be a brood mare for the gods again. I hate it. I never wanted children. I cannot bear to look at them. I won't be driven, not again. Never again."

It was Dorothea they spoke of, not Anna. Yes, Helene had gone—somewhere—and Claire had been afraid. Her father had been so sad, and nothing she did seemed to please him. She barely opened her mouth for fear. And when Helene had returned, freckled from months of sun, of battling the Turkic nomads who threatened to flood the Levant like the sea, she had asked why? She had pushed a cup onto the floor and watched it shatter, and asked why? But, her real question had never been spoken.

Why did you leave us, Mother? Why did you leave me? And why did it terrify me so, when Roderick barely seemed to notice your absence? There was another question hovering at the edge of her mind, one that hurt so greatly she could hardly bear to acknowledge its existence. Claire swallowed and let it come. *Was it something I did?*

Claire knew the answer as soon as she formed the question, knew that Helene's departure had had nothing at all to do with her. Her mother had said as much in the garden, months before. But she had carried the sense of blame within her, the feeling that her own enormous imperfection was the source of both her mother's absence and her father's misery. It had made her first cautious, then careful, and finally bound and gagged her into the prison of perfection. Geoffrey had done his utmost to fill the vacancy created by Helene's departure, to be both mother and father, and he had succeeded in many ways. How could he have guessed her heart was injured, when she had not known it herself. And no one knew her anger, least of all herself.

She felt almost relieved, suddenly, that the unknown man who might have been her spouse was dead and gone, that she would be spared the peril of being a parent. She had rushed into the deathly embrace of Kali to end the terror that confined her, to escape the prison of herself. But the goddess had not been finished with her yet. Disfigured and imperfect, she had sent Claire out to do her work, to destroy the Darkness and to live.

Claire turned her mind back to the immediate problem of water. She wanted a cup of *per-cha* as she had never longed for anything before. All she had to do was choose it. All she had to do was take the risk of an imperfect solution.

Abruptly, she rose and unplucked the ties that held the door flap closed. The wind gusted in, freshening the close air of the tend and scattering ash from the brazier. Claire stepped out into the night.

The sky was bright with stars above the dust-laden, wind driven air. The air sucked the moisture out of her flesh and chilled her to the bone. There was the sound of a step behind her.

Lung and Aurelian had come out of the tent. The man carried her *chuba*, the heavy cloak made of layers of sheepskin and leather. He put it over her shoulders and closed the clasp. His warm breath touched her cheek for a moment. Then he stepped away and fastened the tent door closed.

Aurelian pressed against her. *Do not fear, mistress. I am here.*

Where is a good place for a spring?

The beast looked from side to side, surveying the bleak, rock-strewn landscape with his large, bulgy eyes. Then he padded off towards a tumble of stones that made a little circle near the edge of the campsite. He sat down beside it, and Claire walked over to it. It looked like every other bit of gritty soil to her, and she brushed her forehead and eyes with her sleeve.

The sword hilt in her hand surged, and she could feel its demand that it be withdrawn. She trembled with its power as Aurelian pressed against her right leg. She sensed the strength of the beast, the steadiness and certainty of him, drew a gritty breath, and shut her stinging eyes.

Claire thought of the patterns of the sheath as the sword struggled in her grip. Twice she grasped the vision, and twice it twisted away into confusion. Despite the chill, sweat dripped down her sides and evaporated, leaving her colder and colder. Her *chuba* whipped up behind her in a sudden gust and she staggered backwards into Lung. His arms encircled her, a touch that made her loins blaze with heat for a moment. The sword screamed with desire.

She ignored her body, as she had so often before. Claire stepped away from Lung's embrace firmly, and he did not attempt to restrain her. The excitement of her limbs subsided, and the demands of the sword seemed to diminish a little. She stepped back to where Aurelian had indicated she should work, grasped a portion of the pattern of the sheath within her mind, gritted her teeth, and drove the tip of the scabbard into the dry ground.

Her head felt as if it exploded in light, and she screamed with pain. Her hand shook upon the hilt as the sword strove to release its destruction, its lust for mastery, and Claire felt her arm begin to draw the weapon, against her own intention. She tried to force it back, but it resisted her, then surged and escaped further.

A cold, roughened hand closed around her own, and the sword subsided, shrieking and screaming as it was pressed back into its covering. The tip of the sheath jerked sharply, and dropped downward so fast she would have fallen face down but for a strong, firm arm around her narrow waist. Claire tugged at the weapon, trying to rebalance, and a spout of icy water struck her face and chest.

Lung and Claire tumbled backwards onto the ground as a geyser fountained up into the wind-whipped air, spraying everywhere like a sudden storm. It played, a shimmering column, in the night, drenching them, for perhaps a minute, then sank down. Bubbling merrily, the water churned up out of the earth, as if it had always been there. Claire

eyed it cautiously, and found, to her relief, that it showed
no signs of flooding the campsite.

Claire was abruptly aware that she and Lung were
pressed together in the heap they had tumbled into. It was
very uncomfortable and pleasant at the same time. She sat
up, out of his grasp, then stood up awkwardly. The sword
had fallen a few feet away, and she bent to pick it up. She
closed her hand around the sheath, and ignored the hilt.
She decided she had had quite enough challenge for one
evening, or perhaps a lifetime.

They hurried inside the tent, chilled and soaked.
Claire's teeth chattered as she fumbled the clasp of her
chuba with a hand that was not there. Her stump hit the
metal closure, and it was just too much. She made a little
sound, a whimper first, and then a scream of rage and
frustration that seemed to fill the tiny tent with its fury. Her
left hand, still holding the sword by its covering, clenched,
and the traceries dug into her flesh.

Lung started at the sound, stared at her for a moment,
then stepped over and undid the clasp as if it was the most
ordinary thing in the world. He removed the drenched garment and hung it from one of the wooden supports that
held the sides of the tent while her yowling subsided in her
throat. Deeply ashamed of her outburst, Claire put the
sword down by her bedroll and pulled open her pack. Behind her, she could hear the man moving, adding some fuel
to the brazier and something else. When she felt the icy
blast of the tent flap opening again, she realized he was
going for water.

Alone for the moment, Claire upended her pack and
sorted through her meagre possessions. The lama had provided them with one set of clothing, thick trousers, tunic
shirts, and heavy jackets, plus the awkward *chubas* which
were fashioned as a large rectangle rather than a circle as
she expected a cloak to be. She still had the garments she
had brought from home, the fine linen trousers, now worn
to gauze along the midseam, and the blouse that went with
it, as well as the threadbare garments she had purchased in

Hardwar. Besides these, there was the soft wool robe she had worn when she woke Lung from his deathlike trance, and the rent pieces of the garment she had taken from the remains of the dragon.

Claire removed her wet jacket and the wool shirt beneath it quickly. Her skin went bumpy and she used her linen blouse to dry her torso and arms as much as possible, then pulled the woolen robe around her. It smelled of incense and sweat, of camphor and yak-buter candles, but it was soft and warm. Then she undid her belt and dropped her trousers before she realized that she could not get them off without removing her boots. She spent a futile moment glaring at her missing hand, then began to struggle to get a boot off one-handed while still standing.

She overbalanced just as Lung returned with a filled water-skin, and was sprawled with her unclad limbs imperfectly concealed by the folds of the robe. Claire felt her cheeks flush with heat as she hastily pulled the garment down over her. Lung set the bag down, kept his eyes lowered, and pulled off her boots without comment. Claire pushed her trousers away from her and got to her feet.

After she had hung her clothing to dry and put her boots by the fire, she began to repack her belongings, keeping her back to the center of the tent to afford Lung the privacy to change his clothing. She was acutely aware that they were male and female, aware of him as she had never been conscious of a man before. While traveling with Djurjati, she had never even really thought of it, because he was, in some sense, sexless. And, in being his student, she had become genderless herself. Masquerading as a man for weeks and weeks had worn away her sense of her womanliness, and without the monthly reminder of her lunar cycle, she had nearly forgotten it. It had retreated into a corner of her mind. She had been shocked and almost outraged at the lust the sword had awakened within her.

Her father, in his ruthless, unsparing attempt to set down the tale of his part in the war against the Darkness, had not omitted his own difficulties in confronting his carnal desires while respecting Helene's virginity. They had slept together, the Sword of Light between them, and their flesh had not joined until after the weapon had passed into the hands of Michael ben Avi. What her mother's feelings might have been she could not guess, for Helene had never spoken of it. When she had discovered the sheath of the Sword of Waters, she had believed she would remain separate and virgin for the rest of her days, and, she realized, had assumed she would never be troubled by any yearnings.

But how in the name of Aphrodite had Helene been able to use the Sword of Light without being swept into lust? Was it some quality of the essence of the sword, that light was not so overwhelming as water, or was it simply her mother's fierce, fiery nature which had allowed her to use the weapon so easily. Perhaps Artemis, so determinedly virgin herself, had lent Helene the strength to use the sword. Or perhaps Geoffrey and Helene were so deeply joined in spirit that they could forego the fleshy congress for a time.

Claire shook out the green linen trousers and clumsily refolded them, then put away the rest of her garments. The last things she took were the glorious embroidered tatters of the robe she had found, and she spent a moment looking at the beauty of the work, rather than giving herself a headache wondering about the cursed sword. It was all she had of the man she should have loved, except the small wand of green stone—and the sheath, of course. She did not want to think about that either!

"Where did you get that!"

The sharpness of Lung's question made her jump and startled her out of her thoughts. Claire turned slowly and looked towards him. He was standing, dressed in a woolen robe almost identical to the one she now wore, his long, black hair freed from the topknot he usually wore, so it fell around his face like night. His dragon eyes glittered violet in the firelight, and his aura corruscated silver and jade and amethyst. He looked, for the first time, every inch a monarch and a man. If she could have felt fear, instead of only the memory of it, Claire knew she would have been perfectly terrified. He was not angry, but she could see that his anger would be both magnificent and terrible.

"I found it, just like this. It was foolish of me to keep it, but it was such a beautiful thing. Why?"

"*That* is an imperial robe."

"Is it?" Claire felt a mild disappointment. Then she chided herself for romantic silliness. The dragon had doubtless consumed any number of people, and these glorious embroideries had nothing to do with the sheath. That would teach her to be sentimental. "I suppose I should have guessed. It is much too fine for just anyone, isn't it. I found this too."

She picked up the little stone wand and held it up. Lung gave a hiss of breath like a serpent about to strike. He seemed to swell in size until the tent was too small to contain him. Claire shrank back a little. His eyes gleamed for a moment, and then he subsided. His hands, which were clenched at his sides, opened. The pot of water on the brazier began to bubble, and the tent smelled of wet wool. Everything seemed ordinary again.

Aurelian, who had been crouched out of the way, rose and moved towards her. His soft, warm mouth closed around the wand in her hand, and she let it go. He padded the few feet across the tent, and knelt before the man, lowering his golden body until his flat nose touched the floor. Then he stood up and offered the object to Lung.

Claire could see the man's hand tremble a little as he reached for the piece of stone. His long fingers closed around the tip of the wand, and Aurelian released it. The beast gave a gusty breath of honey-scented air and lifted his curved tail like a fringed banner, radiating smug satisfaction.

Lung held the small jade wand between two fingers for a long time. His face was still, as if he listened to some unheard voice or was lost in memory. Then he lifted the wand towards the ceiling of the tent which was a mere handspan above the top of his head, and his lips moved. The wand glowed with a pale green light that filled the tent, and it began to change. First it lengthened to a cubit, then it became covered with carvings. Claire could not distinguish them clearly. The green light dazzled her eyes, and she looked down at the pieces of robe spread around her.

"I am the Son of Heaven," Lung announced quietly. Then the light faded, and she looked up again. The wand was once again a plain, uncarved length of green stone. He smiled rather gravely, and sat down. "And I need a cup of *per-cha.*"

XIII

Claire woke up and sat up in her bedroll. Lung was already awake, up and dressed, and had made their breakfast. Remembering the glimpse of the emperor she had seen the night before, Claire felt a little awkward that he should be doing domestic necessities, but she accepted a bowl of *per-cha* and a serving of *tsampa* gratefully. He was still the same man, she realized, but her perception of him had changed.

While she ate, he removed a long narrow box from his belongings. It was a beautiful thing, a glossy red surface which had been ornately carved. He opened it and removed a small block of black stuff and an oddly shaped stone dish, a little rectangle with a slope that ended in a depression at one end. He put a little water into the well, and began to grind the block in and out of it. His movements were graceful, and his expression serene. When he was satisfied with his efforts, he removed a brush from the red box, picked up the liquid he had made, and left the tent.

Claire used his absence to dress. It was incredibly cold

this morning, and, after a moment's thought, she pulled the worn green trousers out and put them on beneath her newer woolen ones. When these were in place, she slipped out of the soft robe, yanked her linen blouse over her head, then put the shirt she had worn the day before over it. The extra garments did not add much bulk, but she felt a little warmer. She shoved her feet into the boots, mercifully dry and warm from sitting close to the fire, and rehung the sword on her belt, then pulled it around her narrow waist and secured it. She left her jacket hanging on the tent side while she folded up her robe, packed her bag, and put her bedroll away. A little warmed by the exertion, she pulled on her coat.

She left the tent. It was a crisp morning, and although there was little wind, the cold seemed to go right through her. Lung was kneeling beside the spring she had created, his brush in one hand, the little rectangular dish in the other. He stared intently at a slab of stone which was relatively flat and smooth, a pale grey that shone slightly, as if it had been washed. The shine vanished in the dry air as she watched.

Lung dipped his brush into the spring, then plunged it into the liquid he had ground. The white bristles of the brush turned black, and with a movement almost too rapid to follow, he made some marks on the flat surface of the grey stone. They looked something like the examples of written Tibetan she had seen, but could not read, but they were clearly not the same. As she watched, Claire wondered if it would be possible to create a variation of the spell she had made in order to understand the Tibetans, to be able to read another script. She mused on this while Lung contemplated his efforts.

Satisfied, he washed his brush and smoothed it with his fingertips, then rose. He smiled at her. Claire smiled back. "What did you write?" she asked.

"It says, 'The Spring of the Sword. Drink, wanderers, and be refreshed.'"

Claire was half tempted to ask him who he thought

would ever read the words. Any Tibetan who came this way, unless he was a monk, was likely to be quite illiterate in his own tongue, let alone Lung's. But he so clearly had taken pleasure in what he had done, she let her cavil pass, and nodded. Together, they filled all the water skins to near bursting, took down the tent, loaded the mules and resaddled the ponies.

Claire looked at her patient little steed and indulged in a moment of longing for Absalom, then mounted. Aurelian padded away across the empty waste, and they followed. The pale sun warmed them a little, but she ached with cold. She had never managed to master the yoga which Djurjati assured her kept him from feeling the temperature, and wished she had.

By midday, it was evident they were descending from the trackless plateau. There was some vegetation, short grass as dry as parchment, and little, stunted bushes that were bare of leaf. A small animal of some sort shot out of the shelter of a little bush, and later she saw the silhouette of a bird against the overcast sky. It comforted her. Claire had not realized how depressing the emptiness of the landscape had left her until her spirits lifted at the sight of the bird. It was some sort of hawk, by the form of its wings, and where hawks flew, game flourished.

Perhaps an hour later, they began to hear a faint rumble, like distant thunder, and they both scanned the sky. It was grey and overcast, but there were no heavy clouds. Aurelian led them down a draw, and cliffs rose on either side of them. It was very narrow, and they went single file, the walls of the canyon no more than an armspan away on either side. Caught in a rock Claire saw the imprint of a shell, and then saw others. She recognized a whelk, not too different than the ones which littered the shores around Tyre, where they extracted a dark dye much prized by the weavers of the Levant. She could not imagine how it had come there, unless the sea had once covered this arid land.

The thunder sound had diminished when they entered the declivity, but when they emerged from its lower end, the noise returned, greater than before. A plain lay spread before them, immense and flat, and in the distance, towards the north, there was a faint outline of further ranges of mountains.

They drew to a halt and stared. The ground seemed to tremble, and Claire dismounted, knelt down and laid her ear to the earth. She jerked back abruptly, assaulted by a confusion of sounds which was close to painful. Claire took several breaths, steadied herself, and bent forward once again.

Her hand and her ruined wrist rested on either side of her head, after finding she could not make any sense out of the welter of noise, she reluctantly manifested her mage hand. Despite the cold, she could feel the sweat bead her brow as she brought it into being. If only it did not hurt so much!

The glowing blue hand pressed flat against the dry earth beneath her cheek. The ghostly fingers lengthened, and the tips appeared to burrow into the soil, as if seeking something buried within. At first, all she could sense was something which felt like a scream of anguish, if a scream could be felt. It was so terrible a thing that it made a nothing of the pain of her body. Then she could feel the earth itself, being slain. It was the Darkness, but not as she had seen it in India, where it drove the people it afflicted into madness and destruction. Here it killed the very soil, down to little motes of life she had never guessed existed and had no name for. Somewhere, far away, her ancestor, the Earth Serpent herself, was suffering greatly. A portion of Orphiana was near to extinction. That portion of her blood that descended from the Earth Serpent trembled with fear, and with rage.

Besides this, there remained the thunderous sound that shook the ground beneath her in a very real, immediate fashion. Claire tried to interpret it, and found it came from two different sources. One was hooves, the other feet. And where the feet touched the earth, it screamed and died. She sat up on her heels and let her mage hand fade. The chill, dry air sucked the sweat off her face and out of her body, and left her trembling with cold.

She stood up and brushed the dirt off her knees and looked out across the broad sweep of the plain before them. Distantly, she could just make out a cloud of dust. It was hard to guess how far away anything was on the flat expanse. She watched the cloud for several minutes in silence, and decided it was not coming towards them, but was moving across the plain, from east to west, while they were travelling in a northerly direction.

Lung, still mounted, was studying the disturbance as well, his strange eyes gleaming. "Those are horses, a great herd of horses, with camels and cattle among them."

"Can you see what pursues them?"

"Men, afoot and ahorse, but men such as I have never seen before. They are like beasts, somehow, as if all that was human in them had perished." He sounded puzzled and sad.

"That is the Darkness." *That is what I came to fight, and I cannot imagine how. There must be hundreds or thousands of them.*

"We must stop them!"

"The two of us?"

"You have powers! Use them!"

It had not occurred to Claire that she should do anything in the circumstances, and she looked at Lung as if he had gone mad. She had no intention of rushing into battle with a vast army, and her only thought was to avoid them. What could she do against so many? She swung back into the saddle and looked at Aurelian. He sat, watching the cloud of dust, sitting on his golden haunches, and did not turn his head.

A portion of the cloud broke off, changed direction, and headed directly towards them. Soon, another followed, pursuing it. Claire, cudgeling her brains for some appropriate solution, wished the earth would just open up and swallow the hideous little clot of evil that was perceptible to her eyes now. Or, failing that, that it would swallow her and free her of the problem. She hated the helpless feeling that nagged at her continuously. If only she could be certain what to do.

Her wrist ached with cold, and the scar around her throat began to burn. Her uncertainty was replaced with rage, first a fury that she did not know what to do, and then a greater anger that she was asked to do the impossible. The thunder of hooves became the wild throb of a drum, and she felt her body shake and her blood turn to fire in her flesh. She had a fleeting glimpse of red, gleaming eyes, and a face darker than night, and knew Kali was about to seize her.

Claire struggled to elude the tide of rage that she felt, tried to calm herself, to still her being. The drum throb hammered in her temples, relentless, and she could not escape. She never knew she screamed as the terrible presence possessed her, never remembered kicking her heels into the sides of the patient little pony. All she knew was fury, a desire to destroy everything before her.

She galloped blindly into a maddened herd of terrified animals which parted before her, though she kept a glimpse of lathered muzzles and terror-whitened eyes, a brief memory of a camel, winded, crumpling to its knobby knees. Beyond them was her prey, a band of running men and women and even youngsters, all howling. She could feel the injury they made each time their feet touched earth. Many were shoeless, and their feet bled, and the earth screamed.

Within her body, the goddess raged with the hunger of destruction. Claire kicked free of the saddle and tumbled off her pony a hundred feet in front of the mindless mob. Her flesh body was knocked breathless, but the spirit within cared nothing for that. She was dragged upright with a brutal wrench. One limb extended, and her heel struck the ground. The impact shook her bones, and there was a boom of sound that deafened her to the howls and screams. The dance of death consumed her, her protesting legs moving without her will, without any will except that of Kali.

The earth shook and shivered, and the drum throb echoed in her skull, until a crack opened where her heel struck the dusty earth. Another joined it, spread, widened, that gaped into a chasm before the rushing mob of lightless, maddened people. They tumbled into it, howling, mindless, and began to claw their way up the sides of the declivity even as it yawned deeper and deeper with each step of her deadly dancing.

A minute spark that was still Claire, that watched the milling mob tumble over the edge of the cliff which had manifested itself in the path of the mob, ached. It saw a child of five or six plunge downwards. Its little feet were run to bare bone, and its face was smeared with blood, but it was still a child.

A hand appeared over the edge of the chasm, and she brought her booted foot down on it, smashing the clawing fingers and breaking the rhythm of the dance. Claire stumbled, released for a moment, and began to shake herself free of the terrible being that possessed her. Then she realized she could not, that the dance was not complete, not finished.

Rebelling with every fiber within her, Claire rejoined Kali. It was a surrender, and she fought it even as she submitted. And, within it, she found a sense of welcome, of companionship, which was, in its way, more terrible than anything else. She had wished to ease the loneliness of this fearsome goddess, and as she fulfilled that desire, she partook of the desolation that was Kali.

Claire's arms extended, her battered, aching legs bent and lengthened, and the rhythm of the drum within her changed subtly. Sightless, unmindful of anything but the power she manifested, she danced. The earth shivered, and the edges of the chasm drew together like a great mouth shutting. There was a moan, a shuddering sound, as the lips sealed, dismembering a single, small hand that had crept over the edge just as the crack finally closed itself.

She gazed at the pathetic bit of flesh, then shut her eyes and crumbled to the ground.

She lay on her side, the sword beneath her, her handless arm outstretched, her face resting on the earth. Her ear pressed the ground, and she could hear all the creakings and groanings, and the thunder of the main body of horses and pursuing Darklings some distance away. Claire could feel the whole of earth, from the red burning heart that was its center to the tip of mountain ranges where the snow never left, across seas she had never seen. Every part of it was something of the Earth Serpent, and also of herself. The blood of earth was her blood; the bones of earth were her bones.

Within it, and without it, existed Kali, who was all of earth and all of time as well. The serpent and the dreadful goddess were distinct, but one, two faces of a single spirit, one hearth tending, the other remote and cosmic. Every plow that broke the soil was an injury, a wound that Orphiana, patient and enduring, accepted, and that Kali, quick-tempered and immediate, did not. Would not.

And Kali was not done with her. Claire could feel her, could hear the wild throb of the dance, and she knew she could not rest until she completed her work. She realized that if she died, she would still go on fighting to ease the anguish of the world.

The hilt of that sword pressed against one small breast, and Claire could feel its heat and its lust. She dragged herself upright, away from the persistent, nagging demand of the weapon just as Lung and Aurelian appeared, trailed by a pack of horses and a dozen or so people. Real people. Ordinary folk with good, plain light in them, neither saints nor sinners. She thought they were lovely.

Aurelian stood beside her as she got feebly to her feet. As soon as both her boots touched the ground, she could feel the dance call her, and she shifted from foot to foot, trying to still the itching sensation while she tried to make some sense out of the gabble of chatter which battered her senses. She wished the lovely people would be quiet.

Lung dismounted and gave a curt command. There was an abrupt silence, except for the nicker of the horses. He took her shoulders in his hands. "Are you all right?"

"Yes. No. I have to . . . I have to stop them!" She waved her stump at the still visible dust cloud of the main body of Darklings.

He brushed some dirt off her face, a commonplace, human gesture that touched her with its kindness. It reminded her of how she had stroked the face of Kali once. But the throb of destruction within her would not be denied. "Someday I hope you will tell me what you are. But now is not the time," he answered.

A warm muzzle poked between them, and Claire found herself looking into the warm brown eye of a horse. It flicked its ears and snorted, then nudged her in the chest. She reached up and stroked the strong neck, bemused for a moment, while Lung issued an order. A bridle appeared, and was fastened onto the animal. A thick felt saddle blanket covered the strong shoulders, and a saddle with a wide, flat board where a pommel should have been was thrown across it.

Before she quite gathered her wits, she was tossed into the saddle, and the rest of the group was mounted, some bareback, some on saddle blankets. Lung was on a big grey animal, saddleless but apparently at ease.

Claire looked down at Aurelian, wondered vaguely what had happened to the ponies and the mules, or where the people had come from, but her mind was too consumed with the urgency of confronting the foe that ranged across the plain. It was all she could do to keep from slamming her heels into the flanks of the nameless horse beneath her. Instead, she stroked the mane with her hand, leaving the reins slack, noting the little glints of gold in the brown hair of the animal. She experienced something like bliss to be on a horse tall enough for her long legs, and having her booted feet in stirrups that did not cramp her legs. All the while, she yearned to be killing.

Aurelian put a paw against her leg. *You have done well, mistress.*

There were children I killed!

I know, sweet mistress, I know. But, think, you ended their suffering.

It does not help to know that. I never guessed I would kill babies.

It is not done yet, my compassionate one.

She stared at the dust cloud. *I know. I hate this. I wish I could die.*

I regret that is not possible, mistress, and you will just have to make do.

Claire did not have time to puzzle over this enigmatic reply, because Lung gave a command, and the little troop began to move across the plain, first at a trot, then at a distance-eating canter that brought them within sight of the main body of the enemy as the pale winter sun dropped towards the western horizon.

The collection of animals which the mob of Darklings pursued had run itself out, and the dust had settled a little, so nothing veiled the scene of carnage. Horses, cattle, camels, donkeys, and even a goat or two, were being clawed and hacked with empty, mindless fury by the howling crowd of madmen. They gave little cries that might have been laughter as they gouged out eyes and tore away ears or horns. She watched one man pull apart the jaws of a camel, then reach into its long neck and pull out some bit of flesh and push it into his own mouth.

Claire could no longer resist the urgency of her need to stop this obscenity. Her mind struggled vainly for an instant, and then the blood lust was back within her. She felt the horse shudder, as if it sensed the change in its rider, and she found her hand on the hilt of the sword at her side. A small portion of her protested vainly, fearing the power of the unleashed weapon, but it was out, drawn and eager, before she could resist it. She was too weary to prevent it.

The essence of its nature, of water and cleansing, poured into her. There was no kindness in it. It was the relentless force of floods and torrents, and it swept away all other considerations, like sticks before a wave. For a second she was terrified that she would drown the world in her very effort to save it. She was not strong enough to wield it alone.

And then the Black Mother returned, and was her hand that held the Sword of Waters. Claire was pushed aside, not unkindly, but pressed into a corner of herself, while Kali possessed her, mastered the power of the sword, and waded into the howling crowd of Dark-maddened people, hacking and stabbing without regard to age or sex.

Barely aware that she had dismounted and left her trembling steed to dart away, and hardly noticing an arrow that missed her head by a breath as it buried itself in the chest of an ancient woman lifting a hefty club, Claire slaughtered. Where the sword struck, no blood flowed, but only a pale, brackish fluid that widened into pools as the corpses seemed to melt into liquid. Up to her knees in an ever broadening pond of the stuff, which stank incredibly, Claire waded forward, mindless, her arm rising and falling.

For a moment, no foe stood close enough to kill, and her aching arm dropped to her side, so the point of the sword plunged into the liquid around her. A shock of pain surged into her body, and the fluid swirled around her knees like a maelstrom. The overpowering stench of the foul stuff changed, and the clean smell of the sea swept across the face of the pool, followed by frothing waves that billowed out in all directions, higher and higher, lapping onto the injured earth and curling around the legs of the Shadow-stricken. When it touched them, they screamed and melted, their distorted features sliding away into nothing, and their flesh and bones becoming water.

The pool became a pond, then a lake, and, up to her heart in chilly salt water which threatened to become a new sea, Claire struggled to move. The sword, now in its element, was almost purring with content, and Kali, out of hers, was less present. Claire tried to lift the sword out of the water and could not. The water rose another few inches, lapping under her chin. She could hear shouts, heard Lung call her name, and she turned towards the sound as a wave brushed her cheeks.

Claire could see him, standing on the shore of the new sea, up to his thighs, holding his bow and wearing his quiver, and she could see the frightened men who had ridden with them pulling away from the encroaching waters. It all seemed quite remote as the water covered her mouth. It felt right, that she should lie at the bottom of her self-created ocean, holding the sword, until she rotted away. No more killing. No more death or Darkness. Just silence. No dance, no throb of drums. Only peace.

The water covered her head, closing over her, and she felt the sword rejoice. It would drown the earth, just as it was drowning her. Nothing could stop it. It would sweep the world clean, brush away the Darkness and the Light, end all the questions and the contradictions. Soon, there would be neither pain nor pleasure, neither hunger nor satiety. And there was nothing she could so. She was too small, too tired, too imperfect for the task the gods had demanded of her. Her best would not suffice.

Something gold moved in the waters, a stream of honey in the icy blueness which surrounded her. It moved towards her, familiar and unknown. It had a form that reminded her of something, if she could only remember what. No, it was only the play of waves, like the scales of a snake. A golden water serpent. How lovely. What wonders lay in the waters.

The sword moved back and forth in her hand, sending little curls of colour out, no longer urgent, no longer lusty with destruction. It did not rule her any longer, serene in its own being. The golden serpent moved sensuously nearer, and Claire stepped towards it. Something brushed her leg, something hard, and her stump touched it. And then, without any clear intention, she slipped the point of the sword down into the scabbard which hung from her belt.

A thunderous roar of rage rocked her mind, and her left

arm spasmed. The hilt of the sword froze her flesh as she pressed downwards. She forced it down, without reason, fighting every inch of the way. Claire felt cold, as if her body was becoming ice, and she could not move. The sword in her hand screamed for release, and her mind echoed it, and seemed grimly fixed on forcing the sword to do her will, to be ensheathed again.

The honeyed serpent curled around her, warming her flesh, enveloping her like the sun. She tasted peaches so sweet it was nearly cloying, and the salt of the sea left her. With her last sense of power, she shoved the hilt down against the sheath and drew her hand away from the great, moon-white pearl. Now she could really die without drowning the world.

A soft, warm mouth closed over her shoulder. Claire dazedly guessed the golden serpent was going to eat her, and, all things considered, that did not seem so terrible a fate. It pulled at her, and she surrendered gratefully.

I have you, mistress. She heard the words for only a moment, and then knew nothing.

XIV

Warmth. Claire felt a sense of surprise and enormous pleasure at her first waking thought. She did not open her eyes
for several seconds, just reveling in the experience of being
entirely warm for the first time in forever. There was something heavy on her chest, and softness under her back and
over her legs and arms. Her fingers rubbed against the
softness. It was not wool, and for some reason, this
pleased her. There was no smell of camphor anywhere either, but the scent of honey, of spices and something salty
that reminded her of the sea.

Claire opened her eyes, and found Aurelian's head
resting on her chest, his large, golden body stretched out
against her right side. She pulled her left arm out and
reached for him, stroking the curling mane and the round
ears. For a long time she simply gloried in his presence,
without trying to do more, refusing to listen to the little
questions and puzzles that were rattling around in her
mind like loose pebbles. She was so glad to see him, to
smell the honey scent that always surrounded him, to

feel the coils of his mane under her chapped, roughened fingers. The gods were kind to have sent him to her.

The thought brought back the recent events, of being possessed by Kali, and then by the cursed sword, of nearly drowning herself, and perhaps more. The memories flashed across her mind, and she clung to Aurelian's mane and shivered despite the warmth around her. *What a tale to tell the grandchildren I will never have.*

You are safe, mistress.

Safe! I have a weapon I dare not use, and a foe that makes my bowels turn to water. I will be alone for the rest of my life, except for you, dear one, and . . . oh, to hell with everything. I am never going to move again. I am just going to lie here being warm. I am tired. My bones hurt. I wish I had never come on this adventure.

The choice was not yours, my mistress.

You think I don't know that! You think I don't know perfectly well some fool goddess or other isn't going to drag me out of bed and send me out into the cold again. It is infuriating to be a tool, and not even know why, or what I am doing, or supposed to do.

It is hard to be a servant, mistress, when one is a lord.

Claire stared at Aurelian, looked at his wonderful golden eyes, and soft, flat nose. *You always call me mistress, and never say my name.*

Servants do not address masters by name.

But, Aurelian, you are my friend.

No, beloved mistress, I am your servant. But I do not regret my want of choice, for to serve you enlightens me. But, still, it is hard, for I have long been a master in my own right. You might say it is a new experience for me, as your quest has been for you, and the new is always difficult. Uncomfortable. Think how uncomfortable the gods have been made by the actions of your lineage.

"Serves them right," she said, "dragging us here and there, pulling Eleanor right out of her world and dumping her out of time. I am glad she made them uncomfortable! We are not in a tent. There are walls and a roof. I think a roof is the most beautiful thing in the world, except you."

The door opened and Lung looked in. "I heard your voice. But I did not understand the words, so I thought you might be feverish again, and came to see." He looked worried and relieved at the same time. Claire realized she had spoken in Arabic, and it probably sounded like babble.

"Where are we?" She started to sit up, realized she was naked beneath the coverings, and blushed. Who had undressed her? Her clothing must have been drenched, and her felt and leather boots surely ruined.

"We are in a small town some *lis* from where we first saw the horses and the things which pursued them. It is one of the breeding stations for the Imperial herd, and it was the men from here who found us on the plain. Are you hungry or thirsty?"

"A little. Where are my clothes?" It was absolutely ridiculous. She had been sleeping in a tiny tent with this tall man for weeks, and there was no reason why the thought of him removing her garments should embarrass her. She had barely even noticed his maleness. Much to her annoyance, Claire discovered that she had been acutely aware of Lung for days, and had ruthlessly thrust it down in her mind.

"The women took them away to see if anything could be salvaged, after they disrobed you. Your white skin is the talk of the town. They have never seen flesh so pale before, and are not entirely convinced you are human. I will have the mistress see to your needs, and then we will have some tea and eat."

"Thank you. I am not certain I am human any longer, myself." She added the last, half to herself, for the experience of being a vessel for Kali's energy had left a residue of confusion that demanded examination and understanding, neither of which she had the strength to tackle at present.

A minute or so later two women entered, bowed, and

looked at her somewhat apprehensively. They had several garments hung over their arms, bright, soft things that gleamed in the lamplight of the room. They were tiny, shorter than Anna, black-haired and flat-featured, their skin an almond gold, fairer than the folk of Tibet or the olive complected people of the Levant. Claire could imagine how seeing the portions of her body not browned from the sun might appear peculiar.

"Will you permit us to bathe you, Lady?" The elder of the two women finally asked this question, as if not sure that bathing was a custom she understood.

Claire, who had but moments before been certain she never wanted to see any larger amount of water than could fit in a teacup, found the idea of being clean, of bathing, was extremely attractive. "I would be most grateful for your assistance."

The younger woman giggled and clapped a small hand over her mouth, and Claire realized her poor command of their musical tongue had probably produced a meaning other than the one she intended. The older woman glared. She frowned at herself, pushed mentally at the spell she had created to permit her to use Tibetan, and did what she thought of as tidying. The spell seemed to brighten, to energize, and the slippery, intoned sounds of the language seemed more secure.

"Pray, forgive my heavy tongue," she told them, and knew she had done better. Language is such a barrier to communication, she thought, that it is a miracle anything ever gets accomplished. It was a mental note in Greek, and she nearly laughed at her own absurdity.

The older woman nodded sagely. "Weariness makes the tongue clumsy. We will take you to the bath." The younger girl held up a thin cotton robe, and Claire reached for it. She took the robe and slipped her arms into it, then pulled it around her as she put her legs over the side of the bed. She hugged it around her with her one hand, and followed the women out of the room and down the corridor, shivering a little.

They took her to a room which had an enormous, steaming tub set into the wooden floor. There was a stool, and the girl pointed at it, indicating that Claire should sit. Puzzled, she did so, and found her robe being pulled away. They took small packets of some kind, that smelled of odd spices, and the younger girl hauled a bucket of water out of the tub and poured it over Claire's head before she had time to protest. Then they scrubbed her, quite impersonally, with their scented packets, rinsed her off with more hot water, and helped her into the tub itself. Claire had never thought to have the luxury of soaking her tired body in hot water again, and she would have remained there, quite happily, until she starved, if the older woman had not made it clear that she was to get out. Reluctantly, she abandoned the tub, was toweled dry, and re-robed, then returned to her chamber.

"We have brought you some robes, Lady, but they are summer gowns, left long ago. We had nothing else great enough for your many inches. We pray you will excuse this. My seamstress is creating some winter garb. But, I believe, several of these together will suffice to keep you warm."

Claire thought of the soft woolen robe which was in her pack, and realized that they would not know of its existence unless they had pawed through her personal belongings. She was about to suggest using it, but it was soiled. She preferred the idea of clean clothing on her clean body. It was refreshing just to think about.

"I am certain you are correct." Despite the fact that these two strangers had just bathed her, she was uncomfortable to be disrobed before them. As if they understood, the women lowered their eyes as she removed the bathing gown they had provided. They slipped her into a thin gauze garment, so fine a silk that it did little to conceal her nudity, and the younger woman pulled together two long cords and bound them beneath Claire's small breasts. Another robe, of russet silk, followed, fastened in the same manner, and all three women gave a sort of relieved sigh, now that decency was restored. The sleeves of the russet robe were long, so long that the scarred stump of her right wrist was concealed. These garments had never been made for anyone who had to use their hands for anything useful, and, as they slipped her into a third robe of pale gold stuff, a figured brocade of some bird-like creature, she wondered what great lady they had originally adorned. She must have been a giant, for the hem reached her ankles. Finally, they added a rich, green robe, another brocade, with silver rondels woven into it.

There was no glass for her to study the effect, but glancing down, Claire could see that each robe was fashioned so that the edge of the one below was visible, both across the bosom, and along the fall of the skirt and the drape of the sleeve. Only the gauze undergarment was completely hidden. She found herself feeling disoriented. The clothes were so entirely female, and she had spent so much of her life dressed in male garb, that she was not sure she could walk, let alone eat. She shuddered slightly at the idea of soiling these lovely things with a spatter of food.

"My lady, will you permit us to arrange your hair?"

She just nodded, bemused. Claire rarely gave her hair any attention. She had worn it in a single braid since she had escaped the ministrations of her nurses, and since the loss of her hand, she had not even done that. Lung had bound it into the same sort of topknot he wore each morning after breakfast. Claire had even thought of hacking it off, but somehow had never gotten around to actually doing it.

It was, at present, slightly damp, unbound, and fell almost to her waist. The ends were dry and brittle, but at least it was clean. She stood and waited for whatever happened next.

The older woman produced a small box, a work of art in itself, decorated with a flying bird and a roundel that was a sun or moon, and opened it. Inside were combs and brushes, and several pieces of jewelry, as well as some odd looking implements. She took one, which looked like a cloak pin with small blades at each end, and a comb. The woman combed Claire's hair out, and the younger woman said something about silk. She realized they were amazed at the fineness of her hair. She waited patiently and heard a little snick of metal on metal. The ends of her hair were neatly trimmed away, and brushed off her gown.

The younger woman brought over a little stool and indicated that Claire should be seated. They rubbed some oily, sweet-smelling stuff into it, brushed and combed and divided it, until Claire had the distinct feeling she had traveled backwards in time about two decades. They began to pin it, and the older woman muttered about slippery as silk. She clucked and fussed, and Claire wiggled and was told to sit still. It was as if she was a child again, and it was a good feeling, a safe feeling, to be in someone else's charge for a time. Aurelian, who had retired to one corner of the room, watched the whole procedure as if it was being done for his sole amusement.

When she was finally satisfied with her efforts, the older woman gave a little grunt, and the younger woman held up a highly polished bronze mirror, so Claire could see herself. No wonder Aurelian was laughing. She looked ridiculous.

Claire studied the reflection. Her hair was parted in the center, then mounded into two sections near the back of her head, but atop, not on her neck. It shone like polished wood, due to whatever stuff they had put on it. Small ornaments nestled in the mounds, green stone things almost the colour of her eyes. Except for the scar at the base of her throat, which the robes did not entirely hide, she did not know herself.

She lifted her right arm, to bring her hand to her cheek, saw the long folds of silk that draped over the scarred stump, and lowered it again. Claire still felt there was a hand there, not an illusory glamour, nor the energetic manifestation of the mage hand, but a real, fleshy member that could hold a cup and write in Greek. If all the world was a dream, if all reality was illusion, then her hand still existed as much as it ever had.

Claire lifted her left arm, and the robes slipped back so her hand emerged, and she put her fingers on her cheek. She noticed the fine scatter of freckles across the long nose and the way her eyebrows lifted away like little wings above her green eyes. *Why, I am rather pretty.* She smiled a little. Anna was the beauty in the family, and Dorothea was striking, with her black hair and pale skin, and Helene was always sparkling with animation. She had always felt plain. She did not feel plain now, and it disquieted her.

"Thank you. What a pretty way to put my hair." She touched her finger to the scar at the base of her throat. It was a thin line of red, the skin on either edge a little thickened to the touch. She pondered hiding it for a moment, then rejected the idea. After all, it was only an illusion. Only a dream.

"We rejoice that our poor efforts please you, Lady. Now, we will conduct you to Lord Ts'u." She wondered who that might be, and then realized they meant Lung.

Claire and Aurelian followed the two tiring-women out of the chamber and into a corridor, past several doors which closed quickly as they approached. She caught a couple of glimpses of curious eyes before the doors closed. Then they entered a good-sized room with a table and high-backed chairs, plus an iron stove which glowed with heat. Lung was standing with his back to the door, studying a scroll painting, another of the vague landscapes she found so intriguing. He turned at the sound of soft slippers on the floor, and his strange eyes widened.

"Ridiculous, is it not?" she said in Tibetan, lest the feelings of the two maids be injured.

Lung shook his head and bowed formally. "You are most regal. Those colours become you, and you look like the Autumn Fairy." He replied in Chinese, and Claire blushed and bowed quickly to cover her embarrassment. He walked over to her and helped her to one of the chairs while one of the women put tea bowls and a porcelain pot on the table. A sweet fragrance steamed from the spout, mingling with the smells of wood smoke from the oven and the spicy odor of something cooking. The younger woman poured tea, bowed, and withdrew as Aurelian settled on the floor beside Claire.

Claire waited until Lung was seated before she moved, and then she followed his gestures carefully, as she would have at a meal with a sheik's wife. She let the heavy silk slip back and closed her hand delicately around the thin porcelain bowl, wishing for her sturdy wooden one instead. The warmth touched her fingertips as she lifted the cup to her lips. Sweet, warm steam curled into her nose, and she sipped cautiously. After weeks of thick, rancid yak-butter *per-cha*, it was like the *sharbats* of the Levant, the mixtures of orange blossoms and water used as cooling drinks on hot summer days. But this was hot, and refreshing.

"This is delicious. How you must have missed it in your exile."

"Yes. It is the small things that one yearns for, not the great ones. The smell of tea, the sound of a water-wheel or the rustle of bamboo in the breeze, the cry of a vendor, or the chirp of a cricket in its cage, the carp rising in their pool, gold and silver among the water weeds. What do you miss?"

Claire, who was burning with a dozen questions, realized that she must follow his formality as long as the women were present. And she did not want to think of the many small things she had discovered she missed since she left Baghdad. But, she sipped her tea and attempted to be polite.

"I have missed walls—rooms, chambers, halls. And order." She laughed at herself. "Not that there was a great deal of it, for my father is very untidy. He is a scholar, and he often forgets to put his books away. I miss *kavya*, which is what we drink as you do *cha*. It has a dark, rich smell, and a bitter taste, but good. But, what I miss most is my small room, and the way the morning sun came through the carved screen and made a pattern on the floor. I wonder if I will ever see it again."

Lung nodded. "I cannot say. I hope you will return to your small chamber and see the pattern on the floor."

Claire decided she was not going to cry. She swallowed and felt the scar on her throat burn. "Will you tell me about the lady whose garb I wear?"

There was a little cough from the older woman, and Lung gave her a look, eyebrows lifted, before he turned back to Claire. "She was called Moon Lotus, and she was a wife of the Emperor who was my great-grandfather. She was, as you can surmise, very tall for a Han, and she had something of a reputation as a sorceress. She was exiled here for a time. But, after several years, she was returned to favor, went back to the capital, and bore a son who was one of several claimants to the throne, my grandfather. He never occupied the Dragon Throne, but his son did." Lung reached over and refilled her cup. "They say she had jade eyes—and a heart of stone."

Claire could not help remembering her mother describing her as a lotus made of knives when she was still unborn, a white lotus and Roderick a blue one. It was enough to make her put some credence in Djurjati's tale of reincarnation, and it made her want to run and hide somewhere. It was hard enough being herself without beginning to wonder if she was someone else as well.

The older woman placed a small bowl of soup in front of her, an unappetising mess of yellow strands and soft, white cubes in a brownish broth that reeked of spices and peppers. After the blandness of weeks of *tsampa*, it was like a slap in the face just to smell it. She placed a napkin and a porcelain spoon beside it, and moved away. The other woman had served Lung, and he began to eat, so

Claire took her spoon and pressed a little of the broth into it.

It was hot, spicy in a totally different way than Indian food, and sour into the bargain. Her tongue protested and her eyes teared slightly. All the passages in her head seemed to explode, and she was afraid her nose was going to run, so she sniffed as quietly as she could. It was awful.

Bravely, she took another spoonful, one containing the white cubes, and decided that was not so bad. A tiny bit of unknown flesh came up, and she ate it, hoping it was not snake or horse. Her mouth burned, not unpleasantly, and she carefully put the spoon down and sipped some tea. It washed away some of the fire, and she felt a fine sheen of moisture cover her brow. Then she tried the strange yellow strands, which were crunchy, but rather interesting. Somehow, she got to the bottom of the bowl without either choking or spilling anything on herself. She was more exhausted than after a full day's hard riding.

Claire touched her mouth with the napkin and wished she could wipe her brow as well. The woman came over to refill her bowl with more of the pungent mixture, and Claire swallowed quickly. "It was delicious, but I cannot eat more. I am full." The woman gave one of the sniffs that Claire suspected were a universal expression of displeasure amongst nurses, servants and others devoted to the care of the young. She removed the bowl and walked away, her back stiff, and Claire found herself holding back a grin. It was good to know that people were people, no matter what their customs, that they took offense just as easily in China as in Baghdad.

Lung was grinning at her, as if he understood or had read her throughts. He said something to the woman, and they brought another pot of tea, and also a small earthenware jug with two minuscule cups, bowed, and left the room. "Would you like more tea, or some wine?"

The word wine brought back a flood of memories, of

dark red liquid with the faint taste of resin from the cask, of that miserable, final dinner with her family, of the hills around Aleppo covered with vineyards, and the taste of lamb and rice, heavily spiced, wrapped in grapeleaves and cooked in lemon juice, a dish called *sarma,* which was one of her favorites. Lung was right. It was the little things. "Some wine, I think." He poured, and she stared in wonder at a clear liquid in the tiny cup, without scent or colour. The cup was so small she was almost afraid to touch it, but she picked it up and tasted the stuff. It was a little warm, and had a slight sharp taste which was not unpleasant, but nothing like wine to her.

"I hope I did not offend the . . . the lady who served us." Claire realized she did not know whether the woman was a servant or the mistress of the house, and had never discovered the names of either of them.

"It is not her place to be offended."

"Of all the arrogant, high-handed things to say." Her cup was empty, and she realized it must be a more potent brew than she had assumed to have released her tongue so quickly.

Lung nodded. "Yes. It was. It has been an interesting few days, while you slept like the dead, and I am falling into the ways I had as a child, where my word was law, at least among the members of my entourage. Mistress Ouyang, who is the woman who served us—the other is her daughter, Almond Blossom—is the chatelaine here. She recognized me from this." He pointed to the scar across his knuckles. "We stopped here on our way into the mountains, into exile, and she is caught between her obligation to me, as a member of the imperial family, and her very healthy terror of the Empress. I am glad you are awake to remind me that I am only a man with a great ambition, and not, at present, the Emperor."

"How do I do that?"

"You have no respect for me."

"But, Lung. That is not true. It is so that when we left Lhasa I was very angry, and thought you were a millstone around my neck. But, you have proved to be capable and intelligent, and you have helped me, lent me both your strength and your understanding."

"But you do not respect me as the Dragon Throne."

Claire found that she had emptied her wine cup a second time, and had a pleasant glow that had nothing to do with the warmth of the room. "Well, no. I think it is foolish to want to be Emperor, when it means you will get tied up with duties and rituals." She paused a moment. "You will never have a private moment. You will have a dozen wives, all trying to be the favorite, and you will be surrounded by ministers and advisors and those eunuchs you told me about, that have so much influence—though I cannot see how a man is enhanced by having his balls cut off—all of them wanting favor. Why, you will not even be able to take a pee alone." Her cheeks burned at her vulgarity. No more wine for her.

Lung roared with laughter. He filled her cup again. "No, probably not. I had not understood what a precious thing is solitude. And you are correct. I can order people away, but they will stand just beyond the door, hovering like falcons, to rush in if I so much as belch. And what I have missed, while you slumbered, was that you are never reverential of me, that in your presence I am only a man."

Claire considered this as she drank her third cup, despite her intention not to. She had been surrounded by servants all of her life, and she knew how intrusive they could be in their eagerness to serve. She had danced with Kali, dueled with her, learned her father's magicks and her mother's martial skills, studied Djurjati's philosophies, and been embraced by the mercy of Tara. For all that, she remained herself, a sharp-tongued, fierce girl driven by the desire to achieve some moment of absolute perfection. The experience of Tara had not lessened her sense of loss, for her parents, for Djurjati, and for the nameless man she would never know. Her intimacy with Kali, with the fury of the goddess, had not altered her compassion for the miserable, stricken Darklings she had buried and drowned. She was still Claire, full of doubts and hesitations, still the little girl who learned very slowly and with difficulty. And, she realized, who was now at least half drunk!

"Give me *cha* and tell me what happened. I remember nothing after the waters came over me."

Lung chuckled. "That is my vessel of Pure Jade. To see you contained within yourself, to watch you depart to consider, to reflect, is a wondrous thing to behold. You make no excuses, nor preparations, but simply fold within like a flower closing—as if I was not even here. I treasure that, for no one else ignores my presence. They would not dare. And, as you have so pithily expressed it, will never give me a moment's peace. Are all the women of your people so blunt and forthright?"

"My mother always speaks her mind—at a shout, for she is hot-tempered—and my sister Dorothea, though of a conciliatory disposition, never hesitates to say that dung is dung. But, we are a family of exiles, in lands where females are not much cherished, except as things of beauty. I believe, from what my father has said of his sisters, and of what I have read of his mother and grandmother, that the women of my family are not unlike me." Except they probably never worried as much as I do, she added to herself.

"You do not speak of the sister Anna."

"She is very young, and very quiet."

"Doubtless she will become less so."

"I hope so." Claire realized that she had a small, constant concern over her tiny sister, and what changes her experiences would create. In that instant, too, she realized that if she ever, by some chance, became a mother, she would move heaven and earth to spare any child of hers any adventure greater than climbing an apple tree.

"As for what happened, you stood there as the waters covered you, and I started to come towards you, but the waters boiled, and I could not. Then your golden one pushed past me, sank beneath the waves, and came back several minutes later, holding your limp arm in his mouth, dragging you out like a corpse. Your breast rose and fell, but you did not stir, and some of the men rode back to a village and brought a litter. We took you there, wrapped as well as we could manage. You were cold all through. The women disrobed you and wrapped you in hot blankets and put you to bed. The following day, we moved here, the few *lis* to Taofang. It is not a large place, but bigger than the village. The physician here could not perceive any injury or illness—but then your golden one would not permit him to do more than hold your toe. He tried to take your wrist, but the *keelin* grasped his hand and drew him away. Quite gently I thought, but the old fellow fainted. I decided that the *keelin* knew best, and simply kept watch."

"I regret I was so much bother." Claire felt sick and shame swept over her. She remembered the time she had broken her arm, climbing a tree, and how they had had to find Geoffrey and bring him away from his important duties to heal her. "Thank you for taking care of me."

"I owe you my present existence, do I not? I have balanced the obligation. We Han say that if you save another's life, you are forever responsible for them. So, now we each are in equal responsibility."

"What? Oh, never mind. What happened to the sword?"

"I wound my cloak around it and put it in your chamber."

"Good. I do not know what would happen if it got into the wrong hands—or was lost." She frowned. "I cannot use it again. I dare not withdraw it from the sheath again."

"I understand. How annoying, to possess something of such power, such magnitude, and be unable to use it."

Without thinking, Claire tipped more wine into her cup and drank it. The solution to her problem was so obvious. All she had to do was—she refused to think of it. Who would want to bed a cripple, even for the sword? He who would do such an act was unworthy to possess it. There had to be at least some affection in it, if not love. The whole thing was grotesque. It was just as well the dragon had eaten her mate, for he would have been disgusted if he had ever seen her. She still had her mage powers, painful as they were to command, and perhaps they would be enough to stop the Darkness and restore Lung to his kingdom.

Odd. She had left Tibet with no sense of hope, and now discovered in herself a determination to set this man upon the Dragon Throne or die trying. Why? Always why. Because she dreamed a goddess told her to. No, not that. Because it was her duty. That did not feel right either. Perhaps it was the memory of the moment when their essences had entwined. He was so beautiful, so magnificent. She felt as if she was missing something obvious, but her fuddled mind refused to release it.

XV

The pale light of morning began to silver the room, and Claire, who had been awake for some time, sat up under the covers, tucked her knees up, folded her arms across them, and rested her jaw on her forearms. She had a vague memory of Mistress Ou-yang and the younger girl undressing her, removing the jewelry from her hair, putting her into a sleeping robe, and tucking her into bed like a child. The bed itself, she discovered, was actually a sort of oven, kept fueled with wood or charcoal, and from the width of it, probably intended for several persons to occupy at once. It made sense in a cold climate, but she was glad she slept alone except for Aurelian. She wondered what the women thought of her relationship to Lung. People were people, no matter how they dressed or what tongue they spoke, and a man and a woman together always aroused some sort of gossip. What did she care?

Claire found, much to her surprise, that she cared a great deal, because she respected Lung and she could not bear the notion of anyone thinking badly of him. She chuckled softly. They were much more apt to think ill of her. She found she had, by degrees, come a great way from thinking of her companion as a soft, deluded man, unsuited to rule, except by his lineage. He would probably make a very good Emperor, someday. If nothing else, his exile in Tibet had taught him how to rule himself, which, she decided, was an excellent quality in a leader. Certainly she had seen enough monarchs and sheiks who had none of that capacity, who seemed to feel that their position gave them the freedom to ride over any consideration for the feelings or the needs of others. She had a great longing to write a small essay on kingship, for her father's eyes, but it would have to be in Greek, and her left hand could not manage that. She wished she could grow a right hand out of the severed wrist, not the mage hand of power, but a flesh and blood organ which could hold a pen. She felt more than crippled; she felt incomplete.

The thought brought an unexpected shower of tears, not for her lost hand so much as for the deep, quiet despair that she would never have her partner, her match. How foolish, she thought, snuffling noisily. Just because she was alone did not mean she could not have an interesting, useful life. But she still wished she was a small girl who could curl up in the safety of her father's lap. That was what she really longed for, a sense of security to still the terror which lingered from her mother's abrupt departure. She had dreamed with Tara that she was beyond fear, and, in many ways, she was. She was not afraid to die, but to live was still fraught with all the terror of error and loneliness.

There was a soft knock on the door. "Enter," she answered.

The girl, Almond Blossom, came in, carrying a tray with a teapot and cup, plus a bowl of something. Behind her was a pair of girls, young, anxious looking females, carrying clothing. They eyed her, and Aurelian lolling regally beside her, with curiosity and uneasiness. She watched their dark eyes dart to the corners of the room, to her, then down to the floor. Almond Blossom set the tray down on a tabouret, and bowed, then gave Claire a nervous smile.

"Good morning, Lady."

"Good morning, Almond Blossom."

"I have brought your tea, and also the clothing which the seamstress has completed. They are poor, hasty efforts, and I pray you will forgive us. Lord Ts'u sends greetings, and begs me to inform you that he will be spending the morning over the first dispatches which have arrived, should you choose to join him. He thought, perhaps, that you might prefer some time alone, or to work on your writings. If that is your desire, I will take you to the Lotus Abode, where there is a desk and paper."

"You are most kind and considerate of my needs. I am sure the clothing will be excellent."

The two girls were almost squirming with discomfort, the burdens they bore being held like hot coals, and their tiny feet moving restlessly. Claire could not imagine what was so disturbing as she unfolded her legs and arose from the bed. Almond Blossom slipped an outer robe over her sleeping gown, and Claire sat down on a stool and accepted tea. It appeared that almost nothing happened in this land without it. It was hot and fragrant, but dark and very different from what she had drunk the night before. It was good, very strong, and gave her the kind of a jolt a cup of *kavya* did.

Almond Blossom spoke sharply to the two girls, some rebuke Claire did not quite follow. The bowl on the tray held rice, cold and sticky, and there was a tiny dish of some sort of vegetables that smelled of vinegar. She picked up the eating sticks carefully and realized she really needed two hands to eat comfortably, to hold the bowl close to her chest. She glared at her stump, plucked a few of the greens up, and put them in her mouth. They were crunchy, and not unlike the pickled vegetables she had often eaten in the Levant.

"These are delicious," she told Almond Blossom. She then managed to convey a lump of rice to her mouth without dropping any. Cold and sticky as it was, it was good. Moving slowly, carefully, she somehow managed to complete the small meal, putting the sticks down several times to drink more tea. Then she needed a privy desperately, and had no idea of how to politely convey this notion.

Fortunately, Almond Blossom anticipated or divined her need, shooed the nervous girls out of the chamber, and gestured Claire over to a little wooden box with a lid which lifted, and turned her back while Claire relieved herself. Some small squares of paper sat nearby, and she used them to dry herself. Then she rose and closed the lid, and the sound made the girl turn to face her.

"I beg your pardon, Lady, for those girls. They are ignorant and full of foolish superstition—just stupid country girls."

"I assure you I took no offense. I must appear to them quite strange, and the presence of my golden friend here could not but arouse unease. If I had never seen a woman of Han, and she appeared with a strange creature, I, too, would be frightened."

"You are most gracious, Lady." Almond Blossom shifted on her little feet. You see, they are not sure you are human. They think you might be a demon or a ghost."

"Ghosts do not use privies."

The girl giggled. "I never thought of that! Now, here are the garments. Our seamstress plucked apart those you wore to use as a measure. You must have travelled far, for she said the green trousers you wore beneath the others were of the sort worn by the men of the utter west. She was, I think, a little scandalized. She is very old, and very obstinate, but also knowledgeable."

The girl unfolded the silk wrapped bundles the maids had left at the foot of the bed and held up a white tunic which was an exact duplicate of her thin linen blouse. It had been made of a thick, almost stiff silk, which shone in the morning light. The full sleeves had been pleated into cuffs of white brocade, and Claire looked at the pattern with interest. It was a flower, and, after a second, she realized it was almost certainly a lotus blossom, not unlike patterns she had seen in Tibet. For some reason, this disturbed her, the way Lung's tale of his ancestress had bothered her the night before. She felt as if she was being herded or driven into a place, a place where legend and reality met uneasily.

"It is beautiful. Your seamstress is a real artist. But I wish she had used some dark colour. White shows soil so easily."

Almond Blossom blushed furiously. "Mother told her not to! She said it was wrong."

"There, there. I see nothing wrong with it. What troubles you?"

"It is not an auspicious colour. Mother gave her a bolt of green silk to use. She would not."

"I am sorry that I have caused trouble."

Almond Blossom sighed and opened up the other bundle. Within it were two pair of trousers, duplicates of her green linen ones. One pair was a thin, sheer silk, like the gauze robe which had served as an undergarment the previous night, and the others were fashioned of several layers of fabric, stitched together, so they appeared padded like the tunics that soldiers wore beneath their mail. Again, they were white, and of the same thick brocade used for the cuffs of her tunic. As an outfit, it was magnificent, and totally impractical. She could not ride a horse in white brocade trousers.

Claire looked at the girl. They were about the same age, or Almond Blossom might be a little younger, and she felt sorry for her. Clearly she had been ordered to serve Claire, and just as clearly, she was distressed. "I am ignorant of your customs, so I beg you to inform me of the matter of the inauspicious nature of white. Certainly it is a colour which has never become me, but I am not very vain, so it does not matter."

Almond Blossom thought a moment. "We wear it for mourning."

"I see." Claire nodded. The Hebrews followed a similar custom. "It is also, then, the clothing of ghosts, perhaps?"

The girl looked miserable and nodded. "She insists you must be Moon Lotus. She is a very obstinate old woman."

"Well, see if there is a way to repair my woolen trousers, because I cannot ride a horse in white, but do not trouble yourself over this. Not long ago, I lost a most treasured companion, and I mourn him, so I will wear white for that. I do not mind it." Actually, Claire minded a great deal, but she was too tired to argue the matter. *In a way, that old lady is probably right. I am a sort of ghost of myself these days.*

After she had dressed, and Almond Blossom had put some slippers on her now stockinged feet, she followed the girl to the room called the Lotus Abode, carrying her rather tattered roll of pages, her pen and the bottle of ink which had somehow survived all her adventures intact. It held a thin, brown stuff, but it sufficed. Servants who met them in the corridors averted their eyes or stepped hastily into rooms they had just exited.

The small chamber she was led to had the smell of a room long disused and recently cleaned, a combination of old must and fresh vinegar. It contained a small stove, a kettle for heating water, a table set with a teapot, cup, and a little cannister containing the tea itself, a desk and two chairs. There was a scroll painting of some mountains on one wall, and another with calligraphy on it. On the desk there was a stack of fresh paper, and a slab of ink like the one she had seen Lung use, plus the writing brush and the little stone receptacle used to grind the ink. A small window overlooked a tiny garden, bare now of anything but a few naked trees, and a little pool in the center.

Alone again, except for Aurelian's silent presence, she stood at the window for a time, imagining what it looked like in spring or summer, and wondering if the exiled Moon Lotus had done the same, if she had missed the intrigues of the capital. Then she sat down and experimented with the ink black, trying to copy what she remembered of Lung's movements. She wished she had brought her stinky old Tibetan robe, because at least it would not show any stains.

When she had made some ink, she tried using the brush, but it was too unfamiliar an implement. She picked up the pen, dipped it, and wrote a few lines, pleased with the blackness of the ink. But the things she wished to set down remained determinedly Greek and refused to translate into Arabic.

I want my hand back!

Claire was startled at how angry she felt, and her arm surged, and the glowing mage-hand appeared unbidden. Her flesh screamed. She stared at the shimmering blue thing, the bones clearly visible through the ghostly flesh. If only it could hold something. Ignoring the pain, she flexed the fingers and watched the movement. It seemed both very real and very dreamlike.

"It is a shame I cannot dream my hand back, Aurelian."

The beast cocked his head thoughtfully, then padded over and examined the glowing hand. He was tall enough that his head stood above the little desk, and he studied it with his bulging eyes. *You could, mistress, for a price.*

"And what might that be, my friend?"

Aurelian pondered. It was quite an impressive sight, because he glowed until she had to turn her eyes away. It was too bright, like looking into the sun. The entire room was limned in golden light. Even the shadows were yellow.

You must give up all that you have lost, dear mistress.

Claire stared at him blankly, translated his words rapidly into every tongue she knew, looking for some understanding. How could she give up what she did not have? It was worse than some of Djurjati's more obscure pronouncements. She got up and poured herself some tea, then paced to and fro across the tiny room. The chamber seemed too small, and she felt her breath catch and cease. She felt her body tumble onto the smooth floor, but felt herself continue to pace, almost frantic.

Claire found herself looking down at her still body, just as if she had stepped out of a set of garments. It took her a moment to realize that she had crossed out of the material world into the spirit one, without either preparation or thought. The white clad figure on the floor still showed the glowing mage-hand above the brocaded cuff of the tunic. Beneath the clothing, she could see the lines of power that ran along her bones, all blue, and others, red, that fed along the veins and arteries. They went to her heart, and the blue lines traveled into her head. She had never seen the red energy before.

At the base of her throat, where the red scar marred her skin, she saw a gleam of yet another colour, a green so dark it was nearly black, and she experienced a sense of horror, as if she was looking at something foul. It moved down her body, passed through her heart like a hideous spear, and ended like a barb at the base of her torso, splitting her womb. If she could have closed her eyes, she would have. What *was* it? How could she have anything within her so terrible and not know it.

Mistress! You do know it.

Claire stared at the patterns of energy, and saw the way the greenness was like a fine net that touched every part of her, hidden and nearly invisible. She wanted to tear it out and cast it away, but it was so invasive, so integral. It was not clear and perceptible, like Djurjati's fever had been. She could not imagine where to begin. It almost seemed as if it was all that held her together

Or do I hold it? A name. If only I could name it, I could pull it . . . no. If I could give it up, let it go. But, what is it?

For an instant she knew. It was a creation of all her losses, all her pains and deprivations, which she treasured in some obscure fashion. They were hers, and nothing and no one could take them away. It made a sham of all her tidiness, her order, her control. It made a liar out of everything she had ever told herself about herself.

Forgive me, please, forgive me. I never meant to injure

you like this. I only ever wanted to heal, like my father. But I just hurt my mother by becoming.

All the things, large and small, which had been failures seemed to flood into her. Long forgotten childish, dirty hands and the death of Djurjati, her severed hand, and the heart that had broken when she found the scabbard of the Sword of Waters, even the moment when her spirit had parted from Lung's, all her losses, came together. She held them clutched in her mage-hand now. They were so much of her. How could she be without them? Was a fleshy hand worth this? She had always been a cripple. The severed wrist was merely evidence of it. She could not take the chance.

Claire hovered between what she was, what she knew, however misshapen it might be, and the unknowable being she would be without it. Roderick would have let go in an instant. He was not afraid of anything. Tara had taken away her fear, but not her fear of fearing. Then she looked at the spear that divided her womb, that parted her heart and clove her throat, and let the pain of it pass through her. It was cold, not hot as she had braced herself for, and agonizing.

Finger by finger, joint by joint, her right hand opened. Each cold movement was a struggle and a surrender. And then the palm lay open, empty, the fingers upturned in supplication to she knew not what. She saw the blue lines, the red lines, and, just for an instant, glimpsed a thread of clear silver. Then she knew nothing but rest.

When Claire opened her eyes, she found Aurelian looking down at her, and she felt light-hearted and almost girlish. She reached up and put her arms around his neck, and saw her right hand, neatly banded in the white brocade cuff. She froze. There was a fine, white line, a scar as slender as a thread, against the tanned skin, where the hand had once been severed, and a faint presence of pain. The small crescent scar on her thumb was there, reminding her of Roderick. She flexed the fingers. Then she hugged Aurelian, burying her face in his mane and kissing his flat face.

Rising from the polished floorboards, she stood for a moment, feeling whole and powerful. She dusted off her bottom, though the spotless floor had left no mark on her white garments, and poured herself a cup of tea. It was delicious. Claire refilled the cup, sat down at the desk, and picked up the Indian pen. With a great sigh, she took a fresh sheet of paper and wrote the first words. "My dearest parents. Greetings."

When the soft knock on the door disturbed her, several hours had passed, and the sun had gone across the house, putting the little garden into shadow. "Enter," she answered, without looking up, concentrating on completing a sentence. The stack of finished sheets lay face down beside her, and her hand ached with cramp, but it was a real, human sensation, which she almost savored.

Lung walked in, carrying a red box covered in the shiny stuff they called lacquer. He was smiling a little, and his jewel eyes were green in the light of the lampions. Claire scrambled to her feet, and poured him a cup of tea, the dregs of her last pot, tepid and stewed. She handed it to him as he set the box down on the desk, caught his look of astonishment, and turned away to refill the kettle. She had made several pots of tea now, and knew how to feed the little stove and how to measure the tiny leaves in the cannister, just as if she had been doing it all her life.

"I cannot explain what happened, so it is no use asking me," she said over her shoulder.

"I understand. Woman, you terrify me."

"Nonsense. I am just what I have always been—only more so." Claire spoke the words and knew the truth of them. She was still incomplete and imperfect, but these matters had less power over her.

"That is precisely what terrifies me. A man would be a fool to pretend otherwise."

Claire, her domesticities complete, turned around and looked at him. "Miracles happen all the time. Some are just more obvious than others." She watched his fine features shift as he considered this, and thought what a fine ruler he would be. He gave a little nod after a moment, and opened the box.

"These are such dispatches as have reached us, for as soon as we arrived, I began to gather information from the surrounding districts. After what we saw out there—those people—I realized that I had to have more knowledge before proceeding, and the people here had a great many rumours and very few facts. The response is most disheartening, though whether this is out of terror of the Empress or disbelief that I am who I claim to be, I can only guess. Still, I have gathered enough to have some idea of the state of things, and I wish to discuss it with you. I count you as my advisor, both for your greater experience in matters of strategies, and for the excellence of your mind. The reality is so much different than I had imagined.

"And what was that?" It *always* is, she thought.

"I had a boy's foolish dream that I would return, and be welcomed, that the people would rejoice and I would just ride into the capital at the head of a great force which would spring out of the ground." He gave a bitter laugh. "But an entire generation has been born since I departed, men who never knew my father, or who knew of him only indirectly, are now governors and magistrates. They have no reason to believe I am the Son of Heaven just because I say I am. I grew older in my exile, but I did not mature, for I was surrounded by the faded dreams of old men. I cannot say such things to any but you. You alone I can trust, for you aid me not for reward or favor, but because you have chosen it as your duty."

Claire took her seat and considered this. She did not regard being ordered about by Tara or Kali as being a choice, and the reward she longed for was not to be. It was still painful, the emptiness within her, but different now, because she no longer held it, because it seemed better to live the life she had rather than hold on to the one she had lost. She was once again able to be content in the moments of the present, as she had been weeks before. She knew it would not always be so, that she would have fresh losses to accept, but she felt she could somehow endure them.

"I take it, then, that some of the replies have been filled more with self-interest than with loyalty and devotion."

He nodded. "Most astute."

"My mother told me that any man who will sell himself to you for gold, will just as easily sell himself to another for more."

"She must be a very wise woman."

Claire had rarely thought of Helene in that light, and was unsure if it was true, because she was not clear in her own mind what wisdom was. "Say shrewd. Certainly she understands mercenaries, and mistrusts them. So, what is the state of the empire?"

"Empire!" He made a barking laugh. "The Middle Kingdom is a broken vessel. The pieces are little fiefs carved up by the strongest, and the whole harmony, the government, is in near ruin. It seems that things were fair in the first years, after the Empress bedded her barbarian lover. The country was exhausted from the years of war—both sides were weary. There was a return to order for a time, it seems, and the rice bowls were not empty. Then a fresh war arose, some other barbarians from the west, and . . ." His face creased with sorrow. Claire suspected the same Turkic nomads who had harried the Levant for years were who he meant.

"The south," he continued, "which was ever troublesome, broke away, established their own dynasty, which lasted a year or five, before it crumbled into bickering provinces. The north was busy with the fresh invasion, and, in truth, all that remained of the nation was those areas between the two capitals, the Summer and the Winter. And then this Darkness came. Half the populations of whole cities seemed to go mad, even small children, destroying everything and anything, desecrating the temples and the ancestors." He put one long hand across his breast. "My heart aches. I do not know if I possess the strength to set it right."

"No one ever said being the Son of Heaven was going to be easy!" Claire spoke more sharply than she intended and got up to pour the now boiling water into the teapot. She heard his sigh.

"No, they did not. And I do not know how to begin."

They sat in silence over cups of fresh tea for several minutes. "We will begin by gathering allies," she told him.

"How? Who dare I trust?"

"You must trust yourself, Lung. And I will see to it that none who join us will be disloyal."

"How? Will you bewitch them—as some of the people here believe you have ensorcelled me?"

Claire was livid with rage. Her jaw squared and her lips grimmed, while her eyes fairly snapped with unvented fury. "I would die before I would force a man against his will. I would never sully my power in that fashion—any more than I would fornicate with a camel! What I do is sacred, in the service of the goddess of all living. If you do not understand that, then you know nothing at all about me!"

"Forgive me. It is not simple to believe in such—implacable purity."

Claire, her anger spent, laughed softly. "It is not anything like that. It is just stubbornness and a desire to be perfect. And, since I am human and cannot be perfect, to behave rightly. Which does not permit ensorcelling people. If anyone thinks they are bewitched, it is in their minds, not in mine."

"Yes, you are correct. I think it is the memory of my mother and her intrigues which causes my doubt. You are two faces of a coin, in some fashion. I cannot explain it. So, let me read you what has come to me and tell me what you think."

XVI

Winter had tightened its grip on the land when they left the walled city of Tao Fu, to which they had removed a few days after Claire's recovery. The local magistrate there—sole remnant of the bureaucracy—was a man of utmost probity who had managed to keep his city peaceful despite food shortages, riots and the Darkness-made madness of a good portion of its population. The surviving citizenry were simply terrified and kept to their homes whenever possible, so the arrival of Lung, about twenty horsemen, Claire, and the golden *keelin*, Aurelian, had been taken as only another calamity to be endured as well as possible.

Magistrate Yee, ignoring the ambiguity of the presence of a woman, and a foreigner at that, in the train of Ts'u Meng Lung, calmly turned her over to the charge of his First Lady, a sharp eyed, chill voiced no-nonsense woman who managed to swallow her avid curiosity and keep to the amenities. Only the presence of Aurelian disturbed her to the point of forgetting her manners.

"Where did you get *him?"* she asked after the third cup of tea, termed strange tasting sweet.

Claire turned and looked down at the golden beast who was crouched beside her highbacked chair. "I think he got *me* Madame Yee, and I had no say in the matter."

This broke the ice of formality and they began to discuss ordinary things, the cleverness of the Yee children and the ardent labors of the magistrate. Madame Yee was a well of information, and since she had never heard of Moon Lotus, treated Claire as a strange but human person, not a ghost. After some thought and a little magic Claire transformed the white silk of the garment she had been given to a grey-green which caused no comment. She had also acquired a second outfit made of wool to wear for travel.

Claire and Lung had labored over the messages he received from various warlords, magistrates, provincial governors and others, trying to sift the trustworthy from the suspicious. She, knowing how superstitions could be, tried to limit her appearance as an advisor to the man. But in many ways he was as much a stranger in the land of Han as she was, and he kept her close.

It was simplest to maintain an appearance of distance now. The man who accompanied them had been carefully chosen, not by her or by Lung, but, in the end, by Aurelian, and no one seemed to argue with the choices of the large golden beast. Nor did they seem to have much problem with the presence of a magical animal in the company of the would-be Emperor. On the contrary, Aurelian lent Lung an air of authenticity.

They left Tao Fu after two days with a dozen more men and a hearty peasant girl called Willow to act as a maid and chaperone to Claire. She was cheerful and unlettered and the two of them got along easily. Willow had never been further than ten *li*s from Tao Fu, and clearly thought the whole thing a pleasant adventure, despite the cold and the hardship of the travel.

It was, Claire guessed, near the middle of December

when they finally reached the more heavily populated region of the province, the medium sized cities between the last of the mountains and the great emporium of Ch'ungch'in on the plains of Zechwan. Most of these were in ruins. Willow's cheerful face sobered, and Claire wanted to scream at the outrages she saw, at her inability to either prevent them or heal them. She had a weapon she dared not draw, which nagged at her constantly, which she would cheerfully have dropped into a well or a river to be rid of. She also had an ordinary sword, a coat of fine mail, and a real shield.

Nothing she had seen in India, and nothing her parents had told her had prepared her for what she saw. Even her brief, horrible encounter with the Darkness-run folk near Kantzu had not given her any real comprehension of the actuality. Each nation, she guessed, had its own character, and the Darkness affected it accordingly. More, she realized, that while she had loved India, she had never come to identify with it, or with its people.

For no reason she could discern, she loved both the land, and more, the Han people themselves. She found that the mountains looked exactly like the scroll paintings that hung in many rooms, and were real and not imaginary. And beautiful. Even in the cold of winter, there was a beauty here that moved her.

The Han themselves, strange at first, touched her more each day. Perhaps it was their sense of order, evident in even the smallest things, or just their simple courage in the face of disaster. In a few brief weeks Claire came to feel at home with the mist-clad mountains and the short, passionate people. The Levant was a distant dream that no longer touched her except briefly. She suffered no more bouts of homesickness, other than the persistent desire to tell her father what she saw, and when she wept at night, it was for the injury of China.

They passed through city after city, smoking ruins where mindless bands of Darklings hunted any unafflicted survivors, and, failing that, turned on themselves, as if some killing fever forced them to destroy. She saw babes smashed against the jutting edges of stone walls, and men and women torn to pieces without sense or reason. Armed with her good, plain sword, she hacked them down to death, while her heart ached with anguish.

The worst, she thought, when she could bear to think of it at all, was when she watched some unafflicted father or mother, son or daughter, slaughter kinfolk who had become creatures of the Shadow. She understood now the great value the Han put on the family, and she knew how terrible it must be. Claire did not think she could ever have killed Anna or Dorothea in similar circumstances.

The waking nightmare went on and on, and the nights brought no refreshment. Lung was haggard, deep shadows beneath his gleaming eyes, always calm and always at the head of his growing cadre of followers. He handled a sword, if not with any elegance, at least with competence, and she stilled the terror that something might happen to him. It was not the memory of fear, as it had been from her dream of Tara to the recovery of her right hand, but the actual emotion. In surrendering her losses, she had regained the ability to be truly afraid. It was, she felt, a reasonable bargain, possibly the only fair one since she had left Baghdad. She was too weary, much of the time, to think at all, let alone conceive any strategy beyond destroying any Darklings that crossed her path. She was afraid and tired, and she never knew how she went on.

As Lung's force expanded, adding a few men from each city as they went, he created sub-sections in his tiny army. Claire had been given a dozen horsemen, and about sixty soldiers, a banner, and badges to issue. She had marveled that in the midst of chaos such order could persist, and had only smiled quietly to herself when the badges and the banner was brought to her. A small green field with a white lotus blossom unrolled before her. The gods were still having their joke. She hoped they choked on it. But how Helene would have chuckled.

If any of her battle-scarred cavalry found a difficulty in

addressing her as Captain White Lotus, they concealed it with Han impassiveness, and the foot soldiers just did as they were told. They knew her to be a capable fighter, and perhaps assumed that where she came from, the women were warriors as well as the men. She let it be known that her mother had trained her, to reinforce the notion. It made a change, to talk of Helene, from the horror of the days and nights.

During the long wars against the barbarians, many barracks had been built, and enough of these remained to shelter in from time to time, to get in out of the cold and the snow. Willow told her it was actually a mild winter, so Claire wondered what a hard one was like. The barracks were often still in the charge of some captain or colonel who, like Magistrate Yee, had laboured to maintain some sort of order, who looked askance at Lung's force, as if they might be brigands come to pillage what remained. Some accepted their arrival with joy, but others required a good deal of convincing before they would permit Lung's men inside.

Still, for Claire, it was all a haze of days of slaughter and nights without sleep. Her eyes ached from the smoke of burning cities and from weeping, and her heart ached from too much death. If only there was some way to heal the affliction of the Darkness without death. But even her father had not been able to do that, with all the powers of his flute and his many magicks. More, she was beginning to have small doubts that this was the best way to go about solving the problem. It might take years, an entire lifetime, to destroy the Darkness in the vast reaches of the Middle Kingdom. If only she could make a light so great it would burn the disease out of the bodies and souls of those poor people.

She had this thought over a cup of tea in the barrack of a city whose name she did not know, and smiled at her own vaunting ambition. First she wanted to relieve Kali of her fury, and now she wanted to heal the nation in a single flash of brightness. Was there no limit to her vanity? It was well-meant, but utterly foolish. She was one woman, and mortal. Even the gods could not destroy the invading Darkness and had to force their human servants to do it for them. For some reason she found herself recalling one of Djurjati's stories, about some pure soul about to achieve the longed-for release from the wheel of rebirth, about to ascend to the pure lotus light of Heaven, and who had refused, at the last moment, to go until all people could come with him. Such compassion was exemplary, but she was hardly any saint on the brink of *nirvana*, but merely a confused young woman with an apparently boundless ambition, lacking even the advice of a matron deity to guide her. All she had was two very wind-chapped hands and a brain that felt like a bowl of *tsampa*.

Two mornings later they received word of an enormous gathering of Darklings a day's march ahead, a force outnumbering Lung's as greatly as ten to one. Lung called a meeting of his captains, and Claire was disturbed to see how haggard he appeared. He held himself like a man going on by will alone, and she wished she could walk over and embrace him and give him strength. Instead, she bowed in the correct manner and took her seat.

A Colonel Wang unrolled a map and began a detailed discussion of the lay of the land, with which he was apparently very familiar, suggesting deployment of troops for the greatest advantage. Claire listened intently, memorizing as much as she could, and barely noticed Aurelian, who spent his days near Lung and his nights on the floor beside her bed, when he left the man and came to crouch beside her. She coiled a hand into his mane affectionately and went on listening.

Mistress, look up.

Claire did as she was bid, and saw a pale, white figure wavering in the air. The men in the next chair followed her movement, and gave a little gasp, then whispered a word. Colonel Wang frowned at the sound, looked up, and dropped the long stick he had been using as a pointer. It hit the floor with a clatter, and everyone jumped. The figure seemed to solidify a little, though it was still possible to see the walls through the graceful draperies of the robes.

The room was absolutely silent except for the crackle of the stove and the hushed breaths of the dozen people staring at the vision. She was beautiful, serene-faced and shimmering. The room slowly filled with the light of her, and with her grace. It was like a vast refreshment, and Claire could feel the weariness and despair within her dwindle away. More, she could see the same effect on those around her. What a mercy, she thought.

The figure seemed to expand at this thought, to become yet more solid, and the draperies of her gown fluttered in an unfelt breeze. The chamber smelled of spring, of blossom and new grass and freshness. Several of the men overcame their wonder enough to stagger upright in order to bow reverently, so Claire did the same. She heard a name whispered. Quanyin.

A sound like a flute came out of the air, and it took her a moment to realize it was a voice, not an instrument. The words wafted out.

The White Lotus must provide the Light. Then the shimmering figure began to fade, and was gone. The sense of renewal remained, however, as several pairs of dark Han eyes turned to look at her with interest. Evidently she had not been the only one to hear the cryptic command, which was both a relief and an irritation. After a moment, Claire decided that solitary experiences of the goddess were easier to deal with than what must appear to her fellow soldiers as an outright miracle. You might have been a little more specific, she thought crossly, as the air of expectation thickened around her. How do I get myself into these messes?

And how do I get out of this one, she wondered, as she realized they were waiting for her to speak. Lung gave a little throat clearing cough and Colonel Wang bent down and retrieved his pointer. The other men resumed their places while Claire racked her brains. She would have enjoyed giving the gods a piece of her mind, but at the present she had none to spare.

"We know the force which awaits us greatly outnumbers our own," she began, her voice wobbling, her mouth dry. Someone handed her a cup of tea, and she smiled gratefully at him. Captain Woo. "We also know, from all previous encounters, that these Darklings are ordinarily like a mob, without order or organization. When there is nothing nearby to destroy, they turn on themselves. For this reason, we have not before encountered any group we could not overcome. It has been difficult, but we have prevailed as much due to the very actions of the enemy as to our own hardihood."

Thoughtful nods came from several of the captains. "But, here we have report of an enormous force of these Darklings, and they are clearly not destroying themselves or behaving in the manner we have come to expect. We must therefore assume that one has arisen in their number who leads and orders them in some fashion—else they would not be so large a group together."

Colonel Wang smacked his brow with the palm of his scarred hand. "A most brilliant insight! Our former tactics will be of little use against such a force, for our advantage has always been their disorganization. We need better information before we proceed. Clearly we must identify the head, and concentrate our effort against it, for if we can destroy the head, the body will collapse."

Claire resumed her seat, hoping that her explanation would be interpreted as the light she was expected to provide. She was quietly certain that while what she had pointed out was perfectly true, and even relevant, Claire was just as sure that the beautiful goddess had not made her dramatic appearance merely to cause her to state anything so glaringly obvious. They were all tired, and their minds were numbed with the daily horrors of their task. No, there was more to it than this.

She had not used her mage talents much since her hand had been restored, and in one sense felt this part of her life was done. Or, rather, that she could abjure her magic now, because she was whole once more. Claire smiled mentally at her own self-deception. She was hardly whole, except in body, and only her exhaustion had allowed her to pretend that the surrender of her losses was a complete healing.

There was a pattern there, if only she could grasp it. Claire stroked Aurelian's mane abstractedly, and listened with half an ear to the discussion around her. She noticed that Lung was watching her, his eyes now violet, now green, and she wondered what he saw and what he thought. She barely recognized him any longer. The frustrated boy she had wakened in Tibet, and the stalwart companion she had discovered as they traveled together were both gone as if they had never been. Now he was a leader, a general, a commanding force who extracted loyalty both by his lineage and by his actions. In a way, she thought, these attributes hung on him like poorly fitted garments. Why?

Dispassion and duty are a poor substitute for a heart, mistress.

Claire started a little, not certain whether Aurelian spoke of her or of Lung. It was true of both of them. My heart has not been in the venture since I found the sheath, and maybe Lung's never was. But I care about this country. I hate to see its suffering, under the Darkness. *I wish this were my country. But it is not.*

Claire saw something about herself then, something she had never noticed or refused to see. She was not sure. She saw everything in what was not. She was not a man, and had envied Roderick all her life. She was not small and pretty, like Anna, or striking, like Dorothea. All her self-definition was based on lacks. She had a long list of what she was not—and no real notion of who she was. As she had told the lama at Shigatse, she was a dream. And dreams did not have hearts or countries. She had no personal stake in restoring Lung to the Dragon Throne or order to China. All her compassion was, she decided, remote and impersonal, and she would fight to the death for the cause because it had been bred into her to do so. She saw herself as two distinct people, the dutiful Claire who would endure anything fate cast in her path as best she could, and another Claire who was a creature of all that she was not. Every vessel has an inside and an outside, as Lung had pointed out. And she felt empty on both sides. She longed, she realized, for the kind of single-minded passion that sustained her parents through a quarter century of marital conflict. She might have surrendered the loss of her unknown other half, but she had not even begun to give up the yearning to possess him and to be possessed.

There was a scraping of chairs around her, and she realized the conference was over. Claire began to stand up, to leave with the others, but Lung motioned her to remain. When they were alone, he poured cups of tea.

"People are going to gossip if I stay here very long," she said.

"Yes, they are. If only you were not a woman."

"I have that thought myself, too often to count."

"No. You misunderstand me. I am glad you are a woman—and, more, that you are the very woman you are. Not any modest, simpering creature eager to entrap me with airs and graces. I merely meant that we Han have some customs which create awkwardness. I have wished to confer with you in private, as we were able to do previously, without creating any small-minded questions. I have not wished you to be regarded as my concubine, to have your person demeaned by censure."

"Well, you have succeeded. The other captains treat me as one of themselves, and even tell lewd tales or lie about their conquests in my presence. My own men appear to feel it is an honour to serve under the banner of the White Lotus—enough to bloody the noses of any who are stupid enough to disparage serving under a female. And, I think, we are all too weary and heartsick at what we see and do each day to have much time for worrying over custom. What did you want to tell me?"

"I had a dream last night. I dreamt of a great battle, and I saw above the combatants a great lotus of light which . . . burst." He flung his long hands up expressively. "It made me fear for you. And the manifestation of Quanyen did nothing to allay that fear. So, please, be very careful. You are most precious to me—my Pure Jade."

Claire nodded and smiled. No wonder she did not know who she was. She had too many names. Claire, then Gauri, plus White Lotus, and Lung's private nickname for her. "Thank you for telling me. It gives me an idea—which I suppose was its purpose. Do not fear for me. I will survive until the job is done."

"And then?"

Her smile faded and she looked at him in despair. What would her life be after she restored Lung to his throne and the Darkness was driven out of China? "Why, I shall follow the family tradition and write my memoirs, of course." Claire spoke as brightly as she could, but the words sounded hollow, and she doubted Lung was fooled

Back in her chamber, Claire ate the delicious meal which Willow had prepared for her without tasting it. The girl chattered happily, and Claire replied without any clear sense of what she said. After the meal was done, she opened up her belt pouch and removed the little stone Helene had given her and put it upon the table. It had come into her mind as she ate her rice. She had the sensation of great weight when she touched it, of holding the world in her fingers, as she had had when she had taken it months before, in the garden. Why it had come into her mind she did not know, but she was determined to find out.

Willow looked at it. "Where did you get the sky-stone, mistress?"

"Why do you call it that?"

"Oh, there are a lot of them around where I came from. The village people think they are good luck. Some say they are pieces of Heaven that fall down when the gods get drunk. They do not look like any other stone, and they will not melt if you thrust them into the fire. Every twelve years a few more fall in our district, always during the seventh month, and always in the Year of the Snake." She giggled.

"The last time, one struck the tax collector, and he died, which we all agreed was a fortunate thing indeed."

"And what year is this, Willow?"

"This is the Year of the Cat, mistress." Willow was always mildly astonished at the things Claire knew and did not know.

"And next year?"

"Why, the Year of the Dragon, of course."

Claire heard her and understood her, and had the slight startlement of realizing that not only did the would-be emperor have a pair of eyes which had formerly graced the bearded face of a dragon, but it was also his name. And because she had not understood that the Han put the family name first, she had cheerfully assumed that Lung was a patronymic until it finally dawned on her that everyone called him Lord Ts'u, which she had quickly mimicked. It made perfect sense to her, because the Han put family and ancestry before the individual, but it was also backwards to her own customs. She had not grasped the intricacies of the calendar yet, but the weeks were not of seven days, and the months were the term of a moon cycle, like the Hebrews, so their year's beginning was not fixed, but moved around a little.

Forcing herself to ignore this fascinating distraction, Claire returned to her study of the stone. It was, if Willow was correct, not a piece of earth at all, but a portion of another world. Perhaps this was why it seemed so heavy in her hand. She wondered what sort of world it might be, or if it was indeed a piece of Heaven. All she was certain of was that she was intended to use it in some fashion, and she could not imagine how. She touched it with a tentative finger, trying to feel its properties.

Even so light a touch brought a sense of weight. She paused, aware of Willow's presence and interest. She considered the girl, who was both ignorant and intelligent, and whose loyalty she had come to depend upon. Should she send her away?

"Are you afraid of magic, Willow?"

The girl shrugged. "I do not know. I never saw any— except once a man came to our village who did funny tricks and made scarves come out of air. If you mean sorcery, which I have heard of, all I can say is it sounds frightening."

"What does sorcery do?"

"Oh, like turning people into animals or making someone die by saying secret words."

"Yes. I see. I am going to do some work, and some remarkable things may happen—or nothing. But if you don't want to be here, get along and go flirt with Sergeant Fang."

"Pah! He has a wife and four children back in his village. I am not afraid of anything you will do, because everyone knows you are . . ."

"What do they say, Willow?" Gossip could be deadly.

"Oh, many things. Some say you are a witch who had enchanted Lord Ts'u, and others say you are a fairy from Heaven come to help him. But all agree you are no ordinary mortal."

Claire laughed. "A fairy! And what do you think I am, Willow?"

"I think you are wonderful. Go on. Do your work. I promise I will not chatter about it in the kitchen—or even in the couch of clouds."

Satisfied with this avowal, Claire returned to her examination of the stone. She let her energy flow down her arms, into her hands, and felt the familiar twist of agony as the mage-hand blossomed within the flesh one. Glowing blue fingers brushed the surface of the walnut-sized piece of rock, and Claire had a fleeting vision of violet-tinted skies and broad, rolling plains with grass the colour of old blood. A herd of creatures, neither horse nor camel nor deer, raced across it, their hides a dusky bronze with spots of purple. It was beautiful, and stranger even than the landscape of a dream. If it was Heaven, it was one unrecorded by any people she knew of. Then the vision was gone, and she focused on the stone itself, feeling in it the presence of her mother, who had carried it, and, beyond that, the numinous shimmer of a goddess and of the thousands of worshippers who had come to her with prayers and plaints.

Artemis! I beg your grace to guide me. Let me know your desire, oh, Lady.

Claire felt another personality possess her for an instant, as cool as Kali was fiery, as calm as the Black Mother was furious. The blue light of the mage-hand turned moonwhite, then gold, and it hurt, as if her own energy was being reshaped without any consideration for the limitations of mere flesh and bone. It was mercifully brief, but she felt her muscles spasm in protest and her gorge rose. Even as the wonder of it swept her, a little piece of Claire wished she had not eaten dinner.

The sun-gold hand touched the stone, closed around it, hiding it for a second, and there was a sensation of change that was agonizing, as if the stone was being transformed against its will, into something unnatural to it. Claire felt her legs jerk and light paled to white, and she felt the withdrawal of the other without any loss or regret.

I thank you, Lady of the Moon.

Her mage-hand returned to its normal glowing blue, and retreated into her flesh like a tortoise into a shell, with a little flash of anguish that was nothing compared to what had gone before. Claire found her heart was pounding and her lungs were aching, because she had held her breath without realizing it. She was soaked with sweat and had wet herself like an infant. No one, she thought, would ever want to do magic if they knew how it abused the body.

Gasping to catch her breath and ignoring the stench of her skin, she lifted her flesh hand aside to see what lay below it. Willow, ever practical, put a cup of tea in her left hand without comment, then peered at the object which lay on the smooth surface of the table. It was a barb, like a spearhead, and it shone with a silver-blue colour.

Claire gulped down her tea and looked at it, then picked it up and turned it over. One of the barbs pricked her skin, and a drop of blood darkened the silver metal. It was heavy, heavier than silver, she thought, ignoring the cut, and smaller than a spearhead. Of course! A slow smile moved across her mouth.

"Willow, my quiver, if you will. And then see if the bathing facilities are free." It was, she thought, a great boon to be amongst a people who took personal cleanliness so seriously. Every barrack had a room for bathing.

The girl put the quiver of arrows down on the table, then vanished into the corridor. Claire pulled out several arrows before she found one that felt right, then began the painstaking task of removing an arrowhead and replacing it with what she had made. She had no idea what the arrow was for, but she would find out. It had such a strange feel to it, as if some of the virtue of that world or heaven where the stone had originated still lingered within it. Her hands trembled, and she swore, but finally she had it done. Tired, no, exhausted, she leaned back contentedly.

Willow returned, a cotton robe draped over her arm. "I chased those lazy scoundrels out, and the room is all ours. Get out of those things," she scolded. "I never knew magic was such stinky work."

XVII

It was cold, but no snow had fallen for three days, so the ground was a grey and yellow muck that slowed the wagons and the horses and made the foot soldiers complain. Claire barely noticed. She was straining her senses, reaching out ahead with such farsight as she could manage, to study the dark mass that was the foe. The effort made her aura expand and glow, and her men eyed the corruscating white light with a combination of pride and unease. She wondered, with an unoccupied portion of her mind, if this was how Helene had felt when she had faced the forces of Darkness, and decided it was not. Helene had been able to use her elemental weapon, and Claire could not. It hung, useless and demanding, from her right hip, the great pearl in the hilt pressing against her side, while her nice, ordinary sword hung on the other.

She could see the mass of Darklings, thousands of men and women, and she could tell they had been somehow tamed into a single, vast unit. They were not bent on immediate destruction the way the others had been, but were somehow harnessed. They were quiescent, almost torpid, and barely moved within their encampment. It was as if their strength had been banked like a dark fire, and this was so unlike anything she had seen before that she hardly knew what to make of it. It looked as if Lung's army could just go in and slaughter the entire hideous nest of maggots.

Finally, after some searching, she found the being which had somehow achieved domination over the thousands of Darklings surrounding him. He had been human once, but he had lost that long before the Shadow found him. She probed delicately, though the action revolted her, and she felt his awareness of her immediately. Only his own darkness limited him, so he saw her with no clarity, but only as a nimbus of light that aroused a hungry hatred within his spirit. But he was powerful, unbelievably powerful, and he began to penetrate the veils of utter darkness of himself, and reached out to ensnare her.

It was so quick a mental shift that she barely had time to ward herself. A flash of blazing whiteness exploded around her, casting huge shadows on the muddy ground, and causing her men to shift anxiously in their saddles or on their mud-clotted boots. The little banner of her troop moved though there was no wind, and the lotus on it seemed to open, until the embroidered petals stood out from the cloth like an actual flower.

In that instant, Claire caught a glimpse of who the man had been, and it shocked her. She knew his name, Aiming, his entire, tortured history, from the village where he was born to the thing he was at present. He had been a monk of the Buddhist creed, a man not unlike Djurjati, devoted to meditations and the search for *nirvana,* and in his austerities he had discovered the power to override the wills of others. He had become an abbot, a sage, famous, and a near saint. Students had flocked to him, feeding his strength, and he had become an advisor to warlords and governors, his influence reaching even to the capital. Only the Empress's refusal to bear rivals had thwarted his ambi-

tions to make all of China serve his will, to think rightly
and act rightly. All he had wished was to heal the world.

The aims of Ai-ming were so nearly identical to her
own that she gave a mental flinch. The nation, the world,
stubbornly refused to be healed, to be good and whole, and
as many followers as he created, there were still untold
thousands who eluded him, who went on their merry, corrupt ways, eating and laughing, cheating and fornicating,
until his vast compassion turned to bitterness, and he
thought the world would be better dead than soiled with the
vileness of humanity. Even before the Darkness came, he
had preached death, and thousands had destroyed themselves to humour him.

The left flank drums rolled, and Claire snapped back
into the present as several hundred of Lung's men charged
out to destroy what appeared to be a defenseless foe. No
order had been given, so she guessed that the powerful
mind of Ai-ming she had glimpsed so briefly had entrapped
one of the captains in his dreadful nets.

The Darklings, still one moment, were alive the next,
thousands of them, organized and deadly. They moved as
one, rushing to engulf the charging companies, giving
Lung the choice of watching his men be slaughtered or
rushing in to join them. In seconds, swarming Darklings
surrounded the soldiers, and while they died, hacked down
by cavalry, they were so many that it was a lost cause
almost before it began.

Lung gave the signal, and the rest of his small army of
followers began their charge. The entire Darkling camp
was in motion, and the well-conceived strategy which the
captains had created was nothing more than a whisper in
the wind. Two companies, Woo's and Yee's, did as they
should have, and used their bows rather than rushing in
directly, and Claire ordered her own men to do likewise.
They hesitated.

She could see Lung, on his big bay-coloured horse, riding towards a line of well-organized Darklings. Had he lost
his mind? Probably. She had to stop him! She could see

Aurelian's golden shape trying to slow Lung's headlong progress. What would Helene do? She did not have time to decide.

Claire rose in the stirrups, focused her mind on herself, drew a long, deep breath and lifted her arms above her head. All the sounds of the battle vanished for a second. She felt her fingers tingle, and a globe of power filled her cupped palms. She could sense the heat of it. A moment she flung a ball of fire with all her strength, then prayed her aim was true.

It arched up, glowing and growing, casting golden light into the greyness of the day. She kicked her horse while it began its descent and raced towards the banner of the dragon which was the mark of Lung's troop. The fireball hit the ground just ahead of the advancing Darklings and exploded, making the horses rear and wheel. The Darklings scattered, breaking their ranks to escape both the light and the heat of the fireball.

Perfect! Claire barely noticed her self-congratulation as she reached for the reins of Lung's horse.

"You idiot!" She screamed into his startled face above the din of confused foe and frightened friend. "What the hell are you doing!"

Lung looked dazed, blank for a moment, as if he had just awakened. "Sound the retreat," he bellowed at his drummer.

Claire ignored him and pulled another fireball out of herself and tossed it into another sector of the Darkling force. It was not enough, but it gave them a chance to pull back. She could not create enough fire to make any big difference, to do more than delay the enemy. There had to be another answer.

Aurelian appeared beside her, pressed a paw against her leg. *Light, mistress.*

I know, I know, but how?

The retreat was sounded, but there was almost as much confusion in the ranks of Lung's forces as there was in the Darkling camp. Finally, Colonel Wang, by the strength of

his considerable voice, got some archers organized to harry
the enemy in its disarray, and the rest of the captains managed to get themselves regrouped. A number of foot soldiers tried to rush into the Shadow camp and were brutally
seized or beaten by their fellows.

Claire, pulling back, realized that Ai-ming, the unhappy
monk who led this Darkling force, was using his incredible
powers to influence Lung's men, and she wished she could
put a wall between them, to give herself time to think. If
only she could stop time for a few minutes. *Kali! You are
Time. Help me! Oh, Mother, help me!*

Everything stopped. There was a stillness, a flatness to
the world for some unmeasurable moment, so that everything appeared to lack any dimension. It might have been a
painting. Horses stood with one hoof lifted, and men
paused as they drew their bows or reached for their swords.
Nothing moved, not so much as a blade of dried grass, as
far as the eye could see.

Only Aurelian. As she racked her brains for some tactic,
Claire saw the golden shape of the *keelin* run. It was so
quick her eye could not distinguish more than a blur of
gold, like a single thread, a skein of yarn unreeling in a
line that went out of sight. She had a wrench of loss. He
was leaving her. She did not question why.

She had to create light. The fireballs were not enough.
Claire stared at the picture of the forces around her, feeling
the incredible stillness. Across the field, she could sense
the distorted mind of Ai-ming, and knew that he too was
using the pause to plan. And she knew, with some small
satisfaction, that what she had done had frightened him just
a little. He was afraid of the Light.

Her banner bearer sat on his horse, and the little green
silk flag with the lotus upon it extended from the pole. The
flower was still a bowl of curved petals extending outwards
from the silk. It glowed, and she remembered the words of
the graceful goddess.

The White Lotus will provide the Light.

Claire grasped the memory as Time began again, as

chaos and confusion returned to both friend and enemy.
Drums pounded, men shouted, horses reared and neighed.
And Aurelian was beside her again, just as if he had never
moved. She blinked, glanced over her shoulder at the
Darkling camp, and saw the golden thread that ran around
the huge army.

Hurry, mistress. It will not hold them long. As Aurelian
told her this, a thin sheet like beaten gold appeared where
the thread had lain. It reached up into the overcast sky, and
even as she saw it, an arrow pierced its delicate substance,
and a Darkling fell. She could see the small hole and knew
what a fragile wall it was.

With a jerk, she urged her horse over to the banner
bearer and snatched the pole from his hand. He was a boy,
no more than sixteen, if that, but he shone with a sweet,
clean brightness of spirit. It was so beautiful, so simple and
so humble that Claire felt her heart swell. This was what
she was fighting to preserve, and it was worth anything!

Then she yanked the green silk off its pole and focused
on the flower. She touched its petal with her grubby hands
and watched as they thickened. With every moment the
flower became both more real and less so. Even as she
watched the flower expand until it filled her lap, she found
herself bemused by the question of the nature of reality,
much to her annoyance. This was no time for silly philosophical ponderings. Why couldn't her mind behave? And
what in the world would she do with the flower? Why were
the gods so cryptic?

The lotus floated off her legs and expanded further,
drifting above her head while around her her troop fired
their arrows. As she worked, Claire realized she knew
what to do, but lacked the strength to do it herself. She
remembered how Lung had told her she never asked for
help, and she realized that she had, of late, and had always
received it. And now she needed all the help she could get.

Claire lifted her arms. "Hold your fire!" Her eighty or
so men paused, stared at her, and lowered their bows. "I
need your help." They eyed her, and the floating flower,

cautiously, and waited. "I want you to look at the flower, look at the White Lotus, and I want you to think of all that is precious to you, all that you honour and love."

They looked at her uncomprehendingly. What should she be asking for? "Think of the reverence you have for your ancestors!" Her voice carried above the din of the battle, so that troops on either side of her turned and looked. That was it!

Claire drew a deep breath and called upon a lesson she had learned slowly, and with great difficulty, the Voice of Command. Dorothea had learned it in a minute, but she had never used it except in practice with her father. She did not know if she could do it here. But, she must try. "Let the Light of your reverend ancestor fill the Lotus."

For a second, every man in Lung's army stared at the flower. Then a mass of Darklings penetrated the now arrow-rent golden shield which Aurelian had created, and the battle roared around her. But the flower expanded, and Claire could feel its strength and its power. She prayed she had done enough, and sent it towards the swarming Darkling foe.

It was huge, and it spread light as it passed above the heads of the enemy. They did not, as Claire had hoped, drop in their tracks from its effect. In fact, they barely seemed to notice the presence of the enormous, shining lotus, and she guessed the mind which guided them blinded them to it. It was not enough, and she knew it. What more could she do?

The masses of arrow-struck Darklings formed a barrier which slowed those behind it, and it grew as those who clambered over it fell to fresh flights. But this could not last. There were not enough arrows in their quivers to slaughter the vast numbers of the enemy, and even now small bunches were breaking through to attack Lung's companies.

Claire watched for a moment, pulled her sword and hacked a Darkling down as he leapt for her, and saw that the lotus had stopped moving. It shone above the center of the camp, pure and bright. She could sense that its presence weakened Ai-ming, but he was so strong. And the lotus, like the world, was but a dream.

A dozen Darklings swarmed towards her, and Claire knew she would be engulfed if she did not finish what she had begun. But how? As quickly as she and her men cut them down, more enemy broke through, until her little troop was surrounded. It was like a flood. She felt her hand jerk and reach for the hilt of the useless weapon of power which hung from her side, as if her thought had aroused it.

No! She could not wield the Sword of Waters. She would not drown the world. Claire stabbed a Darkling, and her horse reared and smashed another in the chest, rattling her quiver against her shoulder. She dropped the reins, beheaded a Darkling, then let her sword fall as she snatched the quiver round and plucked the arrow she had made three days before. A Darkling grabbed for her, and she kicked his face as she took her bow up.

Artemis! Give me true aim, I pray you!

She barely felt the knife that cut her left calf as she fitted the arrow to the bow and aimed. Her horse shied, and something pierced her thigh. A Darkling died as one of her men cut him down. Suddenly she was encased by four of her own cavalry, as if they understood what she did not know herself. A strong hand grasped her horse's reins, steadying the animal. It shuddered, and out of the corner of her eye she saw the shaft of a spear sticking from the chest of her protector. His death grip held the reins.

Claire swallowed, gasped, and let her arrow fly. It was an arch of silver as it lifted into the air and sped across the leaden skies. Its descent was a long, slow curve, as it plunged into the heart of the hovering, shimmering lotus. There was a flash so bright that she was blinded and a sound like a single tone of music, absolutely simple and infinitely complex at once. And within it was a cry of anguish. Sightless and deafened as she was, Claire felt the pain of Ai-ming as he perished. Her heart sorrowed, for she knew that but for the grace of the goddess, she might have become just such a creature as had the monk.

There was a burst of golden light that Claire felt rather than saw. A wind whipped across the field, and it smelled of apple blossom, drowning out the reek of blood and death, a breath of spring so sweet it was almost painful. For no reason she could understand, Claire thought of her sister Anna in that moment.

The earth shuddered under her, and as her sight returned she saw a violet landscape, headed with the corpses of a great army. The light shifted to blue, and there was a blessed silence, except for the moans of the wounded. The battle was over, and the presence of the Darkness was gone. It was, in some sense she knew she could never explain, the end of the world. Her mother had been right. Then she turned to count her casualties, to do her duty to the living. Everything was altered, and yet the same. And Claire was too tired to even ask why.

XVIII

There was a good deal of noise in the street outside, and Claire listened to it as she lay in bed, enjoying the luxury of doing absolutely nothing. She had been doing it for several days now, since they had reached the city of Wangshin the evening after the battle. Her wounds, a cut on the calf and a stab in the thigh, had been roughly tended by their doctor immediately, and then more thoroughly treated upon their arrival by another physician. She had been ordered to bed, lodged in an inn which had been turned into a hospital for the injured, and moved to another the day before when Doctor Yang had decided she did not require his further ministrations.

It was, she decided, excellent noise. It was the sound of people going about the business of living with great enthusiasm, the normal clatter of a city. Several hawkers cried their wares, a street minstrel intoned a song, and two people were engaged in a vociferous disagreement about some piece of merchandise. There were no screams of pain, no smell of burning stone and flesh, no thunder of horse or drum. She could barely believe the peace of it. More, she could hardly digest the fact that she had had something to do with it, let alone the truth, which was far greater. She, Claire d'Avebury, had destroyed the Darkness. When the arrow she had made struck the earth, the terrible Darkness had departed, leaving only the ordinary, normal evil and good that all humans had as part of their natures. And she had not the slightest notion of how or why, except that there had been some great healing virtue in the barb she had made from a piece of another world. Maybe Willow was right, and it had been a bit of Heaven.

Lung came into the chamber, grave and happy all at once. He had visited her once before, in the make-shift hospital, to tell her the news that everywhere he could get word from reported the same thing. All the mobs of Dark-lings had simply dropped in their steps and fallen to ash. She had nodded sleepily. It all seemed very remote, a dream of a dream. Her task was done. She was glad, but in an uninterested, distant fashion.

"How are you, my friend?" He asked the question solemnly.

"Fine. I am only malingering after the way of soldiers everywhere. And you?"

"Harried, and missing my most trusted councillor. I read piles of reports every day, gathering such knowledge as I can upon the state of the empire. The Darkness took as many as a third of our people, and our strength was already sapped by the struggles with the barbarians. China had suffered greatly without a true Son of Heaven to execute its mandates, and it is not done."

Claire had a sickening feeling in her belly. She had managed to banish from her mind any goal but destroying the monstrous evil which had ravished both India and China. Returning Lung to the Dragon Throne had not seemed very real at the quietest of times, and during their long march, it had faded into irrelevancy for her. Not so, of course, for him. And she knew perfectly well she still had a role to play. Why did she wish she had not? Why did she yearn to do nothing more demanding than begin her memoirs? She loved the land of Han as much if not more than she had cared for her native countries, and she wished it well. But she did not care to see Lung as its ruler.

She would lose him then. Claire saw it quite clearly. There would be no place for her once he took the throne, except as some sort of exotic pet or concubine. He would be fenced in ritual and ceremony, a gilded servant of the state. She gazed at her right hand, at the thin white line of scar that encircled the wrist like a bracelet. *I have not learned to accept my losses as well as I believed*. And she knew that she had come to care for him over their time together, not the wild, fierce passionate caring of Helene and Geoffrey, but something just as moving, for all its quietness.

"I have thought deeply," he said, interrupting her musing, "and I believe that it was intended that the Sword of Waters should be . . . bedded."

Claire stared at him and felt her face redden. Why didn't he just say, "Give me the sword"? Why did he have to muddy things up? Then she remembered the ruined face of Michael ben Avi, the king of Jerusalem, and the price he had paid for taking the Sword of Light as he had, ungiven. There was precedent, she realized. Her great-grandmother, Eleanor of Avebury, had taken the king, Arthur, as her lover and given him the sword, after the death of her husband Doyle. She had to respect Lung's sense of propriety. He could have tried to rape her, or simply commanded that she pass the loathsome weapon into his hands after she had nearly drowned the world. It was quite logical. It followed the pattern. So why did she want to reject his gently worded idea out of hand? All he asked was that she do her duty, as he wished to do his.

And that was precisely the problem. Claire was sick and tired of doing her duty, of being possessed by goddesses and dragged around like a sack of rice, from one painful task to another. She could not bear to submit to a bloodless, passionless, obligatory couching, just to please the gods. It was not her virginity which mattered. It was her heart that still yearned to be partnered, to be companioned.

A large tear rolled out of her eye and slid down her cheek. Lung reached out and brushed it aside gently. "Forgive me, Pure Jade. I have asked too much of you already. We say that when you save another, you are ever responsible for them. And you have saved me, and more, you have saved my beloved country from the scourge of the Darkness."

"Well, I do not mind being responsible for you, but I do not feel up to the task of bearing the whole weight of China on my shoulders," she blubbered, touched by his tenderness. She found herself sobbing against his shoulder, as if it was the most natural place for her head to rest, smelling his clean, smooth skin and feeling the long, thick fall of his hair resting across her cheek as he bent over her.

"Neither do I," he whispered.

Claire looked up, the sudden shower passed, and touched his cheek. "You are going to be a fine emperor." The thought of him in this position threatened to bring about another bout of weeping, and she swallowed quickly. She had to be practical. The fate of an entire nation was in her hands. She did not want to be practical! She wanted to be loved. "I suppose we must do our duty."

"I hope there is more to it than that." He sounded hurt.

"What do . . . " A light kiss on her lips cut off her question. Startled, she pulled back.

"Do you find me repulsive?"

"Oh, no! But I have never been kissed by any man but my father and my brother. I do not have any idea of . . . how to behave." So close, still encircled by his arms, she knew she lied, because her body was giving every indication of lively interest, if not expertise. "And I had hoped for . . . " Claire could not speak the word.

"Yes. I understand. It must sound very heartless of me, to come to you and ask for your surrender, for my own selfish ambitions. Will you believe me if I say I care for you as much as I have ever cared for any person, that you are most dear to me, that I would trust you with my fears and doubts, which I would never tell another." His eyes were deep violet now, like the sky of the strange world she had glimpsed while making the sky-stone into an arrowhead. She could feel the throb of his heart where her hand now rested against his chest.

"Well, you have never lied to me before, but I understand that men will say almost anything to get under the covers."

"I would not know. I have never attempted this before."

"Oh." Somehow, Claire discovered, she had assumed that one or more Tibetan ladies had shared his bed. She wondered, for a moment, what the man who had borne the sword's scabbard had been like, if he had been fierce or gentle, wise or impetuous. But he was a dream, and Lung was as real as anything in the world. She put a hesitant, clumsy kiss against his cheek, then found his mouth. He tasted of tea and warm spices.

Lung's hand cupped her small breast, and Claire felt her loins heat as they had when she had used the sword to create a spring in the wilderness. Her breath quickened and her heart pounded. She pushed the covers aside, and his hand drew the robe away from her body, revealing her pale skin and long legs. She heard his catch of breath and felt his hand slide down the long line of her flat belly and beyond, to touch the fire that raged within her. She listened to the slip of silk as his robe fell away, and felt the warmth of his skin against her own.

She felt his finger trace the scar around her throat with infinite tenderness, as if he had yearned to touch that injured part of her. His lips kissed the line of Kali, his tongue flicking out to taste her wound. Then his hands and mouth seemed everywhere, and everywhere he touched her she was alive with desire. His long black hair fell across her face, then moved to her breast as his mouth warmed a stiffened nipple. There were no duties, kingdoms or swords. There was only Lung, only the dragon, drawing her into an endless moment of complete pleasure, a surrender which was a triumph over all her losses and her defeats.

There was, later, an instant of doubt, of loss and fear, as they lay with their hair, golden brown and inky black, tangled on the pillow, and their arms still around each other. She stiffened slightly, and, as if he read her thoughts with the eyes she had given him, he laid a finger across her lips.

"No. No matter what happens, you will always be, to me, Pure Jade. Remember that."

To Claire's surprise, Lung did not take the Sword of Waters with him when he left some hours later, or even speak of it. It was as if, for the moment, it did not matter, and that pleased her in an odd way. It left her with a quiet sense of worth, that what had passed between them was a precious thing, not a matter of state. She puzzled over it while she soaked in the inn's bathing facilities, and concluded, tentatively, that for once she had not been used. The goddesses had used her, had used her family for generations, and she accepted that because she understood necessity. But she did not like it, she decided, and she would be glad when her work was done, when she was not needed any longer for any purposes but her own. That she lacked even a hint of what those might be did not bother her overmuch. Perhaps she would go home, or remain in the land of Han and make a garden. She was too much at peace with herself to fuss, a state so new and unknown that she barely dared to believe in it.

The following morning she was up and dressed in a heavy silk robe that Willow had procured for her. It was a soft green, her favorite colour, and fell in graceful folds around her slippered feet. She had just sat down to begin some writing when the girl came in. Claire looked up, annoyed at the interruption, and Aurelian, who had been lolling on the bed, jumped down.

"The Lord Ts'u would speak with you, mistress."

"Show him in, then." Claire found herself immediately unsettled, her tranquility gone. She reminded herself sternly that the previous day had been a wonderful dream, not the beginning of a lifetime. For some reason, this did not comfort her. How would they meet?

Lung walked into the chamber, tall, stern, and remote as the mountains of the gods. He wore a stiff, brocaded robe of a blue which did not become his sallow skin. Claire rose and bowed deeply, to hide a sharp pain of her heart. When she stood up again, his eyes were glittering green, as if he was angry, and she drew back a little. Where was the tender man who had possessed her, who had touched the scar around her throat as if it were precious, not hideous? What had she done wrong?

Something of her feelings must have shown, for his expression softened. He glanced at the bed, the covers rumpled by Aurelian's recent vacation, and a hint of a smile touched his mouth. Willow made a disapproving cluck and hastened to smooth the quilts. What the maid knew, or guessed, Claire was not sure, but the girl had been watching her like a falcon since she had returned the previous early evening, after Lung had left.

"The bastards believe me an imposter!" Lung spoke in Tibetan, and Claire realized he did not want her maid to understand their conversation.

"Which bastards? There are so many in the world."

Lung chuckled briefly. "Several fence-perching dogs' heads whose support I require. While you rested from your wounds, I have gathered much intelligence, as I told you. I have, as I did before, sent word to various governors and warlords, and the replies have ranged from uncommitted to downright insulting. It seems I 'died' twenty years ago— or so they pretend to believe. They are afraid of taking sides, the dirty cowards—afraid of the Empress." He calmed down and gave a small shrug. "I cannot entirely fault them. I am not unafraid of her myself."

"Surely you did not really expect all to flock to your banner in a moment, Lord."

"Yes, I did, because sometimes I am a fool. And I did not have you near me, to remind me of simple realities, of facts and truths. With the Darkness gone, the nation is weary, sick of conflict and anxious to return to peace. To become embroiled in a battle for the Dragon Throne must seem to these men like madness. The Empress has a son by her barbarian lover, and there appears no reason to restore the previous dynasty."

"But you still want to be Emperor."

"I still believe it is my duty—and my destiny."

"Those are very different things, Lung. Would it be so terrible to have freed China from the Darkness and do no more?"

"*You* did that. That was your destiny. Mine is otherwise."

Claire nodded. "Willow, bring us some tea, please." The maid, who had been listening to what must have sounded like babble, looked relieved and bustled off. "This is really a matter between you and your mother, Lung, and not about the Dragon Throne at all." Claire spoke from her own hard won knowledge of how much of what she did was due to things that had happened in the past, the pain of her mother's abandonment and her desire to be perfect, and had little do do with what she was doing in the very moments of her life.

Lung seized her, kissed her so hard it was nearly hurtful, then released her. "I loathe it when you are right. It is not a pleasing habit in a female."

Claire rubbed her bruised mouth and realized she was furious. "I was not created to please you," she replied tartly, keeping her flaming temper firmly in hand. "I do not care if you are the Son of Heaven or the King of the Cosmos. Do not presume—ever!"

"Shrew!" He made the word sound like a kiss. He knew she was angry, and he was not the least bit afraid of it. "Forgive me, Pure Jade. I have been reading letters and reports, writing replies until my hand shook. Perhaps I should just give up the whole thing—except that I hold the Imperial Sceptre. I cannot believe it was given into my hands by chance, without reason. And, I am impatient, and can show it before no one but you." He patted a small pouch which hung from his belt.

Claire sat down and nodded. She had not forgotten that she had dreamed that she must help Lung regain his throne, but she regretted now that they had shared a couch for whatever purpose. She could no longer pretend she acted out of duty. And, for no reason she could put a finger to, she had to be sure that his motives in achieving the Dragon Throne were clear and understood. It had been simpler before. Her only satisfaction came from the certain knowledge that he was as confused and conflicted as she was by the results of their previous afternoon.

"The sceptre is not sufficient proof of your authenticity."

"It might be. No one knows I possess it but you."

"Why?"

"Because it is never revealed—has never been revealed before—except before the Temple of Heaven in the Imperial Capital. It is not just something to wave about casually. It is a sacred thing. And I have never found any moment which seemed right to reveal that I possessed it. It is a shame the robe is ruined. If it were intact . . . can you sew it for me?"

Claire laughed, glad to be back on their former, easy footing. "I am a terrible needlewoman." She held out her sword-calloused hands. He touched one palm with a finger and she felt her whole body quicken. The ease was gone almost before she could enjoy it. Their couching had decidedly complicated matters. Why did she have to come to care for the one man she would never have?

Willow came back with a tray of tea and sweets, glanced from one to the other, and gave a little shake of her head. Then she retired to a corner of the room, clearly determined to chaperon them, whether they wanted it or not. Lung took a seat and Claire poured tea for both of them.

"Why is the robe important?"

Lung answered slowly. "There are hundreds of imperial

garments, of course, for every occasion and ritual. But, if I am correct, the tatters you have in your pack are from a robe... out of legend. It is said that the Queen Mother of the West, Xi Wang Mu, herself made it for the founder of our dynasty, over six centuries ago, and it was worn at his ascension to the throne. So, to ask you to repair it was foolish of me. I am grasping at straws. No needle in the world could mend it."

"Was it lost?"

"Oh, no. As far as I knew, until I saw it in your belongings, it was in the capital, along with the sceptre. To see those sacred objects scattered across your bed nearly startled me out of my wits. I did not know what to think. And I have no idea how they came to you."

"I told you. In the forest, I met a beast, which I later discovered was a dragon. I slew it, though I did not wish to, and it went up in smoke, leaving behind the sheath of my sword, two jewels where its eyes had been, the robe pieces, and the stone wand. Oh, yes, there were a few things like flower petals which were scales once, I suppose. I gathered them up. Aurelian instructed me to do so."

"What did you do with the gems?"

Claire shifted uncomfortably. "They are your eyes, Lord."

"Why did you not tell me! I am surprised your family did not strangle you. You must have been an impossible child!" There was no anger in the words, just astonishment and affection.

"I was not certain how you would feel. It never seemed the right moment. It is not like handing someone a bowl of tea!"

"No. And it would not have served me to know earlier. You keep secrets well, Lady."

"Say rather that I am so much in doubt, always, that I have learned to keep my own council, Lord."

Lung touched his breast and bowed slightly. "I am rebuked." As he straightened, he added. "As usual."

Why are we being so formal, she wondered. Then she

remembered how sometimes her parents, after some vio-
lent disagreement, followed by reconciliation, would be a
little distant with each other, as if to restore a balance that
had been shaken by the strength of their feelings. She
smiled quietly. It was, she decided, a matter of respect,
that neither of them wanted what had occurred to alter what
had become, over the weeks and months together, a part-
nership which served them both. How wise Lung must be.
Or perhaps he was just more aware of the difficulties their
couching could create, aware enough not to let it be treated
as a commonplace event. They were not any man and
woman. If he was to achieve his goal, he would not be free
to wed as he chose, but would marry some proper Han
princess, chosen by court astrologers, no doubt. Well, I
still have Aurelian. She put a hand on the golden mane.
For once, it brought her no ease.

"The sceptre and the robe together would establish your
authenticity, then?"

"Let us just say they might sway the indecisive."

"Do you really want a pack of fence-sitters for allies?"

"No, but I am not in a position to be as picky as I would
like."

Claire nodded. She had heard her father often enough
on the subject of expedient alliances. "I am not the Queen
Mother of the West, but I am, I suppose, a competent
mage. Let me see if I can repair the garment."

She heard his sigh of relief. "Thank you, Pure Jade."

Claire looked up abruptly from her study of Aurelian's
wonderful curls. "That was what you wanted to begin with,
was it not!"

"Yes."

"Why did you not ask me outright!" She was on the
edge of a towering rage.

"I have asked you for so much already, Lady. I could
not bring myself to ask for more."

Claire glared at him. "If you ever do that again, I will
pull your eyes out and stuff them down your throat. Save

your pretty, polite games for those who need them. Too much has passed between us for less than plain speaking."

Lung drew back a little at her fury, then laughed. "I suppose I should count myself fortunate you did not threaten me with castration."

"Certainly not," she replied primly. "There is the dynasty to consider, after all."

"Of course," he answered, and roared with laughter. She joined in, after a moment. A little knot in her chest unwound. They were friends, and that would always remain.

Claire stood up and went over to her battered pack. Beside it lay her sword, and the Sword of Waters, the latter wrapped in a length of silk. She unwound it and put a finger on the hilt. She could still sense its powers, but they no longer commanded her. What effect it would have upon Lung she could not guess, but she did not doubt that he would manage to control its awesome energies. She was glad, relieved, to be free of its burdenage.

Then she removed the pieces of the robe from the pack and unfolded them. Claire spread them out on the bed like a puzzle, using the pattern of the waves to guide her. The waves seemed to move, dazzling her eyes. As she laid the pieces together, she felt the little thrill of magic tingle along her fingers. She passed a hand over her eyes, rubbing them. She swayed, dizzy.

This was not magic as she knew it, and she was suddenly doubtful that she could mend it. Then Aurelian was beside her, pressed against her hip, his goldenness mingling with her aura, steadying her and strengthening her. She "saw" the robe as it had been originally, a picture from the *keelin*'s memory. It had been seamless, not so much made as grown, spring from the mind of the Queen Mother of the West as a thought made manifest. All she had to do was reconstruct the original thought! It was absolutely simple—and totally out of her powers.

Wholeness, mistress.

What?

Wholeness, as your guru instructed you, mistress.

I never understood what Djurjati meant. I never grasped it.

It is not grasping, mistress, not holding, only wholeness.

Claire tensed, then let go. Everything was in pieces, like the robe. Her life was made of pieces, moments, losses. To accept it as an entirety seemed impossible. There was not enough time in the cosmos to do such a thing. No, that was not true. Once, for a moment, she had been Time itself, had been one with Kali. But her human mind thought of that as a piece, when it was, in truth, an entirety. She kept trying to distinguish the dancer from the dance.

In her mind she saw a tiny silver thread, so slight it was nearly invisible, and she knew she had glimpsed it before, just at the moment when she had regained her lost hand. She knew it was herself. She followed it mindlessly, pursued it back to the instant where it began, where Geoffrey and Helene created her. She could see the thread of blue which was her twin, and was distracted for a moment, following it away across a nameless horizon, before she dragged her attention back to the thread of her own life. It was slender, and where it was most recent, ghostly thin, but it was whole and continuous. Curious, she started to examine where it changed, but Aurelian shifted against her, and she lost interest, as if she had had a thought and lost it.

The robe, mistress.

Oh, yes, the robe. The picture of the original, seamless garment returned, and with it the sense of her self thread as a continuity. It appeared to her mind's eye that her thread was embroidering itself within the robe, darting in and out, needleless, and that all she need do was relax. That, she discovered, was very difficult. She was so well-trained to act, to do, to control, that to do nothing was a struggle. It was exactly the opposite of all the magic she knew, all that she had learned with such struggle. She could feel Aurelian helping her, lending her his own great submissions, humbling her with what he had foregone to be beside her. Finally, as quietly as it had begun, it was done.

Claire felt the process cease, softly, painlessly, and yet with a slight wrench of anguish. She was cold to the bone as she opened her eyes and found Willow and Lung watching her curiously. Her knees wobbled, and Lung was across the room and beside her, his strong arms around her, supporting her. She could feel the warmth of his body and the good, clean smell of him. She rested her head against his shoulder and wished she could remain there forever. He brushed her hair with a tender hand, and put a light kiss on her forehead, but she could feel him tremble.

"You vanished," he whispered.

"What?"

"For just a moment, you were gone. And I was terrified."

She raised a finger and put it across his lips. "You need never fear for me, Lord."

"Do not tell me what I can and cannot fear, woman. You cannot say be direct one minute and demand my silence the next. You are cold." He led her back to her chair and poured some tea as Claire's teeth began to chatter audibly. Willow bustled over and draped a quilt over her legs and glared at Lung. Claire gulped the tepid tea down. She had never felt this cold in her life.

Aurelian leaned against her side. *You put a great deal of yourself into the work, mistress.*

Did I? Claire glanced indifferently at the now intact robe which lay across the bed. She could see, here and there, the glint of her thread among the pattern of the waves. And she sensed that her work was almost done. It was a relief. Perhaps she would not have to watch Lung become emperor. Perhaps she would not have to lose him. It seemed preferable, in her weariness, to several decades of unrequited passion.

Willow hurried off to get fresh tea. Claire gestured at the robe. "There it is. Now you can claim the Dragon

Throne. Take it." She paused. "The sword, too. That is yours now."

"All I do, it seems, is take from you."

"Life is not always fair, Lord." She staggered up, the quilt tumbling to the floor off her knees, crossed the chamber and picked up the Sword of Waters. The sea lapped against her palm, soft and deceptively gentle. Claire turned to carry it back, but he had followed her, and she turned into his arms, so they stood with the sword between their bodies for a long moment. His eyes searched her face, glowing violet. She wanted to scream, but whether at him, or herself, or all the gods in all the heavens, she did not know. "Leave me now, please. I am weary."

Claire pressed the hilt of the Sword into his hand, and he took it reluctantly. "I will go, as you ask, Lady. But, know this too. I will never leave you, my Pure Jade. Not even for China."

Then, picking up the robe as if it were no more than an ordinary garment, he left. Aurelian padded after him. Claire crawled into the bed and wished she could die. And, somehow, she knew she was not going to be that fortunate.

XIX

Much to her surprise, and a little to her horror, Claire discovered she had acquired an entourage. She had been quite content with Willow and Aurelian, and the fact that several of her men from the White Lotus troop had come by the inn to inquire after her health and left pieces of stiff red paper with incomprehensible characters on them, which was apparently the custom when calling. Willow could read just enough to distinguish a silk merchant from a goldsmith by the sign above his shop, so the written word remained a mystery, and Claire was in no mood to do any spell making. Lung's parting words had left her depressed and weary.

But two mornings later there was a great bustle in the inn, raised voices that interrupted her at her desk, where she was continuing to record her adventures. She frowned as Willow came in and bowed. The girl looked flustered.

"What is it, Willow?"

"Lady, there are people here."

"I can hear that! What has that to do with me?"

"They are here for you, Lady."

"Here for me?" Was it more of her men? She would like to see them, now that she was up and about. But Willow did not have a tray of cards. Was she under arrest? Perhaps the forces of the Empress had seized the city while she slept. "What do you mean?"

"In the reception hall, Lady. Please, come with me."

Claire stood up, and the soft folds of the gown she wore fell about her long legs. Willow had gone out and had the robe made at a silk store, and it fit well enough. It was a violet colour that reminded her of Lung's eyes, and she wore it with both pain and pleasure. At least it was not white, and Willow did not think she was a ghost. What she did think, having been present while Claire repaired the imperial robe, she kept well hidden behind her broad, peasant face.

"Very well." She did not add that it had been important to interrupt her work, because Willow knew that. Claire had come to appreciate in a fresh way her father's work, because she found herself swept up in the act of setting down her experiences, the struggle to choose exactly the correct turn of phrase, to capture a moment in words as a painter might in pigments.

Claire followed Willow down the corridor, around a courtyard muddy with melting snow, and went to a large room in the front of the inn, close to the street. The room appeared crowded, after days of being alone with her maid. Two faces she knew, those of Lieutenant Lee and Major Wang, for they had been two of the four who had protected her while she shot the arrow into the lotus and sent the Darkness out of the land. Their mail coats were polished, and they wore their White Lotus badges with obvious pride. They bowed along with the others, but they grinned at her too. Comrades-in-arms. She wished it was proper to embrace them. They had saved her life. She had a moment's sorrow for brave Major Yee, who had died with a spear in his chest, still clutching the reins of her horse, faithful even as his spirit had departed.

The rest of the group were strangers, and by the look of them, not military men. One stepped forwards and bowed again, then spoke. "Greetings, Lady. I am Sun Dee An, and the Lord Ts'u has given me the privilege of serving you as your major-domo. I beg leave to present the others in your service."

Bemused, she nodded agreement, so he continued. "This is Mr. Dee, who will serve as your secretary, and this is Scholar Yang, who will be your tutor. The Lord Ts'u wishes that you will become familiar with our written word." The two men bobbed as their names were spoken, and Claire took an immediate and incomprehensible dislike to the secretary, and an equally powerful liking for the tutor. She knew his sort, and had since she was a child. Sun continued, introducing under-secretaries, sub-tutors, her military friends, and several whose presence seemed quite mysterious and unnecessary. What did she need with a keeper of the chests and a victualer? A stable-master? Had Lung lost his mind? She did not want people fussing over her day and night.

But Claire had learned enough in her brief time in the lands of the Han to realize that persons of consequence had servants, lots and lots of servants, and that an entourage established one as someone important. And, she supposed she was, in a way. She suspected that the tale of the mysterious White Lotus was already making its way into the folklore of the people, that it was being told and re-told in whatever the Han used for a bazaar, becoming enlarged and embroidered, so that she would not recognize it in a few years. Lung was making a lady out of her, in more than name.

The entourage took over the inn, and Claire became a prisoner of a merciless schedule of reading lessons in the morning, until her eyes danced with brush strokes, and afternoons with Dee, listening to him drone over dispatches sent from Lung's headquarters for her to consider, interspersed with visits from various merchants of silk, horses, chests and jewelry. She acquired three more maids,

a full-time seamstress, and a staggering number of belongings. After months of her pack and the clothing on her
back, it was overwhelming, and she felt breathless and stifled. If only they were not so polite and deferential.

After a week of it, she was ready to burst. She was
sitting patiently while Dee read her a dispatch, a copy of a
document which Lung had sent to her in red lacquer boxes
each day. Something in his manner still made her itch, and
she fidgeted with her sleeves while she listened. She had
made good progress with Scholar Yang—amazing progress, according to the elderly fellow. Claire had not explained that she was using skills acquired long before, both
linguistic and magical. In her sleep, she dreamed of Chinese characters, dancing merrily, because they possessed
both pattern and an internal logic. The difficulty was not in
the characters, but in their vast number. There were thousands, some differing so subtly, by a mere brush stroke,
that it was easy to mistake one for another.

Something in Dee's voice arrested her attention, a slight
hesitation. "May I see it, please, Dee? I need the practice."

"Oh, Lady, this is hardly worth your . . . "

"Give it to me," she snapped, releasing some of her
pent-up frustration on the hapless secretary. He surrendered
it with great reluctance, and Claire stared at the sheet. For
a second it looked like chicken scratches. Then her memory clicked in, and she matched the characters to the words
he had spoken, so she could make sense of it, even with
characters she was not yet certain of. It was slow, halting
reading, and she creased her brow, but she could follow it.

And then she found an entire section where her memory
supplied no voice. She paused, Claire went back to the
previous sentence, re-read it carefully, then looked for the
next place where Dee's words rang in her mind. She found
it, read it slowly, then returned to the omitted section. She
squared her jaw and worked through it, matching characters from previous sentences where she did not know them,
until she made enough sense of it to comprehend the sup-
pressed information and grasp its significance. It was not

terribly important, a half-hearted promise of support from a minor warlord, but it made her wonder what else Dee had not read to her. More, it made her suspect the replies she had dictated to him, which had then been sent to Lord Ts'u.

"Bring me the copy of the letter I sent to Lord Ts'u yesterday."

Dee went pale. "I . . . I am not certain where I put it, Lady." He pawed the papers on his desk. "The clerk, perhaps, has filed it already."

"Tell me, Dee, what is the usual punishment for a servant who betrays his master?"

"Flogging, mistress." He was sweating profusely now.

"And if that master is the Son of Heaven?"

"State traitors are drawn and quartered, and their entire families are slain as well," he hissed, caught between terror, and now undisguised hatred. He spat at her.

"Master Sun!" She bellowed the name, and footsteps pounded down the corridor. The door flew open, and Sun, his cap askew, was there, followed by Major Wang, a hand upon the hilt of his sword. They looked around the chamber, wondering what was amiss. Dee cringed beside his desk.

"Yes, mistress?" Sun bowed and Wang relaxed his grip.

Claire considered her words carefully. "How did Mr. Dee come into my service?"

"Why, when the Lord Ts'u conferred upon me the honour of forming your entourage, Mr. Dee came forward and offered his services. Many did, Lady, for it is deemed a great privilege to serve the White Lotus. Mr. Dee was chosen because of his excellent qualifications. There have been no literary examinations in several years, of course, for the Emperor suspended them, and the the terrible Darkness disrupted everything, but in the last examinations, Mr. Dee did very well, and in peaceful times, would have gone into the civil service immediately. I felt fortunate to have so able a man to serve you."

"Did you, or anyone else, instruct him to omit portions of the documents which Lord Ts'u had wished me to see?"

Sun appeared scandalized. "I would never do such a thing. Do you mean . . ."

"He was reading me this, and I asked to see it, for I sensed some hesitation. I found, I believe, that he had omitted a portion. Now I have asked to see a copy of the reply I sent yesterday, and he cannot seem to find it. I cannot but suspect that some mischief is present. I do not wish to accuse a man wrongly, but if he has been altering my replies—you see my predicament. If my advices to the Lord Ts'u have been other than I have intended, it would dishonour me, for I am devoted to his cause."

"All know the loyalty of the White Lotus. Perhaps you misunderstood."

"Fine. Let us look at my replies and see."

Dee screamed. His pale face reddened and a stream of vileness flowed out of his cultured mouth. Then he fainted. It was a quiet slither of silk and paper onto the floor. "I do not think that will be necessary," Sun answered, staring at the crumpled figure.

"No, it is absolutely needful. Send Yang to me, and the under-secretaries. We must undo any harm immediately. I cannot bear the thought of the Lord Ts'u depending on men who conspire against him, and for the Empress, or in their own interest."

"I will take care of this dog's-head," Major Wang said, picking up the still unconscious Dee and flinging him across a broad shoulder like a limp rice-bag.

"Be gentle with him, Major."

"Why, Captain?" he asked, reverting to their easier and earlier relationship.

"Because no one conspires alone, Major. Do they?"

He gave a rough chuckle. "Your arrow is always true, Lady. I will treat him like a day-old chick."

The inn blazed with light far into the night, until Scholar Yang's old eyes were red with reading over a week's accumulation of documents, and the two under-secretaries' hands trembled upon their brushes. Dee had done some damage, conveying the impression that Lung might trust several about whom Claire entertained serious doubts, and she prayed it was not enough to matter. But she was hard pressed to imagine a worse situation than leading an army full of traitors ready to turn upon their master once the battle was well begun. Lung trusted her, depended on her, and she treasured that more than she cared to think about. She was grateful that she was too busy and too tired to think about it very often.

It was the final week of the Year of the Cat. Willow had told her that, as they had set out from Loyang, heading for Chen-an, the winter capital. Claire, after weeks of reading dispatches, was happy to be back on the move, in trousers and mail, on her horse. Her entourage, having gotten used to seeing her dressed in robe and coiffed like a lady, had been rather shocked, but the survivors of her little company welcomed her back with genuine delight. Their number, like that of all Lung's force, was increased, for the tale of the White Lotus had been enlarged and embroidered in barracks for leagues around, and she was regarded as a fortunate commander. Nothing succeeded like success, she thought cynically, as she reviewed her troops. Captain was a more comfortable title than Lady, if only because she could swear without offending any sensibilities. She had found the management of her entourage rather exhausting at times.

After the intricacies and complications of choosing allies, the petty intrigues and the larger ones, it was a relief to return to the simplicity of military life. There was no more doubt or ambiguity, just an enemy to face. It was not really that clear or simple, and Claire knew it. Nothing had been clear or simple since that last meeting with Lung. But at least she understood the demands of war, and it felt good to be ahorse again, to ride into exhaustion, and to have dreamless sleep.

Messages had been exchanged between Lung and the

Empress. She had repudiated him in the most precise and insulting terms, calling him an impostor, and had sworn to destroy him. What her puppet Emperor thought remained unknown. Claire wondered how the man who had conquered China felt when he found that the Empress had conquered him. There was no question who was the power in the state, no matter whose bottom warmed the Dragon Throne. She wondered too what sort of woman could deny her own child.

So much had happened so quickly that she could not take it all in. Aurelian had departed, gone to Lung, and was his constant companion, a golden shadow wherever the man walked or rode. She had felt deserted for a day, but she knew it was right. Claire had given everything she could, everything she had. Now all that remained was to see if he would succeed. In a way, she merely wished that it was over, so she could go home. Her job was finished the day she passed the Sword to Lung. She told herself this several times a day, despite a sneaking suspicion that the meddling deities had a few more tricks to play on her. If Lung succeeded, she would go back to Baghdad, marry some man, and settle down to raising fat babies. If he failed, she would be dead, and it would not matter. The only problem was she did not find either conclusion to her liking. She wanted to stay among the mist-draped mountains and rivers, wanted to see the season pass in this strange, wonderful country which had stolen her heart so effortlessly.

The two forces now faced each other, two armies where few if any of the combatants understood why they prepared to battle. The Empress had left the capital to meet Lung, her commanders heading a huge assemblage of what Claire's eye perceived as ill-trained recruits with a few hardened veterans. She was mounted, scanning the companies, their brave banners before their little tents. In the center there was a vast pavilion, where the Empress presumably waited. The Spider Empress, her own people called her.

Claire, curious, tried to learn something about this mysterious woman whom Lung both loved and hated. She set her far-sight in motion, and saw a face of such inexpressible beauty that it caught her breath. There was something more than beauty, and Claire yanked herself out of far-sight with a bone-aching wrench. She had had the sensation of sucking, of being drained of her immediate admiration, as if it fed something.

She had never encountered anything like that before, and it frightened her. She tried to decide what she had seen, what it meant. Lung and several of his immediate subordinates, his generals, rode up and grouped themselves around her. Aurelian sat between her horse and Lung's, lolling his pink tongue. Claire leaned down and stroked the beast.

I have missed you, Aurelian.

It is good to see you, mistress. He rolled his eyes up at her, and exhaled a honeyed breath. *Beware of the Spider. She feels even the lightest touch upon her web.*

I noticed. What is she? Is she human?

As human as you are, mistress.

She is very beautiful.

Can you see beyond the beauty, mistress?

I did not stay long enough to try. Is it a magic I do not know?

That is difficult to say, mistress. In a way, you know everything, and in another, nothing.

Claire scanned the troops slowly, ignoring the Empress, just studying the lay of the land and the deployment of the army. *They all adore her, do they not?*

Yes, mistress. Everyone who looks upon her adores her.

What would happen if they could not see her?

They would still remember, mistress.

Claire recalled how she had altered the memories of the sailors, months before, and decided that befuddling several thousand men was beyond her abilities. And there were Lung's men to consider. What would happen to their loyalties if the Empress revealed herself? Which she assuredly would. So much for her task being done. She glared up at the overcast sky for a second, trying to peer into Heaven and scowl.

A fresh question emerged in her mind. What would Lung do when he saw his mother? Claire shivered. Whatever the Empress was, she was potent. Now, she had to think of a way to protect her friend.

"Lord, do you recall the Empress well?"

"Oh, certainly, Captain White Lotus."

Claire caught the edge of his memory, felt the sucking sensation again, and nearly vomited. She remembered her fiery avowal never to ensorcell him or any man. That would teach her to make sweeping promises! But, Lung must be protected, or the battle was lost before a single sword was drawn. It was a dilemma, a moral question she felt unable to solve without dishonour.

Claire hesitated. What would Geoffrey do? That was the wrong question, for her father always took the compassionate course, the healing path, no matter how difficult. What would Helene do? Her mother always did what was needful, and accepted the consequences. Helene never worried about moral questions, and had often said that honour was something men had invented to allow them to kill each other with reason. Across the continent that lay between them she could almost hear her mother scream, "Do what you must," and behind her, Geoffrey saying, "My dear, you never did have any scruples." But, they were present for an instant, standing behind her, as if they were sure she would do the right thing.

Swallowing a mouth full of bitter bile, Claire called up the spell she had created on the pitching deck of a ship. It came like a lamb, and she realized how greatly her capacities had grown over the months. The spell itself seemed larger and more powerful. *I guess I do not know my own strength anymore.* Then she saw that she was different in the magic, not only by her experience, but by her body having known another's. That surrender had enriched her somehow.

She sighed, released the spell, and tried to forgive herself. She felt the shudder of his mind as it touched him, and the slight shivers of the minds of the men who surrounded them. Lung turned towards her, dazed for a moment. At the same moment, she felt something snap, a little silken thread in a great web vanished. And with it went some portion of the Empress herself. Claire could not guess if it was great or small, but neither Lung nor any of his generals would be worshippers of the Spider ever again.

Claire wondered if he grasped what had happened, if he knew what she had done, and if it would destroy his trust in her. It was rather late to be worrying over the last, she chided herself, as she realized how much his trust mattered to her. She could not win in any case. If Lung lost his contest with his mother, it would not matter at all where he trusted her or not. If he prevailed, he would be engulfed with the ritual and ceremony of his great office, and he would be firmly, politely prevented from consulting her on any matter whatever, by his councilors, eunuchs and advisors.

For a moment she had a terrible sense of desolation, a return of the wretched loneliness that had followed her mother's brutal departure after Dorothea was born, that she was alone and would always be alone. Even Aurelian had left her. The scar around her throat burned and her wrist ached. She could feel the wild drum of Kali, somewhere, and she sighed. No, she was not alone. She would never be alone. She just wished for some companionship that was a little less fearsome and a bit cosier. Claire swallowed a bubble of hilarity. She was sad, but also profoundly amused, and she could not explain to anyone her desire to laugh at the absurdity of the entire cosmos. She could not lose Lung or Aurelian or anyone, for she had never had them to begin with. It was all a dream, a terrible, painful dream, from which she would never awaken. There was no reason to be sad. Or happy. All she had to do, or could do, was be, and that was almost more than she could bear.

The sky was overcast, heavy with an imminence of snow, the air cold enough to mist at every breath. The two camps were bristling with preparation for engagement, but they had done that for two days, until tempers were frayed and arguments broke out. Claire would have worried if she had not known perfectly well that the Empress's troops were in the same foul mood, and that the battle and the killing would begin soon enough to satisfy the most bloodthirsty.

The Empress had returned Lung's final emissary in pieces—an act of such barbarity that the outrage was nearly palpable within the camp. Claire, dressed for battle, but sipping tea in her tent, sensed the tenor of the army as the news spread, and pondered some means of turning it to Lung's advantage. She had not seen or spoken to him since they had met upon the hill and she had broken the thread that bound him to his mother. Her fear that she had done wrong was dismissed, for Lung seemed more whole, as if by rending that thread she had inadvertently healed a wound she had not suspected existed. And, having already broken her word not to use her powers to enspell in the only place where it really mattered to her, she was eager to find any opportunity to utilize her mage skills. She was not prepared to begin any sweeping magicks, but enhancing a prevailing mood seemed a useful thing to do. This, at least, was the excuse she told herself as she reached out with her senses, testing the temper of the force around her, seeking a means to use their natural outrage to blind them to the glamour of the Empress.

Claire had barely completed this working when the drums rolled and the command came to mount up. She was ahorse and ready in seconds, thrusting her cup into Willow's hand and giving the startled maid a quick hug around her square shoulders. Her banner man rushed up, pulling on his helmet while he struggled to unfurl the silk. Claire reached out and pulled the ties that bound the banner, and the White Lotus glowed. In the grey overcast, it was like a beacon.

Claire caught a glimpse of the expression on his face, and on the faces of her troop, and her breath stilled. Such admiration. Such blind adoration. You fools, she wanted to shout at them, I am only human, only mortal, like you. She could nearly taste it, and it was so delicious that she longed to gulp it down. It was so tempting to fall into the dark pools of their eyes, to become the magnificent creature they imagined she was. It would, no doubt, fill up all the empty places within her. *Turn away from me, I beg of you, most sweetly, this curse of eyes.* She would not become any creature dependent upon adoration, even to ease the desolation that filled her.

In a flash of insight, Claire understood what made the Empress so powerful, and saw how she fed on the eyes of all around her, like a leech. She was so startled by this realization that she barely noticed she was mentally bellowing this picture of the Empress all across the camp, like a shout of disgust. When she noticed what she was doing, she shrugged. A great many good, decent men were going to die defending a creature she could have become herself. Anything she could do to lessen that number was forgivable.

The troops moved forward to engage, as the sky paled a little, and the first flakes of snow tumbled downwards. Claire wished she was any good with the element of air, because a battle in a snow storm seemed perfectly insane. Why don't we wait until spring, like civilized people? Why couldn't she be solemn and serious? Claire realized that if she let herself be truly serious, her heart would shatter for the sheer, utter stupidity of the killing and dying which was about to take place. It was not like riding down hapless Darklings. These were men, with wives and children, and they were going to perish over a piece of furniture. Calling it the Dragon Throne changed nothing. It was something to sit on, not to die for. Claire felt a little jolt of startlement. She had set out on this journey expecting to die, and now she could not think of anything worth dying for. She had changed so greatly she barely knew herself anymore. She had no sword of essence, no magic arrow, nothing but herself, and even that was subject to the whims of the gods.

The snow began to fall in earnest as the two armies came together. For a moment the muddy ground was cloaked in soft whiteness, and then it was hideous with the red of fresh blood, with the shouts of men and the screams of horses. She lost all sense of any order in the confusion of snow and fighting.

A sudden sharp sense of danger penetrated the fog, and Claire extended her far-sight almost before she knew it. There was a dark blot alongside the large pavilion where the Empress waited, and it was moving. After a second, Claire realized it was a huge machine of some sort, being dragged by men and horses, something she had never seen before. It was metal, a long cylinder, mounted on wheels, and ornately fashioned, so it resembled a beast. It was enormous, and the mud and snow had mired its wheels.

There was nothing of magic about it, but she could sense its threat. Claire examined the thing as well as she was able in the midst of the fighting, and watched as the men swung its snout about to face Lung's advance. It looked rather like the dragon she had slain in the forest, complete with bronze horns and beard, and she could see something being poured into the lower end of the tube. A man ran up carrying a torch. He started to thrust it into the stuff.

There was a roar like the end of the world, and fire billowed out of the opening, followed by flaming stones. They flew into a rank of Lung's men, and struck horses and soldiers who promptly burst into flame. They line wavered, bellied, and broke in terror as the smell of burning flesh swelled into the snow freshened air. Claire noted abstractedly that it smelled like cooking lamb. The screams and confusion increased as men rolled in the snow to put out the terrible fire which consumed their flesh.

Outrage filled her. A wisp, the merest tendril of Kali flickered, but the anger was her own. This was obscene. What sort of mind could conceive such a thing? They were filling the base with stuff again. With a mental flick, she smothered the torch as it reached for the explosive. Even across the field she could feel the surprise of the man as the fire died in his hands. But there were other torches, other fires to ignite whatever hellish mess they poured into their engine.

Claire stared at the beast-shape for a second. She put herself into the ornate metal work, feeling along the joins and welds. Then she began to push the bearded jaw shut. It creaked, and resisted, but, a finger's width at a time, it began to close. And, in the noise and confusion, no one noticed the upper end of the cylinder was behaving oddly.

When the next torch was brought, the mouth of the tube was less than a handspan wide. She watched it touch the stuff which burned, and felt it ignite as she pressed the metal lips together. Then she tore herself away as fire roared up the long body of the machine. She was almost too slow, and she had a fearsome sensation of unbearable heat for a moment.

The metal shrieked like a living thing. Then fire bloomed, both from the lower end, then everywhere, as the tube burst, showering fire in a circle that consumed the men who tended the machine and everything around them for a hundred strides. A glowing chunk arched into the roof of the huge pavilion, and fire licked the cloth, despite the snow, and began to spread.

Whole troops of the Empress's army took to their heels, running or riding away from both the battle and the field. With a certain grim pleasure, Claire watched. She cast about, to see if any other dreadful engines remained, but it had been unique. She wondered if its maker had perished with it, and rather hoped he had died the death he planned for others. But other minds would make other such monstrosities.

The Imperial Pavilion was ablaze now as the snow thickened, a bonfire in the middle of the encampment. There was a knot of people streaming out of the doorway, maids and servants, men-at-arms, and finally, the Empress herself. Claire watched the unique, distinctive aura as it flickered in the snow.

Lung's army surged forward, taking advantage of the confusion, slaughtering the companies which remained willing to fight. The pavilion collapsed in flames as people scurried into the snow. She kneed her horse forward and towards the remaining fighting.

There was a man on a horse, and he rode towards Lung, firing arrows from the saddle so rapidly she could barely follow their flight. The snow deflected some, but others found their mark, and the men around Lung fell, wounded or dead. She could see the golden glow of Aurelian beside Lung, mingled with his own shining blueness. It charged the snow with colour, like a pillar in the swirling air. She was too distant, too far away to do anything but observe, for the press of men around her impeded her, and the field was growing more littered with the dead and dying with each passing minute.

Then she saw the Sword of Waters leave its sheath, so different in his hand than it had been in hers. That he had not used it earlier surprised her, but he was, after all, a man of remarkable restraint. Perhaps it was worth it after all. He would be a splendid ruler.

The other man fired an arrow, and Lung cut it in two as it arched down towards him. The sword flickered white against the snow, eye-searing brightness. Then the man who had been firing arrows was close enough to engage, and he dropped his bow and drew his sword. They circled, two men in a globe of unearthly light, and Aurelian stepped out from between the two horses as the men closed. Even at the distance, and through the snow, Claire knew that the other man was the better warrior, that he sat his steed as if he had been born on it. The weeks of fighting had strengthened Lung, and taught him much, but he was no real match for the other.

Claire felt her heart catch, and reached for a fireball. She "heard" a stern "no" that rattled her brains. The goddess—which one she did not know—stayed her hand. She must let Lung fight this battle alone. With a wrench, she tore her attention away, and looked around the rest of the melee.

The Empress was rallying the remnants of her forces, by the sheer force of her personality. Claire nodded. She gave a little query at the forces which guided her, and felt a warmth, like a kiss, like approval. Let Lung do what he must. She had her own task, her own fish to fry.

Claire rode towards a regrouping of the Empress's army, hardly aware of her banner bearer on her left, or of Lieutenant Wang just behind her. The white lotus shone in the snow-swirling air, and they were within the ranks of the enemy almost before they knew it, with confusion on both sides. The way seemed to open before her, without a sword being lifted. The enemy turned away, their eyes fixed on a small figure glowing in the snow, and they were like men entranced, as if they had lost their essence or sense of purpose.

There was a kind of quiet then, except for the crackle of the fire amidst the ruins of the pavilion, and the cries of the wounded. All fighting ceased, except where Lung circled a small, doughty warrior, a blaze of auras that pierced the veil of snow. Claire gave a quick glance, then focused on the woman before her.

She was lovely. Much too lovely to kill. Claire could sense the web of glamour that radiated from the Empress. Such beauty demanded reverence, protection and awe. The snares curled into her mind, and Claire found that she believed that she loved the fragile little figure standing calmly before her, unafraid and dignified in a way Claire knew she could never be. She was such a big, clumsy oaf of a girl. So stupid. So ugly. How could she think ill of this adorable creature? Too late Claire realized that she had protected all but herself from the particular talent of this female.

Then the boy, her young bannerman, who shone with such sweet innocence, made a wretching sound, a rude vomiting noise that broke the spell. She heard something wet and horrid hit the roiled snow, and a moment later one of the horses released a warm, scented stream of urine. Claire remembered how she had thought a short time before of the admiration as a curse of eyes, and the little prayer she had uttered to prevent it. With calm, pitiless compassion, she turned it round.

Take away from her, I beg of you, most sweetly, this blessing of eyes.

There was a silence, a moment of stillness, and then the web of glamour shriveled up and collapsed. The Empress gasped and staggered, as if the supports had been yanked out from her. She screamed into the whirling snow, a sound of such horror that Claire felt it would haunt her dreams forever. Then she tore a small hand mirror from within her sleeve and looked into it, patting her perfect face with small, graceful hands, as if she was not certain she still existed.

The beautiful face contorted, and she pointed a finger at Claire. "Beast. Why did you not kill me? How could you rob me of . . . I cannot exist without . . . on your knees . . . adore me, worship me . . . I must be fed. I must be fed."

Her entourage drew away, her men-at-arms sheathed their swords and stepped back, as the tiny female raved on and on, peering into her mirror and howling her demands for adulation. Claire swallowed, glanced at the now rather ordinary appearing middle-aged woman dressed in heavily embroidered garments, and dropped her head. She heard the madness swell as she turned her horse away.

Murkily she could distinguish the riderless shape of Lung's big bay, and she urged her own across the body strewn field, using Aurelian's glow to guide her. It seemed to take forever, and the snow seemed to increase with each step. There was barely a flicker of Lung himself to be seen.

Finally, she reached her goal, jumped off her horse, and ran to the long form which was a dark blot in the whiteness. The other man lay a few feet away, headless, and the Sword of Waters rested beside Lung's hand. She knelt beside him, touching his body, seeking some hurt. He was so still! Exhausted and shaking with cold, she could barely think.

Claire pulled his head up and hugged it to her mailed breast. She could still hear the screams of the mad Empress and the cries of the wounded, but all she could think of was the unmoving burden in her arms. She was suddenly furious in her weariness. The gods were toying with her again!

Angry, she sank her chilled fingers into Lung's long top-knot and yanked viciously. "If you die on me, I will never speak to you again!" Then she cuffed his cheeks roughly.

An arm, strong and alive, jerked around her narrow waist. She felt the warmth of his breath touch her cheek. "I will never leave you, Pure Jade—even if you box my ears," he murmured.

XX

He did, of course, for China, and Claire was surprised at how bereft she felt. She stood, with several thousand other people, the remnants of the aristocracy, the highest level bureaucrats, the generals and colonels and captains of Lung's victorious army, on the second day of the second month of the Year of the Dragon, and watched the installation of the Emperor. They were in the northern capital, called Datu, and the geomancers had chosen the day and the place.

Claire could see Lung, towering above various officials and priests who assisted in the ceremony. Aurelian crouched on his right side, and the great, pearl-hilted Sword of Waters hung from his left hip. He wore now the sacred robe she had repaired for him, and it fitted perfectly. But it had never been intended to be worn with a sword, so the lapping pattern of waves was broken by the line of the belt. She wondered how he had managed this unconventional touch. If she squinted against the pale spring sun, she could still catch the little glints of herself, the thread

269

that held the garment together. I helped put the land of Han back together. I wish it gave me a greater pleasure, she thought to herself.

They had only seen each other once since she had slapped his face in the snow on the battlefield, and that had been so brief an encounter, surrounded by maids and advisors, that nothing had passed between them but the most commonplace courtesies. Then China swallowed him up as sure as the dragon creature had eaten her lover, and she was alone again. Claire tried hard not to mind, to understand that promises given by the man she had come to know and cherish were nothing to the Emperor of this vast land.

The ceremony proceeded, the words inaudible across the enormous courtyard that surrounded the Temple of Heaven. There was a lot of bowing and saying of long, clearly memorized invocations, pounding of drums and ringing of great bells. She discovered she had a splitting headache and that her slippered feet hurt. Claire, dressed in the manner of a high court lady, let her mouth curl in a wry grimace. Here she was, witnessing a great, historic moment, and all she wanted was a cup of *cha* and to take to her bed.

Lung withdrew the little stone wand from the pouch upon his belt, and held it in his slender fingers. She tried to banish the memory of those fingers touching her breast and exploring the line of scar which encircled her throat, and was unsuccessful. The sight of the little wand brought back too many remembrances; the first time he had held it in the little tent and revealed the Son of Heaven to her eyes; his private name for her, Pure Jade, like the object he now held; the gentle ways he had poked at her, until she had learned to ask for help; the vulgar jokes they had made going over dispatches from various warlords and governors. In a way, he was the only friend she had ever had. Everyone else was family or servant or teacher. As for the goddesses, she had no more time for them. She had done her job, done it well, and she did not anticipate any reward or pleasure from those incomprehensible beings.

The stone wand, no longer than a finger, lengthened, and Claire found herself blushing furiously, remembering every second of Lung's embrace. Even at this distance, she could see the ornate carvings which revealed themselves as the wand became a sceptre. It shone in the pale sun, casting a green light over Lung and on those around him. Aurelian alone was unchanged by the glow of the sceptre. He remained his wonderful, golden self, and appeared, if anything, bored by the entire proceedings.

The crowd gave a gasp as the sceptre extended itself, much larger than it had been in the tent. It was huge, a good three cubits long now, and she could not imagine how Lung had the strength to hold it steady in one hand. And it looked like a mace, like the thing the dragon had struck at her with, long ago. The light it cast made huge shadows around the priests and advisors who were part of the ceremony, and Lung's strange eyes seemed to gleam and enlarge in his face as he looked up at it.

Whispers hissed around her like the brush of silk on skin. The whole crowd rustled like leaves in an unseen wind. Lung turned his eyes away from the sceptre and swept his gaze from one side of the assemblage to the other. Claire saw people cringe in their ornate robes, and one man clutched his chest and crumbled onto the cold stones. Perhaps he saw their souls, their hidden weaknesses. As his eyes passed her, surrounded by her now enormous entourage, she had only a sense of warmth, of a light kiss on her brow, and she felt Sun, her major-domo, straighten slightly, as if with sudden pride.

His examination completed, Lung placed both hands on the sceptre and lifted it above his head, setting the winged hat he wore trembling. A great shout, a cheer of rejoicing, burst from the throats of the audience. Claire joined it, releasing the pent-up excitement that was a knot in her belly, but letting loose the sorrow that choked her throat as well. She would have wept, but years of self-restraint allowed her to forego that exposure.

Finally, it was over, and she was helped into a palanquin, and borne away to the villa which was at present her home. Claire sat numb amongst the cushions, hearing the cries of her servants and the steady rhythm of the footfall of her bearers.

"Make way. Make way for Lady White Lotus." They had left the Imperial enclosure and were back in the streets of the capital, and she could hear the chatter of the people celebrating the return to order and the restoration of the true Son of Heaven. Other than the fact that she wished she could die, she shared their delight. They were all getting gloriously drunk.

The ceremony had taken most of the day, and it was close to dusk before they reached the villa on the outskirts of the capital. As Sun swept the curtains which hid her from the gaze of the vulgar aside, she saw a blaze of light pouring from the windows. A servant crouched on his hands and knees, to provide her a step to descend the litter, and Sun extended his smooth hand to assist her. Claire felt smothered and stifled.

Oh, gods! The banquet. She had somehow forgotten there was to be a formal meal upon her return. How was she going to get through it? The men who had survived the long fight against the Darkness and the final battle in the snow against the Empress had been invited to celebrate with her the success of their venture. Her officers, her sweet banner bearer, and the remnants of her troop, would be there. Was there no end to her duties and obligations?

Weary from hours of standing on a cold stone pavement, and heartsick for no reason she could name, Claire straightened her back and walked into the villa. Willow was waiting in the entry hall, and whisked her away to her apartment immediately. Despite her peasant origin, Claire had been politely insistent that Willow remain her personal and most intimate servant. She was not comfortable with the city-bred and lettered girls whom Sun had provided to care for her needs. She did not want their dainty fingers in her hair or rubbing her stiff shoulders. She wanted only Willow, who was like the nurses of her childhood; Willow, who knew that magic was stinky business and was not the least impressed by Claire's sudden elevation to some sort of aristocracy.

There was tea waiting, and her robe was laid out across the bed, a green brocade with a pattern of silvery clouds or waves over its surface. Willow chased the chattering, gossiping cluster of undermaids away with a curt order, and undressed Claire as if she had no hands to loose the ties herself. Once in her fine underrobe, she sat Claire down, tucked a soft shawl around her shoulders, and wordlessly handed her tea. She did not fuss or chatter.

Claire looked at her, at the rather plain face, the stocky shoulders and large, splayed feet in their slippers, and knew that in a way, Willow was the real China. Stubborn, patient, and hard working, she was Han. It made it all seem worthwhile again. Some of her sense of loss faded. Willow, and the men like her banner boy, these were the ones who mattered. Without them, the Emperor was nothing. She hoped Lung would remember that as he ruled, that he would not be swallowed up by favor-seeking sycophants. But he was no longer her problem or her task. It was a shame she felt so empty about it, but she was just tired from a long day.

Willow repaired her coiffure, and put the little jade hairpins which had once adorned the head of Lung's ancestress, Moon Lotus, into place. The sight of them brought back the memory of hot-and-pungent soup and warm rice wine. It was like a dream, but a very nice one. Then she was redressed and ready to face the banquet. She grabbed the girl and hugged her fiercely.

Willow returned her embrace, then patted her cheek. "I know, mistress, I know."

In the reception hall, her officers and men waited, all dressed in fresh uniforms with their company badges. They bowed formally, but grins kept popping out on their faces.

Claire smiled back and ignored the horrified shock on the faces of some of her servants as she embraced her friends. It was just good to see them.

Taking her place at a table on a raised dais, with Major Wang on one side and Lieutenant Lee on the other, she leaned back into the tall chair. Servants began bringing platters of appetisers. Of her original ninety men, only forty remained. She grieved for those who died, some before she even learned their names.

"A little different, isn't it, Captain—I mean Lady— than that barrack at Kwanti where we had to fight the rats for our rice?" Lieutenant Lee slurred his words a little, and she suspected he had been celebrating with wine already.

"Captain is fine, Lee. We are comrades in arms here, and always, as far as I am concerned." Wang filled her wine cup and she emptied it with a little gesture to her men, a small toast. Like Willow, these soldiers would always be China for her, and she was glad.

"They say you are going to be Duchess, Captain." Yes, Lee was definitely several drinks ahead of her.

"What? That is just barrack's gossip."

"No, Captain." Wang nodded as he filled her cup again. "'Tis true. Now he is Emperor, the Lord Ts'u will reward you with a duchy."

"Well, of all the stupid . . . what do I want with a title? I can barely support the posture of a lady as it is!" She had not eaten much since the morning meal, and the wine was releasing her careful control. Claire did not care. Every man there had heard her curse like a trooper.

The meal passed in a haze of dishes and heady wine. A troop of dancing girls and an orchestra appearing between the courses performed. Claire got introduced to a poetry game, the rules of which were not ever clear to her, but the loser had to empty his cup, and she lost a great deal. When she finally bade farewell to her men, and Willow took her back to her chamber, the pain of loss was dulled to an ache.

"Did I disgrace myself completely?" Claire asked this

question as Willow undressed her and began to take her hair down.

"Well, I think you startled them a little when you got up and did one of the dances of your homeland, but there was no disgrace, mistress."

"Did I do that? Oh, no. I cannot remember." She wondered if she had done one of the wild, blood pulsing dances of the nomads, or the strange, gestured one of India. The earth had not shaken, as far as she could recall, so at least she had not awakened the Kali within her. Then it came back. She had performed one of the highly mannered tersichores that the Greek women did for one another. That was all right, dignified even. There was nothing in it to offend any sensibility.

Tucked beneath silken quilts, her face washed free of cosmetics, her hair unbound, she lay still until Willow blew out the lampions and left her. Her head swam, and the tears she had held back filled her eyes and slipped down onto the pillow.

It was a little warmer a few days later when Claire found herself once again standing in a crowd, observing the nuptial ceremony of the Emperor and his new Empress. The tiny Han woman barely came to Lung's chest, and she struggled not to imagine the two of them in heated embrace, while her belly felt as if it was full of broken glass. She had thought that the coronation would be the last painful scene she would endure, and was outraged at how much the sight of the joining of their hands hurt. The new Empress was no beauty, but a rather plain girl who looked perfectly miserable as she stood beside Lung. Claire realized she felt a little sorry for her, even in the midst of feeling very sorry for herself.

It was a briefer ceremony, and shortly after she returned to her villa, a very large entourage drew into the courtyard. There were half a dozen palanquins, bearers, a mounted escort of Imperial troopers, and who appeared to be a mob of lesser officials. Claire, who had been drinking tea and pulling herself out of her dark mood, heard the racket and got up for a look. It was terribly impressive until she noticed the worn state of the litters, their curtains shabby with mildew, the gilding rubbed away in places so the wood beneath was visible. She caught the implication, the subtle insult, and was surprised at how angry she felt. For a moment she did not understand why. Then she realized that she felt the insolence was aimed not at her, but at the new Emperor, and that she could not bear.

Sun appeared beside her. "Lady, will you perhaps wish to change your robes before you greet the Imperial party?"

Claire grinned at her major-domo. She had grown fond of him, for he was both intelligent and tactful, and she had come to depend upon him to lead her through the labyrinth of Han custom. His suggestions were always polite "orders," and she accepted them as such. "And how long may I make them wait?"

His face impassive, Sun answered, "It will take at least a half hour for you to complete your necessities, I believe."

Claire swallowed a laugh and scurried off to her chamber where Willow was ready and waiting. Several robes had been taken out of their boxes by the undermaids, Poppu and Sapphire, who were waiting expectantly. The room fairly bristled with excitement, and she wished she could enter into it. She rejected a blue gown, then a green one, and finally settled on a violet silk that reminded her of Lung's jewel eyes when they rested upon her. The brocade slipped around her shoulders, and Willow bound it into place. Then she sat Claire before the mirror, smoothed her hair, and removed the green hair ornaments. Claire started to protest. She had gotten very partial to those little jade lotuses.

"These arrived while you were out, mistress." Willow opened a beautiful box. Claire stared at the pins, and caught her breath a little. The jade was violet, changing into white, carved into lotus flowers, so the white flower rested on pale purple petals. Aside from being masterpieces of the jade workers art, they were also a play upon her name, both White Lotus and Lung's private name for her, for violet jade was regarded as both the rarest and the purest form of that precious stone. Scholar Yang had told her that.

She looked at them and wondered why she wished she could scream and toss them across the room. Why did she feel so furious? And why did Lung lack the good grace to let her go without remembrances? Claire told herself that a set of hairpins and a title were perfectly acceptable forms of gratitude for all that she had done. So, why did she feel like a cast-off mistress? Why, just once, could things not be clear and unambiguous. How dare he!

Claire glared green-eyed into the mirror as Willow put the pins in her brown hair. She wanted to smash something. She wanted to run away from all the bowing and politeness, to fly home to the Levant. She was sick and tired of doing her duty, of doing the right thing. The scar at her throat burned. She reached out her right hand to cover the image in the mirror, no more than a touch, and watched the shiny surface star and shatter beneath her finger.

It was over. She was not White Lotus or Pure Jade or Gauri. She was Claire d'Avebury, plaything of the capricious deities, and she would depart at the first opportunity. At the thought, she had the sensation of a golden paw on her thigh. *Just a little longer, mistress.* The room reeked of spice and honey.

Sun was waiting to escort her into the reception hall, to receive a title she did not want. He took one look at her expression and flinched. Claire swallowed her rage and frustration, made her face as inexpressive as she could, and followed her major-domo down the corridor. As she walked, she toyed with the idea of refusing the gift, just to show Lung. *How petty I can be,* she thought.

The reception hall was as crowded as it had been for the banquet, but it was, to her eye, a much less worthy group. These men had not fought the Darkness, had not risked their lives for the state. They were, she recognized immediately, the sort of boot-licking advisors who flocked to anyone with power. She had seen many of their sort in the courts of the Levant, and it took her only a moment to have their measure. Inwardly, she shuddered at Lung being surrounded by creatures such as these, expedient men whose loyalty could be bought over and over.

Then she saw it. Claire nearly gasped aloud as she realized that these men had been sent, unwilling, to present her with an empty title, not to reward her, but because Lung had not other means to get them into her presence. He still needed, and expected, her support, her knowledge, and her advice. It was all a sham, a device, and she was both gratified and irritated. She was still the only person he really trusted. But what, she wondered, can I possibly do when we cannot even communicate directly?

As the introductions were made, she studied each man in turn, most particularly the scholarly looking Imperial Censor, a eunuch named Song Li Fan. He had an aura like vomit that made her queasy just to look at. She had promised never to use her mage powers to ensorcell anyone against their will, and broken her word by making Lung forget his mother, so he could accomplish his desire. But she had not done anything to make him other than what he already was, a brave man.

A small smile played across her mouth. There was more than one way to achieve an end. There was falsehood and there was also truth. Sometimes it was difficult to see between them. She had prayed not to be adored, so that she might continue to be herself, and not become a creature trapped in the mirror of eyes. She had destroyed the power of the Empress by removing that very same support. It was a choice between curse and blessing.

Her hands hidden beneath the long drape of her sleeves, she could still feel the presence of the mage-power pulsing along her bones and into her fingers. And, knowing what a terrible thing she did, Claire blessed the entire assemblage with truth.

Song, in the middle of a flowery speech, stuttered and halted. His thin mouth gaped. His eyes rolled. "You filthy barbarian bitch!" He shrilled the words, then spat at her, dropping the scroll he had been about to extend. "You deserve nothing!"

The others drew away as if he had a disease. Claire held her hand out to Sun, and he put his handkerchief on her palm, immediately. She wiped the spittle away in silence. Unconscious of her regality, of how potent a presence she presented, she smiled. "Very well. Now, go back and tell your master. I ask nothing but some peace—and I give you leave to depart."

Dismissed, the courtiers practically ran over one another in their eagerness to be away from the situation. The scroll, calligraphed with the Vermillion Brush, by the hand of the Emperor himself, lay on the stone floor, forgotten. And Claire, believing she had done her final service to both the man and the office he now served, turned away to her chamber, to savor her defeats.

XXI

In the courtyard of the villa, Claire was practicing stick fighting with her friend Major Wang, under Aurelian's benevolent, golden gaze. The creature had reappeared two days before, and Claire, after a long stony stare of rebuke, had fallen to her knees and put her arms into his curly mane and breathed his honeyed scent deeply. He had offered no explanation for either his defection or his return, except to say *I missed you also, mistress*.

It was a chilly morning with the taste of spring, several weeks after Claire had blessed a number of officials with the unwanted gift of speaking the truth. She and Wang had worked up a good sweat from their exertions. They practiced together daily while the nation shuddered with yet another series of upheavals, as advisors and councillors were dismissed, executed or exiled to distant provinces. She was not certain whether she was a duchess or not. The only thing that was clear was that she was a prisoner of sorts. The stick fighting helped release the fury that knowledge created.

Claire had become good friends with Wang, and she enjoyed their bouts together. He was shorter than she was, but broad shouldered and quick, so the differences in their heights were evened out by his skill and speed. Some of her entourage were rather shocked by the activity, but it had become accepted. Lady White Lotus was eccentric. It broke the routine of the day up a little. This included further study with Scholar Yang, calligraphy lessons, and, to her delight, dancing instruction with a retired professional entertainer, Miss Fan. She had everything she needed except the freedom to depart.

As so often happened, they had an audience. Willow was seated on a stone bench, her eyes on Wang, as they often were these days and several other servants stood or crouched above the paving stones. Claire was barely aware of them as she swung her stave and blocked her opponents' rapid blows. She almost always ended the sessions with a bruise or two, but these did not bother her. She simply fought to weariness, for the healthy release of tension. It was better than brooding and feeling sorry for herself, and she could almost forget her profound loneliness while she sweated and struck. The ever-present ache in her breast diminished a little.

Concentrating fiercely on Wang, she did not notice a sudden stir amongst the audience. She heard Sun's voice distantly, and she ignored it. She ducked under a blow, spun around, and caught Wang firmly across the lower back, the wood smacking his light mailed shirt with a metallic clang. It was a dancer's move, and Wang had been threatening for several days to start joining her lessons with Miss Fan, to keep up with her. Wang turned to face her, whipping the speeding tip of his stave towards her chest, and she caught the blow with the middle of her stick, just as she saw a tall figure standing in the entry of the courtyard, flanked by Sun and several strangers.

The stave dropped from her clenched hands and struck the paving stones with a clatter, as Wang snapped his stick back in mid-air and turned to see what had distracted her.

When he recognized the visitor, he bowed, but Claire had lost all power of motion whatsoever. She stood, frozen, the sweat cooling on her skin, as she stared at Lung, memorizing every feature of the man she had never expected to see again.

He was dressed in a plain robe, a scholar's garb, and he looked tired. His jewel eyes were shadowed, but she could see the soft violet light of them, and her heart pounded, not from exertion, but from a combination of joy and fury, a mixture of emotions she could barely contain, let alone control. She ignored all the bowing around her. How dare he open that wound again! She would box his ears into the following month!

Lung crossed the courtyard, paying no attention to the bobbing servants, and took her in his arms, brushing a wisp of sweat-matted hair off the wide brow beneath the small helm, then yanking away the metal cap and dropping it onto the paving stones. Claire stood stiffly in his grasp. If he had come to offer her in imperial concubinage, she would rip his heart out. He put his long, slender hands on either side of her face, and looked at her as if he were thirsty. He probably was. There had not yet been the inevitable cup of *cha*. Then he kissed her mouth, gently, and a concerted gasp came from the watchers. There was a soft scurrying of slippered and booted feet, and they were alone, except for Aurelian's shining presence.

Claire would have liked nothing better than to put her head against his shoulder, to stand against his tall body. Instead, she drew back. "What do you want from me now?"

"Nothing, Pure Jade. I have abdicated the Dragon Throne. I have set the nation right, and now my half-brother can have the woe of governing it."

"You what! After all the trouble.... But, you *are* the Son of Heaven."

"Heaven has many sons. Not all of them may occupy the Dragon Throne."

"You mean, after all we did, after all the battles and

death and . . . why?" It was incomprehensible. She had laboured so diligently to put him on the throne, and now he
was just going to walk away from it. It made her work a
nothing. No, that was not true. The Darkness was no more,
and that was worth all her efforts.

"There are reasons. The primary, which I did not immediately grasp, is that I cannot continue the dynasty."

Claire gaped at him. Her skin flushed. "You cannot
what?" Her voice squeaked. She shivered in the cool spring
air. "Why not? My single experience of you would have
led me to believe you could father half a province and still
have the strength left to write an excellent treatise on the
tenets of Confucius. I assumed you were plowing the Imperial harem like a . . ."

"How I have missed your vulgar, tart tongue! You have
no idea how weary I have become from unflagging agreement! Let us go inside. You are getting chilled. I will explain as much as I am able, I promise."

"You said you would never leave me, and then you
did." She spoke as a child, but though she understood the
reasons for what had happened, she had never managed to
still the pain of that abandonment. It hurt, just as much as
her memory of Helene's departure ached in her mind and
heart. "Then you locked me up in the gilden cricket cage
and made me into a duchess," she went on, determined to
leave no grievance unaired, "which suited me as well as
slippers on a cat, and those horrible men came. You sent
them, because you knew I would do something, did you
not!"

"Let us say I have never known you *not* to act, beloved."

"Don't you dare call me that! You are married, and I
will not be any man's concubine!" He pulled her gently but
inexorably into the villa.

"My widow does not miss me, I assure you. Poor girl."

"Widow! How can she be a widow when you are still
very much alive?"

"But, I am not, Pure Jade. I am . . . well, I do not quite

know how to describe it myself. But, when, in the forest, you slew the dragon, you killed me."

Claire felt a ringing in her ears, and the corridor swirled before her eyes. His words made no sense. She could never kill Lung. She loved him so much. Her mind seemed to fold up, like a flower closing, and she plunged into insensibility.

When she opened her eyes, she saw the familiar surroundings of her sleeping chamber. What an awful dream she had just had. A nightmare. She looked up at the embroidered curtains above the bedposts. Then she laughed a little. How foolish to dream that Lung had come back to her. He was the Emperor now. Was she going mad? Claire shivered under the covers. She could not bear the thought that she could no longer distinguish the real from the unreal. She pulled her hands from beneath the covers and looked at both of them. She turned over the hand she had lost and regained, at the white scar around the wrist, and then noticed how disgustingly dirty her palm was. She could smell her own sweat, now dried on her skin.

Claire sat up and saw Lung, sitting on a tall chair, sipping tea and eating a small sweet, chatting quietly with Willow, who looked worried and confused. Aurelian sprawled at the foot of the bed. She clenched her hands and forced herself not to faint again. He said she had killed him! How was that possible?

Pushing the covers aside, she got out of bed and realized she was completely unclothed. She lifted a hand to cover her breasts, then paused. It was unimportant. Willow saw her nude every day, in the bath, and Lung was a ghost. So, why was he sipping tea and munching sweets? Why did he not have the common decency to take himself off wherever ghosts belonged?

Willow clucked and hurried over to put a robe on her mistress. The slip of silk across her skin seemed real enough. The cup of tea now in her hand felt warm. Lung watched her in silence, a slight smile playing across his mouth. Aurelian leapt off the bed and rested against her side, familiar and real. Except, of course, he was not real and had never been, because clearly he belonged in another realm, one where he was a master, not a servant. What place had he come from? Was all this too a dream? Would she, in a moment, awaken in her small bed in Baghdad and see the clear morning light making a pattern on the floor as it shone through the carved window screen? Had she ever left Baghdad at all? Claire touched the scar at the base of her throat, feeling the slightly roughened edges of it against the smoothness of her skin. How could she tell the dreamer from the dream? And why could matters not be neat and orderly and perfect?

"You appear extremely well for someone I slew in a forest half a world away."

Lung grinned, nodded and patted his chest. "I have never felt better," he responded. "But this does not change the truth, that I was that beast. Say, perhaps, that it was that part of me which perished. We all have a beast within, do we not?"

Claire thought about it. She came from a line of shape-shifters. Yes, everyone had a beast within. And a goddess and god as well. Fortunately, few people had to experience either of these aspects directly. She nodded slowly. The inexplicable presence of the scabbard of the Sword of Waters in the remains of the dragon now made some sense. She had killed its bearer and brought him back to life! Or whatever state he was presently in. But, why? Always, why.

Mistress, it was needful. The gods themselves had set their face against your venture. Alive, you could be harmed. The goddesses had no choice but to change your state, to protect you while you completed their work.

Aurelian's statement rang in her mind. *Then I did die in Kali's arms.*

That is one way to see it, mistress.

If this is a joke, I am not seeing the humour in it. I am either alive or I am not. I feel, I grieve and rejoice. Surely,

*I would not do those things if I were dead. Surely, I would
have noticed.*

*If you had been permitted to notice, perhaps, but you
were not, mistress. You were always companioned, seen
and believed in. Nothing is ever what it seems.*

Am I a ghost then?

*No, mistress. But you are no longer what you think of as
human. You no longer belong here in the world. You are,
as you told the abbot, a dream. We are all dreams in one
sense. Your task is done—well done. Now you may rest
from your labours. I will take you to a place where you
may dwell in peace. I have been waiting to bear you away.
It is what I came to do, dear mistress.*

Claire sat quietly puzzled for several minutes. Meta-
physics, she reflected sourly, had never been her best pursuit. But, as she thought of the things which had happened,
how she had drowned in her self-made sea, how she had
lost and regained a hand, she accepted, reluctantly, that she
was certainly not the girl who had left Baghdad with Djurjati, all those months before.

She thought of her father, and she wished she could see
Geoffrey and speak to him, and tell him everything. She
longed to sit in the garden with her mother again. She
looked at Willow, so real and faithful, her broad, peasant
face so calm and cheerful. And then she looked at Lung.

Claire rose and walked around the table and sat in his
lap, as she had longed to for weeks and weeks. She rested
her head against his shoulder. She could feel the steady
beat of his heart. His arm gripped her waist, quite real and
solid. He had come back to her, and that was really all that
mattered.

No, she could not be dead. She was too substantial. She
could not bear to leave the world, to leave her father. But,
if she believed the golden beast, she had no choice. What
had Helene told her? That the gods were unable to communicate with men until all the swords were brought into the
present, and the Darkness was banished.

Roderick! Claire had a sudden terror that her brother

was no longer alive and well, and she stiffened in Lung's warm embrace. The gods were going to pay dearly if they had harmed her little brother! After a moment it struck her as odd that she had no thought for Anna. But, she knew, on some deep, wordless level, that Anna was safe.

Godfather! I need you! It was a peremptory command, not a prayer or a plaint. She knew what was needful, and she had not time to worry about courtesies. There was a strange stillness in the room.

Then the air thickened, and the familiar figure of Mercutio di Maya, the ever young Hermes, materialized beside the table. He gave her a mocking smile. She glanced at Willow, but the girl appeared to see nothing. Lung was staring at the small, slender god. Claire slipped out of his arms and stood up.

"I do not imagine that Chinese is one of your accomplishments, Godfather," she said in Greek.

"No, actually it is not. I was wondering when you would call me. I am glad to see you, this final time. Where you will journey is not a place I can enter."

"And where might that be?"

"You will see. Now, how may I serve you?"

Claire was furious, but she knew it was useless to rail at him. "I have written down my adventures, as well as I could. Will you take them to my father? And, there is a small jar of ash I wish sprinkled on the Ganges. Can you do these things?"

"Certainly, child. You were always so tidy, and I see that even to the last, you are. The words will be cold comfort, you know, for Geoffrey, but comfort nonetheless."

"Tell me of my brother."

"Roderick is well. His work has been accomplished."

"And Anna?"

"Anna has found her place in the world."

Claire noted the ambiguity of his reply, and knew she could get no clearer answer from her devious god parent. Was he not the master of lies? But she remembered how she had thought of Anna when the lotus had exploded, and was certain that in some way she, too, had been part of that strange moment. She let it go, and took the bundle of manuscript, the poor quality Indian paper covered in pale, brown Arabic script, and the finer stuff she had written on since she had come to the land of Han. It was a thick pile, and she took a length of silk up, a brocaded piece which had been intended for a robe, and wrapped it up. She found her hands shook as she tied the ends, and that tears brimmed in her eyes. She handed him the little clay jar which held the ashes of her teacher, and found she was full of words, but could barely speak. If only she was calmer, in less pain. If only she could speak her heart.

"Give this into Geoffrey's hands, and tell him how much I love him, and Mother and Dorothea. I will never see you again, will I?"

"Only in your heart, daughter."

Claire hugged the young god, and kissed his cheek. She did not understand at all what was going to happen, but she had the sense of having completed some errand, of really finishing her tasks. "Farewell, then."

"Child, you have done a great thing, a great deed. You have given us, the gods, and man, the chance to dance hand in hand once more. Be glad. Your labours are done. Now, enjoy the reward."

She would have demanded he tell her more, but Hermes was gone, the manuscript and jar with him, so Claire turned back to Lung and Aurelian and Willow, who was gaping.

"Who was that?" Lung demanded.

"A very dear and old friend, and my. . ." Claire realized she had not word to convey the god-parent relationship. "He is a messenger at times. I asked him to serve me. I would have presented you, but he speaks no Chinese, and you not Greek or Latin."

Aurelian pressed against her side. *We must leave now, mistress.*

I am not going anywhere before I wash up.

Aurelian rolled his bulgy eyes and gave a little sigh

while Claire poured some water from a ewer into a basin and washed her hands and face, then removed the robe and laved her breasts and thighs, washing away the sweat of exercise. She took a gauze underrobe, slipped into it, and let Willow help her into a dark green brocade of flying cranes, just as if it was an ordinary day.

Lung rose when she was dressed. "Do you have any idea where we are going?" she demanded.

"To see Xi Wang Mu, the Queen Mother of the West, if I am not mistaken."

"But, she lives in Paradise!"

"Does it really matter where we are, Pure Jade, so long as we are together?"

"When you put it that way, no. You came back!" She let herself accept it, and felt her heart rejoice.

"I said I would never leave you, and I meant it."

Claire was too confused to argue. And, after all, it was a dream, was it not. Aurelian stood up, and enlarged his body until it filled most of the space between the bed and the table. Willow shrank back a little. The scent of peaches and honey filled the room.

Claire gave Willow a long hug. "You marry Major Wang soon, you hear me. He needs a good wife, and you will be the best."

"Yes, mistress." The girl stared at the huge golden beast, at Claire and Lung, and burst into tears. "I'll do what you say."

Lung helped Claire onto the golden back of the strange beast. Then he mounted behind her, clasping his hands around her waist. Claire leaned back against his chest, content. No more adventures, no more terrors. She barely noticed the room vanish around her. Sweet air brushed her cheeks, and she wondered what Paradise would be like. But it did not matter, because her work was over, and she would never be alone again. She had never felt more alive or happier. It was, she decided, a wonderful dream from which she prayed she would never have to wake.

EPILOGUE

Geoffrey d'Avebury stood before a lectern, reading a passage he had written. The smell of spring blossoms drifted up from the garden, and from the streets he could hear, faintly, the sounds of revelers. It was the third week of March, and the festival which marked the arrival of springtide was in full rout.

A sound made him turn, and Hermes, his young face solemn, stood in the middle of the room. He held a heavy bundle wrapped in cloth. Geoffrey stared at him nearsightedly for a moment. "Don't you ever knock?"

"No. It is a custom I have never learned. This is from Claire."

Geoffrey took the package from the small hands of the god. It smelled of sandalwood and unfamiliar spices. "Where is she?"

Hermes made no reply. Geoffrey set the package on his littered desk, and sat down slowly. He had known, somehow, that he would not see his first-born and dearest child again, but it was no less painful for having been anticipated. Six months before, on her birthday, he had felt a severance, as if a cord had been cut with a sharp knife. And then, at the winter solstice, he had sensed a light in the world that had seen so much of his daughter that he had convinced himself his earlier feeling had been a phantom.

"She sent her love to you, and to her mother and sister."

"Her love! What is that! What good is that!" Geoffrey felt a blood vessel pound in his brow.

"It is all that men have to give one another, old friend."

"I want her back, here, where I can keep her safe. I don't want her love."

"Safe, Geoffrey? Or prisoned in endless childhood?"

"You always have had a gift for seeing through my devices." He coiled a finger in his beard. "I cannot say I like it. She was so precious a babe. All of them were precious."

"I know."

"I wish they had never grown up."

"Yes." Hermes's voice was soft with care.

Geoffrey opened the package and pulled out the thick stack of paper. He began to read, unable to resist the written word, and for a time there was no sound in the room but the rustle of pages, as he turned them over, and the breathing of the two occupants. The sun passed over the house and the shadows changed, until the afternoon was gone, and blue twilight tinted the walls and floor.

Hermes watched as Geoffrey finished the last page, then walked over and poured two goblets of wine. He handed one to Geoffrey, who looked at last every day of his nearly fifty years, old and worn, careworn and desolate. Loving mortals, Hermes reflected, was such a painful, fruitless pursuit. And this one had captured his heart years before. They suffered so.

"She changed the world, Geoffrey. Be proud. By her efforts and her resolution, she made it possible for the mortals and the immortals to once again commune. She did a great healing, greater than any god in all the mansions of heaven could conceive."

"Proud. What use is that? My little girl is gone." His

blue eyes filled with tears and he wept for a long time. Finally he brushed his sleeve across his face and drained the cup of wine. "Is it over yet? Are the gods finished toying with us?"

"I think, rather, that your wild, unpredictable line has finished disturbing our peace, Geoffrey. It was not a one-sided thing, you know."

"I still never know when you are lying."

"The swords are done. The world is safe from the threat of soulless Darkness. That does not mean that all will be well, that everything will be perfect. But, the balances are restored, here, in this earth, so that men and gods may strive and change and further. That, my friend, is the best we can hope for or achieve."

Geoffrey looked at the stack of manuscript, full of sentences begun in Greek and completed in Arabic, a stylistic mare's nest, brimming with a passion he had never imagined his daughter possessed. He had never known her. On some of the later pages there were vertical characters made with a brush which he could not read. He wondered how he would unravel their secret. But, even in his grief, he felt immensely proud of her.

"Thank you for bringing this."

Hermes gave a sharp laugh. "I did not have a choice. She ordered me about like a servant. It was . . . educational."

"She was a remarkable girl, wasn't she?"

"No, Geoffrey. She *is* an incredible woman."

ADRIENNE MARTINE-BARNES is of Arabic-Hispanic heritage, which may explain her lifelong interest in the hijinks of various deities and her mild irreverence for the stuffier forms of sacredness. Her rather off-the-wall interpretations of Celtic and Mediterranean gods—in *The Fire Sword*, *The Crystal Sword*, and *The Rainbow Sword*, all available from Avon Books—continue into fresh areas: the Orient in *The Sea Sword* and Nordic myth in her future endeavor, *The Sword in the Tree*. She wishes to be openhanded in giving offense.

Ms. Martine-Barnes was born in Los Angeles in 1942 and spent an ordinary childhood talking to trees, cats, and other sentient beings. She has written a monograph (*Nekobana, Or Zen and the Art of Cat Arrangement*) which reflects some of these experiences. She is also the author of *The Dragon Rises*, possibly the most peculiar use of Arthurian material yet to see print, as well as two contemporary novels. When she is not writing, she paints, quilts, costumes, makes dolls, and adds to her collection of over 200 hippopotami.

RETURN TO AMBER...

THE ONE *REAL* WORLD, OF WHICH ALL OTHERS, INCLUDING EARTH, ARE BUT SHADOWS

ROGER ZELAZNY

The New Amber Novel

SIGN OF CHAOS   89637-0/$3.50 US/$4.50 Can
Merlin embarks on another marathon adventure, leading him back to the court of Amber and a final confrontation at the Keep of the Four Worlds.

BLOOD OF AMBER   89636-2/$3.50 US/$4.50 Can
Pursued by fiendish enemies, Merlin, son of Corwin, battles through an intricate web of vengeance and murder.

TRUMPS OF DOOM   89635-4/$3.50 US/$3.95 Can
Death stalks the son of Amber's vanished hero on a Shadow world called Earth.

The Classic Amber Series

NINE PRINCES IN AMBER 01430-0/$3.50 US/$4.50 Can
THE GUNS OF AVALON   00083-0/$3.50 US/$4.50 Can
SIGN OF THE UNICORN   00031-9/$2.95 US/$3.75 Can
THE HAND OF OBERON   01664-8/$3.50 US/$4.50 Can
THE COURTS OF CHAOS 47175-2/$3.50 US/$4.25 Can

Buy these books at your local bookstore or use this coupon for ordering:

Avon Books, Dept BP, Box 767, Rte 2, Dresden, TN 38225

Please send me the book(s) I have checked above. I am enclosing $_____ (please add $1.00 to cover postage and handling for each book ordered to a maximum of three dollars). Send check or money order—no cash or C.O.D.'s please. Prices and numbers are subject to change without notice. Please allow six to eight weeks for delivery.

Name _____

Address _____

City _____ State/Zip _____

AMBER 10/88

UNICORN & DRAGON
By LYNN ABBEY

illustrated by
Robert Gould

A BYRON PREISS BOOK

An epic tale of two very different sisters caught in a fantastic web of intrigue and magic—equally beautiful, equally talented—charged with quests to challenge their power!

UNICORN & DRAGON *(volume I)*

75567-X/$3.50US/$4.50Can

"Lynn Abbey's finest novel to date"—*Janet Morris*
author of *Earth Dream*

AND IN TRADE PAPERBACK—

CONQUEST
Unicorn & Dragon, (volume II)

75354-5/$6.95US/$8.85Can

Their peaceful world shattered forever, the two sisters become pawns in the dangerous game of who shall rule next.